Sandy Monroe
Office Sluts
The Collected Edition

Sandy Monroe
Office Sluts
The Collected Edition
This bundle contains the collected stories from the following Office Sluts books:

1. *The First Weeks*
2. *Wild Adventures*
3. *Travels Abroad*
4. *Dirty Diaries*

and the extra short: Cuckold Shoot for Onlyfans
For adult readers only
Copyright 2024 Sandy Monroe
Published by Sandy Monroe
Smashwords Edition, License Notes

Cover: Sandy Monroe
Email: sandy.likes.to.write@gmail.com
Follow my blog[1] and my Twitter account[2]!

---

1. http://sandylikestowrite.blogspot.com

2. https://twitter.com/SandyMonroeXXX

Office Sluts 1

The First Weeks

Chapter 1: Lurking Around

"Did you see her?" Carl pointed to the girl who just walked by our cubicle. She definitely had nice legs and a round hard ass swinging as she walked through the corridor. "This is why I love this place," he continued. "The women are beautiful and sexy, they wear business casual which usually means short skirts and large cleavage. They walk around here all day, bend over at the copy machine, show their large breasts when they choose lunch at the cafeteria and do stuff like that – they flirt with us all the time and make every guy horny."

Carl was a sex-addict asshole, but he was right. It was fine to work here at Walden, Inc. And of course, it needed a lot of sacrifice, self-discipline, concentration, teamwork, and other shit like that. But it was an ideal place for a guy like me.

My name is John Smith. I know what you think; who's this nobody? And you're probably right. I got here right after my graduation in law at the university. I was really happy with my average diploma and didn't really know what to do with myself in my average life. Just like in that old Def Leppard song, 'Let's Get Rocked':

"I'm your average ordinary everyday kid
Happy to do nothin', in fact, that's what I did"

During a long and hot summer, I answered a lot of job ads and after a series of job interviews, I started to work here, at one of the biggest law firms in the country.

As with every workplace, Walden, Inc. has its good and bad sides. It's great to work here because of the hot chicks, the excellent pay, and the chance to make independent decisions. But it's bad to work here because of the long and boring meetings, amateurish leaders, and the horrible buffet.

And there are the overtimes. Man, I hate them. There is no one else in the whole building, everything is extinct, like in a bad horror movie. And my boss chose me on my first week to stay here after working hours to wait for an email from Japan.

"We'll pay for every minute you spend here," he said after lunch when I was already planning my weekend already. "You just have to wait for the letter, print it, and stamp it with our official stamp. Even an idiot could do it."

Now that was nice. I decided to send him to hell on an anonymous ranting site. Then I loosened my tie and poured myself another coffee.

As the afternoon went by, everyone went home to spend some quality time with their family or friends. Since I've only been working here for a week, I didn't know where to find stuff. The restroom on our floor had a breakdown so I had to search for another for a long quarter hour. The offices and halls were dark, and everyone was at home, watching football. It was only me left here as a rookie, and I had to wait for the official answer from our client in Japan. They think I've got nothing better to do...

When I got back to my office, I sat in my office chair. With a daring idea, I took off my shoes and then stretched my legs. I leaned back in my chair and closed my eyes for a while. I thought over what was waiting for me at home: an empty fridge, and a cold bed. If I considered it, it wouldn't matter if I stayed here overnight.

I was startled by the sound of high heels in the hallway. I straightened up and put my shoes on. It was about time; my door opened and Bonnie stepped in. She was a black-haired, cute, sexy woman. I had been working at the office for only a week, but I quickly found out the whole department had a thing about her. When she dropped something on the floor, my colleagues almost fought one another to give it back to her. We talked a few times, but I didn't think I was good enough for her, so I didn't really care.

But now here she was, leaning against the door frame with gleaming eyes, and asked me in a trembling voice,

"I can see you're still in, too... Do you want to see something interesting?"

"What would that be?" I asked. I was hoping she would invite me somewhere interesting, ask for my number, or something like that. Maybe she would use the good old "I need a little help" trick.

"Come with me," she said.

We stepped out to the dark hallway. I wanted to turn on the lights, to see where we were going, but Bonnie stopped me by holding my hand.

"Don't turn it on, we don't want to scare them away," she whispered.

"Who exactly?" I whispered as well, but Bonnie just flashed a smile and turned around.

She led me through the maze of dark corridors. She stopped at a corner, took off her high heels, and walked along on her bare feet. I followed her in complete silence. There was a little hall after the corner and a conference room behind a glass wall. That's where our staff meeting took place every week. Even I had to take part in these, although I have been considered as a trainee. There were lush tropical flowers and little palm trees in front of the glass wall - none of them originated from this clime but if the HR came out with the idea that these have to grow in our offices, they won't spare any money. Bonnie took my hand again and pulled me among the palm trees. This way we could peep into the conference room between the palm leaves.

A man was fucking a woman inside the conference room, on the elliptical table. Both of them still had their clothes on. He was doing her from behind. I stepped close to the glass wall very carefully, to get a better view. Bonnie tried to pull me back, but I didn't let her do so; I pulled her beside me.

The scene could have been from a kind of an old Playboy movie; the woman was bent over the table, her long blonde hair was spread on the table, her skirt was tucked up, and her panties were on one of her legs, but she had both of her high heels on, of course. The man was dressed in a gray suit with his white shirt unbuttoned, his tie loosened, and his pants on his ankles. He was fucking her with abandon from behind. The woman grabbed his tie and pulled him closer to herself with it. I could even hear their moans in the silence of the building.

"He's got a really big cock", Bonnie whispered to me, causing me to stir a bit. I don't know how she knew that because his clothes almost hid all of his body. Bonnie had probably seen this more than once before. I saw her watching the scene with sparkling eyes. She swallowed once, probably because her throat had gone dry.

The man in the conference room leaned on the woman and fucked her like a well-oiled machine. It was really exciting to watch, and I started to feel my arousal. The man grabbed her thighs and gasped something in her ear, but I couldn't hear what. She nodded at him. The guy stopped, stepped back, took his cock in his hand – he really had a big one – and slapped her ass cheeks a few times with it. The woman was laughing, I could hear that even from here, on the other side of the glass wall. The man said something, like teasing her, slapped her ass cheeks with his cock again, then put it back, this time really slowly, and started to move inside her.

"He just put it in her ass," Bonnie said. I was looking at her questioning, so she continued, "I watched them some other times as well. A little suckie under the table, a little lickie on the table, then cowgirl, and at the end, from anal behind. They always do it the same way," she shrugged.

"So you were peeping, right?" I whispered to her. She kinda blushed as I could see her face in the dim light, between the leaves of the palm tree.

"Of course," she said. Her hot breath was warming up my blood. "I wouldn't miss to see a good fucking like that..."

The man started to really give it to the mystery woman. He fucked her ass really hard; both of them panted very loudly, and the woman even screamed. They probably thought they were alone in the building at this time of the evening. He straightened up, pulled her ass cheeks apart with his two hands, and watched the view in delight. I could tell he really enjoyed his cock moving in and out between her round ass cheeks. Of course, this caused my groin to swell more, and I imagined myself behind the woman. The man released her, spanked her light brown ass cheeks hard, and fucked her harder, grabbing her hair with one hand, her breasts with the other, and pulled her close to himself.

"This is really dirty," I whispered to Bonnie, whose eyes were sparkling like diamonds.

"I think they stole these ideas from some kind of a porn movie," she answered, but couldn't get her eyes from the view. "That's where people do it like that... Especially at the end, just watch it!"

They were panting really hard. The woman grabbed his neck from behind. They were moving like a couple who knew each other well. The woman cried out, and as he would just have waited for it, penetrated her asshole deeply. She was trembling, cried out loud a few times, then fell on the desk. The light was really dim, but I could see both of them were covered in sweat. The man bent over her and slowly started to move inside her again.

"That's my favorite part," Bonnie said, partly to herself.

The woman seemed to come to life. She snapped away from the man, turned around, and got on her knees before him. She grabbed his cock and started to jerk him off. The man hung onto the table and enjoyed the fondling he got from her. She took his huge cock into her mouth a few times, but didn't really work on it, she just made it wet and slippery. She jerked it really hard and seemed to know how to deal with it. And the man screamed loudly, trembled, and sprayed his juices on her face. She jerked it off gently for some more and held it above her breasts. That's where the next drops were sprayed. Their white color seemed to glisten in the dim light of the floor. Finally, she licked his cock thoroughly, cleaned it with her wet tongue, and the man moaned like a really satisfied lion.

While they were dressing, I backed off from the plants. As I tried to adjust my pants to hide my erection, Bonnie spotted it and touched it gently through my fly.

"I can see you liked it, too...," she said to me, then turned around and walked away. I still had a glance at her putting on her high heels, then she waved goodbye and disappeared.

I hurried back to my office. I sat in my chair, leaned back, and smiled. This is a good place, I thought, I will really enjoy working here. And I didn't know yet what in the next weeks would happen to me.

Chapter 2: Team-building

I was curious about the team-building. My colleagues were talking about a lot and sometimes we got an email about the plans. I think they had tried to make us interested in team-building so they gave us information about it only little by little. There was a poster in the elevator, showing who was in charge of the registrations. Of course, I sent my registration a long time ago. I wondered if I could get to know the strangers with whom I worked. And I was hoping I could get to know Bonnie a bit better after the team-building itself, at the party. Who knows, maybe we could have a special exercise together during the day...

But nothing works out as you planned it. As I found out, the location of the team building was a little camp in the mountains west of the city. Back in the old days, it was a student camp, but somebody bought it and remade it. He organized outings for big companies like ours. There were a few log cabins around a lawn and a big main building made of bricks and glass, where we could get together for lunch or dinner.

The team-building itself was a huge disappointment. The whole day was spent with idiotic things; we were searching in teams of five for some kind of hidden treasure in the woods; we had to solve lots of one-horse tasks. I lost all my spirit when I had to dive into a wet, cold cavity of an old tree elbow-deep – I'm no Indiana Jones, for heaven's sake!

Later on, I became friends with two guys from the IT department, so we laughed about everything from then on. Our team leader, sent by a professional team-building firm, was nearly crazy by the end of the day. He promised to tell our bosses everything about our 'bad attitude' as he called it. But we were just laughing since we wore a nickname on our T-shirt, a nickname that "described us." This was another of the team-builders' ideas.

I was really glad when the night came. I occupied an empty corner with my food. I was searching for Bonnie but I couldn't find her anywhere.

During the evening, the managers told us how proud they were to have us as members of their team, how much good work we had done, how satisfied our clients were, and so on. The beginning was sort of entertaining, but when they were telling us the same bullshit the twentieth time, I got bored and I didn't care anymore.

At least the food was good. I was eating dessert when I saw Bonnie. She was sitting among her colleagues, with the other hot chicks from the real estate department, and they were really enjoying themselves. I figured I'd ask her out for a little chit-chat. I ate my dessert, took my plates out, and wanted to go to Bonnie but I bumped into Carl. He was an arrogant, grease-haired, tall but slim man. I never really liked him.

"Hi, Johnny boy, how's the food?" he asked.

"Good, I guess," I said, and tried to sidestep him, but he stopped me.

"Do you want to have a little fun?"

I saw something in his eyes that made me wonder what he was thinking. I checked the real estate girls above Carl's shoulders. I didn't see Bonnie there anymore.

"What is it?" I asked a little disappointedly.

"Come with me," he said and hurried out.

We went around the building. Carl was behaving very mysteriously, he checked whether we were followed by someone and answered none of my questions. But he stopped at the pool,

"Listen up, you're still new here so I thought I would put you up to this. You don't have to thank me, let's say I'm doin' you a favor. And when you have to do a favor for me, you remember what a good friend of yours I am, comprende?"

I didn't like his Godfather take-off too much, but I nodded. He continued in his arrogant tone,

"Do you know Helen? From HR?"

"The small, black-haired girl? Of course! She organized my job interview when I came to the firm..."

"Okay, okay..." Carl said, but didn't really listen to me, he was watching the surroundings behind us. "Listen, mate," he leaned to me like a conspirator from the Middle Ages. "Helen's got a... little strange obsession. At these team buildings, she always hides in a room and welcomes a little group of insiders there."

I was looking at him with a dumb expression on my face.

"You don't get it, do you?" he tapped my chest. "She sucks off all the guys! This gets her off! I don't know what is good in it for her, but she never lets anybody do anything to her, you can't even touch her breasts or her ass. It's a shame since she's got a real...," he motioned with his hands how he'd grab Helen's ass.

"She's got a really nice rack, for sure..." I admitted.

"That's not the point! I'll work you in, you will have a nice evening. But there are rules, brother."

"What kind of rules?"

"The first rule – you can't touch her, she really hates especially when you grab her head during the face-fucking. Just let her do her job. Now what do you think the second rule is?"

"Er...," I was thinking. "Discretion?"

"You will go very far, brother. This little adventure has to remain between us. Don't mention it to Helen at the office. You talk with her about the stock exchange or the weather. That's how she wants it, enough said. And we won't be fools to miss out on a good little suckie like this, will be, mate?"

He didn't even wait for the answer and took off toward the trees on a little pathway. I recalled Helen; she really was a very sexy girl. A little small, but her body was really neat, with nice, round breasts and ass. Just the way I liked them. I'd heard some rumors about her and the director, but you don't have to believe everything they say. But now what Carl told me... Can this be true? Is she really a whore like this? I became interested.

We walked to the furthest log cabin. From the outside, it seemed abandoned. Carl checked the area again then we went inside. The ground floor was really quiet. Some jackets were lying around on the floor. Carl showed me the stairs to the upper floor. There was a little corridor. Carl confidently opened a door.

It was warm inside, the fire was burning in the fireplace, and that's where all the light came from. Helen was kneeling naked on a huge bear skin in the middle of the room, just as Carl promised me. Three guys were standing around her, all of them from different departments. I barely knew them. Each of them had their cocks in their hands and they were waiting to be the next to be blown. Helen was sucking the man before her with her eyes closed, in her very rhythmical, very routine way. She let the cock out of her mouth once in a while, smiled, patted it playfully, like a little stick, then grabbed the ass of the guy and pulled him back between her beautiful lips. Aside from being naked, there were some traces of sperm glistening between her breasts already.

"She is really good," Carl smiled. "Come on, brother, try it out!"

He pushed me to the end of the short row. I watched for a while how Helen sucked a guy then like the others, I unzipped my trousers and got my dick out. Two guys just finished in front of me, they sprayed their white jets on her tits and some fluids landed in her hair. The men stepped back, grabbed their clothes, and hurried away. Only one guy remained and Carl was behind me, but he already got his dick out and jerked it furiously. Helen pulled the guy deep into her mouth. The guy was moaning loudly and his knees went weak. I think Helen must have swallowed every drop because when she let the cock out, there was just her saliva dripping from it.

"Now that was juicy," she said, smiling. "Next!"

The guy stumbled away, and Helen mopped her lips like a fighter after a match.

I was next. Helen eyed me up and down, but I wasn't sure she recognized me. She pulled me closer to her by my knees, and gently slid my cock between her beautiful lips. She licked along the head of my cock, while stroking my cock up and down with her hand. It felt really good to be in her hot little mouth, especially when she twirled her tongue around my cock head. She let it gently deeper and deeper, sucking and licking it like a lollipop. When I was halfway in her mouth, she started bobbing on me. I let out a satisfied moan, she was doing it so well. Her wet tongue was moving quickly around my cock, and her saliva was flowing wildly around my cock, down to my balls.

Suddenly she let my cock out of her hot mouth and spanked her cheeks with it. Then grabbed it again and started to jerk it off. With her other hand, she smoothed out her hair from her face. She bent under my sack and licked my balls with her small tongue during the jerk-off.

"She's a pro, right?" Carl patted my shoulder. What could I say? I enjoyed the girl's work on my cock without a sound. She swallowed my cock again, sucked it really hard, and when it was deep in her throat, she swallowed some more, to make the sucking feeling stronger. She was really a pro, the head of my cock touched the back of her throat once or twice. I enjoyed it very much. I instinctively grabbed her hair to take her onto my cock, but I recalled what Carl had said before - no touchy! So I enjoyed the hardcore suckfest, moaned and sighed loudly and the girl was just sucking and sucking me off. And she did it really well! She lightly grabbed my balls and gently stroked them as if they were plums, meanwhile, her head solidly bobbed on my cock.

I closed my eyes and let it go. My orgasm hit me like a shock, the sperm broke out in thick, hot, aching waves from my body inside Helen's eager mouth. She continued sucking, but at a bit slower pace, she hardly touched the head of my cock, she licked it very slowly instead. She gently sucked every drop out of me and swallowed it all. When she let my throbbing cock out of her hot mouth, I could hardly stand on my own two feet.

"It was juicy...," she giggled and fondled my cock with her palm.

"Thanks...," I sighed.

Some drops of sperm and saliva fell down on the bear leather beside her knees, but neither of us cared about it.

"Let me here," Carl said and stepped to the girl. He didn't hesitate, quickly shoved his cock between Helen's lips, and she started bobbing on him. I felt it was time to leave so I dressed up, and stumbled out, down the stairs.

I sat down for a little bit and thought over what just happened to me. So, this was Helen's obsession. Using Carl's words annoyed me a little bit but I didn't know how to say it otherwise. And I had to admit, she was really good at it. If there is something like that at every team-building, it would be worth coming to them.

Chapter 3: Changing The Batteries

When I started to work at Walden, Inc., I didn't think I would be lost for weeks in the cruel world of registration and subscription sheets, signings, and countersigns. The long and boring donkey work was broken only by some winks from Bonnie now and then, but we didn't really have time to talk. I felt sorry because I wondered since when had she known about the couple whom we were peeping at a few weeks ago. I also wondered what excited her about it, and most of all, how could I excite her.

But things didn't really work out, at least not the way I wanted them to. There were some office parties at which our bosses told us how well everything went and how lucky we were to work in such an able and agile team. After these speeches, there was always a little buffet table in the office building, so I could get together with Bonnie, but apart from that, I couldn't get closer to her.

These overtimes will kill me. The problem is not really the late work hours, but the idle sitting and waiting sessions till the Japanese clients wake up in the other part of the world and answer our emails.

That's how I spent this night again. The whole office was empty, I was the only one working like a dog. Or that's what I thought. I turned on a radio station on the net and leaned back in my ergonomic chair. I was going over what I had at home, what I should buy for a delicious dinner, and what to eat in the morning to get kinda fresh again. There was an old Beatles song playing on the radio when I heard something.

Bonnie stepped into my office in her little black skirt and knee-high boots. Her cheeks were slightly red, and she was holding something behind her back. I turned off the radio.

"I thought you might be in tonight," she said, smiling. "Are you waiting for the answer to the real estate deal?"

"Yeah, and I'm really having fun. Kinda."

"Well," she said, "could you please help me a little? I really need your mechanical skills..." She stepped closer to my desk, but her hand was still behind her back.

"What is it?"

"Well... could you change the batteries in this... I wouldn't like to be laughed at..."

"Shoot it..." I said with a sigh. "Let's get over it."

"Okay, but don't laugh at me? And you can't tell anybody!" she said very seriously, and after I nodded, she showed me the device.

I was really surprised. Because Bonnie, the professional real estate expert, this sweet little bimbo, held a pink vibrator in her hand. It was kinda big, with artificial veins on its surface. The end was a little curvy with a big head on it. I took it in my hand, smiling.

"I didn't know these feel so soft," I measured it in my palm.

"It's made of silicone," Bonnie said, with burning red cheeks. Then when I started to eye her, she blurted out, "Now what? I knew I shouldn't bring it to you..."

"You did it right!" I told her. "I just tried to imagine you in the sex shop searching for the appropriate dildo..."

"It's not mine, smartass!"

"Then whose is it?"

"Clarissa's!"

This made me excited. Clarissa was a really sexy bitch. Nobody knew what she was working on. Sometimes she appeared, leaned over a folder to somebody who just started stuttering right away in surprise, trying to be funny for this super hot bitch, but Clarissa disappeared right away. She didn't seem to be impressed by anybody. She had long, blonde hair, full lips, serious eyes, and a wonderful, slim body. She didn't have large boobs or ass but everything on her was absolutely round and curvy. And the top of it, she knew all this about herself, so she wore black, patterned stockings on her long legs all the time, with a pink mini skirt. When she showed up, everyone was checking her out, the men did it hornily and approvingly, the women jealously and deprecating.

So that's why I got excited by the news. I was holding Clarissa's vibrator in my hands!

"Well, she must have been a hot as hell scene in the sex shop among the fake cocks...," I said smiling, but Bonnie stopped me.

"She ordered it online. It was just a few bucks. Will you change the batteries or not?"

"I'll change them, of course," I nodded with my dry throat. There was a small panel on the bottom of the tool. I opened it and took the batteries out.

"I'm gonna need two pencil batteries. Did you bring any?"

Bonnie handed over the two new batteries. I put them quickly in the proper place, closed the panel back, and turned it on. I only wanted to try it out. It started vibrating in my hand. It felt kinda weird. I turned it off quickly.

"You don't like it?" asked Bonnie, smiling. She wanted to take it away from me.

"Hey!" I stopped her. "I didn't do it for free! What will I have in return?"

"Well... someday..."

"No-no," I told her. "I'll give it back to you only if you tell me what you are going to do with it."

Her face turned totally red. She tried to argue with me and told me a few times the vibrator belonged to Clarissa, but I didn't change my mind. But her phone rang, and she answered it angrily,

"Yes... Almost ready... I just have a little... Okay, I'm going right now..."

She hung it up and looked into my eyes.

"Clarissa needs her toy right now," she said.

"Okay, let's take it to her!" I nodded and set off. Bonnie shrugged and followed me.

We went to the highest floor of the building, into a small office. I visited this place only once when my contract was signed. Bonnie took me to an oak door and let us in. The Venetian blind was down, and Clarissa was lying on the black leatherette couch. She was wearing beautiful, black, flowery pantyhose and red high heels on her long, neat legs. Her pink mini skirt was up, and she was fondling her groin through her pantyhose. She didn't seem to be disturbed by us at all. She didn't even take her hands away from her groin, she just looked us up and down.

"Who the hell is he?" she asked Bonnie.

"He's the one who changed the batteries," Bonnie pointed at me. "But he asked to be here in return."

Clarissa shrugged and took the vibrator from Bonnie.

"Sit down there," nodded Clarissa to me, and turned to Bonnie. "Can we start it?"

I sat down in one of the ergonomic chairs. Bonnie quickly kneeled down in front of the sofa. She bent toward Clarissa, grabbed her pantyhose between her legs, and tore it apart. I could see there were no panties on the blonde girl, her wet pussy was glistening before us. Bonnie bent down and started to lick her with her little tongue.

It was hot as hell. There lay Clarissa, the mistress of the firm, every man's fantasy, her legs spread wide, and my favorite colleague was licking her pussy! I was sorry I had no camera with me to record the whole scene. Bonnie's small head was moving up and down. Clarissa was enjoying the licking with eyes shut tight, as though I wasn't there at all. The vibrator was still in Clarissa's hand. Bonnie was leaning on her elbows on the leatherette and started to finger-fuck the blonde bitch. She was working with two fingers in the girl's pussy, turning them around and around and her tongue was circulating on the blonde girl's clit. She was using a lot of saliva to make the girl really wet. Her fingers were stroking into the blonde's pussy with steady motions which made Clarissa moan loudly and gave the vibrator to Bonnie. She licked the head of it and winked at me.

"Okay, Bonnie, no time for a show," Clarissa panted impatiently. "Put that thing in me!"

And she did. The pink dildo easily slid into the blonde girl's pussy, but Bonnie shoved it a little further with her palm. Clarissa let out a satisfied moan. Bonnie continued pushing it with a smile. She turned the vibrator on and let it tremble a little in Clarissa.

"That's good," Clarissa moaned. I would never imagine her relaxed like that.

Bonnie grabbed the vibrator like a knife and started to fuck her wildly with it. Clarissa pressed her palms on her face and enjoyed the drilling. My cock was starting to move in my pants, I had to adjust it. Bonnie bent down to the blonde girl's groin, fucked her with the vibrator, and licked her clit with her small wet tongue. I saw her other hand was working in her own panties.

Bonnie adjusted her hair and pulled her hand out of her panties. I could see her fingers were wet. And then she pressed the tip of her middle finger into Clarissa's asshole.

"Ouch," Clarissa hissed, but Bonnie didn't care, she pushed her finger deeper, then pulled it out, made it wet with her tongue again, and pushed it back into the hot blonde girl's tight asshole. This turned me on very much, it even made goosebumps on my back. Bonnie was fingering the blonde girl's asshole smiling, and she was working with the pink tool in her dripping pussy. Clarissa was practically screaming, turning her head back and forth on the leatherette. Her whole body started to tremble.

"I'm coming!" she screamed. She grabbed the arm of the couch and she came with a loud scream. I looked at the door, hoping it was made of real oak.

Bonnie fingered her for a while but Clarissa calmed down. Bonnie pulled the pink vibrator out, turned it off, and stroked and fondled the blonde girl's thighs a bit.

Clarissa opened her eyes.

"You know what I want, don't you?" she said, smiling at Bonnie, who only nodded. Both of them stood up. Clarissa bent on her all fours on the couch and pressed her ass high. I could see her pussy and her beautiful asshole through the split of the pantyhose. Little shining drops of pussy juices fell from her slit on the black leatherette couch. Bonnie took off her own panties and with a smile, she threw them into my face. Then she turned back to the blonde girl, who lay her head on the back of the couch and waited for the next round. Bonnie kneeled beside her, and tore her pantyhose some more, making the hole larger. That's when I realized there was a tattoo on Clarissa's back. Some kind of green, curly figure like in an old pirate movie. A pretty beautiful tramp stamp, if you ask me.

"You like it, huh?" asked Bonnie and fondled the blonde girl's magnificent ass.

"Come on...," the blonde girl moaned, so Bonnie bent over her ass. She pulled the round cheeks apart and started to lick her. She must have pressed her tongue really deep into her asshole because her head was moving back and forth. Once or twice she took a deep breath then she continued licking her asshole. It was really hot. I took out my cock and pulled it a few times. Bonnie started to finger her ass, first with one, then with two fingers.

I figured out this wasn't some sensual licking. This was preparing. Bonnie was preparing Clarissa's asshole to push the vibrator inside her! Sometimes she licked her clit too but fingered her asshole with abandon.

When Clarissa's asshole loosened up nicely, Bonnie pulled out her fingers. She pulled the round, nice cheeks apart again so I could admire her work. The pink hole was gaping. Then she took the vibrator from the couch and pressed the head of it against Clarissa's puckered asshole. I watched breathlessly as she shoved it halfway inside easily. The blonde girl didn't seem to be bothered by the pink tool in her asshole, she let out the same husky moans as before. Now Bonnie turned the thing on and started fucking her asshole with maximum power.

I was jerking my cock so loudly Bonnie glanced back at me,

"Don't you dare to jerk it off!" she said to me rigorously. "Who do you think I'm preparing this beauty for?"

I froze. There she was in front of me, Clarissa, the blonde demon, everybody's fantasy bitch, with a pink vibrator in her ass, and she was being readied for my cock. I almost shot it. But I took a big breath and stepped towards them. Bonnie pulled out the vibrator, licked it with delight, then threw it on the couch. She pulled apart Clarissa's ass cheeks once again so we could admire her gaping pink asshole. Then she looked at my cock,

"I'd better make it wet," she said and bent over it.

I thought she would take it between her full lips, but I was disappointed; she oozed a big amount of her saliva on my cock and smeared it all over my throbbing member. Then she steered me behind Clarissa and guided my cock to her asshole.

"Now show me what you got, cowboy," and she slapped my ass. I didn't need to be told twice. I shoved my dick in Clarissa's anus. She let out a big moan but didn't protest. I waited for a minute to help her get used to my throbbing cock in her tight little ass. It was tight, hot, and wet, even slippery with Bonnie's saliva. Clarissa looked back above her shoulder,

"Come on and fuck my ass!"

I felt as if some kind of red fog ruled my brain. I saw only Clarissa and started to fuck her like I never fucked anyone before. She was pushing her ass back onto my cock.

"That's it!" she cried. "Harder! Faster!"

I was balls deep in her but this wasn't enough. I stepped above her, to have my groin above her ass. I hung onto the back of the couch and fucked Clarissa from above like a monkey. Bonnie must have been crouching somewhere below us but I didn't care. I was into the blonde's tight, hot asshole only.

It was better than I expected. It was hot and tight and slippery. It was perfect. I felt Bonnie spanking Clarissa's round cheeks below me. She was urging her,

"You like to be fucked in your asshole, huh? You like that thick, hard cock in your ass?"

Wow. I had to pull out to hold back a little. Bonnie bent over right away, plunged her tongue deep into Clarissa's gaping asshole and licked her a little bit, and spanked her round ass cheeks hard. Then she looked up at me,

"Fuck her, you stallion!"

I didn't need to be told twice. I plunged my throbbing cock back inside the blonde girl's tight ass and fucked her with abandon, with hard and steady thrusts.

"Don't shoot it in her, she really hates that," Bonnie whispered in my ear while she was slapping Clarissa's ass again. She probably felt I couldn't take it much longer. I fucked the blonde girl with all my power. I wanted her to have the ass fucking she deserved.

I must have found some secret spot because Clarissa began to whimper below me.

"That's it, you fucker!" she screamed and came in strong waves. Her hand and knees went weak, but I held her strongly and continued the fucking. I wanted to fuck this beautiful ass well and as I could see it, she didn't mind it at all.

When I felt I was on the edge, I pulled out. I wanted to jerk off on Clarissa's ass myself, but Bonnie stopped me; she placed her black, lacy panties on my cock and used it as a grip to jerk me off. This girl was full of surprises! For a moment, I wondered where she got her ideas. She was jerking me off like a real pro while looking into my eyes.

This was too much. I let out a loud cry and came like a stallion. The first shot went on Clarissa's tattoo, the huge, thick, white drops almost covered it. The other shots rained on the blonde girl's ass cheeks, and some of them poured on her asshole. Bonnie jerked me off some more and milked every last drop out of me. I had no time to admire my work because Bonnie bent over, and licked everything off of Clarissa's back. She collected every drop, then went on the blonde's beautiful ass cheeks. I stepped behind to let her do her job. She was a real pro. She even pulled Clarissa's cheeks apart and licked her red, gaping asshole for a few minutes, which Clarissa enjoyed with closed eyes and some loud, tired moans.

I panted for a while. The girls dressed. Bonnie took her panties from my cock, and pulled them up. Clarissa adjusted her skirt, then nodded for us to go away. Bonnie came back to the corridor with me. I asked her if I could take her home, but she said she would call a cab since she still had some work to do.

When I got back to the office, I got the answer from the Japanese clients. I just had to print it, sign and seal it, and I was ready. I put the earphones back to my ears. The radio was playing Lynyrd Skynyrd's "Things Going On." I wondered if I could tell anyone in the office what had just happened to me, but it seemed too risky. So I started to plan how I could get in touch with these girls again. Well, I wasn't really interested in that blonde bitch. Of course, I liked to ass-fuck her but my real interest was Bonnie, with her lots of erotic and perverted ideas.

Chapter 4: The Call

Many people hate Mondays, but if you ask me, Fridays are a lot worse. Someone hit my car on Friday morning, so I spent all day arguing with the garage on the phone. I stopped for lunch only. It was sushi and I hated it. I hated everything, maybe even myself.

On top of that, I had to participate in a phone meeting with Japanese clients. I didn't even know what to say, but my boss told me I only had to take the meeting minutes. They would send somebody from the real estate department to deal with the meeting. Furthermore, it wouldn't be too important. Maybe that's why they chose me.

Anyway, this meant I had to spend another evening here, in this shitty building. I wished it was the Nakatomi building with the terrorists capturing anybody. With no John McClane present.

But you can't always get what you want, just like in that old Rolling Stones song. The Japanese clients didn't cancel the meeting, so I had to go to the conference room. My mood brightened up a little when I found out the real estate department sent Bonnie to the meeting.

"Same shit?" she asked. Her sexy voice made everything a bit easier.

"Let's get through with it," I said, and we entered the room.

There were just the two of us. We sat in the big office chairs and Bonnie was dialing the number while she asked me how I was doing and I complained to her about my car.

"Shit happens," she said with a sad smile.

It wasn't long till Mr. Tagamoshi from Japan answered. We heard his voice through the phone on the table. It was on speaker so everyone could hear him.

"Mushi-mushi!"

"Mushi-mushi!" was our chorus. That was almost all we knew about Japanese, so we switched back to English.

"How do you do?" he asked us.

"Really fine, thanks. You?"

"Me too, thanks," he answered. Bonnie and Mr. Tagamoshi chit-chatted about the weather and stuff. I got bored fast, drawing circles in my notebook.

Mr. Tagamoshi was speaking about this week's results. Most of them were well-known, but the other ones weren't important. Bonnie was drawing as well, and she ran her finger through her beautiful black hair a few times.

I thought I'd take my chances and wrote a message in my notebook, and showed it to her,

"So did you like my sperm?"

She read it with eyes wide open. She looked at me and said nothing. I smiled.

"Can you hear me?" Mr. Tagamoshi asked.

"Yes, Mr. Tagamoshi!" she answered, "Loud and clear. Please continue!"

While he went on, she quickly sketched something on the notebook and handed it over,

"I would like to taste it again!"

I really liked the idea. She pulled the notebook back. I thought she got scared or something but she wrote another line under the previous one,

"From my ass!"

Now that got me wild. I looked her up and down. She was wearing a white blouse, a black mini-skirt, and black high heels. She had her legs crossed and her sole was wobbling in her shoes which meant by the body language books, she needed a serious fucking.

I stood up and quickly pushed her chair a bit from the table.

"What did you say?" Mr. Tagamushi asked.

"It was probably something with the line," Bonnie answered quickly. "How did you find this week's results given our synergy?"

I knew I had time. When I hear synergy I know there will be a quarter hour of bullshit coming. And I wasn't wrong, our client started to speak about the synergy – whatever it was.

As for me, I knelt down on the rug in front of Bonnie. I slipped under the table so I couldn't be seen from outside. She looked at me with surprise but didn't object. She didn't object at all. She pulled herself closer with the chair and sprawled her legs. I got to see her beautiful pussy through her panties. I pushed her skirt up, pulled her panties away, and buried my face into her groin. She let out a sigh.

Her pussy was already wet. I licked it from the bottom to her clit.

"Ohhh...," she moaned.

"Pardon?" Mr. Tagamushi asked.

"Nothing at all. Please, continue."

He continued talking and I continued licking. I pressed my tongue deep into her slit, collected as much fluid as I could then pulled back and spread it all over her clit.

I pressed my index finger into her pussy. She moaned but did it very quietly. I used her fluids to make her clit wet then I pulled her lips apart and licked her all the way up and down. I shoved my tongue deep into her pussy and enjoyed her sweet aroma.

I entered her pussy with two fingers and turned them around a few times. I could feel she had some strong muscles down there. I found her G-spot easily and started to fondle it with my middle finger. While doing it, I was licking her clit in circles.

She pulled my head strongly to herself. I sucked on her clit and fingered her harder. Then I continued to lick her in a downward spiral. Slowly, I reached her asshole with my tongue and licked over it.

"Ooohhh...," she moaned.

"That strange sound again," Mr. Tagamoshi said.

"I... don't know... what it was...," Bonnie said to the phone on the table.

"Are you sure?"

"I've read about... a coronal mass ejection from the Sun, and that it will probably... affect our communication...," I heard from above. How the hell could she concentrate like this? I had to speed things up.

I pulled my finger out, and slid lower, to her asshole. I used her pussy fluids and my saliva as a lubricant and started to enter her tight back door. She gritted her teeth not to cry out loud and she pushed her butt towards my hand.

I pressed my finger deep into her asshole. She hissed a little but didn't object. In fact, she lowered her ass for me to have better access to her asshole. I checked her face; she was lying back in her chair with closed eyes. I really hoped nobody was watching us from the corridor because she looked like she was in a seizure or something.

But I didn't care about it. My instincts controlled me, so I continued to finger her asshole and sucked her clit. I had the wild idea to fuck her ass here and now. So I wanted to prepare and relax her. She was so hot and my cock was so hard. I really needed to fuck her. And the strange voice speaking from the phone made everything more exciting.

As I fingered her asshole, I entered one free finger into her pussy. I must have hit some secret spot because she immediately started trembling.

"That's it...," she moaned loudly.

"Really?" Mr. Tagamoshi asked. "Could you please repeat again?"

"Yes, Mr. Tagamoshi.... Yes!" she cried out loudly and she came. Her whole body was shaking in the chair. She gripped my hand and pushed my fingers deep in herself. She trembled for a few seconds, then came to her senses,

"Sorry, Mr. Tagamoshi," she said into the phone, looking into my eyes. "I thought there was something with the line, that's why I was so loud."

"Strange...," we heard. "I can hear you clearly now... Nevermind. I think that was all for today. Thanks for your time."

"Thank you very much," we said. Bonnie hung up the call, and we looked into each other's eyes again. She was coming down from heaven, but I had a throbbing cock in my pants.

"Let's skip writing the meeting minutes," I said and stood up, before her. "I think it's my turn now."

I unzipped my fly and my cock sprung free. It almost slapped her face.

"Wow," she said. "I didn't have the opportunity to tell you last time how I admire your member," she said, smiling, and took me into her warm palm.

"You can admire it now," I said, and grabbed her head and pulled her mouth onto my cock. When I felt her hot, wet mouth, I closed my eyes.

And that was when I heard the creaking. Bonnie looked up and let my cock out of her mouth. We both knew what it was. The janitor.

We had just seconds. I quickly pulled my pants up, she pulled up her panties, and we adjusted our clothes. The creaking got louder and the janitor's cart appeared in the corridor. He was listening to music on his earphones and he was pushing the cart with dance moves.

"Hi, everybody!" He came into the conference room. "Did you finish?"

"Yeah," Bonnie said and looked into my eyes. "At least I did."

"Cool," the janitor said, not noticing the sexual frustration coming from me. "Then shall I start cleaning this room?" Not waiting for an answer, he got some antiseptic wipes and started his cleaning process.

We walked out to the corridor.

"It was really hot," Bonnie said. "I haven't come like that in a very long time."

"You're welcome," I answered. "Too bad we couldn't continue."

"What about your car?"

"It's damaged, you know..."

"Come on," Bonnie said and started to search in her purse. "I'll take you home. Let's continue it there."

Chapter 5: On The Road

We were taking the highway going out of the city. Bonnie was driving her Porsche. The radio was playing "I Will Possess Your Heart" by Death Cab for Cutie.

"Nice car," I said.

"Oh, it's my uncle's," Bonnie answered. "I couldn't afford one with my salary, no."

She turned the volume on and sang with the music aloud,

"You gotta spend some time, Love.
You gotta spend some time with me.
And I know that you'll find, love
I will possess your heart."

I watched her sing. I was so excited I would have had her suck my cock right then and there, but since she was driving, I had no chance of getting it. The big city lights were moving behind us.

Suddenly I saw police lights flickering in the mirror.

"Shit," Bonnie said. "I totally forgot about him."

"Forgot? What are you talking about? Is everything alright?"

"Yeah, it will be. Open the glove compartment. Give me the lipstick."

"The lipstick?" I asked. "What about the registration?"

"Never mind!" she said, checking her make-up in the mirror. "And trust me on this. Don't make any stupid moves."

She pulled down to a minor road among the trees. We slowed down, and she unbuttoned her jeans. The police car followed us. After half a mile Bonnie stopped the car and looked at me,

"Just let me do the talking. And anything else."

The uniformed cop got out of his car and walked near Bonnie's window. She opened it.

"Good evening, Ma'am," he said with his bored voice, chewing gum. He didn't take his sunglasses off which I found a bit weird at this late time of evening.

"Can I see some IDs, please?"

She handed our IDs over. He examined them carefully and then gave them back.

"I couldn't miss you're guilty of offending at least three traffic regulations," he said. " I'm afraid you're going to get some traffic tickets."

"Come on, officer," Bonnie said with her sweetest voice. "Is there any way we can sort it out?"

"Given these violations...," he adjusted his belt with the gun and the radio. "I'm afraid you're in serious trouble, Ma'am..."

"Please, officer...," Bonnie begged. "I would do anything..."

"Oh yeah? Anything?"

It was enough.

"What the fuck are you talking about?" I shouted to the arrogant cop. "She wasn't speeding! All the lights were on! We didn't do anything!"

"Ssh...," Bonnie hissed at me, but the cop was faster. He got his taser out,

"So you're a smartass, right? I'll show you how we deal with smartasses around here!"

He aimed at me and shot. The taser hit my shoulder then I felt the electric shock. My last thought was he has to be good at this - then I passed out.

I don't know how long I was unconscious. When I came to, the inside of the car was in dim light. I was alone sitting inside. The lights of the car were on. Bonnie was bent on the hood of the engine and the cop was fucking her from behind. I slowly became aware of all my senses and I understood what Bonnie was screaming,

"Fuck my ass! Deeper!"

The cop adjusted his sunglasses, gripped her hips, and fucked her even harder. He was chewing his gum with a poker face.

"That's it!" she cried. "Split me in half with your big black cock!"

He slapped her beautiful ass cheeks a few times which made Bonnie laugh out loudly. She looked back to the guy above her shoulders.

"You like it, huh?"

"I love your hot white ass, you little black cock slut!" he shouted.

"That's right! I'm a black cock slut!" she cried and fell on the hood. Her whole body was trembling. She cried out loudly with her eyes closed. The black cop showed no mercy, he fucked her like a black terminator.

"That's it, honey!" He slapped her ass cheeks again. "Cum on my big black cock!"

As far as I could tell, he couldn't take it anymore. He stopped moving and came with big shudders.

"Wow!" he shouted and thrust a last one into her body. "Now that's what I call a good end of a week!"

He stepped back. He bent down to Bonnie's ass, spread her ass cheeks with his big black hands, admired his work for a second, then slapped her cheeks again,

"I hope you liked it, slut!"

"It was perfect, as always!" she said softly, with her head still bent over on the hood. Her head hid her feelings but her tremblings showed me she was still in heaven. Yeah. Black heaven.

The cop grabbed her panties and showed them to her.

"I think this belongs to me," he said and put it in his pocket. "I'll secure it as evidence of a crime."

Bonnie buttoned up her jeans as well and adjusted her shirt. She checked her butt but nothing was visible. Yet.

The cop put on his pants, adjusted his gun and the radio on his belt then walked to the side of the car and stepped toward me,

"Bonnie told me you are a good guy," he said to me through the open window. "Sorry for the taser earlier."

"Yeah, whatever," was my answer.

"So next time, as usual, Ma'am?" the cop asked Bonnie.

"You bet," she said and patted his groin, then got into the car. The cop turned his car's lights off and drove away.

She looked at me from behind the wheel,

"I'll take you to my place," she said. "I think we have a lot to discuss."

She started the engine, and I looked out into the dark night. Yeah, we had a lot to discuss. This was a very long Friday. I touched my aching shoulder. I felt I'd fall asleep as soon as I could find a bed.

Chapter 6: In The Condo

When I woke up I was alone. The sun was shining in through the glass walls of the house. I only had my pants on. I sat up on the bed and looked around. White walls, white furniture, white sheets. The interior design wasn't too sophisticated.

I walked outside through the glass door. The sun shone in my eyes and my head started to ache. I was standing poolside. The water seemed calm and cool. Well-kept trees protected the garden from the heat of the sun.

There was a rattan table with a continental breakfast on it, with four rattan chairs around it. The breakfast included black tea, sandwiches, bagels, jam, and milk. I sat down in a chair facing the pool and I felt like I was in a hotel or something.

Bonnie emerged from the pool. The water was flowing down her body. She was rising like Venus from the sea. Her beautiful black hair was attached to her head and neck. She wiped some of the water from her face so I could admire her perfect, round breasts, her lean body, and nice legs. She climbed out using a pool ladder. Like a Baywatch girl. Yeah, she could have definitely played in Baywatch.

"Good morning, sunshine!" she said in her sexy voice and sat down in a rattan chair beside me.

"So you're awake!" I said.

"I've been awake since dawn. I took a shower, washed my hair, drank some grapefruit juice, and took a swim. "

"Did you make all these?" I pointed to the breakfast.

"No, I'm not really good in the kitchen. It was made by the maid."

"Nice," I said and took a bite of a sandwich. It was like salvation for my stomach. Then I sipped some tea and started to feel a little better.

"Is this all yours?" I asked, waving around.

"Don't be silly," she said and drank some juice. "All of this is my uncle's. He's working overseas and he lets me stay here. I can use the whole house."

We just sat there for a while and had breakfast. I was eyeing her up and down. I really liked her hot naked body, but I felt I had to talk with her about the events of last night.

"So...," I started, "what was this all about yesterday?"

"The thing is," Bonnie admitted, "I love black cocks. Especially when they are big and juicy."

"Yeah, I figured it out yesterday," I nodded and fondled my shoulder where the taser hit me.

"You had to find it out the hard way," Bonnie said, with her adorable smile. "Of course, I have nothing against white cocks, either," she looked at me. "But I have this thing, maybe a fetish for black cocks."

"Do you know when it started?"

"Well, I think back then after high school. After I graduated, I wanted to have a tattoo. I walked into this tattoo parlor, started to chit-chat with this black guy and we spent a really good hour or so together. After closing time, I was still there and I was sitting in the tattoo chair, trying out in which position the tramp stamp is made, with my ass up. And he went down on me, nice and slow. He licked my ass really well, so when I spotted a tube of lubricant on the desk, I said to him I want to try it out."

"And he was in?"

"Yeah, he was in," Bonnie laughed. "He fucked me really good. And that's when everything started. Later on, I had to study a lot at college, so I had to suppress my needs. Sure, I had two boyfriends during my college years, but they didn't last long if you know what I mean..."

"Where do you know Sergeant Hancock from?"

Bonnie laughed.

"His real name is Patrick Donovan. He's nicer than he shows himself to be. He's a really nice guy, actually. He stopped me on a rainy night on the highway and I was in real trouble. I tried my charm on him and it worked so we spent a hot night together in a hotel nearby.

"Let me guess – with his big black cock, right?"

"I was horny, okay? I hadn't been properly fucked for ages. Wait a minute...," She bent to me and looked deep into my eyes, "are you jealous?"

"A bit, yeah."

"It's just sex, silly boy. And I wouldn't be jealous of you."

"Not at all?"

"Remember, last month I organized a threesome for you."

"Okay...," I said, thinking about the wild night with Clarissa, and leaned back into the chair. I wondered about this for a while but Bonnie shrugged,

"Anyway, we meet now and then, and since he knows what I like in him, the story is basically the same at every time. He stops me, and we argue for a while about the speed limit or something like that. It is unnecessary, really, because my panties are wet when I stop the car already."

"Then what? He fucks you on the hood?"

"Basically, yes, but not always on the hood. Sometimes we go deeper among the trees, and sometimes we sit in the police car. Once he even handcuffed me and fucked my face, now that was wild..."

We just sat there in silence for a minute.

"So this is my story. I found out I adore big black cocks. Sometimes I just need one to fill my ass. I don't wanna spend time with the guy, chit-chat with him, or have a romantic dinner. Once in a while, this little booty here needs to be fucked by a big black cock. Even if I can't walk straight for a few days after that. I hope you don't think of me as a whore."

"A whore? No. A black cock slut, maybe."

Bonnie was laughing. I bent over and kissed her. She pressed her wet tongue into my mouth then pulled away, stood up, and jumped into the pool. I took down my pants and followed her for a minute.

We were laughing and chasing each other around in the pool. Then we went inside the house. We took a shower; we took turns fondling and caressing each other's bodies. I really enjoyed soaping her tits, her thighs, and her beautiful round ass cheeks. After I finished, she turned around and watched my throbbing member.

"Wow," she laughed. "I can see you're really happy to see me."

Then she washed my body with circling motions. She worked from my chest down to my cock.

She got towels and we dried ourselves.

"Wanna warm up a little?" she asked.

"Sure."

She led me into the sauna. We were sitting in the hot air covered by our towels only. She leaned to me with her back. I caressed her body. My hands went under her towel, I fondled her sweaty tits.

"So did you like Sergeant Hancock's cock in your butt?" I asked.

"Very much," she moaned, enjoying my palms on her tits.

"Did he fill your ass properly?"

"Yeah...," she moaned and her hand went under her towels and started working on her clit.

"Did you like his sperm in your asshole?"

"Yeah...," she moaned with eyes closed.

I raised her jaw to look into her eyes.

"I'm gonna fuck your ass right now," I said.

"Do it!" she answered with gleaming eyes.

I stepped before her, and my towel fell on the hot floor. My cock sprung in front of her face just like it did in the shower. But now she didn't laugh.

"Finally...," she said and leaned over, taking it into her mouth. Her wet lips seemed cool in the hot air of the sauna. She shoved her fingers into her cunt and sucked me all the way in, making it wet with her cool saliva.

"Now that's hot...," I moaned. She just hummed a little and started bobbing on my cock. I grabbed her head and controlled her movements. It was tempting to fuck her mouth and shoot all my seed in it or to spray it over her sweaty face and tits, but I had other plans.

She took my cock out of her mouth, fondled my balls with her free hand, and licked them with her small tongue.

"That's it, baby," I sighed. "Lick it good..."

She took my balls gently in her mouth and jerked my cock with her free hand. With the other one, she spread some of her own juices on the head of my cock then licked it off. Her hand moved back to her twat and she sucked me again with a lot of saliva.

I stepped back and helped her up.

"Please be gentle...," she looked into my eyes. "I'm still sore because of yesterday evening..."

"Don't worry...," I murmured. "I'm gonna relax you a bit. Sit on my face!"

"Oh yeah...," she sighed, smiling. I lay on the bank, but it was too hot so I put my towel under my back. She climbed on top of me, sat down on my chest, and slowly slid to my face. My head was between her thighs. The sweat was pouring down on me from her hot skin. I took a big breath and licked her swollen pussy a few times. She sighed loudly. I raised my head to lick her clit as well. She enjoyed it with her eyes closed. Then she raised her hips and slid forward. She pushed her asshole into my face. I reached it easily with my tongue and licked around it with big wet circles.

"Oh my God it's so good...," she moaned. I supported her ass cheeks with my hands and shoved my tongue into her asshole. I circled inside, spread her cheeks wider then licked her deeper.

"That's it...," she murmured. "Lick it good... Oh shit..."

Her asshole was relaxed. I guess she was still under the effect of my last night's licking, then the hardcore pounding on the highway by the black cop. These images made my cock twitch and I licked her deeper and deeper.

"I can't wait any longer," she admitted, then stood up. I sat up as well and turned my back to the hot wood of the bench. I wanted to fuck her ass really bad but didn't want to hurt her. "Sit in my lap so you can control the ride."

She nodded, then sat in my lap. My cock jumped between her sweaty ass cheeks. She leaned back and set it to her asshole. She sat down on it slowly, gently.

"Oh... my... God...," she moaned with her eyes closed. "I really needed this..."

After a minute of relaxing with her hot, tight asshole on my cock, she started to ride me with a steady rhythm. I couldn't believe how hot she was. After weeks of daydreaming about her, here I was, sitting naked in the sauna and fucking her butt. My cock was balls-deep in her hot asshole. She was loosened up really well and our hot sweat made everything slippery.

"That's it," she cried. "Fuck me! Fill me!"

"I'm gonna fill you up, baby!" I shouted and slapped her ass cheeks a few times. She laughed but enjoyed the fucking with closed eyes. I fondled her sweaty thighs, her boobs, and I wiped some sweat out of her face. She kissed my fingers and pushed herself deeper and deeper onto my cock.

With a sudden idea, I pulled out. She looked at me with surprise but I made her stand up and sit on the wet towel on the hot wood. She instantly understood my plan and took my cock into her mouth. She sucked it like candy. I grabbed her head and fucked her face real good, shoved my cock deep into her mouth, to her throat. She used a lot of saliva to make my cock more slippery. I pulled out and slapped her face with it a few times. Her saliva was dripping on her wet sweaty face.

"That's enough," I said. "Turn around!"

She kneeled on the towel with a laugh. I pressed my cock to her asshole and entered her with a single, powerful thrust.

"Oh yeah...," she moaned. I didn't say anything, I needed all my strength and self-control to keep up with her. I started to fuck her with strong, long thrusts.

"You like it, huh?" I grabbed her head by her hair and pulled her close to me. "You like my hard cock in your slutty asshole?

"Yeeeah...," she cried. I was glad the condo was outside the city so nobody could hear our animalistic fucking. "Fuck my ass!"

I slapped her ass a few times just like I saw the black cop do last night. This made her wilder; she was bucking on my cock with her hips.

"That's it, you anal slut! Take it in your asshole!" I tried to talk to her as dirty as I could. "Take it hard and deep! I hope you can't walk for days after me fucking your hot tight ass!"

That was enough. She let herself loose and came with her whole body trembling.

"Come in my asshole!" she cried with a sore throat. "Fill my slutty ass with your hot cream!"

I was fucking her through her orgasm like crazy. I came deep in her ass. My whole body was trembling. With three or four thrusts, I shot like a gallon of my hot seed into her hot tight asshole. She enjoyed it with her eyes closed.

I pulled out with an audible 'pop' sound. My cock was glistening in the dim light of the sauna. It was covered with my cum and her sweat. I tried to catch my breath but she came to her senses and kneeled before me,

"Let me clean it properly," she said and swallowed my member into her hot mouth. She sucked and licked everything off of it, and she was doing it really gently. She probably knew how sensitive a man's cock can get after a good old butt fucking session.

"Now that's what I call a perfect weekend," she said. "Now come on, let's cool down in the shower."

I followed her out as I watched her round ass cheeks jiggling before me. A small stripe of my cum was dripping from her ass to her beautiful thighs.

Chapter 7: The Video

It's really annoying when on the computer system of the company they hide the sheets you need in a hidden folder on a hidden drive. There is a document every week which can't be found anywhere.

I should have prepared a mortgage contract for a real estate. I was searching all the folders for the document I needed, but I didn't find it anywhere. I logged into the shared network drive wondering whether I'd find it among the common files. Somewhere deep in a folder, I found a folder called "Summer house." I opened it. There were no documents in it, only a large video file.

I started it. It was an amateur recording; the camera was moving. It was Janet, the blonde secretary of our department sitting in the scene on a yacht dressed in a bikini. The wind was blowing her blonde, long hair. The sun was shining. Somebody told her something, but the wind blew into the microphone so I couldn't understand it. Janet was laughing. She looked at the water behind her and stretched her arms, she was enjoying the sunshine.

Cut, sizzling, and there was another location, maybe the interior of the yacht. That's what I guessed based on the beautiful wooden walls and furniture. Janet was sitting on a couch, with two seniors in law on both sides of her, two huge black men. One of them was Ule, from South Africa; I worked with him a few times. I didn't know the other one. There had to be a third man in the cabin who held the camera in his hand. The two black men were paddling on Janet's lean body and they were telling jokes which I couldn't really understand. The blonde girl was laughing loudly and slapped the men's hands when they pinched her thighs and ass. But I could see she really enjoyed it.

Another cut. And what I saw now, made my blood hot. Janet was on her knees in front of Ule. The camera was zooming slowly onto her face. Janet was smiling and fondling the black man's huge hard cock. It was only inches from her full red lips. She held up a tube with whipped cream, shook it up, and released a thick stripe of white cream on the black cock. She put down the tube and started to work; she licked his balls. When the man moaned out loudly, she stopped, looked into the camera, and smiled. Her nose was white from the cream.

"Your nose is white, you little bitch," someone said very loudly, probably directly to the microphone. I recognized it; he was the boss of the department. We called him the Worm. And no, he was no Dennis Rodman. He was only a stupid guy with a bad attitude. So it was he who organized this little trip? This is how you build business relationships?

Janet was going down on the big black cock. She was licking the cream from it, and the man was begging for a little harder sucking. But Janet laughed out loud, and licked the cream all the way at the length of the cock, till the head, and left a little there.

"And now the best part of the show, my fellow gentlemen," I heard Worm's affected voice. But he was right; it was beautiful how Janet licked the white cream with the end of her tongue from the throbbing black cockhead. The two black men were laughing and applauding, with their eyes gleaming.

Another cut. Janet was sucking the same huge black cock. Her full lips were moving up and down on the rod, she sucked as hard as she could and jerked it with her hand. The man enjoyed her sucking with loud moans.

"You can fuck her face, Ule," the Worm cried into the microphone. "That's how she really likes it."

The man didn't hesitate, grabbed the blonde girl's head, and pulled her with a steady motion onto his cock. He started to fuck her face, but she really liked it, her saliva was flowing out onto his balls.

I began to get excited but there was another cut. Now Janet was hunkered down at the front of the couch. She was totally naked except for her high heels. This has to be very important on a yacht. The camera was showing her heels then her open pussy – that's when I noticed her piercing in her pussy lip. It zoomed out and it showed the two black men naked as well, standing at both sides of Janet, their cocks standing beside her face. Janet was turning from one side to another to suck them. She was holding the two huge black cocks in her two hands and she was jerking them off wildly. It was interesting to see the contrast of all these colors: the black men, her blonde hair, her pink tongue, and her white skin. The camera zoomed on her face. She looked into it, then tried to press both cocks into her mouth at once.

"That's it, sword game!" the Worm shouted. I didn't really like this part, I wanted to flash forward, but Janet had to have enough as well because she let out the cocks from her mouth and took a deep breath with a smile. The two men wanted more, they slapped her face with their cocks a few times. Both of them were covered by Janet's saliva so it got on her cheeks as well. She was just laughing.

In the next scene, she was on her knees on the couch. One of the black men was doing her from behind. And as the camera moved to another angle, I could see he was fucking her ass. Yes, her tight ass was pounded by a big hard black cock. It was fucking her with powerful thrusts. I guess he fucked her pussy before because it was wide open down there and some white fluids were dripping from them – I couldn't say it was whipped cream, pussy fluid, or sperm. Janet was screaming, the guy pulled her closer to himself by her hair and fucked her with no mercy.

New scene. It was like a hardcore porn movie. Janet was riding one of the black cocks with legs spread wide, in reverse cowgirl. The big black rod was in her ass. Janet's pussy was gaping hungrily for the camera. She was moving up and down, and her blonde hair fell onto her face. She was breathing heavily. The camera was put on a small table so it didn't move anymore and I got to see the boss, the Worm, in the background. He sat at the end of the couch, pulled his cock out, and watched with an evil smile how his secretary's ass was being taken by a big black cock.

Janet was pushing herself onto the huge cock. She didn't say anything but moaned some when all of the huge hard cock was fucking her tight ass. I could tell she was really enjoying it. The Worm was jerking his cock in the background, with empty eyes.

That's when the other black man showed up. I could see only his ass from this angle. He got between Janet's spread knees and waited for them to slow down. When they did, he pushed his cock into her pussy. Janet grabbed his neck and shouted out loud, "Do it!" and she closed her eyes as he entered her. The cock in her ass must have filled her already but now she had two of these huge throbbing organs in her body. Janet moaned out loudly but in a good, satisfied way. Like she would have waited a month to have two big black cocks inside her body. The men were moving slowly; they let her stretch to the max. Her moaning slowly lowered, so they started to really give it to her. The two cocks were moving separately, one of them was always deep in her. Janet let out a sigh; she was clearly enjoying herself. She even bit the shoulder of the man fucking her pussy, but when she let it out, only her saliva was glistening on his black muscles.

Then they switched and started to move together. Like a two-piston machine working in a hot, slippery material. This made Janet scream. The men were fucking her like hell.

That followed the classic DP scene. I wasn't surprised at all. Janet was lying on Ule, facing him, he was fucking her pussy really hard, and the other guy was pounding her ass from behind. They were working in the same rhythm. The sweat was dripping from all three of them, I could hardly see which limb belonged to whom. Only Janet's groin was well visible, and the two huge black cocks moving in her pussy and ass. Both members filled her balls deep, then pulled back again.

Janet was practically screaming. She bent on Ule's chest, her blonde hair spread on his black muscles. She didn't try to move or to control anything, she just enjoyed the hardcore fucking. And the two men really gave it to her.

First, the unknown man came in her ass, then Ule in her pussy. They were fucking her further, but they were yelling loudly and their cocks were trembling. Some white fluid came out of Janet's pussy and asshole, it was glistening on their black cocks.

They continued fucking her for a minute, then the unknown black man stood up, walked over to the couch, and put his cock into the blonde girl's mouth. He was breathing heavily, but Janet seemed to be fresh, she sucked off everything from his huge organ. Ule fell back onto the couch.

The video was over. I copied it to my hard drive, to a hidden folder. It was a good decision, because two days later the original file was missing from the shared server. I thought it could be a good blackmail leverage against Ule. Or maybe against Janet...

Chapter 8: The Private Party

It would have been really elegant to arrive for Bonnie in a red Ferrari, but I still didn't have the fortune for it. Maybe later. That's why I used my good old Mustang to get to the front of Bonnie's place. I sounded the horn as we agreed. The rain was pouring from the clouds up above. Bonnie ran out, hopped in beside me, and kissed me lightly.

"Let's go," she said, pulling off her raincoat, and showing her beautiful, brown thighs. She wore a black mini skirt, as always, and a frilly, white blouse. I took delight in admiring her for a minute, but when she glanced at me, I started the engine and we set off.

The castle, our destination, was outside the city, in the mountains. I could hardly see anything in the pouring rain, but I hoped this weather wouldn't have any effect on the private party.

Bonnie set me at ease,

"I don't think we can go out to the lake," she said, "but we will have a very good time in the castle.

The trip took an hour. The rain almost covered the whole castle. Only some light from a few windows was shining through the darkness as floating frames. When we got a better look, I understood why it was called a castle; it had to be a copy of a small castle from somewhere in Europe. The roof was hidden among the trees. A small lake spread behind it. We stopped in front of the main entry. A servant took the key, and we ran into the hall.

It was another, enchanted world. The hall was warm and bright. Friendly light was pouring from the antique lamps on the walls. I could hear moans and music from the inside of the building.

"The party has already started," Bonnie said as another servant took our coats, and then we entered the main hall.

We went upstairs on semicircular stairs. There was another small hall. Our boss, the Worm, was sitting in a beautiful mahogany chair, and Janet, the blonde, big-tit secretary, was kneeling in front of him.

The Worm was fucking her face with a satisfied smile on his face. Her blonde hair hid the scene, mostly because the Worm held her head by grabbing into her hair, that's how he controlled her movements. The girl was wearing a short, black velvet dress. As she was kneeling in front of her boss, her ass came in full view. We could see she was wearing no panties, her wet pussy was gleaming in the bright lights. To make the view hotter, she grabbed the heels of her shoes; she let her boss control her completely. And he did. He was shoving his cock deep into her throat, again and again, balls deep.

I bent down to Janet's pussy to check the piercing which I saw in the video. But Bonnie grabbed my hand,

"Come with me, you'll have nicer things to see."

She took me with her. I followed her but took a last glance at the door. The boss' cock was deep in the blonde girl's mouth. She was sucking him with eyes closed, but with a kind of a smile on her face – as it was possible with a cock in her mouth.

We stepped into the following room. My eyes went wide because of the surprise. The lights were red, as in a traditional sado-maso room. Britney Spears's music was coming from the walls, but not the virgin shit she was singing at the beginning of her career, but the one screaming "Britney, bitch!"

Helen was on her knees in the middle of the room. The black-haired, small girl from the HR. The one with the cum addiction. She was wearing a black leather dress. It covered her body completely, only her nipples were free. The hottest piece on her was a black collar by which she was secured by four long black leather straps to the floor. A black leather whip was beside her knee on the floor. A few naked men were standing around her. Helen was jerking a cock in both of her hands and she was sucking a third one, a big strong black guy standing in front of her. The man was enjoying it really much, his hands were in Helen's hair and she fucked her mouth with slow, but strong movements.

"Wow," I said with a dry throat. I recalled how she sucked me off at the team-building party, but back then she didn't allow anyone to grab her head. Something had changed – maybe she got wilder.

"I never saw her this hot," whispered Bonnie in my ear. "This is a hell of a party..."

Helen was sucking the big black cock with abandon. She must have done it well because the guy cried out loudly and his knees went weak. His cock was throbbing in Helen's mouth, and the girl was swallowing. Two other guys sprayed as well; they unloaded the white drops on Helen's leather suit. The girl jerked them off wildly, she didn't even want to stop, the men had to break out of her grip. All three of them stepped back.

"Who's next?" Helen asked, with the well-known gleam in her eyes. She took up the whip beside her and caught the leg of a man with the end of it like a cowgirl, then pulled him closer to herself.

"I've got something for you!" Bonnie said to her which made Helen smile. Bonnie pushed me in front of the kneeling girl, near the other man, then she bent down to Helen and took a small amount of the cum onto her finger from the drops between Helen's breasts. She held her finger to her mouth and tasted the white thick fluid. The other guy was watching her with surprise.

"Not bad," she said with a sparkle in her eyes. "A little salty but not bad. But I bet you'll like this one so much better..."

"Let me have it!" Helen told her. She probably didn't remember me from the team-building.

Bonnie opened my fly and got out my cock. It was hard already, the things I saw so far had their effects on me. Bonnie slapped it against Helen's cheeks a few times. Helen would have taken it in her mouth but the leather straps didn't let her reach me.

"Don't fuck with me," she said, which made both girls laugh. Then Bonnie pulled me closer to Helen and put my cock into her mouth. I felt as if I had become the girl's toy. But I wasn't complaining. I enjoyed Helen's wet and hot mouth. She started sucking me in her rhythmic, professional way, meanwhile, she removed the whip from the leg of the other guy.

"Let me help you, I'll take over," Bonnie said. There was a flash in Helen's eyes, she dropped the whip to the floor and grabbed my ass with both of her hands. She pulled my cock into her throat so strongly her pink nails almost hurt my skin. It was so good I let out a loud moan. She didn't fuck around, she was sucking me really hard with her hot mouth. Her saliva was dripping to my balls, then down to the floor.

Bonnie beside me held the other guy's cock in her hand and started to jerk it off. She was doing it gently, moving her wrists, but she was watching me. She looked into my eyes.

"You like it, don't you?" she asked me, smiling.

I couldn't say anything. I closed my eyes and enjoyed the sucking. Helen let my cock deep into her mouth, and the head touched her throat. Her head was moving in a hard, steady rhythm on my dick. Bonnie patted my chest, and then I felt her hand on my balls. She lightly gripped them which made me cry out. Helen let my cock out of her mouth and jerking it, asked Bonnie,

"Do you want some?"

"Not yet...," Bonnie answered, so Helen went back onto my dick and sucked it really hard.

I couldn't take it anymore. I shot like a volcano, and Helen swallowed it all. I felt like I was flying. I must have come a lot because I felt it coming out of me like from a hose. Helen said nothing; she swallowed every drop.

I would have enjoyed myself in Helen's mouth more, but she let me out and concentrated on the other guy beside me. Bonnie pulled me with her.

We went to another room. There were some huge armchairs in the dim background and light romantic music. Some guys were kneeling in the front of the armchairs, mostly interns, as I recognized them. They were licking out the MILF bosses sitting in the armchairs.

"If you didn't graduate from Oxford, you'd have to earn your promotion here," Bonnie explained to me.

"I would do so, it depends on who I have to lick out," I said, smiling. "Is there any chance you can promote me?"

Bonnie was smiling. We stepped to one of the armchairs. I didn't know the woman sitting in it, but she was hot, her face was nice. Her dress was open, and I could see one of her breasts which were fondled by an intern kneeling in front of her. His head was hidden under her skirt, but even this way it was visibly moving up and down. There were some goodies on a small table beside them: whipped cream, strawberries, a banana, and some small dildos. Now his hand reached out from under her skirt and placed a string of anal beads on the table.

"It was in her pussy?" I asked Bonnie.

"I think it was in her ass," she said, smiling. "I would prefer so..."

The guy continued his work under her skirt. He really needed that promotion. Or a better salary, who knows...

"This guy is doing it really well!" said a woman sitting at the wall to another. "Wanna try him?"

"I will, I just let this cutie finger my ass here...," moaned her friend. "He's trained so well..."

The whole room seemed like a sweaty brothel to me. The ladies were moaning, enjoying themselves, one of them was sipping a pink drink through a straw while being licked out.

"Do you want to...?" I motioned toward an empty armchair, but she took my hand,

"I want something else," she said and led me out of the room.

We went up on a spiral staircase and reached the second floor of the castle. There were some small tables and chairs covered with red leather. Thousands of candles lit the room around the walls. And what we saw there was a real orgy. At least a dozen couples were fucking. To the left of us, two hot girls were licking each other. There were two young guys next to them, licking a law executive girl's pussy and ass at the same time. I could tell what they were planning to do since both of them were fingering her holes really hard. The main receptionist of the building was fucking a red-haired girl in the background. I can't imagine how he got invited here. Another man was standing in front of the red-haired girl, he was fucking her face with apparent pleasure.

Bonnie was watching the bodies moving in the room with a sparkle in her eyes. I knew what she wanted. I decided I would satisfy her completely tonight. I'm gonna give her anything she wants. I took her hand and led her to the middle of the room. There was a free hassock covered with red leatherette. I pulled her there and let her go.

"Now it's your turn," I said. I motioned a naked, muscular guy to the hassock. I chose him because I saw Bonnie checking him out when we entered the room. Bonnie pushed him on his back to the long hassock with a smile. She dropped her clothes, leaving only her high heels on. She looked into my eyes, knowing how much she excited me. She stuck a finger into her pussy, then showed it to me. I quickly licked it and she laughed out loud.

"Let me fuck you!" the guy on the hassock said, watching her beautiful ass. Bonnie turned around, climbed upon him and adjusted his cock to her pussy, then slowly sat down on him.

"Oh my god...," she moaned and closed her eyes. "I really needed this..."

She enjoyed the rod with slow, circling movements. Then she opened her eyes, looked at the guy beneath her, grabbed his chest, and started to ride him with loud moans. She rode his cock balls deep in her pussy at every thrust, and only the head remained in her when she rose. I wondered how he could keep up with her but it didn't seem a problem for him at all.

"Oh fuck....," she sighed again and again. "Fuck fuck fuck...."

She then rested a bit, bent down on the guy, hid his face with her hair, and moved slowly on the cock. I felt now it was my time. I climbed behind her and pressed the head of my aching cock to her asshole. When she felt what I was planning to do, she turned her head around. I could tell she was ready. The guy behind us stopped, and let me enter Bonnie's asshole slowly. She sighed loudly, her head bent down, her black hair spread on his chest. I remained still for a while, to let Bonnie adjust to the feeling of having two cocks in her. My cock was throbbing in her hot ass, and I felt the other cock staying still in her pussy. When I felt her relax, I entered her deeper, and when she let out a loud moan, I pulled back. I was moving slowly, enjoying Bonnie's hot and tight ass. The guy below us was moving slowly as well, I could feel his cock through the thin wall of Bonnie's pussy. I had a strong temptation to shove my cock balls deep into her asshole, but I didn't want to hurt her, so I fought the feeling.

Bonnie looked at me and gave out the order,

"Fuck my ass!"

It was clear and loud. I grabbed her shoulders and started to fuck her in a hard, slow, but steady rhythm. The man lying on the hassock sped up as well. Bonnie was moaning wildly, her fingers grabbed his chest. Her fluids made our cocks really wet so our fucking had a smacking sound.

A girl was getting it in her ass in front of us as well, but she was sitting in reverse cowgirl in the guy's lap, so I could perfectly see her ass stuffed with the huge cock, and her gaping pussy. And I could see perfectly how she started to finger herself.

Bonnie was moaning louder and louder, I felt she would come soon. It would have been nice to come with her at the same time, but I couldn't take it anymore. I shoved my cock balls deep into her ass and pumped her full with my hot sperm. Bonnie was moaning with closed eyes, and the man below her was fucking her wildly. The cum was coming out of me in big amounts. I was trembling like a tired stallion. I bent down on Bonnie's back and kissed her neck. She lost control completely.

I took a deep breath, and slowly, carefully pulled my spent cock out of her asshole. It came out with an audible pop. It was covered with my sperm.

I stepped back and watched as Bonnie straightened up, leaned on her elbows, and enjoyed the other cock fucking her pussy. Her gaping asshole closed slowly, but a few drops of my sperm dripped out of it.

I could see she still needed some serious fucking. I looked around to find my replacement. Ule was sitting in the corner, the black manager who fucked Janet on the video. I guessed he was recovering from a hard pounding. He was fondling his cock slowly, and he was watching the couples fucking in the room.

I caught his glance and waved him over. He got it, walked to us, then looked Bonnie up and down. He grabbed her ass with his large hands, pulled her ass cheeks apart, and saw drops of cum in her gaping asshole. He nodded, then climbed above the couple and signaled the guy below to stop for a while. He pressed his big black cock to Bonnie's tiny asshole. Bonnie opened her eyes in surprise, and looked at me, but I fondled her back and whispered in her ear,

"Let's try it!"

Bonnie gritted her teeth and nodded. I nodded to Ule and he entered her instantly.

"Oouch...," she hissed with closed eyes. Ule stopped, watched her with an evil grin on his face, then grabbed her breast with his one hand, grabbed her hair with the other, and pulled her head back so her whole body stretched. And that's how he entered her deeply.

"Ooooohhh," Bonnie moaned, but Ule showed no mercy. He shoved his big black cock in her with some really powerful thrusts.

The two men started to fuck her. They were moving together like a well-oiled machine. Bonnie's face turned wild, she started to scream, but no one cared since everyone was doing the same in the room.

I wanted to get in on the action so I stepped to the end of the hassock and put my hard cock into her open mouth. This gagged her screams, but of course, she couldn't really suck me since the two men were fucking her with real abandon. I'd never seen a perfect sandwich like this. All she could do was to press her lips on my cock. I grabbed her head by her hair and moved her head on my cock in the same rhythm as the other two men fucked her two other holes. Sweat and saliva covered our bodies, and as the music just got louder, our rhythm got faster. I fucked her face watching how Ule filled her perfect ass with his big black cock.

That was when she came. When I felt her well-known trembling, I pulled my cock out of her mouth. She screamed with her eyes closed. I jerked my cock as the two guys fucked her through her orgasm. She collapsed on the guy below her.

The two men didn't care. They fucked her like a doll. The two rods were stretching her two holes wide. She let out some tired moans but hardly moved at all.

They finally came. First Ule – he stopped moving and his whole body was jerking. Then the unknown guy below her came as well with a loud cry.

I couldn't take it anymore, I had to come for one last time. I plunged my cock into her open mouth and fucked her face with a few thrusts. The scene before me was enough, I came like a stallion again. I let my cum drip into Bonnie's mouth. She didn't swallow as vigorously as usual, probably because of the two cocks spasming in her pussy and ass.

Finally, all of us pulled out. Cum was dripping from Bonnie's pussy, ass, and mouth. Some of our sperm fell onto the black leatherette of the hassock. Bonnie's hair was messed up; she was covered with sweat and sperm. She was beautiful. She looked into my eyes, and I could tell she was grateful.

Office Sluts 2

Wild Adventures

Chapter 1: In The Bank

"What's this?" Bonnie asked.

She was holding a black thong; we were packing my stuff in my flat.

A few weeks ago she introduced me to her uncle, the owner of the house she lives in. We got to like each other, and later on, he offered to let me live in his condo with her. I thought about independence and shit like that, but the cost-effective reasoning won.

So we spent a Saturday organizing and packing my stuff before moving. I threw the trash out in the alley and when I returned to the flat, she was waiting for me with this sexy black thong in her hand.

"Well..." I started but she stopped me,

"And don't bullshit me! Who does this belong to?"

"Okay, sit down and I will tell you all about it."

We sat down on the bed, and I began my story.

"When I moved here, I didn't know anybody. I didn't have a car yet so I had to take the bus. I was reading ebooks and fantasizing about every hot woman I saw on the street. One time I ran into Andy, my crush from high school. She was in a hurry, running somewhere. My bus stopped a few steps from her. I stepped off and hurried to her. She recognized me instantly, so we greeted each other and talked about what we were up to. She told me she was working in a bank office not far away. She was running late, so I walked her to the office. It was a large bank with security and everything.

"We said goodbye, I got a kiss on my cheek then she hurried away. I checked her out from behind, and I could tell time made her only prettier. She had a nice round ass with long, muscular legs. Her white skirt and white high heels just made her body even sexier.

"I couldn't get her out of my head all day. In fact, not even for the night. I had fantasies about her body, her silky black hair, her moans...

"When I woke up, I knew what I had to do; I had to fuck her."

"Oh, you pig," Bonnie said, smiling.

"I am, but isn't this why you like me?" I answered. Then I continued with my story.

"Two weeks passed. I bought the stuff I needed, called her, and told her I had to meet her for business reasons. I told her I wanted to have a safe deposit box at her bank, and I requested her personally to handle the account. She told me it wasn't her area but she would help me anyway.

"So on a foggy morning, Andy and I went into the safe at the bank. She closed the door behind us, stepped to one of the walls of the safe, and bent over at the waist. I admired her magnificent ass again. I could even see the line of her thong along her hip. She opened a small safe in the wall, put the safe deposit box on the table, and then gave the key to me. I put my bag on the large mahogany desk and eyed her up and down."

"'Take your time, put anything you'd like in the storage,' she said. 'This is the only room in the building without any cameras in it, to keep the privacy of our clients secured. The doors are soundproof so you can check any recordings here. As a result, we have no cell signal.'

"'Thanks very much,' I said as she stepped toward the door. 'You can stay,' I said and looked deep into her eyes. 'In fact, I want you to stay.'

"I watched her as she wondered about what I said. My whole plan depended on her decision."

"'Okay, if it doesn't bother you,' she said.

"'Not at all.'

"She smiled and stepped beside the table.

"I opened up my bag and put my stuff on the table, beside the steel box. They looked strange on the shiny mahogany surface: a small bottle of lubricant, a huge black butt plug, and red anal beads on a string. Andy didn't say anything, but sized up the toys with her large brown eyes and then looked at me, questioning.

"I let her think about it.

"'Choose one,' I pointed to the toys on the table, breaking the silence. She thought for a moment, curious if I was serious.

"'I think I'll go with these,' she said with a shrug, pointing to the beads.

"'Good choice,' I nodded. 'They are the smaller ones. They'll go into your pussy.'

"Wow," Bonnie interrupted. "This story gets hotter and hotter."

"Are you sure you want to hear the rest of it?"

"But of course!"

I went on.

"Andy's eyes widened but she didn't say a word. She straightened, looked into my eyes, smiled, and I knew I won.

"'Turn around,' I said. 'Lean over the table.'

"She did. She bent over the desk, presenting her magnificent ass to me.

"I knew she submitted herself to me and for a short time, I could do whatever I wanted with her. And if it meant destroying her beautiful ass, then so be it.

"I lifted her skirts to her waist. She was wearing a black lacy thong. It showed her round ass beautifully.

"'That's nice,' I said with a dry throat. 'But I have to take it down.... For security reasons...'

"I pulled her thong to the side to reveal her pussy and her ass. Her pussy lips were swollen. The sight was beautiful. Her ass was gleaming in the light. She looked back at me and I could see a little sparkle in her eyes as she licked her lips with her wet red tongue. The little bitch.

"'That's nice,' I repeated. I spanked on her ass hard. She hissed but didn't say anything, just kept looking back at me, smiling. I pulled her head up to me, and we kissed for a minute. Her appearance, her red lips, and her wet tongue had their effect on me, I could feel my cock hardening."

"Just like now?" asked Bonnie. She touched my groin and pointed to my hardening cock.

"I have to admit, all these memories..."

"Don't admit anything. Just tell your fucking story!" she said. "And I will take care of this," as she opened my fly, took out my cock, and gently fondled it in her hands. I leaned back into a large pillow and continued with the story.

"'You like it, right?' I asked and spanked Andy's round ass cheeks again. I did it harder this time, loving the feeling of her hot skin on my palm. The spankings sounded strange in this marble-and-oak environment. I wondered how many spankings this room had seen. Maybe this was the first one, more than I suspected...

"Pulling her cheeks apart, I admired her asshole for a moment. It was tight and pink and made my cock twitch. Then I leaned over and quickly kissed it. Her body trembled, as I smelled the scent of her skin.

"I straightened and spanked her once again.

"'Ouch!' she said this time. With a grin on my face, I kneeled behind her and pulled her round butt cheeks apart again. With a quick move, I licked all over her wet pussy and asshole. This made her moan loudly, so I buried my face into her twat and started licking her out. It was easy since she was dripping wet.

"I found her clit and sucked it between my lips. It was already swollen and I circled with my tongue all around it. My tongue dipped into her pussy as well, enjoying her sweet aroma. I could tell she was enjoying it since she was pushing her pussy into my mouth.

"'Deeper...' she moaned. 'Please lick me deeper...'

I continued eating her out, and I spanked her nice round butt again. I grabbed it and pulled it even closer to my face. As I shoved my tongue deep inside her pussy, my nose pressed into her asshole. I moved it sideways a bit and enjoyed her hot flesh on my face. I penetrated her dripping wet pussy with my tongue again and again."

"That's so hot!" Bonnie said. She was practically jerking my cock now. With her other hand, she dived into her jeans and was rubbing her pussy.

"I pulled back to get some air. Andy was standing before me with her hungry pussy and ass. It was time to get more serious.

"'You won't need this,' I said and pulled her thong down on her beautiful long legs. It came to a halt on her high heels.

"I spread her cheeks again and started to lick her ass this time. I began with small circles around her asshole, then entered deeper. She moaned and tried to move closer to me so I grabbed her ass tightly and pulled her ass to my tongue. I licked it wet and deep. My saliva was dripping all over my face, but I was hoping I could make her ass loose enough for a good fucking.

"I moved back and pressed my index finger to her hungry asshole. She pushed herself on it. The first knuckle disappeared into her ass easily. I felt her hot flesh around it and pushed further a bit. She leaned her head down and relaxed for a few seconds. Then she moved further on my finger. I felt this was green light, so I made circles with my finger inside her ass, trying to ease her back door as much as I could. Soon I felt it loosen enough to push my middle second finger in as well."

"Oh..." Bonnie moaned. "I hope you fucked her as well..." She bent down, letting my cock slip between her wet lips to wet it a bit. She pulled back off of it and ordered me to continue the story.

"With my other hand, I found her clit and fondled it lightly. That was when she came for the first time. Her whole body tightened, then trembled slightly and she let out a quiet cry.

"I waited for a minute, then I released her. I opened the lubricant and took the big black butt plug in my hand. I smeared some lubricant on it and pressed it to her asshole. I made small movements at first. She enjoyed it, her eyes closed as she enjoyed the sensation. The plug's small end slid easily for a while but then it widened so I had to slow down. I made more small circular movements with it, then rested for a moment. Again, I pushed it into her ass, and to my surprise, it slid in easily.

"'Oh my God...' she sighed. I released the butt plug; it stuck straight up her ass. I admired it for a moment, then with a smile, spanked her ass again.

"'Give me the other one,' I asked her. She took the anal beads from beside her and gave them to me. I immediately pressed the first bead to her wet pussy and slid it inside. It slid in quickly and easily, the huge butt plug in her ass didn't seem to affect her pussy. So I pressed another bead inside, then another. Only one remained between my fingers and I gripped it tightly so as not to lose all the string. Instead, I gently pulled it out a bit, then pushed back again. She clearly enjoyed how the beads massaged her pussy from the inside. I started to fuck her with the anal beads, moving them in and out of her pussy. It became really wet soon, her juices gleaming on the beads. Some even dropped on the marble floor below. I could feel her arousal. She started breathing faster and even let out some quiet moans.

"I started to give it to her really hard.

"'Do you like it?' I asked. 'Do you like to be double stuffed? It's like being fucked by two hard cocks, isn't it?'

"I don't know whether she'd ever tried being double-penetrated, but the idea definitely hit her because she came again. Her whole body shuddered from the orgasm, and she let out a loud cry. I was glad there were no cameras in the room, and because the room was sound-proofed.

"I left the toys stuffed inside her body and stood up, grabbed her by her hair, and raised her face to me.

"'Now it's your turn, bitch!'

"She knew exactly what to do, she turned around and knelt before me. She opened my fly, took out my cock, and swallowed it deep. A real bitch in heat. She was doing it just the way I liked it – with a lot of saliva and a hungry mouth. It was so good I almost came so I had to switch; I pushed her away and helped her sit on the mahogany stool.

"'Let me fuck your boobs,' I said, hoarsely. I opened up her blouse and stripped her out of her bra. She let some saliva drool between them, pressed them together, and then gently pulled my cock between them. Her flesh was hot but her sweat and saliva seemed cool at the same time. She moved her tits up and down my cock. She even licked the tip when it reached her mouth.

"That was when I noticed her thong stuck on one of her heels. I pushed my cock deep into her throat and got an idea. I pulled her face from my cock and looked into her eyes.

"'Gimme your thong!'

"She didn't know what the hell I was talking about, but looked around and found her thong. She pulled it from her heel and gave it to me. I smelled it, admired her pussy's smell for a moment, before throwing them on the table."

"This thong?" Bonnie asked. She held it to her nose, very carefully. "I can't smell anything."

"I washed it," I admitted. "I didn't exactly know what to do with a stolen thong..."

Bonnie smiled and I went on while she jerked my cock.

"I pulled Andy away from the chair. She got it and kneeled on the marble. I almost felt sorry for her because of the cold floor on her knees. But only almost.

"I grabbed her hair and started fucking her face. She obediently let my cock free, put her hands behind her back, and grabbed her high heels. Her body tensed just like a bow on my cock.

"She swallowed my cock deep into her throat. I thrust into her and enjoyed the hot feeling of her engulfing my cock. Then I pulled back and she sighed loudly. She released her heels, grabbed my dick with one hand, and started jerking it while leaning between my thighs and licking my balls.

"'That's good,' I moaned. I closed my eyes and enjoyed her wet tongue on my balls. 'Wanna have a tea bag?' I asked, which made her gently swallow one of my testicles and very lightly sucked it. 'Wow,' I sighed, and when she switched balls, I closed my eyes again. I was in heaven. She jerked my cock in her fist but it was so wet it almost felt like a pussy. And her licking and sucking my balls...

"I opened my eyes and stepped a bit closer to her.

"'Now a double ice cream,' I ordered. She looked up, not being sure what I meant. But I motioned her to open up again. She did and I lowered my groin and let my two balls on her full lips at the same time. She got what I meant and widened her mouth, then, again gently, swallowed both of my testicles. Now that really was something. Nobody ever did that to me. I almost came as she sucked my balls so eagerly and licked my sack with her wet tongue at the same time, but I wanted to fuck her. I pulled away and sat on the chair. She wanted to follow me on her knees but I made her stand up. I admired her long naked legs again and slowly pulled out the anal beads from her pussy. They were dripping with her juices. I dropped them on the table beside us and pulled her into my lap.

"She almost jumped in my lap and guided my cock into her. With all those juices and the effect of the beads, it slid easily in. She closed her eyes again. Her breasts slid lightly in my hands. It felt so good to hold them.

"With the butt plug still in her ass, I felt her really full with my cock. As she started riding me up and down, I buried my face between her swollen breasts and inhaled the sweet scent of her skin.

"Her hungry pussy swallowed my whole length. She was riding me so hard, fucking herself with my cock. I could see I wasn't the only one who wanted a piece of ass; she wanted to get fucked really bad.

"And I intended to give it to her. Burying my face between her breasts, I grabbed her ass with both of my hands and helped her ride my throbbing cock.

"'Oh... my... god...' she cried. 'I needed this... so... bad...'

"She was so loud I was glad the room was sound-proofed. With a sudden idea, I picked up her thong and stuffed it into her mouth. She looked surprised but continued moving up and down on my cock."

"Wow, you nasty boy!" said Bonnie. "I didn't think you'd do something so nasty!"

"But you like it, right?"

"Hell yeah!" she said, and she pulled out her hand from her jeans. She wrapped the black thong around my cock, and started to jerk me with it.

"And you like this, right?" she asked.

I nodded. She dived with her free hand back into her jeans and told me to go on.

"Andy was a fucking machine in human flesh. She leaned down to me and her long black hair covered my head, she pressed her face to mine while riding me really hard. From this angle, I could feel the butt plug in her ass through the thin wall of her pussy. As she was impaling herself again and again on my hard cock, the plug made pressure on the end of it again and again. I really enjoyed her kinda-DP'd body this way, and I could tell she was enjoying it, too.

She straightened up, leaned back and I held her in my arms so she didn't fall back completely. She moved like that for a few thrusts and with a loud moan, came again. Her whole body trembled, and she was enjoying herself with closed eyes for a good half minute.

"I let her come down from seventh heaven, then pulled her back to me by her arms. We stood up and looked into each other's eyes. She still had her thong in her mouth but I could tell she was smiling. She bit on it like a wild animal. So I used the thong in her mouth as a collar, turned her around, and bent her over on the chair again. I pulled out the plug from her ass, slowly and firmly. I pulled her round, hard cheeks apart and admired her gaping asshole for a minute. Then I spanked her again. She was laughing, waiting bent over so her hair covered her face.

"I stepped behind her and pressed my cock head to her asshole. It only needed a little push and entered her tight back door easily.

"'Mmmmm...' she sighed with her thong in her mouth, which made me even hornier. I was finally in her asshole. How I longed for her for years! And I wanted to make it the ass-fuck of her life."

"I bet... you did...," Bonnie said, with her eyes closed. I could tell she was getting close to her orgasm and she jerked my cock really hard, so I decided to tell the story as dirty as possible.

"I started moving in and out. My cock entered deeper and deeper. It was a bit tight, but so hot I didn't care. When she started to push herself back on me, I turned it up a gear and started fucking her harder. My cock entered her ass like a knife in a piece of melted butter.

"I was fucking her ass balls deep. I grabbed her by her hair and impaled her ass on my throbbing cock again and again. We were moving with such passion that her thong fell out of her mouth, so with my other hand I covered her mouth – sound-proofed room or not, I didn't want any security guards to hear us. In a porn movie, they would probably join me and bang this little slut, but for now, I stayed in reality and stuffed this bitch full of my cock.

"'That's it, bitch,' I hissed into her ears. 'I'm gonna fuck you in half.'

"'Fuck me...' she cried out loud. 'Fuck my ass!'

"I grabbed her by her waist and fucked her with all my power. I didn't even care about whether anybody heard us anymore. We were both screaming with lust.

"I felt my balls tighten as my orgasm took over, and I came. I pumped all my sperm into her hot ass. It was a big release after a long long time of waiting. Finally, I pushed a few last thrusts into her, then, with weak knees, pulled out and stepped back."

That was when I came into Bonnie's palm. I shot my sperm up, and the white cum dripped on the black thong wrapped around it. Bonnie watched my orgasm with a smile and jerked everything out of me. I sighed and told her the rest of it while she finished herself.

"Andy was bent over on the desk for some moments but when she turned around, she was the old professional office girl. She picked up her bra again, adjusted her clothes quickly, and combed her sweaty hair with her fingers.

"'Can I have my thong back, please?' she asked in her totally cool voice. I held her thong in my hands for a moment,

"'Nope,' I said. 'I will keep it as a memory. Plus, I want you to walk upstairs with my cum dripping out of your ass.'

She said nothing and adjusted her high heels, but I could see her face was burning red.

"'Yeah...' I continued. 'I want you to work today with my sticky cum dripping out back there. I want your colleagues to smell it on you and to suspect you of having sex with somebody. Even when your boss orders you in his room, he will smell my sperm oozing out of your ass.'

"She didn't say anything but I could tell she liked the idea.

"I'm sure she enjoyed it," Bonnie said to me. "Did the two of you meet again?"

"Later on I saw her with an ugly dude at a party. As far as I know, she's with him now and they live happily ever after..."

"Too bad..." she murmured, and I watched her putting the thong away in a box with all the other stuff she brought here for the nights she spent at my place.

"You like her, don't you?" I asked.

"Hey..." she said, looking at me. "I listened to how she let you fuck her ass. I jerked you off with her thong. Of course I like her."

"And what will you do with the thong?"

"I'm gonna wash it," she said, smiling. "And I'm gonna let you fuck me in the ass while I wear it."

Chapter 2: The Japanese Teacher

Carl and I were enrolled in a Japanese language class. Our bosses thought we needed basic lessons to understand our clients better. So here we were, sitting at a desk in a large meeting room with the new intern girl, Lori, and the Japanese teacher, Asa. She was an Asian girl, having recently started at our firm to teach dumbasses like Carl and me. Her appearance was the silver lining in this whole lesson; she was hot, with nice perky breasts, long legs, and silky long black hair. She even dressed to show off her hot body: she was wearing a short black dress with silver buttons, black high heels, and geeky glasses. She was talking to us about kanjis and their roles in Japanese culture and shit like that.

Carl was making notes on his laptop, just like Lori in front of me. Maybe it was the lunch, maybe it was the lack of sleep last night, but I couldn't concentrate on the lesson. I have to admit, I got lost after a few minutes, so instead, I admired our teacher's hot body. I eyed her up and down, tried to imagine her naked, on her knees, maybe with a collar on her neck...

Carl pushed his laptop in front of me on the desk.

"Did you know our teacher started in porn?" he whispered in my ear. I looked at the monitor. He'd found a movie on a porn video-sharing site in which our hot teacher was on her knees sucking a huge black cock. I leaned closer to the monitor, then looked at our teacher, then back to the monitor. Yep, it was definitely her. A couple of years younger, maybe. But she was there, on the scene, on her knees before this black dude, sucking like there was no tomorrow.

I scrolled down to the bottom of the page. There were more previews of other videos, with Asa in a variety of positions and situations, but based on their titles, each and each one of them involved hardcore sex.

"O... kay..." I said, but I couldn't take my eyes off of the site. That was when our teacher stepped in front of me.

"Could you please repeat what I was telling you about the readings of the kanjis, Mr. Smith?" she asked me sternly.

"Well... er..."

"What are you watching there?" she turned the laptop to her. When she realized what we were watching she didn't even blink, but straightened and adjusted her hair. "So you found these videos, right? Okay, I admit, I did some gigs in porn movies before. Are you satisfied?"

"Actually, it wasn't me..." I said, but she didn't care,

"Yes, I was doing porn, yes, I had sex for the money, and yes, I was really enjoying it. Okay? Any more questions?"

"What the hell..." asked Lori, but Asa motioned her to be silent.

"It will be better if we talk about it. I don't want to have any awkward misunderstandings later." She sat down next to us at the round oval table. "Okay, ask your questions."

Neither Carl nor I could say a word. We were looking at each other, then to the monitor, then to the teacher. But she didn't stop.

"Yes, my stage name was Asa. Yes, I have a loving family. My parents know about my whole movie career. My dad refused to see any of it, my mom always says I have to take care of myself and she's happy if I'm happy. Yes, I love sex, I love doing it in public, I like to be fucked, I love a little side-play with women. What else?"

I could see Lori watching us with eyes widened.

Carl had a question. "What was your favorite..."

"Scene?" finished Asa the question. "Okay, which ones have you found so far? I liked the one in the porn theater, I also enjoyed the anal on the stairs, and I liked being licked by two girls at the same time... Oh! If I had to choose an all-time favorite, I would say the blowbang."

"Aw..., gross," Lori said.

"What's gross about it?" Asa turned to her. "There's nothing wrong with being in a circle of hot muscular men while you are on your knees, with hard cock everywhere."

"Doing it with a lot of strangers?" Lori asked.

"So what? Haven't you ever dreamed about doing it with a stranger before?"

Lori's cute cheeks turned red. She tried to write something in her notebook. Then she attacked again, "What about the taste of the cum?"

"What about it?" Asa asked. "Haven't you ever tried it?"

"Not yet."

"Never?"

"Never."

All the four of us remained silent. This escalated quickly.

"Well, you should," Asa said. "Men love it. Do it and they will adore you for life. Isn't that so, guys?" she turned to us. We nodded, smiling. "Do you see? They are animals..."

"Okay, I simply haven't had any opportunity to do so," Lori said.

"Then you will do it right now!" Asa said.

"What?"

We didn't know what her plan was. But she made it clear, "You're gonna suck Mr. Smith here," she pointed at me, "and you are going to taste his cum!"

Lori didn't seem to like the idea, but our hot teacher stood behind her, took her hand, and pulled her up as well.

"Come on," she urged her, "do it and you'll be over it for life! Plus, these guys will always adore you!"

"But what if somebody..."

"No one has to know," Asa said. "Unless you want to, of course."

"No..." Lori said with a blush. "But I never really..."

"Oh, I will show you how," our teacher said, then she turned to us. "Push your chairs back, gentlemen."

We did as she told us. She stepped in front of Carl and pressed his legs apart with her high heels.

"Come on, let's show her how it's done!" she said. Carl shrugged, "Why not?"

He released his belt, pulled his zipper down, and took out his already hard cock. Lori and I just watched him but Asa dropped to her knees and held the cock in her hand.

"See?" she told Lori. "They don't need much persuasion."

And with that, she took Carl's cock into her mouth. Carl sighed out loud, leaned back in his chair, and closed his eyes. Asa started to slurp on his cock loudly, with visible abandon. She closed her eyes as well, and let the cock slide deep between her full lips. Then she glanced at us, who were watching them. She let the cock out of her mouth, grabbed it with both hands, and gently jerked it up and down."Come on, get on your knees, Lori!" she said, with some saliva dripping out of her lips. "I'm sure Mr. Smith wouldn't mind you sucking his cock!"

"Not at all!" I admitted and opened my pants as well. I figured this could be a good adventure for this afternoon. I took out my cock. Lori looked at it, her eyes widened, then shrugged and knelt, looked at Asa again, and took my rock-hard cock into her mouth.

It was fantastic. When I woke up that morning, I didn't imagine a young hot intern would suck my cock in the afternoon. I could tell she had no experience but she really seemed to like it, bobbing her head up and down just the way she must have seen it in porn movies.

I looked at Carl and Asa. She was licking his cock from his balls all the way up, and looking into his eyes. Carl watched her with a happy smile.

I felt a little bite on my rod.

"Slow down," I stopped Lori. "It hurt a little."

She took my cock out,

"Sorry," she said. "This is my first and I want it to be..."

But I didn't wait for her to finish her sentence, grabbing her head by her hair and pushing her back onto my cock. She laughed a bit but continued her sucking.

"Easy, girl!" Asa told her. "Lick around the little arrow on the bottom of the head. Cocks are really sensitive there, and guys really like it."

She did and it was fantastic. While working with her tongue, she let some saliva pour on my cock which made it wet and shiny. Then she swallowed me back to her throat.

"That's right, suck him good!" Asa said, jerking Carl's cock. "Try to take the whole length into your mouth!"

Oh, she did! It was so good! Her saliva was dripping to my balls. She was bobbing up and down again, eyes closed. I could see Asa's hand under her skirt, furiously working down there. I glanced at Lori's body but she was concentrating on sucking my cock. And she was doing it really well!

"Lick the balls!" we heard our teacher say. Lori released my cock, held it in her petite hands, and licked my balls. She was working fast with her small tongue. I moved her hand on my cock hoping she would jerk it just the way Asa did with Carl's, but she didn't get it, instead licking my sack energetically. I couldn't blame her, being her first time, doing it in an international office. So I enjoyed her gently kissing my balls and watched Asa deep-throated Carl next to me.

"Oh... my... God..." he panted which caused Asa to release his cock from her mouth and jerked it in front of her face.

"Come in my mouth!" she grinned wildly. "Come between my fucking lips! I want to taste your fucking sperm!"

She really was a professional. His first spurt landed on her face but she quickly took his jerking cock between her lips and sucked it again. Carl's body jerked a few times, as he pushed his cock deep into Asa's mouth. She held it there and massaged his balls carefully.

Lori released me totally and watched how Carl came into our teacher's mouth. She gently fondled my cock but watched Asa getting a mouthful of sperm. Her eyes even widened when Asa stood up, stepped to her, and held her face in her hands. She made Lori open her mouth, then just like starting a friendly kiss, she opened her lips and let Carl's cum and her own saliva flow out into Lori's mouth.

"That's so hot..." Carl said beside me. As for myself, I couldn't believe my eyes. The young hot intern on her knees, getting snowballed by our Asian teacher? As Lori started getting to feel for it, she sucked and swallowed the cum quickly. They even shared it with a kiss, with tongue and everything.

And when I thought this can't be hotter, Asa pointed at me,

"Now suck out his sperm!"

Lori turned to me again, let my cock deep into her mouth, and started sucking me again. This time I couldn't hold it back, I grabbed her hair and fucked her face.

"That's it, honey, suck it!" Asa said, grinning at her like an evil little devil. This whole situation, Lori's hot mouth, and her dripping saliva had their effect on me. My balls tightened, and I sprayed a huge amount of cum into her mouth. She swallowed it with her eyes closed.

"It's good, isn't it?" Asa said.

"Yeah..." I sighed even though I knew she wasn't asking me.

After half a minute, Lori wanted to release me but Asa pushed her head back on my groin. "Suck out everything, but gently!"

She did, sucked, and licked my softening cock for a little more. Then she let it out, cleared her lips with her palm, and looked at Asa.

"It wasn't bad... Just like saliva."

"See?" our teacher asked. "There's nothing wrong or dirty about it!"

"Oh it was so so wrong and dirty," she answered. "That's why it was so good."

<u>Chapter 3: Evil Clowns From Outer Space</u>

It was three AM. I woke up to a sudden noise in the bed beside me. I opened my eyes and found Bonnie sitting next to me.

"I can't sleep," she said.

"Close your eyes," I told her. "And count sheep…"

"Please…" she told me. "I had a nightmare."

I sat up. Having a bad dream can affect your whole day. I recalled all the stuff I read about it on the Internet. I turned on the lava lamp. Bonnie was covered with sweat. I got up, found her a dry T-shirt, and brought her a glass of water from the kitchen.

"Thanks," she said after drinking a little. "It's better."

"Was it the movie we watched?" I asked.

"Definitely!" Bonnie said. "I've been dreaming about evil clowns!"

"But I told you the Killer Klowns from Outer Space is just a bad horror flick from the '80s. I thought it would be funny to watch it."

"Well, it seemed funny last night, but I've been dreaming about evil clowns."

"From the movie?"

"Well, not exactly… They were no aliens but hung black guys dressed as clowns."

"I've never seen a black clown before," I tried to joke with her.

"There were two in my dreams! And they were wearing the same strange masks with the evil smile as in the movie."

I had to admit, that wouldn't be something I'd want to dream about.

"Okay," I sat down beside her, "what exactly happened in your dream?"

"Well… there were these two clowns. They both were huge, muscular, bald black guys with their faces painted white and a red nose. Oh, and a red hat."

"Were they sad clowns or happy clowns?"

"I think happy ones. And they had those strange, colorful ragged clothes on. And boots. Black boots."

"What were you wearing?"

"Well... some kind of latex stuff... And a cap just like the soldiers wear in the old soviet movies!"

"Wow, sounds sexy... And what were these clowns doing?"

"They were chasing me around a haunted town. And they had their cocks out. They were huge, like long black snakes. I was running in my high-heeled boots but I couldn't get away, so I was screaming like hell! I fell on the ground many times but they were chasing me so I had to get up and run for my life... I was running by a big Ferris wheel, then a cemetery with two scarecrows in it, and an empty street with houses with blank windows... And the next thing I know one of the clowns was sitting in a steel chair. I was kneeling in front of him, sucking his big black cock. And it was huge!"

"I thought you liked black cocks."

"Oh, I do! But this was so strange! I had a collar on my neck, with two thin chains attached to it and the clown controlled my movements with these chains. So he was basically fucking my mouth in his evil way."

"I wouldn't think that was evil. I think that was hot!"

"Okay, it feels hot now when I think about it. But in my dream, he seemed to be evil! His cock was really big, I could fit only half of it in my mouth. My saliva was pouring around it, I tried everything to make it wetter. He was fucking my mouth like a pussy! Then he pulled my head back by the chains and kissed me!"

"Wow! An evil yet sensitive clown!"

"Of course he was evil! He stood up, reeled some of the silver chain on his cock, then pulled my head back on it! And shoved his cock to my throat! I could feel it throbbing inside my mouth like a big black snake!"

"Now that's disgusting!"

"Actually it wasn't... It felt kinda good! It was kinda good kneeling in front of him and letting him fuck my mouth like an obedient slut... Especially when he pulled out, and flapped my face with his huge black dong! I even took his balls in my mouth. They were huge but I managed to take them in both at the same time."

"You got a double ice cream from him," I said, smiling.

"If you say so... And he was jerking his cock while I was blowing his balls! Huge drops of pre-cum dripped onto my face and I could smell his strong scent!"

"What did the other clown do?"

"He was standing beside us and was jerking his huge cock! The head touched my cheeks sometimes and it was warm and hard. And at one point he grabbed my hair and pulled me from the other clown's cock onto his... And he was fucking my mouth just like the other clown did... It felt so good..."

"It wasn't really a nightmare, was it?"

"Wait for more! The next thing I recall I was on my knees again, and one of the clowns was fucking my ass from behind, the other one was fucking my mouth! The one in my mouth pushed his cock into my throat. It was tasty but he pulled out and pressed his balls into my mouth. I had to lick his sack like a good little kitten. I did it and he was really enjoying it, shouting things in a strange language I didn't understand. When his sack was dripping from my saliva, he pushed his cock back all the way into my mouth and started fucking my mouth just the way the other clown was doing me from behind. They were moving like two pistons in me. And when I started to enjoy it, they started to turn me around like a fried chicken on a spit..."

"They were spit-roasting you," I corrected her.

"Whatever! My whole body was hanging on these two cocks and they were rotating me upside down. First slowly, then faster and faster. I even got dizzy about it. And they were fucking me at the same time! Their cocks stuffed my ass and my mouth balls deep! And while they spun me, they fondled my ass cheeks, my tits, and my belly... Their big strong hands were everywhere..."

"So all your senses were overwhelmed by them. This is not unusual in a dream."

"But that wasn't all! Next, I was DP'd by them! I was on my knees on one of these huge guys, and one of those huge black cocks was fucking the hell out of my pussy, the other one was pounding my ass!"

"Just the way you like it..." I said, smiling.

"Yeah..." she smiled as well. "I like to be DP'd sometimes... But these cocks were really huge and hard ones! I never felt so full in my life! Plus, they were moving at such the same tempo I never felt anything like that in reality. And their rods were so hot! I must have come a few times..."

"Did they come, too?"

"Hell yeah! The last thing I recall before waking up is being on my knees, and jerking their huge cocks with both of my hands! And they've been standing at the sides and shooting! Can you guess how they came?"

I sighed, thinking of the bad jokes on the 9gag website.

"Their cum had the color..."

"Of the rainbow!" finished Bonnie my sentence. "And it wasn't funny! There were all the colors flying everywhere! They covered my face, my breasts, my hair! And the taste! Can you guess how they tasted?"

"Maybe... like toothpaste?"

"No, it was candy! Their cum tasted like candy in a variety of flavors! Strawberry, pineapple, raspberry, banana..."

I sat there for a moment, wondering if she was still horny from her dream. Hearing her talk about it really made my cock hard like a stone. She looked pretty tired though. Her eyes were already closed.

"I think you like all this shit you told me," I said gently. "Big black cocks, latex, anal, a lot of cum..."

"Yeah, I like it... But they were laughing all the while! With their loud, evil laugh! It was terrible!" she murmured with her eyes closed. And that was all, she fell fast asleep. I turned down the lights and lay beside her on the bed. I hoped I wouldn't dream about evil clowns. Or at least, if I will, I hoped I'll be one of them and will have a chance to fuck Bonnie dressed in latex.

Chapter 4: The Job Interview

"This is unbelievable," I complained angrily. "This bitch brought me the wrong documents again."

Bonnie and I sat at my desk, looking at the black folder that Janet, my ditzy blonde secretary, had just brought in.

"I wrote up the document IDs just for her and told her where to find them. You can't even miss it."

"Leave her alone," Bonnie said, smiling. She was sitting across from me in a leather-covered armchair, playing with a letter opener.

"How can she be so stupid? I can't believe it. How low is her IQ? How did they hire her?"

"Do you want me to tell you?..."

I swallowed hard. I felt I was going to hear a tasty bit of gossip. I leaned back and looked at Bonnie. She started her story.

"We got her CV a year ago. It wasn't hand-written as we asked for this position but printed so we would throw it out if the boss wouldn't check her pics. She'd done some modeling..."

"Well, I'm not surprised," I said. I imagined Janet's perfect, long legs and pert, round breasts under her white blouse.

"She had really nice pictures, I have to admit. But that was the only thing going for her. She'd been employed two places before that, for a few months at both of them, and had been promoted at both places, but her qualifications... She graduated from a small college somewhere in the south, I think Texas, I'd never heard about the place before. She hadn't attached her transcripts even though we asked her to."

"I wonder if she even knows how to read," I said.

Bonnie shrugged.

"Maybe she does, but she couldn't answer any of our questions. When we asked her about her IT skills, she just talked rubbish. She knew nothing about relational systems or organizing things. Carl was present at the interview, too, because the Worm alone can't decide anything. I should have taken notes in the background, but these two men couldn't take their eyes off of Janet's miniskirt.

"There we were sitting in the conference room, examining her resumé, and couldn't get any reasonable answers from her. There was an awkward silence. Janet must have felt it because she started to insist,

"'You won't regret it if you hire me, I will be a good employee... I will do anything...'

"She was watching our eyes. I saw this case was dead so I wanted to make a little joke, 'Really? And what if you have to suck off the boss every evening?' I pointed to the Worm and that's when the real job interview started.

"Instead of running out hurt, her eyes caught fire, 'I thought you would never ask.' she said and before we could stop her, she was on her knees in front of the Worm, opening his fly with a fast, practiced move. She took out his cock. He was really hard by then, I think he was imagining through the whole interview how to fuck this little hot bitch in the ass. That bastard...

"So Janet bent over his cock and started sucking it. Carl and I were watching in amusement. I didn't know what I was thinking about, but the Worm was enjoying it a lot, so I closed the door and pulled down the shades of the conference room so nobody would see. When I turned back I found Carl with his fly open, jerking his cock and watching the hot young blonde sucking the boss. And she was doing it so well, like a bitch in heat, I could tell she was in practice."

"You're so slutty..." I told Bonnie, but she just flipped me off.

"This bitch was sucking like a pro. Now I knew why she was promoted at her last two jobs.

"She was bobbing wildly on the boss' cock, fondling his balls with her manicured fingers... Well I'd never take the Worm's cock in my mouth, but it was her business… Then she let it out and slapped her face with it. The saliva on the cock started to smear her make-up but the little whore didn't care about it. She let the cock back into her mouth really deep, I'm sure it even touched her throat. She was using a lot of saliva, just the way you have to do it. I felt sorry for Carl so I bent down and…"

"Oh no…," I moaned.

"Now what? I didn't know you back then, honey," Bonnie said, smiling. "I had some good nights with him, that's all. I knew what he liked and what he didn't so I sucked him a little, made him wet to turn him on.

"Then I sat in his lap, adjusted my skirt, pulled my panties over, and let him inside me. It was very exciting, we could have been discovered anytime, with Janet sucking the boss near us. Carl couldn't even keep up with me, I moved some and he shot his load in my pussy."

"Quick firing asshole…," I said, but Bonnie continued.

"I felt Carl's dick go soft inside me, But I got almost nothing so far. I looked at him but he didn't really care about me, he was watching Janet, and she was still sucking the Worm like a real pro. He had to be at the end because he was moaning loudly, pushing his cock deep into Janet's mouth again and again.

"I was a little disappointed in Carl, and I had my desires, too. Suddenly the Worm moaned out loud, and Janet swallowed instantly. The first shot had to go into her mouth. Then she let it out, jerked it off, closed her eyes, and cum sprayed her bitchy face. She enjoyed it, obviously. White drops fell everywhere, on her nose, on her cheeks, on her red lips…

"And I could see Carl's cock coming to life because of this hot scene in front of us. He just turned me around, pressed me down on all fours on the table, and put it in my ass! Like he would fuck a doll! Okay, I'm not complaining, he fucked my ass a few times already…"

"I should have thought that..."

"Yep, he did, no big deal. Can I continue with the story or do you get jealous of me?"

"Go on..."

"Where was I...? Yep, Carl was shoving his cock in my ass like a madman. He knew I didn't need to be persuaded to be fucked in my butt, maybe he didn't even think about it there and then. He just wanted to fuck me. So there I was on my knees, Carl entering my ass, and Janet stood up, got a Kleenex from her purse, and cleaned her face like a real pro. She sponged up the Worm's cum in front of me which made me think this wasn't the first time she'd done this.

"Then she looked us up and down, watched Carl fucking my ass, so she took off her jacket and climbed under me. Her head went right under my pussy."

"In a 69?" I asked, excited.

"Oh, I couldn't lick her, Carl was fucking me so hard. He's a real fucking machine sometimes... He was always good with second rounds.

"So Carl was fucking my ass hard, grabbing me by my shoulders. Janet was lying under me and licking Carl's sperm from my pussy. It was so good! She even grabbed my ass cheeks, and tried to pull me closer to her face but Carl was fucking me like a machine. The Worm was sitting behind his desk, fondling his limp cock, with a satisfied, evil smile... You know how he is. So Carl was fucking my ass hard and then Janet pushed her finger into my pussy.

"I was in heaven! It was like two cocks moving in me! I would really like to try that out sometime..." she wondered, but then she continued. "I think she plunged two or three fingers in me. It was incredible... It was soo good, I almost screamed, but I didn't want to be heard, so I clenched my teeth. My pussy fluids were spread on Janet's face, and when she fondled Carl's cock with her finger through my pussy walls, I couldn't handle it anymore. I came hard and fast.

"My whole body was shaking; my asshole gripped Carl's cock deep inside. He pushed some more then he came, too. He filled my ass with his hot cum. I think Janet licked my pussy clean, so she got to the next round."

"You made her lick your ass out?"

"But of course! If she wants to work here, she will have to do things like that all the time..." Bonnie said, smiling, and I nodded. "Carl sat down beside the Worm, and Janet began to lick my butt. She pressed her tongue deep into my sticky asshole as far as she could. After the hard fucking I got, it was good to feel this fondling. She entered my asshole with her tongue and let Carl's thick sperm flow over it, into her mouth and she just swallowed and swallowed... Then I felt her sucking the remains out of me. She was professional in this as well; she didn't push any of her fingers into me, and she let me calm down.

"When I caught my breath, Carl and the Worm were sitting relaxed in their chairs. Janet climbed out from underneath me. The guys were adjusting their ties. I laid on the table, my knees were so weak. But this blonde bitch got a little mirror out of her purse and fixed her make-up. And when she finished, Carl and the Worm handed their cards over to her and they made her promise that she would see them right on her first day about her duties."

"So that's how this bitch was hired?" I leaned back into my chair.

"Yes," Bonnie answered. Her cell rang, so she answered it and hurried out of my office.

Chapter 5: In The Elevator

It was going to be a long and boring night, some extra hours, as always. And I had to stay there because of the Japanese clients again, who can't answer some simple questions in an email, they have to be contacted via a video call, and you have to bow, and talk about bullshit for a quarter of an hour. We ended kinda early tonight, I even was surprised at how quickly we agreed on every item on our meeting list. They might have seen the determination on my face, but it could be that they were only tired as well. Anyway, we finished the call after half an hour, parted with mutual politeness, and closed the line.

I shut off my laptop and leaned back in my chair. It was dark outside; there were some dim lights in the other building across the street as well. Some maverick cabs were driving along the streets. It was time for me to get home from this hell.

I didn't have anything to bring home, so I took my jacket, shut off the lights, and stepped out to the dark corridor. I went to the door of the elevator, pressed the button, and leaning my head on the wall, I was waiting for it to arrive.

The door opened with a ring. Two girls were standing in the elevator. I was familiar with them; they worked in accounting. I didn't speak to them much, but I had some encounters with them already.

One of them was Clarissa, the blonde ice queen, who let me fuck her ass a month ago. She was hot as always in her high-heeled black leather boots and tight jeans. I recalled she was from London, maybe that's why I liked her accent so much.

The other girl was Lori, the small, sexy brunette intern, the one who tasted my cum a few weeks before, during the Japanese lesson. She had an ass which made me think about spanking her. She didn't have huge breasts but she had a nice face, with cute, geeky glasses.

As I stepped into the elevator, I eyed the women up and down, and as I saw, they checked me out as well.

"Hi," Clarissa said. I said hello as well; Lori murmured something with her full lips.

The door closed, and we watched the numbers going down one after the other. We started at the 40th and descended slowly.

"Now you could try it out," said Clarissa from behind me on floor 36.

"Come on..." said Lori.

What the fuck are they talking about?

32nd floor...

"Why not? He's kinda cool..." Clarissa said. Suddenly I felt her arm on my side; she stopped the elevator on the 30th floor. I turned back to them but they didn't seem to care about me.

"Are you sure?" Lori asked.

"Don't take it so hard, honey!" Clarissa said. "Now you will get to know how it feels, and if you don't like it, you won't do it anymore. But you have to try it out at least once!"

"What is it, girls?" I asked. "Why did you stop the elevator?".

"Listen up, cowboy," Clarissa said to me. "Do you like this girl?" She pointed to Lori.

This was a surprise for me, so I didn't say anything, only swallowed a big one. Clarissa continued,

"Look at her hot body. Lean waist, perky tits." She showed her to me, like a horse at a rodeo. Lori was listening to her with red cheeks. "Wouldn't you fondle her body? Wouldn't you slap her round hard butt?" She gave it a big slap, which made Lori hiss out loud. Lori looked at me with red cheeks. "Look at her beautiful face! Wouldn't you kiss her? Wouldn't you touch her? Wouldn't you spray your sperm on her?"

Neither I nor Lori could say anything. Clarissa was clearly enjoying the situation.

"Come on guys, do you really want me to start this?" she asked, and leaned to me, grabbing my groin. She opened my fly easily. "Mmm... This will be perfect," she murmured when she took out my hardening cock, and held it in her soft, warm hand. She fondled it for a minute, and nodded, when she saw it growing harder and harder. Then she looked at Lori.

"On your knees, honey!" she ordered. Lori obeyed, kneeled in front of me, took my cock in her hand, opened her mouth, and took my dick between her tender, wet lips. She closed her eyes and started bobbing on my cock.

"That's it, honey!" Clarissa patted her hair. "Suck it! Deeper! That's how guys like it!"

Lori sucked me like a pro. I don't know how many guys she dated in the last few weeks, but her technique improved since the Japanese lesson so much. She used a lot of saliva, and she deepthroated me easily. And Clarissa was grinning beside us like an evil genius, watching how Lori let my cock balls deep in her mouth. I put my two hands on both sides of the elevator and I enjoyed the nice wet sucking.

"That's it, jerk it a little, let the blood run in it, it will be harder that way," Clarissa ordered. Lori obeyed; she sucked and jerked my cock, and her other hand went into her pants.

"You little bitch," I moaned. "I'm... gonna... cum..."

"Be careful!" Clarissa said. "Take it slow, Lori! This isn't what we want, you know..."

"You should try out how it feels when I unload on your faces...," I panted.

"You'd like it, won't you, cowboy?" Clarissa asked. "But I have other plans with you. Stand up, Lori!"

Unfortunately, Lori obeyed again. She let my cock out of her mouth and stood up.

"Take down your pants and bend on the bar," Clarissa pointed to the horizontal pole screwed to the wall of the elevator. Lori turned around, opened up her gray pants, and pushed them down. I took my cock in my hand instinctively and started to jerk it when I saw her round ass covered by her ruffled panties.

"Shouldn't we use some...?"

"Lube?" Clarissa ended my question. "No, that's why I made you suck his cock a bit, to make it wet and hard." She examined my cock. "Shit, it isn't wet enough. Next time you have to use more saliva, Lori. I'm gonna show you how it has to be done!"

She knelt before me as well, reclined next to the wall of the elevator with her hand, took my cock with the other, pulled it into her mouth, started to jerk it, and smeared her saliva on the head of it with her tongue. This made my flesh creep. I straightened and enjoyed her work on my throbbing rod. I wanted to grab Clarissa's hair to fuck her face wildly but she chose this moment to let my cock out of her mouth with a loud slurp. She looked at me, and ordered,

"Come on, cowboy, fuck her ass!"

I heard the words, and they got to my mind but I acted slowly, like a robot. I stepped behind Lori, pulled the panty away from her ass, and put my wet cock into her hole. I tried to press in, but my cock slipped down, between Lori's legs.

"She's tight, isn't she?" Clarissa asked. "Come on, cowboy, fill up this young innocent bitch!"

My throat had gone really dry. I set my cockhead to Lori's asshole. I pushed it in. Lori was concentrating with her head bent down, her teeth gripped together, and I felt she was relaxing, she let me in deeper so I stopped for a while to let her adjust to my throbbing cock.

"How do you like it?" Clarissa asked her.

"Kinda... good..." Lori moaned so I entered her deeper, and deeper, with half of my cock first, then a bit more. I heard her moan from somewhere but I couldn't care, I simply had to move, so I grabbed her hips with one of my hands, embraced her shoulders with the other, and started to fuck her ass hard. Clarissa started murmuring in our ears,

"Hard, isn't it? This is how a real ass fucking is! Fuck this tight little slut! Fuck her in half, let her know how it is when a real hard cock fucks her ass!"

This was more than enough. I thrust a few more, then came. My whole body trembled, as I pumped her ass full of my sperm. I felt my balls emptying in her hot flesh. Then I stepped back and leaned to the wall of the elevator. Both of us were panting. Only Clarissa was calm, grinning wildly.

"Now that's much better," she said, pleased. "It was good, wasn't it?"

Lori nodded, trembling. Both of us dressed up quickly, which caused a little silence in the elevator. I realized it got really hot in the small place. Meanwhile, Clarissa started the elevator again, we descended with a quiet buzzing.

"I only have one question," I said, adjusting my tie. "Why do you think the emergency bell didn't ring when the elevator stopped?"

"Oh, I made the handymen turn it off long ago," Clarissa said with a laugh. "Some people would do anything for a piece of ass..."

Chapter 6: The Pirate Girl

"Hey!" Bonnie said, as she burst through the door. "Look what I found at the club."

She leaped into my lap, waving a flyer. "We have a sexy Halloween party to go to."

Since we'd moved together in her uncle's condo a couple of months before, we hardly had time to go out together.

Bonnie calmed down enough to show me the flyer. The headline said,

"Dress up for the sexiest night of the year! Spend Halloween Night with fun and games!"

The graphics on the flyer suggested sex. Lots of sex. Silhouettes of people fucking in a variety of positions.

Bonnie gave me a big smoochy kiss and said "Let's go. It's a lot better than sitting at home in front of the TV on Halloween. It looks like fun, and besides, maybe we can meet some new people there."

So I spent a few hours in town choosing the best black tuxedo just like the one Pierce Brosnan had been wearing in 'The World Is Not Enough'. I spent a good amount on clothes and shoes and even bought a huge toy gun to put under it.

While I was dressing, Bonnie stepped out of the bathroom, wrapped only in a towel after her shower. She dropped the towel, twirled around, and said, "How about I go as Lady Godiva?"

"I'd love it," I said, "but you'll get us both arrested."

Seeing Bonnie's naked body gave me a hard-on. I couldn't get enough of watching her walking around the house nude. Her nipples always seemed to be erect, sitting on those soft, perky B-cup breasts.

She walked across the room to me and gave me a hug and another smoochy kiss. As she did so, she grabbed my cock through my trousers.

"Looks like someone is excited about the Halloween party," she said.

"How about we fuck before we go?" I asked.

She laughed, "No, you'd better save your prick for the party. Who knows what kind of surprises we will have…"

Bonnie walked to the closet where her costume was hanging on a hanger. She slipped the long, black witch's dress over her head and pulled it into place. It appeared to be pretty snug around her breasts and waist. She turned her back to me and asked me to zip up the back.

She looked at me above her shoulder. "Like what you see?" she asked.

"Of course," I said. "And I'm wondering who else will see it tonight."

Bonnie stood up and pulled up her thong.

"Jealous, huh?" she asked. "As far as I know you don't have any reason to complain."

She was right. Since we've been together, Bonnie did everything to be sure I was sexually satisfied. We had an open relationship, that's right, but it was for both of our benefits. We tried out all the fantasies we wanted. And sometimes she even helped me organize stuff like when she asked me to repair the vibrator and I ended up fucking Clarissa, the ice queen of the office in the ass. Or when we were invited to the private party of the firm and she let me DP her with another guy. Yeah, that's right. I didn't have anything to complain about.

We were finally ready to go. Bonnie was wearing her sexy witch outfit with the authentic black hat, her naughty black dress that matched her glossy black hair, high black heels, and thong, underlined by black and yellow striped panty. I had my tuxedo on with a red bow tie and a huge gun under my armpit.

We called a cab. The driver eyed us up and down but didn't say anything, he opened the door for Bonnie and helped her with her long dress. He drove us to the industrial part of the city, where many factories were renewed for loft flats inside them.

I paid the driver, left him a serious tip, then got out and held the door for Bonnie.

"Shall we?" I asked and held her hand like a true gentleman.

"Yes, Mr. Bond," she giggled. "Please take me to the world of tales."

We got to the huge black steel door. The same sign was painted on it as on the flyer.

Halloween Night Party

"Welcome to the club!"

The tall, bald tattooed bouncer met us at the door and collected our entry fee. After he let us into the club, we walked down the dimly lit hallway. There were the typical Halloween decorations: pumpkins, huge fake spiders hung from the ceiling, and a ghost made from a sheet near the entry. From some speakers at the end of the hall, we heard the Halloween sounds of wolves howling, owls hooting, and witches laughing hysterically.

From the side rooms off the hallway, we heard some laughing and moaning. They were the unmistakable sounds of sex.

After a corner, there was a man fucking a girl's mouth. She was dressed as a French maid, in a dress black and white. She was on her knees, hand tied behind her back by a pair of pink handcuffs. The guy was dressed as a soldier from the II. World War. He was holding her head by grabbing her hair and he was thrusting his cock deep into her mouth.

"That's it...," he moaned. "Deeper..."

And he thrusted his huge rod to her throat again and again. Then he pulled out and spanked her cheeks with it a few times. A lot of saliva and his pre-cum was dripping from the end of his cock.

"Please put it back," the maid sighed. The fluids from his cock were smeared on her face and strained her make-up. The guy grabbed her head tightly and pushed his cock back in between her full lips. He fucked her face faster this time, with full power and abandon. She moaned quickly and in a high voice like a small bird.

The guy stopped and we could see his body twitching.

"Don't swallow it yet...," he moaned. "Keep it in your mouth, honey."

She took all the guy sprayed inside her mouth. Some drops even dripped out of her mouth.

"Now open it," she ordered. She obeyed and he leaned down to check his cum collected on her tongue. Then he nodded: "Now you can swallow," which she happily did.

"That was so hot," Bonnie said. "It made me crave some man-sauce," she added.

"Maybe you could ask her to leave some to you next time" I nodded to the maid who was still on her knees, smiling happily at the soldier before her.

"Oh come on," Bonnie held my hand and pulled further down the corridor.

We found a room with a door left ajar. Inside there was a girl on her knees, dressed up as Catwoman. The black latex covered her whole body, only her cleavage was visible: she didn't have huge tits but the look of her skin made the whole image even sexier. A matching black mask covered her eyes. She was surrounded by a bunch of guys in a variety of costumes: a Superman, a Zorro, a cop, a doctor, and a fireman. She was sucking Superman's cock with all her abandon but she already had some strains of cum shining on her black latex.

"Suck it!" the guys cheered.

She was working on the steel-hard cock with eyes closed. The other men were jerking their cocks, and the cop held a small bowl in his hand. With a loud groan, he sprayed his cum into the bowl. He jerked everything into it, till the last drops, then gave it to the fireman. I could see the bowl was half with cum.

The fireman took the bowl and wanted to jerk off into it, but Superman finished fucking the Catwoman's face:

"Give it to me, I'm coming!" he cried, and after he got the bowl, he shot his thick, huge drops in it. The Catwoman was on her knees, giggling. When he emptied his cock, he poured the contents of the bowl on the Catwoman's face. She quickly opened her lips and tried to catch every string of white cum dripping on her.

"Good kitty!" someone said.

"Drink your milk, Catwoman!"

"Lick it up!"

The men loudly cheered and laughed watching her.

"Mmmm..." Bonnie purred beside me. "What a nice cock tail," she emphasized the two last words for the sake of the joke.

"Oh yeah," I said, grinning. "Maybe I should prepare something like that for you."

"Good idea! Maybe for my birthday?"

I grinned and made a mental note.

We moved further. The next room was furnished as a medical room. There were two white beds in it, with two guys lying on them. A hot chick dressed as a nurse was riding one of the patients, jerking the other beside her. She had the slutty white costume and hat on, without any bra, and the costume slid up at her waist. I could see her red thong pulled away from her pussy and the cock entering her again and again. She was really in heat, moaning out loud and riding wildly. Her white dress was halfway open, leaving the patient below her to fondle her large, full tits which were bouncing wildly up and down as she rode him.

"Come on, let's go!" Bonnie said. "I don't feel comfortable in hospitals."

So we went on. We found two cheerleaders 69'ing on a large steel table. A huge black guy dressed up as Dracula jerked his cock on a chair beside them, and whispered obscenities to them:

"That's right... Lick that cunt, bitch.."

The girls wore the typical cheerleader outfit: short skirts and white T-shirts with huge football logos on them. The girl below was holding a large pink dildo in her hand and tried to stuff it into the other girl's pussy.

"I've never seen a black Dracula before," Bonnie told me. "Look, he even has his fake teeth!"

He sure had them and they made his grin even more evil. He watched closely as the pink dildo slid into the cheerleader's pussy. He licked his index finger and slowly pushed it into the cheerleader's asshole. The girl moaned out loud with her eyes closed.

"Excuse me?" I heard a tinkling voice and somebody touched my arm. I turned around. A blonde girl was standing there, dressed up as a pirate girl. She was smaller than me, dressed in shredded clothes showing off her sexy brown skin. She had black boots on her feet and a black eyepatch pulled up to her forehead, on the colorful head scarf.

"Can you help me?" she asked, with her green eyes glowing at me.

"What can I help you with?" I asked, like a real gentleman. She looked me up and down, then explained,

"We just have had some fun with some friends of mine, and we would like to continue but we're one man down."

"One man down for what?" I asked.

"For being full," she said with a smile which made me understand she was talking about her body. She turned to Bonnie and asked, "Do you mind if I borrow your man for a while?"

"Not at all," Bonnie answered. "There's a lipstick party anyway," she pointed to the next room, the door left ajar. I saw a row of guys with a row of girls on their knees before them, sucking and slurping their cocks diligently. Bonnie took out a red lipstick from her purse and adjusted her makeup. "I wanna see how this red looks on black" she winked at the pirate girl and the two of them shared a smile. "Good luck!" she said to me, then entered the room with the lipstick party and closed the door behind herself.

I didn't have time to wonder because the pirate girl held me by the hand and led me up some stairs.

"I planned everything," she explained. "I selected the guys, talked it over with them, and made them promise this would be our little secret. And you know, how guys are: they had their orgasm, now they would turn around and fall asleep and leave the poor girl unsatisfied. By the way, do you like sloppy seconds?"

I had no time to answer since she led me into a dimly lit room. There was a huge king-sized bed in the middle, with the bedding cockled up. There had clearly been some action going on here. I even smelled sex in the hot air of the room.

A guy dressed up as a football player was lying on the bed. He was huge and sweaty, his T-shirt torn to pieces so his muscular chest was visible. His helmet was on the bed beside him. Down there he was naked, so I could see his huge cock pointing at us. He had his eyes half closed but watched us as we moved into the room.

"Who is this?" somebody asked. My eyes got used to the dim light in the room slowly. I could see a guy sitting in the armchair near the door. He was dressed like a pilot, in a gray coverall with some badges and huge sunglasses on his head. He was chewing gum and he had his soft cock out, jerking it in his hand. He looked like Tom Cruise from Top Gun, without the handsome face, of course.

"He's the one who will take your place, honey," the pirate girl answered. The pilot spitted one aside but said nothing. "Come on, guys, let's do this!" she said to the other side of the room. One of the shadows parted from the corner: it was a guy dressed up like Batman!

His costume was perfect: black rubber clothes with a mask and a belt. But he didn't move like the real Batman; he was staggering as he stepped to us. He held a bottle in his hand with only a few whiskeys on the bottom.

"Do you want some, mate?" he looked at me with a blank stare from his mask.

"A drunken Batman? Really?" I asked the pirate girl but she shrugged:

"He's a good guy. And he's still hard, unlike my boyfriend..." She waved her hand to the pilot in the armchair.

She climbed on the bed and sat on the football player's lap. She adjusted his cock into her pussy, and slowly settled on it.

"Oh that's still good," she moaned. Then she looked back at me and gestured to get behind her,

"Come on, Mr. Bond," she said, giggling. "Get your weapon ready." But she bit on her lips because the football player held her hips and shoved his cock deeper into her.

I took my cock out. When I bought this tuxedo, I didn't really think it would feel tight when I would climb behind a hot girl with a desire to fill her ass up.

I climbed up behind her. The skin of her beautiful round ass showed up between the shreds of her pirate costume. She leaned back against me as she slowly began sliding herself up and down on the football player's cock.

She winced a couple of times, then said, "Oof," as she finally had his cock fully inside her. The pirate girl bounced up and down a couple of times, then lay on the guy's chest. She looked back at me, and said,

"Fuck my ass with your huge cock!"

I put my legs above the guy's thighs, adjusted my cock to the pirate girl's asshole, and slowly slid it in. It went easier than I thought. Even though I could feel she was full with the football player's cock in her pussy, my cock slid easily into her hot asshole. I even sensed something fluid on my skin. I reached down to check: it was cum.

"What the fuck?" I asked. The blonde girl looked back at me and winked:

"Is there something wrong?"

That was when I realized why she asked me whether I like sloppy seconds. Somebody just fucked her in the ass!

"Whose cum is this?" I asked. I could see the pilot spitting again to the floor.

"Does it matter?" the girl asked. I saw her big green eyes and I decided she was right. It doesn't really matter at all. If this is the price I have to pay for double penetrating this hot chick, then so be it.

I pushed into her deeper. She grabbed my head,

"Oh god... That feels good," she moaned.

The football player began fucking her ass and only the membranes between her rectum and vagina separated my cock from his, and I could feel the head of his cock bump against mine, almost as if I was wearing a condom. He also held her by her hips so I could build up a steady rhythm and started fucking her ass.

The pirate girl was going, "Ungh... Ungh... Ungh...," every time I bottomed out.

We fucked her steadily. I grabbed her hair and pulled her closer to me. With my other hand, I spanked her ass a few times.

"Helly yeah!" she cried out. "See?" she told her boyfriend. "It's easy. Even this guy can do it."

"Yeah, after I eased the back door..." the pilot said but the girl didn't pay any attention to him. She enjoyed the hard fucking she got from us.

That was when Batman stepped in front of her. He gulped from the bottle and then pulled his cape away. I could see his cock was out and hard already. He grabbed her head and pulled her mouth on his cock. He pushed balls deep into her. She started bobbing on her immediately.

"Oh yeah!" he shouted. "Suck my cock, honey!"

We fucked her in a good rhythm. All her holes were filled, and her body tensed on our cocks like a bow. I thought I would speed things up a little by some nasty talk.

"Do you like to be stuffed?" I murmured into her ears while I fucked her ass hard. "Do you like these cocks in your body?"

"Mmmhmmm..." she moaned as she could with her mouth full with Batman's cock.

"Yeah? Would you like to get your holes filled with our sperm?"

"Mmmhhmmm..." she moaned again but that wasn't enough for me. I pulled back her head letting the cock in her mouth free.

"Say it!" I ordered.

"Yeah..." she murmured.

"Come on man!" the Batman said, whining. "What is your fucking problem?"

This drunken Batman was a little disappointing. A real illusion breaker. But I wanted to hear the pirate girl speaking dirty.

"Say it!" I ordered her again.

"I love your cocks!" she cried out.

"And...?"

"And I want you to fill me with your cum!" she cried again with eyes closed.

That was enough for me. I pushed her head back to Batman's cock. He greeted it with a grin and pulled another gulp from the bottle. Then he threw the bottle to the floor, grabbed his cape, and covered her bobbing head with it. I could hear she was giggling under the blue cape but in a muffled voice so she probably continued the sucking. The drunken Batman was laughing and he moved her head under the cape, fucked her face with large thrusts. Then he pulled the cape away. The pirate girl raised her head, and jerking his cock, laughed at the guy before her:

"You're a fucking animal!"

"I'm the fucking Batman!" he shouted, with his arms spread. The girl laughed, and I was grinning. But the football player below us didn't say anything, he just pounded the girl's pussy with his huge cock. The Batman grabbed the pirate's blond hair again and pulled her mouth back to his cock.

We fucked her with all our power. Now all the three cocks pounded her open and gaping holes. She closed her eyes again and cried out loudly.

"That's it! Fuck me!"

The pilot was watching us from the armchair. He didn't jerk his cock anymore, he even put it away. But I could see he bit his upper lip a few times.

This made me fuck his girl even harder. I leaned on her, grabbed her tits through her costume, and pounded her balls deep.

"Ohhh..." she cried out, "that's so goood..."

I could tell she was close to her orgasm.

"Oh fuck... Oh fuck, I'm cumming," she cried out.

I could feel her ass clamping down on my ass as she rode out her orgasm. The football player let go with his load, and I could feel his cock pulsing inside her. That was enough to make me unload, too. I pushed deeper and let all my juices shoot out into her hot, tight ass. I could feel my balls tighten and empty their load into her body.

But we didn't have time to enjoy our mutual orgasms. The Batman pulled her from us and helped her to her knees on the floor. He grabbed her head and jerked his cock on her panting face furiously. He needed a couple of strokes only, and came like a pornstar; with a loud groan, he sprayed his huge load on her cheeks, on her nose, on her lips, on her jaw, everywhere.

He backed up and sat in another armchair beside the pilot.

"See?" the pirate girl said. "That's why I like him so much. I can always count on his big cock."

"Did you enjoy yourself?" her boyfriend asked.

"Oh yeah... I've never come like that before."

After we put our costumes back on, the pirate girl winked, then said to me,

"It was a pleasure doing business with you, Mr. Bond."

I pointed at her and winked with my fingers doing like a shot at her. She smiled and I got out of the room.

I met Bonnie in the corridor. She was waiting for me. Her lipstick was smeared around her lips and she held her shoes in her hands. She clearly recovered from the lipstick party but she still had some strings of some cum in her hair.

"Was it good?" she pointed behind me.

"It was hot as hell," I admitted. "I'm glad you took us to this party."

She acknowledged it with a nod.

"What about the lipstick party?" I asked. "I can see you sucked some lucky guys dry" I pointed to her hair.

"What?" she asked. She reached up and found the white fluid in her hair. She tasted it from her fingers and said, smiling, "Yeah... It was wild."

"What's with the shoes?"

"Oh that..." she looked at it. "A guy asked me whether he can jerk it off in my high heels."

"And you let him?"

"Well, it sounded like a funny idea back then so I borrowed them from him... But now that cold fluid under my skin feels strange and sloppy."

"Sloppy is good sometimes," I said, grinning, and held her hand and took to the exit.

"Wanna share stories?" she asked.

"Absolutely!" I said. "But let me call a cab first."

Chapter 7: The Promotion Party

Bonnie stepped into my office with a bright smile on her face.

"I just got a promotion!" she told me. "I will be the head of the real estate department!"

"Wow," I said, and I leaned back in my chair, starting to unbutton my fly. I was hoping she got excited about the sudden promotion and she would blow me under the table or something.

"You're so wrong, Johnny boy," she waved her hand at me, smiling. "This is not so simple! I still have to earn the promotion!"

"To earn it? Didn't you earn it in the last two years? I don't think anybody worked more than you..."

"It's another kind of earning," she said. "I have to prove to my colleagues that they can trust me, I'm a part of the team, and I'm ready to make sacrifices for the company..."

"And how should you prove all this?"

"With a hardcore anal party!"

***

The party was organized on Friday night. We arrived at around 8 PM. The hall of Walden, Inc. was unusually dead, only the receptionist smiled at us from his booth. He smiled at Bonnie:

"Congratulations!" he said to her. I could tell he knew exactly what was going on.

A private elevator took us down deep underground, to a level I didn't even know about. Bonnie stood a little nervously beside me, I could feel her scent and the aura of her skin that she'd prepared a lot for this night. I leaned back a bit and admired her ass in her mini skirt – her ass which I had fondled so many times. Will this ass be fucked to death tonight? It promised to be an exciting show.

"What exactly will be my role?" I asked, hoarsely.

"Just be there with me," Bonnie said, wondering. "Then take me home!"

We arrived at the secret floor. The door opened and we were greeted by Helen, who had only her black latex boots and matching black gloves on, nothing else. Her naked body looked strange in the industrial corridor.

"Welcome to the Ceremony!" she said, smiling. "It was time. Let's get dressed!"

This was new. I didn't have any peculiar dress to change, but as it turned out, I didn't really need one. Helen led Bonnie away and sent me to the changing room. I wandered around the corridors, under the heating tubes on the ceiling, then I found a steel door labeled as Changing Room and I entered. One of the walls was full of hangers, with black capes hung on them. There was a bench and a small table, and a box full of masks on it.

"If you want to join in, put your car keys in the bowl!" the sign said on a rattan bowl. There were about a dozen keys already in it. I threw mine in as well, I thought I had nothing to lose.

I changed my clothes to a long, black cape, nothing underneath, and walked out to the corridor. The lamps slightly flickered on the ceiling. I could see the soft light of candles coming from the end of the corridor so I went that way.

The room I found was brightly lit by hundreds of candles. I didn't feel like it was an underground room of a skyscraper in New York. There was wonderful carved mahogany furniture in the room, with candles everywhere. Helen was already waiting for me, held me by my hand, and led me to a beautiful armchair that looked like a throne.

"This will be your place tonight," she explained to me. It was hard to concentrate on what she was saying with her perky tits in front of my eyes. "Did you throw your keys in?"

"Yep..."

"Unfortunately, you can't play tonight. The rules are clear: your woman will be fucked by other men tonight. But relax," she patted my knees. "I'll make it worth it for you. Now enjoy the show," she said, smiling, and walked to the center of the room.

Bonnie was on all her fours on a big oak table. Men were standing around her, dressed in black capes. They all had white masks covering their faces, and they watched Bonnie's body without a word. Her eyes were covered with a black silk blindfold, and she had a matching pair of high heels on her feet. Nothing else covered her body, I could even see the reflection of the candles on the sweat glistening on her brown skin. She shivered and her body trembled in the circle of men.

Helen knelt on the table beside Bonnie and pulled apart my girl's ass cheeks with her hand covered by the black gloves.

"Look at this tight ass!" she said out loud which made the men let out a tense sigh. "This woman offers this beauty for three lucky winners tonight! Three lucky men can fuck her asshole!" She turned to Bonnie, saying, "This will be the ass-fuck of your life, believe me, honey!"

Helen pulled Bonnie's cheeks apart a bit more. She licked into Bonnie's ass, then pulled her head back and waited for the effect. Bonnie's rosebud closed tight. Helen laughed out loud and leaned back, started making small circles around my girl's asshole. The groaning men enjoyed the show. My cock started to erect under my cape, and I probably wasn't alone with this.

Helen licked my girlfriend's ass more intensively. Her hair covered the view a lot, but the men around them liked what they saw. They got their stiff cocks out from under their capes and fondled them above the girls. Helen's head was barely moving, I thought she pressed her tongue into Bonnie's asshole deep and licked her tight orifice well.

I used to lick out Bonnie's ass a few times so I knew how much she loved it. She used to moan loudly when I used a lot of saliva on my tongue and twirled it deeply in her asshole. Helen must have done the same since Bonnie relaxed more and more and moaned more and more passionately.

The rattan bowl was there beside them on the table. There were a dozen car keys in it and a tube of lubricant. Helen picked the tube up, opened it, and pushed a good amount from it into Bonnie's ass. She smeared the transparent liquid around the hole and moved her fingers closer and closer with small circles. She worked the lubricant into Bonnie's hungry asshole. When she was done, she smacked Bonnie's ass and said,

"The mare is ready to be ridden, gentlemen!"

Helen took a Porsche key from the bowl, held it up over her head, and walked around with it like those pretty models do at the beginning of a new round at a boxing match. Well, there was a very important difference here: Helen was naked except for her black gloves and high heels, and she didn't initiate a boxing round but a hardcore anal fucking of my girl. There was some clapping, and then the owner of the Porsche stepped out of the circle; a muscular, tall guy as I could see him in his cape and the mask on his face. Bonnie smiled contentedly back at him; he took off his cape, and stepped on the table, beside Bonnie. He fit his huge cock to the entrance of her ass and slowly entered her. Bonnie dropped her head, her hair covered her face and the end of the black kerchief. But I knew she was probably smiling.

The guy didn't move for a while, he just let Bonnie get used to his cock in her ass. But after a minute, his body tensed and moved a little, which made Bonnie moan out loud.

Helen stepped before me; she sat on the beautifully carved arm of the chair and leaned on my shoulder. The Porsche guy was really enjoying his position. He started fucking Bonnie's ass slowly, gently.

Helen was lying on my shoulder and watching Bonnie on the table, she whispered in my ear,

"It's beautiful, right? Her nice, round ass fucked like this..."

"Mmmhmmm...," I whispered back, watching Bonnie.

"His cock looks hot in her asshole," Helen said. Her small hand dived inside my cape and found my already hardening cock.

"Look at you!" she said when she grabbed my erection. "So you like what you see? Are you excited about this stranger fucking your girlfriend in the ass?"

"Mmmhmmm...," I moaned again and watched with eyes wide as the masked man's cock moved in and out of Bonnie's ass. The lubricant proved to be essential since the guy fucked her ass with strong, hard thrusts. Helen watched them, smiling.

The guy fucked Bonnie faster. His cock entered her balls deep again and again. He even grabbed her hair and pulled it like a head-gear. Then he stopped moving.

"Now he comes in her ass...," Helen whispered into my ear. "Look, how slow is he moving! He pumps her ass full of his fresh cum!"

Bonnie enjoyed her ass being filled with sperm by the masked man with her head down. She surrendered herself to the feeling completely; when the masked man pulled out with an audible pop, she raised her head in surprise, just as she would have awakened in another world. She turned her head around and listened to the men murmuring around her. The black kerchief covered her eyes so she couldn't see what was happening around her. But she probably felt the last white drops dripping on her ass cheeks from the masked man's cock; this made her ass waggle which resulted in the men jerking their cocks faster around her.

Helen released my already hard cock,

"Sorry, I have to go!" she whispered, then went to the mahogany table. She picked up the next car key from the rattan bowl and presented it. She didn't have to wait long; the next man stepped out and took off his cape. His long, blonde hair fell to his shoulders. He looked like Schwarzenegger in the Conan movie. His cock was hard, and his sack was larger than the usual. He climbed behind Bonnie, who was stretching on the desk on her fours like a cat. He took the girl by her hips and entered her ass easily.

Helen came back to me and commented on the new round,

"He slid in too easily, didn't he? Well, he's got a thin cock. Plus, cum is the best lubricant..."

The blonde man pounded Bonnie's ass with easy thrusts; his huge sack splashed on her pussy again and again, becoming wet from her juices. He didn't seem to be bothered by being the sloppy second. He just fucked Bonnie's ass with visible pleasure.

"Oh yeah...," he groaned. Bonnie cried out with small screams; the blonde man fucked her ass without mercy just as he would do exercises on a cardio machine. He took Bonnie by her shoulders and speared her ass balls deep again and again. Both of them were panting hard; the blonde man's sack smacked loudly on her swollen, glistening wet pussy lips.

Helen grabbed my cock again and fondled it gently under my cape.

"Have you ever fucked her ass like this?" she asked, musingly. I felt like she wanted to excite me instead of wanting to know anything so I rather remained silent, and enjoyed her small palm on my rock-hard cock. That's how Bonnie did, also; she surrendered her body to the blonde stranger with loud moans. He had to find the perfect rhythm since Bonnie screamed out loud, and came with her body trembling.

"That's it...," I heard the men around her. "She is coming!"

"She enjoys it..."

"I think we have chosen well..."

"Look at her," Helen said, smiling. "She's really enjoying it! The little bitch! She's so fuckable, isn't she?"

The blonde man came. His sack twitched visibly, and his whole body trembled. He even groaned. I thought he screamed inside but he didn't find it manly enough to show it among these masked men, so he just held it back. After he pulled out, he took a deep breath, took up his cape from the floor, and mopped his red cock in it. Bonnie's asshole was gaping because of the hardcore pounding; the girl panted loudly.

Helen got on her feet again and chose the third key. She held it up for everyone to see. I heard a few men sighing in frustration.

The third man was Ule, the tall, huge black lawyer. He was wearing a mask as well, but I recognized his body and his huge cock. He wasn't a stranger in Bonnie's body. He didn't wait any moment, pulled down his cape, knelt behind Bonnie, and thrust his huge, black cock into her asshole full of sperm. Bonnie hissed out loud, but Helen spanked her ass,

"Take it, girl, this will be the best part!"

When Bonnie dropped her head, her hair fell onto her face again. She probably tried to relax her rectum around the huge black cock. Ule made small thrusts. He clearly enjoyed the tight grip of the hot, tight hole. Bonnie moaned. She must have relaxed her ass because the huge black man was getting under his way moving in and out. I could even see a sign of two men coming in Bonnie's ass so far; as the black rod was pumping her, some stripes of white cum was glistening on it.

Helen turned back to me. But instead of sitting on the arm of the chair, she knelt between my legs, picked up my cape, and swallowed my cock deep into her mouth. She was bobbing with her head on it using a lot of saliva. I supposed that's how she kept the companions of the main stars of these seances in check, while the stars themselves were fucked in their asses systematically. I had to admit, it was planned out well, I had my time in there.

Ule grabbed Bonnie's hair, pulled her head to himself, and fucked her ass like hell. She really behaved like a mare now; Bonnie enjoyed the animalistic fucking, she pushed herself on the big black rod again and again, moaning and groaning. Her pussy was gaping and I knew she would do anything to get a nice hard cock in there as well. But this wasn't the time or place for that. Tonight her ass was under attack, the executives of Walden, Inc. wanted the control of her bare ass. And Bonnie enjoyed it very much. She wasn't on her fours anymore, her arms were stretched out on the table, and her ass was bent high so Ule could split her beautiful, round butt deeply.

Meanwhile, Helen was sucking me wildly. She let the head of my cock touch her throat every time she bobbed on it. She was doing it perfectly, like a real pro, wet and hot. I could feel her routine. But I couldn't concentrate on it. I was mesmerized by the view of how the huge black rod split Bonnie's ass apart. Bonnie was screaming in pleasure, her pussy fluids streaming on her thighs. Nobody cared; the men watched as Ule pounded the new head of the real estate department's asshole. They jerked their cocks wildly; watching Ule probably meant somehow they could be part of this wonderful event. But Ule enjoyed it the most, of course; he pounded Bonnie's ass balls deep. As he fucked her, even his mask fell but he didn't care; he just fucked and fucked the young tight ass gaping before him.

I couldn't take it anymore. This feeling, this night, the view of Bonnie's ass stuffed full and Helen's mouth made me cum. I shot out into Helen's hot mouth with my eyes closed. I even raised my hip to push it deeper into her throat.

"Mmmm... it's so good...," I heard Helen murmuring, but I was still enjoying her swallowing my sperm with my eyes closed. "Sorry, I have to go now," she said at the end, letting my cock go. "I'll add this to the rest of it."

What kind of rest of it? I opened my eyes and saw that while I was spraying my seed into the mouth of the best cocksucker of the firm, the huge black lawyer already finished with my girl who was lying in a daze. The white stream of sperm was dripping from her ass. Masked men around her were coming, spraying their huge loads on Bonnie's back, ass, and thigh, and some pervert "colleagues" were coming into her black hair. Somebody even aimed for the black silk kerchief on her eyes. The white drops were glistening in the soft material.

As Helen arrived there, she knelt behind Bonnie and kissed my girl's ass cheeks all over with her sperm-covered lips and licked up every drop of white sperm she could find. After she cleared Bonnie's sweaty cheeks, she leaned over and sucked all the sperm she could out of my girl's asshole. This caused a loud ovation among the men. Some last drops fell on Bonnie's ass and Helen's face but she cleared everything up with her small pink tongue.

Then she crawled on her knees to meet Bonnie, held my girl's tired face up, and let the sperm pour from her creamy lips into Bonnie's mouth. Everybody was cheering and clapping. The girls kissed for a while, with their tongues dancing, and some sperm dripped out of the corner of their mouths. I felt a new pulse in my cock at this hot sight.

I got up. I knew my duties; I had to bring this successful woman home, I had to make her a bath with candles, and let her rest so that in a few days I could fuck her brains out again and again.

Office Sluts 3

Travels Abroad

<u>Chapter 1: Hannah and Dorothy</u>

"Here they are," Bonnie introduced the two girls to me. She just popped into my office dragging these two hot young interns by their hands. I logged out of my computer, stood up, and walked around my desk to shake hands with them.

"John, this is Dorothy" Bonnie introduced the taller girl to me. I looked her up and down. She had brown hair and heavy makeup. "And this is Hannah," Bonnie pointed to the smaller, blonde one. Both girls were wearing mini skirts and high heels, showing off their thighs and legs just like new interns who want to get attention. They were giggling and checking me out. "And this is the marvelous John Smith who I told you so much about," Bonnie continued. "He will teach you a lot of important things to know at this firm. Please do anything he says," she explained, then turned to me, saying, "Please, be gentle with them."

She stepped out of my office and left me there with these two young girls.

Dorothy had a huge cleavage exposing her perky tits in her push-up bra. I found it difficult to take my eyes off them, wondering how they looked without a bra.

Although Hannah was shorter, she was sexier, with a nasty, dirty smile on her face. I silently thanked Bonnie for bringing these two hot interns to me for training rather than to Carl.

"Well, hi," I said after I finished checking them out. "As Bonnie said, I'm John Smith, you can call me Johnny as everyone does. I'm an attorney in law, I have been working for a year at Walden, Inc. I know a few things about how things go around here, so I can teach you a few important things."

"We hope so," Hannah said, and both girls giggled.

"Okay...," I said and motioned them to my desk. "Where shall we start it?"

"Well...," Dorothy said, "Bonnie told us we could help you a little bit."

"Yeah...," Hannah added, "She told us you have a huge load and maybe you could share it with us."

They giggled again. I didn't believe my ears. Had they suggested what I think they had? What the fuck did Bonnie plan for me?

"Well, the fact is I do have a huge load..." I said, very carefully. I didn't want to get involved in a sexual harassment lawsuit with these dangerous sirens standing before me.

"Oh, let us help you!" Hannah said, and if I saw it correctly, she winked at me. They both giggled again and Dorothy put her hand on my crotch. She had long, pink nails and she fondled my groin gently. With her other hand, she pulled my head to hers and kissed me. It wasn't a sensual, gentle kiss; she rather pressed her tongue into my mouth and turned it around.

They had to be an effective team because while Dorothy was kissing me and fondling my groin, Hannah started to unbutton my shirt.

"Are you sure?" I moaned, but Dorothy pulled my head back to her and continued kissing me. Hannah unbuttoned my shirt and pulled it open. She fondled my chest and purred like a cat.

"I love your hairy body...," she panted. "You're so manly..."

I didn't know what kind of men she had done it with so far.

Hannah caressed my chest and my stomach. She leaned down a bit – she didn't have to strain too much since she was much smaller than me – and kissed my chest. I was surprised at how professionally these girls excited me in a minute; my cock was already hardening. Hannah even kissed and licked my nipples as well. Dorothy pressed her tongue deep into my mouth and enjoyed our kissing with her eyes closed.

Hannah went down on me: she kissed my belly button, then my belly. She opened my fly with her small but quick fingers. I wanted to check on her but Dorothy pulled my head back to her and continued pressing her tongue in my mouth.

Hannah knelt before me and took out my cock.

"Wow," she said. "Look at it, Dor'..."

Dorothy released me and checked my cock. I could see a sparkle in her eyes.

"That's really nice," she admitted. "Is it hard?"

"Hell yeah," Hannah answered. She measured my cock in her small palm. "And it's fucking huge. Bonnie was right."

"What?" I asked but Dorothy put her manicured finger on my lips.

"Hush, Mr. Smith," she said. "Let us do what we are here for."

She smiled with an evil grin and she winked at the petite blonde on her knees before me. Hannah winked back and licked my cock all the way from its base to the head.

"Mmmm," she said. "It's really nice. Come one, Dor', you have to taste it!"

Dorothy knelt beside her girlfriend, then she pulled my cock in front of her face and looked up at me, smiling. She was so slutty like this, on her knees, with lust for my cock in her eyes. I could hardly wait for her to swallow my cock between her lusty lips. She probably knew that and teased me by reaching out with her pink tongue and touching my cockhead with the end of it. She slowly licked around the purple head and then tasted it with her tongue, saying,

"It's really tasty!"

And they giggled again.

I pushed my pants and my underwear and sat back in my chair. The young girls followed me on their knees.

"Can I start it?" Hannah asked.

"Go ahead!" Dorothy said and held my cock to her girlfriend's face. Hannah swallowed immediately. I let it enter deeper than I thought she could take in her small mouth. Only half of my cock got in, but I could already feel it was filling her mouth completely.

She started to bob on it gently, carefully. She concentrated on not biting my cock, she even closed her eyes while doing it.

"Suck that cock, bitch," Dorothy said to her, which made Hannah giggle. Since my cock filled her mouth, she gagged a bit; she released it and laughed out loud to Dorothy,

"Oh, you fucking slut!" She even slapped her girlfriend's face with my cock. "What did you just say? Huh?" she slapped her with it again. They both giggled again like pillow-fighting girls at a pajama party. Dorothy slapped Hannah back, and the blonde girl ducked, with my cock still in her hand.

"Woah," I said, "take it easy, girls."

"Sorry, Johnny," Dorothy said, smiling. "We don't want to hurt your precious member," she fondled my cock. "Let me make it even for you," she looked into my eyes again, and slowly swallowed my cock into her mouth. It felt really good to be in her hot mouth; I could tell this wasn't the first time she sucked a cock. I moaned out loud, it felt so good. She didn't just let it in her mouth; she sucked it really hard.

"You're doing it like a pro, bitch," Hannah said. Dorothy giggled on my cock but didn't let it out for a second; she continued bobbing on it up and down.

I grabbed her head and started fucking her mouth. She obeyed with her eyes closed. She let my cock deep in her throat at every thrust; my balls hit her jaw a few times. I could feel my throbbing cock filling her small mouth. I could even feel her throat with the head of my cock at every thrust I made.

"Suck it, bitch, suck it!" Hannah said. She was fingering herself down there, kneeling on the floor as I face fucked her friend beside her. She watched us closely, with her face just a few inches from Dorothy.

I could feel my heavy balls tighten like just before I cum. With these two hot bitches, I knew it wouldn't take long. But I still wanted to enjoy them a little bit. Who knew when I could get two hot interns like them to suck my cock?

So I pulled out and pulled her hungry mouth away a bit. Hannah leaned to her immediately and kissed Dorothy's wet lips. The two hot interns were kissing and kneeling on the floor, and I watched them with my cock throbbing above their faces.

Hannah leaned below my balls and started licking them. Her small tongue flicked over my throbbing balls, making it even harder for me to last longer.

"Now that's something I've never done before," Dorothy said with lust in her eyes.

"Well, Dorothy, I have a feeling we are not in Kansas anymore," I said. She giggled and let me spank her face with my rock-hard cock, leaving glistening drops of her saliva on her cheeks. Then I drove her head back to the head of my cock. She took it immediately between her lips and swallowed it deep. The feeling of having my cock in her hot mouth and her girlfriend licking my balls down there made me feel like heaven. I looked up, and whispered, "Thank you!"

Dorothy started to bob up and down on my cock. Hannah was licking and kissing my heavy sack. She even tried to take one of my balls into her mouth but she couldn't open her lips so wide.

I felt it was time for me to cum. I took Hannah by her hair and pulled her out from under me. Then I grabbed Dorothy's head with my both hands and started fucking her face. She didn't object, she just went along with my moves and let me fuck her pretty mouth and full lips. I leaned my head to the side so I could watch how my throbbing cock disappeared in her mouth again and again.

I couldn't take it anymore. I pushed the last one and shot my hot cream into her hot mouth with a loud groan. I could hear Hannah saying, "Save some for me!" but I didn't care: I shot stream after stream into Dorothy's hungry mouth. It was like flying; the tension was released from my whole body.

I stepped back, totally spent. Some drops of my white cum were dripping from the corners of Dorothy's lips. She had a proud and smiling face. She immediately stood up and leaned above Hannah; the blonde girl opened her pink lips and received the sticky mix of her girlfriend's saliva and my white cum. Their petite tongue danced as they kissed and shared my sperm.

"Mmmm...," Hannah purred like a good kitten and she closed her lips as she swallowed my cum. "You made a cool dessert, Dor," she stated to her girlfriend, smiling.

"Shut up, bitch," Dorothy said and wiped some drops of cum with her red nails from Hannah's cheeks and licked her finger.

They both giggled and I watched these two hot interns in awe, having sucked me to spray all over their nasty faces in such a short time, kneeling before me – I recalled what I stated when I started at this firm: it's good to work at Walden, Inc.

Chapter 2: First Class

I could hardly believe it; we were the only ones sitting in first class. Our flight attendant told us something about the current economy and the night flight, but I didn't really pay her any attention. I enjoyed the large space and I was happy Walden, Inc. paid for the first-class tickets for the three of us.

There were Bonnie, Carl, and I arranging our bags into the luggage racks above our seats. When my boss told me I had to go to Japan to get to know my colleagues better and to participate in some meetings, I wasn't happy at all. But later on, I found out Bonnie was coming as well, and the firm would pay all our expenses, so it promised to be an exciting week.

So here we were on the plane, packing our luggage onto the shelves above the seats. I helped Bonnie with her suitcase. Carl was already sitting beside us, reading a Playboy issue with a grin on his face.

"Is that chick from Two And A Half Men?" I asked, pointing to the cover girl of the magazine.

"Yeah, Jenny McCarthy," he said, checking the cover. "She's hot, isn't she?"

"As I recall, she was on the cover last year," I said. Carl shrugged, saying,

"I don't really have time to read my magazines," he said. "They just pile up on my shelves. But on a flight like this, I usually have time for some reading."

"Some read Schopenhauer, some read Playboy," Bonnie giggled.

"Hey, don't judge me, okay?" Carl said.

We all sat down and fastened our belts. It wasn't long till the plane took off.

***

I was having a very bad dream. I was in a parking garage and Britney Spears was chasing me with a whip. She shouted at me, "Work, bitch!" I couldn't escape her, anyhow I tried hiding behind a Maserati or a Bugatti. She was spanking my bare ass with her long black whip and shouted the same line at me again and again.

I woke up to the sudden trembling of the plane. I looked around. Carl was snoring beside me with his Playboy on his lap. As the cover crinkled, Jenny McCarthy had a grin on her face.

I glanced over at Bonnie. She was asleep. An eye mask was covering her eyes. Her perky breasts rose and fell in slow motion under her blouse. She even snored a bit which made her even cuter. Her legs were slightly sprawled as she slept in the reclined airline seat.

I thought about what she had said earlier, about how she would try to do it in public. I thought about some of her hints – her peeping at the couple in the office, her willingness at the Halloween party, her ass being fucked at the promotion party, and so on. I came to the idea that I had to take my chances here and now, on this airline flight.

I looked around. Carl was sleeping as well, with his Playboy on his lap. His face leaned to the window, but he didn't seem to be bothered by the cool surface.

There were no other passengers in first class. The travelers in the coach class sat behind us in another compartment, separated by a red curtain. The flight attendants probably had their break since none of them were around.

I opened my safety belt. I stood up, looked around again, and checked whether everything was safe. No one was around. I loosened my tie around my neck and took it off. I untied it and leaned it over Bonnie's arms. It was long enough for me to gently tie her hands to the armrests. I was working slowly, checking around again and again. I tied a loose tie on her hands so she would be able to free herself easily, if necessary.

I managed to tie her arms without waking her up. I knelt before her on the carpet. I lifted her skirt slowly, but stealthily. I could see her black thong under her skirt, barely covering her pussy.

Bonnie's reclined seat gave me better access to her pussy. I touched the inner part of her thigh. She twitched a bit, her head turned in the other direction, but she didn't change how she breathed. I thought she was still sleeping.

I moved her thong aside and exposed her slit. With my palm up, I slowly and gently worked my middle finger all the way into her cunt.

She sighed and rolled her head to the side. I thought she might wake up, so I removed my finger and placed it under my nose. Her musky pussy scent caused my cock to inflate. When I realized Bonnie was still sleeping, I put two fingers back in her pussy and moved them in and out. Her lubrication began leaking out on my fingers and her pussy odor filled the air.

When I began moving my thumb over her clit, Bonnie woke up, pulled her eye mask up, and looked down at me.

"What are you doing?" she asked.

"Relax," I told her. "Let me take care of you."

"You're going to get caught."

"I've checked, and the flight attendants are on a break," I answered.

"Well then, you'd better hurry because you've made me horny."

She smiled and sprawled her legs further apart.

"Put the mask back on," I told her and she did, leaning back in the reclined chair and letting me finger her pussy.

I began moving my fingers faster and faster inside her pussy while moving my thumb in circles over her clit.

She lifted her pelvis to give me better access to her pussy. I leaned forward and flipped my tongue on her clit. When she tried to move her hands to pull my head toward her pussy, she realized they were tied to the arms.

I smeared her pussy juices over her asshole and slowly pushed my middle finger in it. It was tight and hot, as always.

"Oh... Fuck...," she moaned. "I'm almost there."

I continued moving my fingers in and out of her pussy and ass and licking her clit until her body went rigid and her orgasm hit her. Bonnie's pussy and asshole clamped down on my fingers about ten times before it ended, leaving her panting for breath.

I looked up at her. She was smiling happily, but to my huge surprise, Carl was awake, standing beside her with a huge grin on his face. His hands even were fondling her breasts in her cleavage. How the hell did he wake up and stand beside her? Was he a fucking Cherokee warrior or what? And Bonnie was enjoying herself, she was smiling.

"Can I join?" Carl asked, hoarsely. I thought it over. Fucking Bonnie in the first class, miles high, in a threesome?

"Why not?" I shrugged. "Let's do her!"

"Cool," he said, grinning. He released Bonnie's boobs which made her moan out disappointedly. He straightened up, grinning, and opened his fly. Bonnie turned to the sound of his zipper and smiled again. He took out his cock; it was hard already. He pointed it at Bonnie's face and pulled his foreskin back. He fondled it for a few times, then touched her lips with the purple, shiny head of his cock. Bonnie followed his cock with the eye mask still on, smiling happily.

In a flash, I had my trousers and shorts around my knees. I placed Bonnie's feet over my shoulders and impaled her with my stiff cock. It wasn't the most comfortable position that we'd ever used, but the airline seat didn't give us any other choices.

I just plunged my rod deep into her hot pussy when I saw a flight attendant slide the red curtain aside. I just looked into her eyes and pictured how she could see us – a young brunette lying in the reclined chair with her skirt pulled up and the eye mask still on her face, being fucked by a horny guy dressed in his suit and she sucking another guy's dick. I saw her wink after she put her hand over her mouth, then she quickly closed the curtain.

I fucked Bonnie harder. She was panting and puffing almost as hard as after her orgasm. When I stood up a little more, Bonnie was folded in half with her feet near her head. The new angle gave me a better opportunity to hit her G-spot with my cock and I got a closer look at how she sucked Carl's erect cock. He even grabbed her head and pushed himself deeper into her throat with every thrust he made. As he was moving in and out, his cock became more and more wet, and her saliva even got smeared around her red lips.

She came again. I knew she could cum really quickly when she had a hard cock in her mouth, that's why we did so much 69. She enjoyed it right now as well. She held Carl's cock deep in her mouth, and her whole body trembled.

"That's it, baby...," Carl murmured. He pulled his cock out of her mouth and smacked her cheeks with it a few times. Bonnie enjoyed it with a smile, and we could feel her afterglow even with her eye mask still on.

"Let me have a bit of her pussy," Carl said to me.

"Fine," I said. "Sit on the chair."

I released the restraints on Bonnie's arms and helped her get up. It was difficult to control her with the eye mask still on her face. We had to move slowly. I nodded to Carl. He sat on the chair, leaned back, and helped Bonnie sit in his lap, facing him. She giggled when she felt his erection between her thighs. He pulled her thong away, guided his cock into her slit, and when he succeeded, she sat on it.

She just sat there for a few seconds, enjoying Carl's cock in her pussy. While she did so, I took her hands, pulled them back behind her back, and leaned close to her ears,

"Do you like his cock in your pussy?" I hissed to her. "Do you like it deep in you?"

"Yes...," she moaned like a kitten.

"Good...," I said. Holding her hands I got to an idea. I picked up my tie from the floor and tied her hands behind her back. She moaned again, smiling, and started to ride Carl. She was moving with long, slow thrusts on him, splitting herself on his stiff cock again and again.

I bent her over Carl and pulled her skirt up a bit more, and pulled her thong sideways. I grabbed her ass and pushed her down on Carl's cock to the hilt.

"Now you're gonna get it, you little slut," I said. I stood behind her and slowly but firmly pushed my cock deep into her asshole. It was so tight and hot that I almost lost it.

"Ohhhh... yeah...," she moaned. Her head dropped to Carl's chest and her hair covered her face. But I could tell she was enjoying it.

"You're a real bitch in heat," Carl said.

"Fuck me!" she ordered, and we obeyed happily.

I grabbed her boobs and started fucking her ass. Her pussy fluids made my cock wet and slippery so I could fuck her tight asshole with abandon. It was so tight I felt like I was splitting her in half. Besides, I could feel Carl's hard cock pounding her pussy. He held her by her face and fucked her hard.

"Do you like it?" I hissed in her ears. "Do you like being double-fucked?"

"Fuck yeah!" She said.

"I bet you like it, you bitch!" Carl said to her. "I bet you like being fucked in your ass and pussy at the same time."

"Yeah..." Bonnie moaned.

Carl fucked her with an evil grin on his face. He checked her hand being tied back behind her and pulled down his own tie as well.

He continued fucking her hard but tied his tie around her neck like a collar and grabbed the end of it like a slip.

"We're gonna fuck your brains out, bitch," he exclaimed then he turned to me, saying, "Here you are, brotha" and handed me the tie sideways. I took the end of it and pulled Bonnie back just like a bitch in heat. She straightened which caused our cock to move into her from a different angle.

"Wow," I moaned.

"Yeah..." she sighed and moved in contrast to our thrusts. We fucked her balls deep with strong, hard thrusts.

"Fuck!" she cried out, and her body started to tremble. I quickly put my palm to her mouth to keep her silent. She came with us sandwiching her – I felt her flesh spasming on my cock. She was breathing hard. But we didn't stop, we pushed our throbbing cocks into her hot body again and again.

The red curtain slid aside slightly and I saw two female flight attendants peeking through the small opening, while we continued fucking Bonnie. That caused me to shoot a huge load of sperm into her hot throbbing asshole.

"Mmmm...," she purred. "Come on, boys, fill me up..."

This did it for Carl as well. I could feel through Bonnie's pussy wall his cock stiffening and trembling in her pussy. He let out a loud groan, and thrust a last one, coming deep into her.

I slowly pulled back. My cock popped out of Bonnie's ravished asshole with an audible 'pop.' I untied my tie around her hands and took Carl's tie from her neck and gave it back to him.

"Thanks, man," he said. "I think I'm gonna keep it as a memory."

Bonnie adjusted her hair back and pulled down her eye mask. Her face was red but I could see in her eyes she really enjoyed the whole session.

"Thank you, guys..." she said. "That was just what I needed."

I saw the curtain open just a bit and both female flight attendants stepped next to our seats.

"Welcome to the Mile-High Club," the first one said. "That was pretty hot."

The second flight attendant gave us some warm, damp washcloths. "You'll need these to clean up," she added.

"Thank you," Bonnie answered.

"I hoped you liked the show," Carl added, grinning.

"I sure did," the first one said, checking Carl out. "I haven't seen anyone fucking like that since I've worked here."

The flight attendants left for a couple of minutes to let us wipe our fluids off and get our clothing rearranged. The area around our seats smelled like pussy.

A few minutes later, the second flight attendant came back with a plastic bag to drop the used washcloths into.

"We'll be serving a meal in a few minutes. You probably need it," she winked.

"Oh yeah," Carl said. "We definitely do." He sat in his chair and opened his Playboy again. "Sorry, honey," he said to Jenny McCarthy on the cover, "I hope you don't mind but ain't got time for culture."

Chapter 3: The Auction

"Believe me, you will enjoy it!" Mr. Tagamoshi said. "Besides, what can go wrong?"

Yeah. What can go wrong? I recalled his last sentence at dawn again and again and wished him hell. But let me tell you about this crazy night from the beginning.

The conference we attended took place in Osaka, one of the largest financial centers in Japan. We didn't see much of the city, only went to the location, Umeda Sky Building, and started working. Carl, Bonnie, and I separated into a series of different meetings. I don't know about theirs, but mine were boring as hell. Plus, I was totally tired because of the jet lag effect so I wasn't effective at all.

We didn't meet until the closing dinner in the evening. We had a buffet table full of strange Japanese food; I could read their names written on small tables before the trays: nikuyaga, gyoza, sushi, sashimi, and so on.

"How was your day?" I asked Bonnie when we finally had a chance to be together, eating our food.

"Terrible," she answered. "They got the whole idea of our contracts wrong. I spent literally hours correcting their mistakes. What about you?"

"Well, I can't exactly remember all the rubbish I talked myself through today. Luckily I made notes," I showed my palmtop to her. "I hope I can work the details out from them next week, at home."

"Yeah, I miss home," Bonnie said and switched to dessert. "And we still have the closing party to attend after this dinner. I wonder what it will be like."

We found it out right after dinner. Mr. Tagamoshi, the head executive of our Japanese associates sat at our table. He was a small, bumptious man with round glasses and a bald head.

"I hope you enjoyed the dinner," he told us. We agreed keenly and made sure we had the best dish of our lives. We didn't tell him a word about how much we hate to eat half-alive fish and cold rice.

"How do you like our office building?" he chit-chatted.

"It's really beautiful," I answered.

"I'm so glad you like it. Did you know the Umeda Sky Building was completed in 1993 and is 173 meters high? The skyscrapers are equipped with superior safety measures such as earthquake-proofing and disaster protection, and have a floating garden at the top," he raised his hand above his head. "With time, the half-mirror glasses that cover the building reflect the sky on their surface, so that the building seems to become one with the firmament and it appears as if the garden is alone, floating there in the blue."

We nodded, sipping from our drinks. I didn't really know how to react to his introduction to the building so we were just sitting there in an awkward silence.

"So... Did anybody tell you the theme of tonight's party?" Mr. Tagamoshi asked eventually.

"No," I answered. "Should we prepare for something?"

"Well, for a few years, we have decided we should support charity at our closing party. The HR department selects each year another organization to support. Usually, a huge sum of money is collected. The HR is happy, the guests are entertained, the reputation of the firm is rising, everybody wins."

"Okay...," I said, "but how is the money collecting exactly going?"

"Oh," Mr. Tagamoshi said, smiling, "we found out a perfect way to do that. We organize an auction."

"An auction, for like, dedicated baseball balls and t-shirts?"

"More like for people."

There was a little silence among us. I could hear the tingling of glasses from the tables around us. We looked at each other with Bonnie.

"Pardon?" she asked.

"Yes, you heard it well," Mr. Tagamoshi laughed. "We organize an auction in which you can bid on our co-workers. The highest bid wins the given colleague for the night."

"What do you exactly mean by that?" she narrowed her eyebrows.

"The winner pays the money to charity, and in return, he or she owns the auctioned person for a whole night. And he..."

"Or she...," I added, cocking my eye to Bonnie.

"Or she can do with her companion whatever she wants."

"What are we talking about, exactly?"

"Well," Mr. Tagamoshi shrugged, "Most people have lunch together. Some of us invite the other one to a tea ceremony. Once, I was invited to an amusement park. So believe me, it can be fun."

"What about..." asked Bonnie carefully, "any... deviant tasks?"

"Well," he leaned back and crossed his finger on his belly, "I've heard rumors about some sexual adventures going on on these occasions, but I didn't believe any of them. It wouldn't be appropriate and it would hurt the policy of our company, wouldn't it?" he said but the light reflected on his glasses so I couldn't tell whether he was joking.

"Yeah, I guess so..." I nodded. "Okay, thanks for the enlightenment."

"Oh, this was more than just an... enlightenment," he leaned over to me and looked deep into my eyes. "To show how much we appreciate you as our guests, I nominated the two of you to the list of attendees at the auction tonight."

"Pardon?" Bonnie asked with her eyes open wide.

"This is a great privilege with which we show our appreciation to our guests. Believe me, you will enjoy it," he patted our shoulders reassuringly. "Besides, what can go wrong?"

With that, he left us to entertain other couples having dinner. Bonnie got his cell out of her purse and dialed immediately.

"I'm gonna ask the Worm about this," she said. "I don't want to participate in any unknown ceremonies here."

I waited for her to discuss the situation with our boss. As for me, I got a bit curious about this evening. Who knows, it can shape even well.

"His cell is dead, as always," Bonnie said.

"Then we just have to go with the flow, I guess," I shrugged.

The dinner came to an end. The waiters cleaned the tables, the lights went dim. A blonde singer stepped to the stage, dressed in chains, and started to sing about the generic bullshit about love: *"There is everything, yet there is nothing"* and so on. The lyrics did not make so much sense but she was nice and hot in her red costume. All the men around us seemed to like her.

"She's Ayumi Hamasaki," Bonnie said, looking her up on her smartphone.

"Is she the Japanese Britney Spears or something?"

"Apparently," she nodded. "And she's singing Wake Me Up right now."

The blonde girl performed one more song then she left the stage. All the men were applauding and cheering. They nodded to each other with a satisfied smile on their faces.

"Thanks to Ayumi for this breath-stopping performance," said Mr. Tagamoshi, appearing back on the stage. "And now, the charity auction we all have been waiting for!" he announced. "As you all may know, the money we collect today goes to support the homes and families ruined in Fukushima. So please go ahead, be noble, open your wallet, and donate!"

Everybody was cheering and applauding. We did it with Bonnie, as well.

"And to spice things up a little, the apropos of the charity donation will be a little auction to our volunteers!"

"Volunteers, my ass," Bonnie said to me. I shrugged and listened to Mr. Tagamoshi.

"The winners of the bids can spend a whole weekend with our lovely volunteers! And remember," he winked to the audience, "don't be naughty!"

Cheer and applause again.

The auction began. To my surprise, Carl was the first to be auctioned. He had a smirk on his face as he stood on the stage, in the bright lights.

"The upset price is ten thousand yens!" Mr. Tagamoshi said. "Who gives eleven thousand for this young and strong man?"

Three young women started to bid on him immediately. The price went higher and higher and stopped at thirty thousand yens. Carl walked down from the stage with a huge grin on her face and started flirting with the winner, a young hot blonde executive. As they passed our table, he winked at me.

"And now, let's see a beautiful brunette, Bonnie..." Mr. Tagamoshi announced. Bonnie got up, whispering to me: "I hope I won't be bought by some pervert." As she hurried to the stage, she had a huge smile on her face. That's my girl, I thought. She always tries to get the best from the situation.

As she stepped up to the stage, the bid immediately started. Mr. Tagamoshi didn't need to work too much, a handful of men raised their hands to show they would like to spend a night with my girlfriend. I kinda liked the situation, but got afraid of what Bonnie told me: she might get into the hands of a pervert, or something.

As her price got higher and higher, most of the men stopped bidding on her. They were watching her beautiful, curvy body, her nice cleavage, and her shiny brown hair. I could actually see a man beside me gulping one as she watched her with blank eyes.

But only one man wanted her enough to pay the highest bid for her. He was a relatively short guy with grey hair, glasses, and a dark suit. He didn't say anything, just raised his hand to Mr. Tagamoshi again and again. I could see Bonnie trying to catch a glimpse of him but the lamps of the stage made it really impossible.

When the mysterious stranger won the auction of Bonnie, I could see some of the men around us leaning back into their chairs disappointedly. The stranger stepped to the stage, held Bonnie's hand, and led her out. I could still see her whispering "Help me" to me, but I just spread my hands, showing, there was nothing I could do.

It was my turn. Mr. Tagamoshi called me up to the stage and introduced me to the audience.

"And here's another of our colleagues from the U.S., Mr. John Smith, or as his close friends call him, Johnny!"

I always hated when people called me Johnny but didn't say a word. I had my usual smile on and hoped for the best.

But it didn't come. Only a few bidders raised their hands and they quickly disappeared when an old Japanese lady raised the stakes so high they couldn't compete with her. What does she want from me? I thought. Maybe a foot massage? Brrr... I checked her wrinkled skin and was disgusted.

"Wonderful!" Mr. Tagamoshi stated. 'Obasan Yakamoto, you've won this beautiful specimen for the night!'

I could hear a weak applause. I may have looked a little disappointed because Mr. Tagamoshi covered his microphone and whispered to me strictly: "Be careful and obedient, Mr. Smith! Mrs. Yakamoto is the widow of our late executive. I hope we don't get any bad news about your performance tomorrow!"

I could see there was no escape for me. I decided I would do whatever it took to attend to a good business relationship. So I followed the old Japanese lady out of the room. At the entrance, she tossed her bag to me, and the porter called her limousine.

We got into her pearly white limo. She eyed me up and down again. I felt like a horse in a corner.

"Call Maria and Aki, Jean," she ordered the driver and lit up a long cigarette. As he made a conference call, she started jabbering in Japanese with the two other ladies in the line. I didn't understand anything that she said but I heard my name multiple times. After she finished, she crossed her legs slowly like Sharon Stone did in Basic Instinct. And I could tell neither was she wearing panties. But she didn't look as seductive as the blonde actress in that movie at all.

"You see what you like, Mr.... Smith?" she asked in her trembling voice.

"Yeah... I think you're beautiful, Mrs. Yakamoto!"

"Don't bullshit to me!" she cried. "I know I'm old but I don't care. I have the same pussy as every 20-year-old bitch around here!"

I thought it would be wise not to say anything. She took out a smartphone from her purse and took a picture of me.

"Perfect..." she stated. "Now we'll have a picture before and we'll make another after... Or maybe more..."

She made another one, this time zooming at my groin. This was the first time I cursed Mr. Tagamoshi for his crazy auction.

The old lady lived in a small apartment. I had to follow her inside.

"Take off my shoes, slave," she ordered. I knelt down and got a look at her wrinkled feet. Well, this wasn't the way I imagined what I would do tonight. But I took off her shoes, anyway, keeping back my breath so as not to smell her ugly feet.

She tiptoed into her apartment, throwing her coat to the floor. It was followed by her gloves and her scarf. I thought I would better take them up and when I was bending for them down, I could see she was checking me from the room.

I put her clothes and my coat on a hanger and stepped into her tiny apartment. It was filled with china and tapestries. Everything smelled of mothball. She pointed to a small door in the corner of the room. I opened it – it was a small room.

"Get dressed in these, but fast," said the old woman pointing to an apron hanging there. "And don't wear anything else. My friends are coming over. We have to prepare everything." And she shut the door.

I got naked and folded my clothes neatly. I had a feeling I would be in trouble if Mrs. Yakamoto would find my clothes left just around. Then I put the apron on. It was the kind you can buy at fun shops, having printed the body of a half-naked, muscular fireman at the front. He sure had a bigger hose than me at that time. I felt like I was waiting for an examination at the urologist.

I could hear chatter. The other witches have arrived. I took a deep breath and stepped out. They were coming into the sitting room, two identical-looking old Japanese women. Aside from their clothes, I couldn't tell them apart from Mrs. Yakamoto, either. When they saw me, they started chatting in Japanese, again. My host showed them to me, detailing some of my body parts.

"Turn around, come on!" she ordered me. I did, and they were having a huge laugh at my butt. I thought I would show them something so I jiggled it like a stripper. They were laughing more loudly, but then Mrs. Yakamoto stopped them:

"Bring us tea, Mr. Smith! Everything is prepared there, just boil some water and bring it in!"

I went out to the kitchen. I didn't really know much about Japanese so I was glad the tea, the pots, and everything else was prepared on a bamboo tray. Even the water teapot was filled with water, so I turned it on, and it turned off automatically after two minutes. I put the teapot on the tray and brought everything inside – desperately paying attention not to spill any hot water on my naked skin. I put the tray on the coffee table and wanted to step back, but my host stopped me:

"You'll have the privilege of preparing our tea!"

"Sorry, but I..."

"You don't know how to make matcha tea? You stupid Americans..." they were laughing at me again. "Now I'm going to teach you, son! Put a spoon of tea powder in my pot... some more... now pure some water in it..."

She grabbed a little bamboo stick from the tray and gave it to me.

"Now mix it with this muddler. Fast! Come on, American boy! Mix it 'till it will be smooth and creamy! That's right! Okay, go on and make the tea for my guests as well!"

I prepared the tea for the other ugly ladies as well. I managed not to spill out anything. I was trying so hard that sweat started to form on my forehead. I had to mop it up with the apron, but it was made of plastic so it was no use. But they took a look at my penis and they started laughing again. I covered it with the apron but it was no use, Mrs. Yakamoto raised the apron with another muddler again.

"What a toy you got there, American boy," she said, laughing. "Turn around!"

I did and I could feel her spanking me with the muddler with short strikes.

"Bend over!" she ordered. I slightly bent over and they were laughing even more loudly. The old witch was spanking me harder, one of her strikes got on my balls.

That was when I had enough. I managed to repress my anger, only hissed and straightened up, turning around, asking them:

"Can I get you anything else, ladies?"

"Sure, American boy!" Mrs. Yakamoto stated. "Get us some wagashi from the fridge!"

I didn't know what the hell wagashi was. I only used the opportunity to escape. Unfortunately, my clothes were in the closet where I had to change to this horrible apron and I couldn't get them without the old witches noticing me. But I got my coat from the hanger in which I had my phone and my wallet – I didn't really need anything else.

I don't want to detail how I sneaked out of the apartment, covered myself with my coat to cover my bare ass and the horrible apron; how were passersby watching me; how the cab driver looked at me when I got into his vehicle. Let's just say I took a mental note not to participate in Japanese auctions in the future. Like ever. Then took a shower, put on a tender bathrobe, turned the TV on, and waited for Bonnie to arrive from her night.

Chapter 4: Bonnie's Initiation

"Okay, I will tell you everything," Bonnie said. "But give me a half an hour first."

I agreed. She looked like she could use some rest; her cheeks were red, and her hair was messy and sloppy.

I helped her undress. She went into the bathroom and took a long hot shower. She was in there so long that steam was coming out through the door left ajar.

I listened as she was singing a song. She seemed relaxed yet tired. I called the room service and ordered two roast beef dinners and a bottle of champagne.

She stepped out of the shower, with her freshly washed body and hair. She sat at the table beside me, with only a short towel wrapped around her body—her boobs were barely covered by the top, and her pussy wasn't fully covered by the bottom. She ate the dinner like someone who hadn't eaten in weeks. After she gorged, she leaned back in her seat and started telling me her night.

"After the stranger bought me, he took my hand and led me out of the room. I could still hear 'you're next,' but I couldn't check who bought you. I was checking this stranger out: black hair, muscular body, dark grey suit. I couldn't deduce anything particular about him.

"'I'm Doctor Surlove, I've been living here for a few years. You can call me doctor, or...' he hesitated, 'Master for tonight.'"

"All right, Master, " I answered. My name is Bonnie and I'm here representing Walden, Inc.

"We stepped into the elevator. There were only the two of us in it. It had glass walls so we could see the whole city below us. I admired the view as he stepped behind me.

"I could feel the Doctor checking me out again. Then he reached out and pressed the STOP button. I turned around and found him facing me.

"'Who's your Master for tonight?' he asked.

"You're my Master, I answered immediately. And I'm your slut."

"'Oh no,'" he said. "'Not yet. You'll have to earn that.'"

"I followed him into the game, asking, 'How can I earn it, Master?"

"'You can earn it right here and right now.'"

"There was a moment of silence. I could feel my heart beating in my chest. If I were to continue this game, there would be no stopping me tonight.

"We were looking deep into each other's eyes."

"'Get on your knees', he said."

"I looked into his eyes once more and I decided I'd play his game. And I knew what he wanted. I got on my knees immediately and opened up his fly. I knew I had to be quick since people were waiting for this elevator.

"I took his cock out. It was a nice, long one, and it was hardening already. I pulled his foreskin back and while looking into his eyes, I licked around the head. He smiled and nodded.

"'Good girl,' he said. 'Now show me what you got.'"

"I opened my lips and took the head of his cock into my mouth. I could feel him hardening in my mouth. He even moaned out loud.

"I took his cock deeper into my mouth. I let my saliva drool around it, then removed it. It was fully erected now, glistening in the bright light of the elevator. I admired it for a moment then reminded myself we don't have much time. So I placed it back into my mouth and started sucking it and bobbing with my head.

"I even closed my eyes. I enjoyed the moment so much. I was on my knees in this elevator, thousands of miles away from home, with the whole of Osaka below us, and I was sucking this stranger's cock who I just met and who just bought me for the whole night.

"He grabbed my head and started fucking my face. He pushed his cock really deep and I swallowed easily.

"He released my head so I removed his wet cock from my mouth so I could breathe. The mix of my saliva and his precum was dripping from it to my cleavage and my neck.

The Doctor was panting as well and looked at me, with uncontrollable lust in his eyes.

"'Jerk it on your face,' he ordered. And I did. I left my lips slightly open and jerked his cock wildly in front of my face. The Doctor leaned back, let out a loud groan, and sprayed everything he had on my face. He must have collected it for several days since I got a huge amount of fresh, hot sperm on my cheeks and my lips. I wanted to lick it up gracefully but he stopped me, saying, "'Let it shine on your face. I want everybody to see you're my slut.'"

"And he pulled out his belt from his trousers.

"'Now you've earned the right to be my slut,'" he said. And I could see his belt even had the word *SLUT* written on it. He had really prepared for this auction! It looked wild and scary yet it was intriguing. I was wondering how far this game would go. And I admit I had fun! This guy was strange but attractive, and he had some nice ideas I could enjoy. So I decided I would go on.

"Yes, Sir," I bent my head towards him and let him put his belt on my neck. I felt like a wild animal on a leash.

"He pressed the STOP button again. The elevator started and within a second, we were at the ground level. When the door opened, a few people were waiting; the Doctor stepped forward and led me out among the people. I held my head up proudly and followed him. I heard whispers behind me but we left quickly, leaving them standing there. I hoped no one took a picture of me – I have to admit, I was too horny to think about that.

"The Doctor gave his card to the valet and waited for his car to arrive. He looked me up and down, and said, "I'm proud of you, slut. You passed the first test.'"

"Thank you, Master," I answered. "I hope I won't disappoint you."

"'I'm sure you won't,'" he said.

Chapter 5: Bonnie's Night

"I sat next to the Doctor in his car. He was driving calmly and relaxed.

"When he stopped the car at the first red traffic light, the Doctor turned to me and checked me out. I could tell he liked what he saw since his eyes were smiling. But he said nothing, only pressed the Play button on the media player in the car. First I thought it would be AC/DC or Def Leppard or some other classic rock, maybe metal but it proved to be Taylor Swift's new album, you know, the Red. I wouldn't think about this guy listening to a country-pop female singer. He was actually thrumming on the wheel and singing the lyrics along!

"Taylor Swift was singing *'We Are Never Ever Getting Back Together'* when we arrived at the Doctor's house. It was a beautiful villa at the side of the city, among the trees. It had large glass walls and a cubic structure.

"The Doctor led me into the house. He opened the door before me and helped me with my coat. He was a real gentleman, even asked if he could give me something to drink. I asked for a Margarita. As he prepared it I checked around the living room. It had huge glasses to the forest around us, an expensive looking black leather couch, and matching armchairs. There were modern, blissful pictures hanging on the walls. The center of the living room was occupied by a large black table.

"'I was planning to have guests tonight,' the Doctor said, handing over my Margarita. 'My friends are coming over to our monthly usual poker night. I had to attend this boring business dinner downtown, but I haven't regretted it since I managed to invite you here.'

"'Well, it wasn't actually an invitation...' I started but he shrugged:

"'You know what I mean. And as far as I could see it in the elevator, you didn't like my "initiation" at all. Right?'

"I didn't say anything but I could feel my cheeks going red. I sipped a gulp from my cocktail quickly.

"'I take it as a yes,' he said. 'And now comes the big question: do you want to be my maid for tonight?'

"'What does this exactly mean?' I asked.

"'First of all, you served me tonight more than perfectly,' he said, grinning. 'Your official duties are accomplished, I'm totally satisfied with today's auction. I got my money's worth, if you don't mind me saying so. You can go home if you want.'

"'What if I stay...?' I asked.

"'If you choose to stay, you'll have to serve my guests tonight as my personal maid. You'll have to fulfill our every wish no matter how nasty or dirty they will be.'

"'Wow...,' I said. 'This really sounds...'

"'Nasty?' he asked.

"'Yeah...' I agreed, nodding. 'Just to make it clear, can you tell me anything about these wishes? Maybe some details or examples?'

"'No,' he said. 'I don't want to spoil the night. Let me put it this way: if you choose to stay, you will have a night you will never forget. You may not sit straight for a few days, but you will definitely enjoy it.'

"I suspected he meant anal sex, and he meant lots of it. Which I didn't really mind. So I looked around, more like to gain the courage to say yes to his wild offer.

"'When do I have to decide?' I asked, sipping another one from my Margarita.

"'My buddies will be here in half an hour,' he said, checking the time on his watch. 'You'll still have to change your clothes and prepare, so this means, you'll have to decide it... about now.'

"I could feel the whole room spinning around me. Do I really want to serve this stranger and his friends? Do I really want to jump on this strange adventure?

"'Yes,' I said, half aloud.

"'Pardon?' he asked, putting down his whiskey on the table. 'I don't think I've heard you well.'

"'Yes, I will be your maid and slave for tonight. And I will serve and fulfill your and your friends' every wish.'

"'No matter how dirty they will be?' he asked, smiling.

"'That's right. In fact, the dirtier the better.'

"'Perfect!' he stated and checked the time again. 'Then please follow me to your room.'

"He led me to a small room with a bench in it. It had two large wardrobes which he opened before me. Checking what they contained made me rethink my decision. They were filled with all kinds of sexual toys: whips, pink handcuffs, dildos, nipple clips, and strap-ons. He stood before the shelves and hand-picked a pair of black high heels for me.

"'Take them on,' he said, and chose other things from the wardrobes: 'And this...' handed me over a black latex dress which was so short I was sure it would cover neither my breasts nor my ass. I decided I would go on and play it by his rules; I took the shoes and the clothes over without a word. I even started to get naked.

"'Oh and not to forget the last, but most important piece...' he added and gave me a black butt plug with a huge grin. It was shiny and curvy; it even had a small piece of jewel at the base of it.

"'What should I do with this one?' I asked.

"'I hope you're only joking,' he answered. 'Please hurry. You have...' he checked his watch again, '25 minutes. The toilet is there,' he waved to a hidden door at the end of the cupboard, 'if you need it.'

With that, he left and I remained there sitting on the cool bench, with high heels and a latex dress beside me, and a black butt plug in my hands.

I took my time. I got naked and tried the high heels on. They matched perfectly and even looked sexy on my feet – I wondered how the Doctor found out my size. Aside from the high heels, I got only the Doctor's belt on my body, serving now as a collar. It was the one the Doctor gave me in the elevator, with the word *SLUT* on it. I didn't take it off since I thought it would match the latex dress on me.

I tiptoed into the bathroom and used it for a few minutes to refresh myself. I found some clean towels and a small bottle of lubricant in the bathroom. I washed the remains of the Doctor's cum off of my face, drank some water, and adjusted my hair and make-up. Then I went back and took the latex dress on – again, it fit perfectly. As I guessed, it didn't cover my breasts, in fact, it raised them a bit. My groin became also naked. I knelt down at the bench and smeared a good amount of lubricant all over the butt plug. Then I pressed some into my asshole as well. I suspected I would need lots and lots of lubrication tonight but I will barely have the time to get new portions of it.

I put the end of the plug into my asshole, and slowly, closing my eyes, I pushed it inside. It didn't manage to enter at first, but I relaxed a bit and pulled aside one of my cheeks with my free hand. I managed to press it in – after it slid through the gate, it easily penetrated my ass deeper, until its base stuck at my rim.

"That's when I heard the doorbell ring. The door of the small room opened and the Doctor found me there on my knees, with my hands on my bare ass, in the black latex dress and his belt on my neck. I could tell he enjoyed the view since he licked his lips and said, 'Come on, my slave, it's time to welcome the guests.'

I stood up, adjusted the latex dress on me, and stepped out into the living room. The black table now was occupied by some sets of cards and chips.

The doorbell rang again.

"'Go on!' the Doctor ordered. 'Open the door!'

I tiptoed to the door and opened it. Two large guys were standing out on the door-still.

"'Wow!' the first one said, checking me out. He was a huge black guy with a bald head and a black suit. Even his tie was black so he looked like a bodyguard.

The other guy only whistled one as he leaned his head sideways and watched me up and down. He was smaller and thinner but muscular. He wasn't dressed so formally; he had jeans and a short shirt that barely covered the huge tattoos on his arms and his neck.

"'Can we come in?' the black guy asked.

"'Of course, sorry,' I made a small pirouette as I could recall from my years learning ballet. 'Welcome to the Master's house. I'm your maid tonight.'

The small guy whistled again. The Doctor was already behind me so I stepped aside and let them in.

"'Wow, Doc,' the black guy said, checking my body, 'you sure got a hot bitch here tonight. What's your name, beauty?'

"'You can call me Slave tonight,' I answered and I could see the Doctor nodding with a smile. 'Wow, man,' the black guy added, 'you surely trained this bitch well.' and he slapped my ass cheek with a grin on his face. 'Hey she's even got the secret collar on,' he said, watching the belt on my neck serving as a collar closely.

"'Wait till I tell you how she deserved it,' the Doctor said, then greeted his friends and invited them in. 'Pour us some whiskey, slave,' he said to me. I tiptoed to the bar and took out some glasses. I prepared whiskey on ice for the men while they were listening to the Doctor's story about how he had won me at the auction and how he had initiated me in the elevator. The guests were grinning and kidding about it, especially, when the Doctor stated I would be their special entertainment tonight.

"'She will be here through our game and will do whatever you guys ask from her.'

"'She will do anything?' the small guy asked.

"'Absolutely anything!' the Doctor said.

"'Wow…' the black guy said.

I served the drinks. I leaned down with the tray and I let them admire my breasts hanging a few inches from their faces.

"'Thanks, slave,' the Doctor said.

"'Do you require anything else, Master?' I asked.

"'You can leave the bottle here', he said and put it on the table. 'I ain't got anything else right now, slave. What about you, guys?' he turned to his friends.

"'Actually, I got here right from the duty so a sandwich would be nice… slave…,' the black guy said. The other one didn't say anything, just whistled again, checking me out. I nodded and tiptoed to the kitchen. I found some food in the refrigerator along with some bottles of champagne and a few portions of olive. I put together a sandwich with a large portion of meat in it, and even managed to roast it a bit with a small electric oven I found there.

I found a good portion of fresh tiramisu in the refrigerator. I parted it into three small bowls and put it on the tray beside the sandwich.

When I got back, the men were already busy playing poker. The small guy and the Doctor were even smoking some thick cigars. I tiptoed to the large black guy and put the sandwich beside his set of cards on the table.

"'Wow, thanks, slave!' he said. 'It smells really good! Did you guys know the word 'sandwich' originated from a night of cards like this? A count named Sandwich was so busy playing cards his butler worried about him and put a piece of meat on a piece of bread...'

"'And served it to the count, yeah, we know that,' the Doctor said, with his attention on the cards. 'Would you please shut the fuck up and play?'

"'Hey, man, just because you have no luck doesn't mean you have to be rude,' the black guy said, putting some cards on the table, and started eating the sandwich I prepared for him.

"The Doctor was really concentrating on his cards. I wanted to have a joke on him so I stepped behind him, leaned over his ears and I blew a hot breath into them. This threw him out of his mental balance: he jumped up to his feet right away and threw his cards to the table!

"'What are you doing, bitch?' he shouted. 'We're playing seriously here!'

"I smiled since he clearly was losing in the game.

"'Don't smile on me!' he continued. 'Make yourself useful!'

"'How may I do so, my Master?' I asked.

"'Yeah, Doc, how may she do so?' the black guy said, with his mouth full of the sandwich.

"'You know what?' the Doctor said, looking at the small guy who was happy with his cards and blowing circles of fumes into the air from his cigar. 'Get on your knees and go under the table: take out this guy's cock and suck him off. I want to see his poker face when you distract him.'

"'Hey, man, there's no need for that,' the small guy said.

"'Yeah, there is,' the Doctor said. I could tell he was angry. 'Get down there, bitch, and show him how to play this game.'

"I knelt down and crawled obediently under the table, although it was hard to move in that tight latex dress. The Doctor sat down and I could hear them continue playing the game.

"It was darker down there and the smoke got stuck under the table. But I could see my latex-covered body had an effect on these guys: each of them had a nice bulk at their groin. I moved closer to the small guys but then I got an idea: I will play a bit with my Master tonight. Besides, I just love black cocks. So I moved closer to the black guy and opened his zip slowly, not to be heard. I managed to zip it open without a sound. I took his cock out: it was huge! It was just as black as his body and had thick veins around it.

"I licked its head around. I could feel him tensioning but I hoped the Master didn't see it on his face. I took his head between my lips and started fondling it with my tongue. I used a lot of saliva to make it all wet.

"Meanwhile, I checked the butt plug in my bare ass with my free hand. It was still stuck there so I continued sucking the huge black cock in my mouth. I let it deeper into my mouth and started bobbing on it up and down. I could swallow only half of it; the tip pressed to the roof of my mouth again and again. I could tell I will have some trouble with this huge cock later if he wants to fuck me but I continued anyway, it tasted so good. I supported myself with my hand on the cool floor. The huge head was throbbing in my mouth; I watered it with my saliva so much it even poured onto his balls making his pants wet.

"I could feel him shifting position; he must have had a hard time concentrating on the cards and keeping his poker face. I hope he finished eating his sandwich, though. But frankly, I didn't care: I just enjoyed his beautiful hard cock in my mouth.

"I could tell his duty spared his cock whatever it was. He couldn't keep up too long and after a good hard sucking, I could feel him spraying his huge hot load into my mouth. I swallowed it quickly, it was hot and fresh, just the way I like cum. I tried to swallow it all, but some dripped out at the corner of my lips.

"'Oh...,' I heard him making a loud sigh and I knew immediately we were busted. That's right: the Doctor looked under the table and when he saw me there, his face reddened.

"'What the fuck?' he shouted. 'That's not what I ordered you to do! Get out of there, right now!'

"I crawled up from under the table and moped up the black guy's cum from my lips with the back of my hand.

"'You've been a bad girl,' the Doctor said. 'A very bad bad girl. You just made me lose a huge amount. Now I'll have to punish you. Guys, help me teach this slut a lesson!'

'I turned around. Both of the guests stood up and threw their cards on the table. The black guy's cock was hanging out of his zip and small drops of cum were dripping from the end of it on his black trousers.

"'Sorry, Doc,' he said. 'She's such a talented cock sucker!'

"'Hey, the Doctor was right, let's do it!' the small guy said, with the cigar still in his mouth. 'It looks like I'm the only one who hadn't touched this nice piece of ass here,' he slapped a hard one on my ass cheeks. 'Wait...,' he said and pulled my ass cheeks apart. 'Wow wow wow, look what we have here,' and he showed the butt plug in my ass to the other men.

"'Wow, Doc, you crazy old motherfucker,' the black guy stated, and I could see his long hard cock hardening again. 'You prepared a nice surprise for us!'

'The Doctor smiled and I felt he was not angry at all.

"'Come on, honey, show us what you got! Get on the table!' the small guy said, slapping my ass again.

I climbed onto the table on all fours. I pushed my ass out a bit and looked up to the guys around me.

"'Check out this little kitten...' the small guy murmured. 'All she wants is to be fucked hard. Is that right, bitch?'

"Yes, Sir!" I said, well, admitted actually. I had already had two large amounts of cum in my stomach tonight; I was almost naked, on my fours in front of these strangers and I had a butt plug in my ass.

"'Look at her pussy!' the tattooed guy said. 'It's already dripping wet! She enjoys this like hell!'

"I do, Sir!" I admitted it, again. 'And I deserve whatever punishment you want for me.' And I let my head down. My hair fell before my face. The tattooed guy smacked my ass again, but this time, he leaned on it and placed a kiss on my cheek. This tenderness surprised me, and it even continued; the guy went on kissing my ass cheek, and I felt another mouth on the other one: it was the black guy. His huge lips and tongue caressed all over my half butt.

"'I'm glad you like my surprise, guys,' the Doctor said.

"'Fuck yeah, Doc,' the tattooed guy said. 'And I think I want another taste of her.'

"They turned me around. I felt sorry because they stopped licking and kissing my ass but I was hoping they would fondle me in another way. I had to kneel down with my thighs apart. The Master bent me back so he supported me from behind. The black guy took my hands behind my back with one hand and grabbed the bottle of whiskey from the table.

"'Take her legs!' he ordered. The tattooed guy sat down on a chair beside the table so his head was in line with my pussy. He admired what he saw down there for a moment, even tasted his tongue loudly. He unbuttoned his shirt and threw it to the ground. I could see the tattoos covering all his chest: a blue dragon and a skull. Then he said, 'Pour that whiskey over her!' and he leaned between my thighs, and parted my knees with his muscular hands. The black guy started dripping whiskey on my breasts. He did it carefully, not to waste any of it. The cool liquid poured down and in between my breasts, on my belly, to my pussy where the stranger licked it off with huge movements. The pure alcohol felt tingling on my pussy but he did a good job and licked it off quickly.

"'Does she taste good?' the black guy asked, laughing.

"'Fuck yeah, she does' the other one said, looking up from between my thighs, but in this position, the whiskey dripped on his face. He shook it off, laughing, and went back to licking my pussy. He closed his eyes and enjoyed the whiskey he was drinking from my slit.

The black guy put the bottle on the table and fondled my wet breasts with his large, warm hands. He even licked the remains of the whiskey from them. And when he reached my nipples with his tongue, I couldn't take it anymore. This night proved to be adventurous and sexy enough for me to come: my whole body was trembling. I came right there, kneeling on the table, my thighs spread wide and a stranger licking my pussy. Luckily the black guy was holding me from behind; my knees went so weak I could have fallen off.

"'She loves it, man,' the black guy said.

"'Yeah, I can see that', the other one added. 'But now I want to plunge my dick deep into her pussy.'

"They helped me climb down the table. The small guy quickly unzipped his pants, sat in a chair, and made me sit on his lap, with my thighs spread wide on his. He guided his hard cock into my dripping-wet pussy. I closed my eyes and slowly sat on it. It penetrated my pussy right away. I sighed out loudly, enjoying the hard cock in my pussy. It filled me easily, especially since the butt plug was still in my ass.

"'You're so tight, bitch,' the guy said. He pressed my breasts together and kissed them. 'And I fucking love your tits,' he said and buried his face between them.

"I sighed out loud again and let my head back. It was so good being fucked and fondled by these guys. I wanted to feel the orgasm again and again.

"The black guy stood beside us. He was now naked, and his cock was hard and ready for another round. I leaned on it immediately and took it into my mouth. I could feel it being even harder than the first time. But now I had more room to get to it so I used my hand to fondle his balls while I sucked his beautiful rod.

"I was riding the tattooed guy with abandon. He was thrusting his hips into me with the same rhythm. I could feel my pussy juices pouring down on his cock and his balls.

"I could feel a hand at my butt; it was the Doctor, he was standing beside me and he managed to grab the end of the butt plug in my asshole. I slowed down and he tried to pull it out from me. At first, he didn't manage to do so, so I stopped riding the tattooed guy, even letting the huge black cock out of my mouth, turned around and asked, "What are you doing?"

"'What are you doing, Master?' he added, actually not really looking into my eyes but being transfixed by the plug in my butt.

"'Sorry... Master...,' I said.

"'I'm trying to... get this thing out of here...'

"I leaned forward and tried to loosen my butt a little. It was a bit hard since the tattooed guy's cock was throbbing in my pussy and he was still fondling my tits just like his black friend did. But the Doctor could better grip the plug from this angle and slowly pulled it out. I sighed and buried my head into the small guy's shoulders; I felt an emptiness in my butt – I missed it, and felt my asshole gaping inches in front of the Doctor's face.

"'Wow...' he said, admiring my asshole, 'gentlemen, I think her ass is ready...'

"'Hell yeah,' the black guy said. 'I wanna fuck it right now! Sorry, dude,' he said to the tattooed guy, giving him a smack on his shoulder, 'I can't wait anymore!'

"'That's okay, put your cock in her, she's a pro!' his buddy said.

"They helped me on all fours on the table again. The Doctor pulled my ass cheeks apart and watched my asshole closely. He licked it over with slow, sensual motions with his huge tongue. I moaned and enjoyed this licking very much. He even pushed his tongue deeper into my asshole and moved it around.

"The black guy climbed behind me and pressed his cock right away to my asshole. I was glad I had prepared my asshole for this kind of penetration earlier; I leaned with my head down and relaxed my ass for the huge black cock. It could hardly fit in, but he entered me anyway. His hard cock filled my ass completely, I felt like I was a stuffed animal.

"'Ohh... yeahh...' the black guy sighed relaxed. It must have been a long time since he fucked a tight white ass like mine. 'I fucking love this bitch, Doc'!'

"The Doctor was standing at my face. He already had his cock out and pushed it to my face. I knew what to do; I was his slave, as a matter of fact. So I let it slide into my mouth and started sucking it as hard as I could. The black guy started fucking my ass, his huge cock was sliding in and out of my hungry asshole. He gripped my hips with his huge hands and was really giving it to me. I could hardly concentrate on the cock in my mouth but I knew I had to, that's what my Master wanted. So I bobbed on it in the same rhythm as the black guy fucked me from behind.

"'That's right, let's roast this bitch!' the black guy shouted and all the men were laughing. The Doctor grabbed my head and started fucking my mouth. He pushed his cock really deep onto my throat.

"I closed my eyes and let these guys use my body. They were fucking me just like a sex toy and I really loved it. I was so excited

I could feel my pussy juices running down my thighs. They fucked me so hard that the whole table was shaking below us; the chips were actually falling onto the carpet.

"But this wasn't enough, the third guy was beside me again, taking a black whip in his hands. The Doctor answered something but I didn't understand it, I was busy with the two cocks pounding my ass and my mouth. But I could feel the whipping on my bare ass. The tattooed guy whipped my back as well but the black latex dress softened the splashes so basically I felt only some tickling. But my ass was more sensitive, I could feel my veins throbbing because of the whipping I got there.

"'Hey, don't hit my balls!' the black guy shouted behind me and all of us laughed; well, my laughing was muffled by the Doctor's cock in my mouth. But from that on, I could feel the strikes a bit higher. I could tell he was doing it for fun; it didn't hurt at all, but excited me even better.

"The black guy pulled out his huge cock from my ass; I didn't expect it so I kind of fell back to him, releasing the Doctor's cock out of my mouth. A thin slide of saliva dripped from my lips and his cock down.

"'Now let's fuck her the way she deserves!' the Doctor cried out. He swept the chips and the cards down the desk and lay on it. He made me sit in his lap and guided his cock into my dripping wet pussy. It slid in easily, deep, until the root. I even leaned back, and let it enter me balls deep. The black guy immediately started fondling my tits, pressing his head between them. My body and his bald head were in hot sweat.

"I could feel the tattooed guy pressing me forward. He climbed behind me on the table and pressed his cock at the entrance of my ass. Luckily he didn't have such a large cock as the black guy since the two cocks would have made serious injuries inside me. But these cocks matched perfectly; I even thought about maybe they weren't doing this for the first time.

"As the small guy slid his cock into my anus, he and the Doctor started fucking me. I felt so full, it was a real double penetration. They started with furious thrusts but gradually synchronized their movements so they started to fuck me in the same rhythm. I enjoyed it with loud screams and moans.

"The black guy released my tits and knelt up on the table. His cock was standing at my face and he gently pushed my head on it. I closed my eyes and let the third cock slide into my body.

"I tried to hold myself and match the rhythm I got from the serious full penetration. My fluids were dripping all over the Doctor's cock, I could feel them each time his cock entered me balls deep.

"After my first orgasm in this position, I relaxed my body. I was nothing more than their fuck toy and they tried to fuck the shit out of me. and I really enjoyed it. I didn't feel any tension, any stress, only release. And orgasm. I couldn't tell how many times I did come with these three hard cocks in my body.

"All the three of them were fucking me with all their power. Their cocks pounded my pussy, my asshole, and my mouth at the same time. My whole body was on fire. I've never felt so full in my life. It was frightening yet wonderful at the same time.

"That was when the black guy couldn't take it any longer. He pulled out his huge cock from my mouth. I thought he would jerk it on my face, but he looked at me, then said,

"'Wait a second!' And pulled the small bowl with the tiramisu to us. I couldn't really concentrate on what he wanted to do with it since the Master was pounding my pussy, and the tattooed guy was fucking my ass. I leaned down on the Doctor's chest and let the two men fuck my brains out. The black guy held the bowl of tiramisu beside my face and jerked his cock furiously for a second. He only needed a few moves and his cock shot out. The first hot spurt shot above the bowl and hit my cheeks. I closed my eyes instinctively, but I felt no more shots on my skin. I opened my eyes again: the black guy was shooting his hot, thick sperm into the tiramisu. That's right, he pushed the head of his cock into the black dessert and let all his juices pour into it.

"Now you may find it gross, but I couldn't think about anything like that, since the two other men were fucking me relentlessly. I watched moaning and groaning as the black guy finished his business with the tiramisu and put it down. He pushed his cock back between my lips. I couldn't really concentrate on sucking him so he just smeared the mix of the tiramisu and his sperm over my lips. After that, he sat down beside the table, totally spent, and poured himself another glass of whiskey. He sat there and watched me getting fucked by his poker buddies.

"The tattooed guy was next. I could feel him pounding my ass as hard as he could. He was using me like a piece of flesh, again, and shouted at me things like 'That's it, bitch!', 'I'm gonna fuck your brains out!' and so on. I felt like a real whore being sandwiched and this feeling put me through the edge. I came again, and this time I felt like I would faint. The world disappeared for a moment, and my whole body trembled. I could see sparkles.

"When I came back to my senses I felt the guy behind me pulling his cock out of my ass. He snapped a loud one on my ass, and shouted,

"'Gimme that shit!'

"The black guy tossed the tiramisu through the table. The tattooed guy got it and pressed his cock into the black cream like the black guy had just done. My eyes were half open as I lay on the Doctor's chest and watched as the tattooed man unloaded all his sperm into the tiramisu. Some of his white drops fell on the top of the cream, but most of it went inside the cream.

"'Hell, yeah...,' he groaned out loud. 'That felt good...'

"Both he and the black guy laughed. They even gave each other a high five above the table. Then a small guy gulped one from the whiskey bottle.

"'Fuck, I've run dry,' he said. 'And I'm hungry!' And he walked out into the kitchen.

"The Doctor didn't give up. He was slowly, but continuously fucking my pussy. My ass was sensible from the pounding I had just received so I decided I would help him finish. I sat up, sank deep onto her cock, and started riding him hard. He immediately released my ass cheeks and grabbed my tits. I really liked his muscular arms, his grip on my sensitive nipples, and the lust in his eyes. And most of all, his moves; he wasn't pounding as hard as he did before. We were moving in a steady, good rhythm. I closed my eyes and enjoyed his cock deep inside me.

"I knew I wouldn't come again so I took the bowl with the tiramisu and showed it to him, saying,

"Please give me your part of the dessert, Master."

"'Okay,' he nodded. I climbed off of him. He jumped up. 'Get on your knees, slave!' I had to admit, he had the strength and the stamina.

"My knees were weak but I managed to kneel before him. I was holding the tiramisu in my hand, and I smelled the fresh cum inside it. I could see the black guy watching us above his glass of whisky. Even the tattooed guy came back from the kitchen, wearing a stripy rope and nibbling a sandwich, leaning to the door frame.

"'Get me off, slave,' the Doctor said. I grabbed his cock and started jerking it at my face. As I moved my hand on it, my pussy juices were dripping from it to the carpet and on my face. 'That's it, slave,' he groaned. 'Jerk me off, I fucking want to give you my present.'

"I held the bowl with the messy tiramisu to the end of his cock and jerked his throbbing member swiftly. My pussy fluids served as a perfect lubricant because his foreskin clashed loudly as I jerked him.

"'Yeeeaaahhh…,' he groaned and sprayed a huge amount of white hot sperm into the bowl. I kept on jerking him till there was no more coming from his penis. Then I licked his cockhead clean.

"And when he leaned to the desk, I happily held the bowl to my face and… Okay, I know, what you're thinking right now. It's gross, isn't it? A ruined tiramisu mixed with the cum of three total strangers… But hey, they entertained me for a whole night! I had dozens of orgasms and their cocks had been everywhere inside of me, fucking my brains out. I thought they deserved a show like this at the end.

"Besides, I was hungry. So I ate the whole bowl of spermy, creamy tiramisu. It was really creamy and sweet. I think it was the best dessert of my life."

Chapter 6: In The Sex Shop

I decided to bring some souvenirs home. Although Bonnie stated she didn't need any because she had just had the best night of her life, she agreed to join me on my gift hunt.

On our way outside the hotel, she asked the receptionist for some hints. He was really polite, as always, but I had a feeling he winked at her at the end of their conversation.

Anyway, we got an address to visit. We flagged down a cab, and Bonnie told the driver where to take us. He started the engine immediately but I could swear I could see him grin like the Cheshire Cat.

It took us more than half an hour to get there. We could take a good look at the center of Osaka on the way. We could see the huge flashing ads in the city center called Minami, the huge variety of dining places, and shopping houses. I watched as people were walking or hurrying on the streets, chatting with each other or talking on the phone.

The place where we arrived turned out to be a sex shop. I don't know whether the receptionist directed us to this place intentionally or not. We were standing at the flashing neon lights of the store window and looked at each other.

"Hey," Bonnie shrugged, "you wanted a souvenir. Now let's get one."

I shrugged as well and we entered the store.

This wasn't the first time we went to a sex shop together. I'd already bought her some toys which we had chosen together – a vibrator, a butt plug, and lubricants. But I always felt some butterflies in my stomach when I stepped into a store like this. Like it was some kind of guilty or bad thing to buy anything from here. Luckily I had Bonnie on my side. I knew she was at least as embarrassed as me but the two of us could always find the humorous point of view of the situation. That was one of the reasons why I loved her so much.

This time I felt it a bit easier since we were not at home; there wasn't even a slight chance of somebody spotting us as we entered the sex shop. So I grinned as the doorbell rang when we closed the door behind us.

It was a huge shop, filled with racks of sex toys everywhere. Pink lamps were flickering and a small cat just ran out from somewhere and mewed at us.

"Hi," a pudgy Japanese woman greeted us. "Do you mind if the cat stays here?"

"No problem, really," Bonnie said. She even leaned down to the kitty and fondled her for a minute.

"Good! How can I help you?" the woman clerk asked.

"We're visiting Osaka and the gentleman here," Bonnie pointed at me, "wants to bring some souvenirs home."

"This is the best place you could have chosen! I've got everything!" the clerkswoman rushed and started pointing to stuff on the shelves. "Dildos, butt plugs, anal beads, strap-ons... Name it!"

"Well...," I looked around, "I was looking for something more... special."

"Oh, I think I just know what you're thinking of, naughty boy," the woman waved her index finger at me. "Follow me!"

She led us through a tight corridor to the back side of the shop. As we followed her we passed by shelves filled with red panties and funny gifts. We arrived at a small hall with a glass booth in the center. There were a few men standing around it. The glass walls of the booth had some hip-high holes. And a girl dressed in a black latex fetish dress was kneeling in the booth, sucking a well-suited man's penis which was shoved in through one of the holes in the walls.

"You were thinking about this, right, naughty boy?" the saleswoman said, grinning. "Nothing is better than a hot glory hole party, right?"

"Well, this isn't what I was..."

"Actually...," Bonnie stopped me, "this is not a bad idea."

"What?" I turned to her.

"Look, honey," she started, "I know you had that terrible adventure after the auction, while I was having the night of my life. I have a terrible twinge of conscience about it. I would like to make it up for you."

"I'm sure you will..."

"I agree, honey, but I still have a sore ass from the pounding I received from the guys at the Doctor's house. I need time to recover and I know you're starving for some sex! Let me handle it this way for you..."

"Well...," I hesitated but Bonnie didn't wait any longer, pushing me closer to the booth instead. I could still hear her chatting with the saleswoman about how much to pay and other details.

I stepped closer and peeked into the booth. I couldn't believe my eyes. The girl in the glory hole booth was Asa, our Japanese teacher. I didn't even know she was in Osaka, yet she was on her knees vigorously sucking a huge cock. She had her eyes closed and sucked the pole halfway into her mouth. She held her hands together behind her back and bobbed quickly on the hard cock in her mouth.

Bonnie stepped beside me and recognized the kneeling domina as well, saying, "Isn't she.."

"Yeah, she seems to be...," I nodded.

We watched Asa sucking this stranger's cock in awe. She was working on it like an expert, a professional cock sucker which she probably was.

"Haaiii...," we could hear the guy moaning. "Haiii..."

Asa looked like in that porn video that Carl showed to me at the office. Maybe she had missed her old days in porn, or just wanted to have a crazy night in her hometown, I didn't know. But she was surely sucking everything out of this guy, bobbing with her head hard and fast on his throbbing cock.

He didn't take it long. He was screaming something in Japanese again. When Asa heard this, backed up immediately, releasing the guy's cock from her mouth. She released the grip behind her back and started jerking off his cock furiously with her right hand covered with the black latex gloves. She held her right cheek in front of the cock so that when it started spurting, the thick drops landed there. Actually, some of them arrived on her forehead and her jaw but most of the white fluid covered her right cheek.

The guy stepped back, being spent. He started adjusting his suit immediately and hurried out without looking at any of us.

Asa didn't waste the time, and turned immediately to the next cock. It was a huge black rod, belonging to a huge, muscular black guy at the other end of the room. Asa seemed to be happy to get such a nice member; she grabbed it and played with it for a while, jerked it, spanked her wet cheeks, and touched her lips with it. I could hear the black dude saying something to her but couldn't understand what. She smiled and put the huge cock into her mouth right away. She swallowed it as deeply as she could, closing her eyes again.

"Fuck yeaaahh...," the black guy moaned loudly. "Swallow it to your throat, bitch!"

She did, she let the huge black cock slide deep into her mouth. I could see a large amount of saliva dripping out of her mouth on her breasts. She pulled a bit back, then continued deepthroating the black guy, swallowing his huge member deep again and again.

"That's it, honey..." he moaned gracefully. "It's perfect..."

Asa started bobbing on it hard and fast. I could hear her humming with the huge cock in her mouth. She even put her hand on the back of her head and pretended she was pulling herself on his cock as if a guy would fuck her face.

"I'm cumming..." the guy moaned. Asa released his cock again and started jerking it off in her latex gloves. This time she held her left cheek to the cock; the other side was dripping sticky with the mixture of the previous guy's cum and her own saliva. The black guy shot his thick white load on her left cheek; some went into her hair, some on her forehead, again. But as she aimed lower, the majority of the fresh cum landed on the left side of her face.

Asa giggled happily, like a girl getting a Christmas gift. She wiped some cum off her jaw and licked it off her fingers.

The black guy put his huge cock away in his pants quickly and left with a nod to us.

"It's your turn, honey," Bonnie said from behind. "Give her everything you got."

I opened my fly, took out my hard cock, and stepped to the glass wall. The hole was a bit low so I had to part my legs to put my cock in it. As soon as I managed to get into position, Asa leaned on my cock like a hungry snake. I don't know whether she recognized me through the glass wall; she didn't seem to care about who she was sucking off.

Anyway, she started bobbing on my cock. She didn't waste time, she was going for the cum right away, sucking me deep and hard. She supported herself with her palms spread on the glass walls and sucked me off with her eyes closed. Her dark sweaty hair was flying around her head as she was working on me.

It didn't take long for me to cum. All the frustration and load released from me. I shot my first spurt right to Asa's throat. As she sensed it coming she moved back, releasing my throbbing member from her hot mouth, and helped me spraying everything on her face by jerking my cock vividly. She didn't seem to care about which part of her face I was shooting at. So I shot spurt after spurt on her forehead, on her hair, on her nose, and her lips.

When I finished, my fresh sperm joined the previous two doses. Now her whole face was covered with sticky white cum.

Bonnie held my hand and pulled me out of the room. I managed to put my spent member away and close my fly on the way. As we left the room, we bumped into two Asian men dressed in sweaty business suits; they mumbled something for apologies but didn't really care about us. Their eyes were fixed on Asa.

"Did you enjoy it?" Bonnie asked in the doorway.

"It was fucking hot!" I stated.

"Consider it as a consolation prize, honey," she said, putting her hand on my shoulder. "I hope this will help to forget your terrible night."

I agreed, and glanced back to the glory hole behind us: Asa was sitting smiling on the floor, with her legs spread wide. She was cleaning her face like a good kitten, and licking and swallowing the huge amount of cum from her fingers. As the two Asian guys stepped into her glass booth, she raised back on her knees and said,

"Welcome to paradise!"

Chapter 7: Travelling Home

"My best sexual experience?" asked Carl behind me. Bonnie was smiling at me, whispering, "They are at it again."

They were really at it again. Carl and Asa were sitting behind me and Bonnie on the plane home. I was a little tired; the adventures I had gone through in Japan were in my head. I had the shameful memory of getting spanked with a tea muddler. I was hoping I wouldn't get in any serious trouble because I left that old witch there with her friends. And when Asa and Carl started their intimate conversation behind us I immediately recalled the image of her being on her knees and sucking off strangers in the glory hole booth. And here she was, asking Carl, the greatest Casanova at the firm, to tell his best sexual experience.

"It happened in the office building, actually," Carl started to tell her after the plane took off.

"Oh, you funny boy!" Asa giggled. "With whom?"

"It was that blonde girl, Brigitte."

"That bitch from accounting?"

"She's not a bitch, she's just sexually overdriven, okay?"

"Please...," I could hear Asa lamenting.

"Okay, she's a bit bitchy. But I like that in a woman. That's why I like you!"

I could hear some playful wrestling.

"So you wanna hear it or not?" Carl asked.

"Okay, go ahead."

"I was doing some overtime at a night because I got a lot of shit to do. Actually, I was having hot coppers that morning, so I was late, that's why I had things piling up. Anyway, I was in my cube, typing like crazy, when this chick Brigitte came to me.

"'Can you please help me?' she asked in her silky voice. I turned to her and could see right away something was going on.

"What's wrong?" I asked. "Something happened?"

"'Well, yes, actually...,' she admitted, with red cheeks, admiring her shoes. 'I've got a problem and I can't concentrate on my job, can't sleep, my hands are trembling...'

"What is it?" I asked.

"Well... I have... a kind of addiction," she admitted. 'I know it's wrong but I can't help it. Actually, I have managed to keep it under control so far and I don't know how I got into this situation.'

"Okay...," I said, waiting for her to tell me more about her addiction. I suspected it would be drugs, cigarettes, and alcohol.

"'Maybe it's because my boyfriend left me a few weeks ago. Since then, I couldn't get my dose and I really miss it...'

"What kind of addiction are we talking about exactly?" I asked her carefully.

"'Well.. I'm... addicted to... cum.'

"Well, I was really surprised. This blonde bitch looked like an attention whore to me. I could tell the way she had dropped a few lines into the conversations we had with our colleagues. And that's how she dressed, as well, just like that night: wearing a sexy pair of high heels, low-cut tops, and tight jeans. The smell of her perfume filled the cubic and I could see the veins throbbing on her neck.

"Pardon?" I asked.

"'I know it's strange and wrong, but please don't judge me. I just like its texture, its fresh taste, its aroma, everything in it. Sometimes I would drink a whole bug of it if I could. But I couldn't get any since that bastard left me for a younger girl,' she said.

"And how exactly could I help you, honey?" I asked.

"'You know, I don't want to hook up with some stranger just to get my dose. I don't want to get any diseases, or if the guy is some loser, I don't want to listen for hours about his job, his hobbies, and shit like that. I just want to swallow a nice load of cum as soon as possible!'

"So...?"

"'Please let me... suck your cock!'

"Now that was like music to my ears. I smiled and leaned back in my chair. We didn't really speak to each other, like... never, but we moved like a couple. I opened my belt and she knelt down between my legs. She immediately zipped down my fly. My cock jumped free from my trousers.

"'Wow,' she said and seized it all over in her hands. 'I hope you got a nice big load for me, big boy,' she added, smiling.

"'Absolutely,' I said.

"She pulled the foreskin back and took the head of my hard cock in her mouth immediately. It was so hot and wet, I could feel goosebumps on my back.

"She licked my cock all over like a good girl does a lollipop. She even went down to my balls and licked them like candy. She rolled her tongue over and over on them, making them wet with her saliva. While she was fondling my sack with her tongue, she also gently fondled my whole dick in her palm. I could feel she builds up for an amount of cum as large as possible.

"Then she backed up and released my cock, putting her hands behind his back. She leaned on the head of my cock and started swallowing it deeper and deeper. Then backed up again, letting my wet cock out of her mouth, and looked into my eyes, saying: 'Fuck my mouth!'

"That was just what I needed. I grabbed her head and started fucking her mouth. She enjoyed it with her eyes closed. She let my cock slide really deep into her mouth, even in her throat, she didn't gag or anything. I could even feel her swallowing a big one when my head touched her throat so the feeling of sucking even intensified.

"I almost lost it but pulled back, out of her hot mouth.

"'Do you like it, bitch?' I asked her, patting her cheek with my wet cock.

"'Fuck yeah,' she said, with a huge smile on her face. I pulled her head back on my cock. She immediately swallowed it deep, like a hungry whore, and started bobbing on it. She released her hand, put them on my ass cheeks, and pulled me by my ass into her mouth deeper and deeper. She closed her eyes and let me fuck her mouth, even helped me by pulling my body to her face. Her saliva was dripping down my balls on my trousers and on the carpet.

"We were moving so fast my balls were slapping on her face. She was sucking me like a real pro, in fact, maybe she was a real pro, at least in the area of cock sucking.

"I couldn't take it anymore. I shoved my cock deep to her throat and I came like a volcano. I could hear her moaning, like when a real addict gets her dose. She was swallowing it all. I emptied my whole load into her hot mouth and enjoyed the sensation as she even sucked and milked the last drops out of my cock. Then she stood up, said 'Thanks, big boy!' and left me there for good."

"And that was your hottest adventure ever?" Asa asked.

"It was! You know, I've been in threesomes and orgies before, but that's what I recall most gladly. I'd never met someone so hungry for cock and cum before."

"You mean, before meeting me, right?" she asked, coyly.

"That's right, baby," he said. "That's absolutely right..."

"Then I have a surprise for you, big boy..."

I could hear some movement behind us and a moment later Asa walked by us to the toilet. She looked back at Carl from the end of the line with a perky wink, then stepped into the small restroom. I could hear Carl counting to twelve and then following her. As he arrived at the door, he knocked, the door opened and Asa grabbed him and pulled him into the small toilet. Carl closed the door behind himself and the "occupied" sign lit up.

"I think they will enjoy the ride," Bonnie said and leaned her head on my shoulder.

"They definitely will," I agreed and prepared my phone to shoot some pictures of them when they would get back from the toilet.

Chapter 8: The Birthday Party

I woke up early on Saturday morning. I didn't mind: I had a lot to prepare for Bonnie's birthday surprise. I checked her sleeping beside me in the bed; she was even snoring a bit which made her cuter than usual.

I slipped out of bed, got dressed, and sneaked out of the bedroom. I went into the kitchen, made a good pot of coffee for myself, and sat down with it, after turning the radio on.

I went through my checklist for Bonnie's birthday party. I managed to check off every item on the list. It had been only a week since we arrived back from Japan. It took us a few days to rest up after the jetlag and to catch up to speed with things in the office. When I realized her birthday was so close, I only had a few days to plan and organize everything. Luckily the maid, Yvonne helped me. We hadn't been talking too much before, since she worked at our apartment while we were at the office. She saw me having trouble organizing the birthday party on one of my days off. We started to talk, and she helped me polish some details and even agreed to attend the party.

Two hours later I stepped into the bedroom with a tray in my hands. Bonnie was still lying in the bed but opened her eyes and looked at me.

"Good morning, sunshine!" I said and put the tray on the bed. "And happy birthday!"

"Wow, thanks," she giggled and admired the breakfast. There was fresh hot coffee, orange juice, pancakes, maple syrup, and a red rose - just the way she liked it. "Won't it be too much?"

"Wait 'till you see the dessert," I added.

"Will there be a dessert?" she asked. Her wide brown eyes sparkled. "You're not serious, are you?"

"Dessert and a present," I added. "But eat this first, you'll need the energy."

"I like the idea," she said, smiling, and started having her breakfast while I slipped out to arrange some final details for her present.

When I got back, the tray was empty and Bonnie was coming out of the shower. She stepped out wearing only a towel, her skin glistening with small drops of water.

"Did you enjoy your shower?" I asked.

"Yeah, it was so good!" she said. "But what are those?"

"These are your presents," I said, showing off the two boxes in my hand. "At least, a part of them."

"Wow! Let me just put something on," she stepped to the cupboard but I stopped her.

"For these, you won't need anything on."

She stepped back and sat on the bed. She looked at me again; her face was flushed red. Then she took the two paper boxes from me.

"Happy birthday, honey!" I said.

"Thanks!" she said and opened the pink ribbons on the top box. There was a thin black silk scarf in there. It smelled of a sweet perfume - I didn't know why the hot saleswoman in the lingerie store had sprayed it on the scarf when she had packed it up but now I could see it had been a good idea because it aroused us a bit right away.

"Wow," she said, pulling it apart with both of her palms. "Thanks... I guess!"

"You can put it on after you open your other present first."

She put the black silk scarf aside and opened the next present. She held it in her palm and looked at it without saying anything for a minute.

"What is this...?" she asked. "It looks like a butt plug but why is it shaped like a curve? And why is it attached to a strap?"

"It's called an anal hook," I answered. "This..." I pointed to the shiny metal butt plug, "really goes into your butt. And the other end..." I pointed to the black strap and the collar at the end, "will fit on your neck."

"But why is the strap so long?"

"So I can walk you like a bitch in heat," I said, with a huge grin on my face.

Bonnie smiled and gave the presents to me.

"You want to put them on me, right?" she asked, coyly. I nodded and took the scarf and the anal hook in my hands.

"You don't have to wear anything else," I said.

"Yeah, I guessed so," she giggled.

"You'll need one more item, though," I added and stepped into the closet. It only took a few moments for me to select the sexiest pair of black high heels she had.

"Oh, I should have known," she said when I gave them to her. She dropped her towel and put on the high heels, adjusting the straps of them carefully. I could still see some water drops glistening on the skin of her back.

"Good... Now get on your knees, honey," I said. She slipped to the floor on all fours immediately. She looked gorgeous with only her high heels on. I could feel my cock hardening at the sight. I was tempted to fuck her right there and then but I had other plans with her. I knelt down and covered her eyes with the black scarf. I tied it gently behind her head and checked her face. She looked like a girl next door who had some dirty fetishes which was definitely the case.

I knelt behind her on the floor and leaned into her ass. She was shivering in anticipation.

I grabbed and pulled her ass cheeks apart. Her tight asshole became visible. It looked pink and fresh and virgin; not like it had been stretched out a week ago in Japan by three horny men. I tried to imagine those cocks jammed up in there, and the thought made the bulge in my pants larger and harder. I recalled her promotion night when those colleagues of hers fucked her ass really hard. The mental image was so intense it made my cock twitch a little.

But the sweetest memories recalled by the view of her pretty round ass were those endless crazy hot nights when we made sweet love. When she sat on my face, jerking me while I licked her ass out, or when I fucked her ass from behind. My mouth started watering so I leaned down and started licking her asshole long and deep just as I knew she liked it.

"Ohhh...," she moaned. "Is this part of my present?"

"This is only the beginning," I answered, then leaned back into her round butt and pushed my tongue into her tight asshole with my tongue. I pushed as much saliva as I could in there. She moaned loudly, letting me know how much she liked it.

I felt her rosebud relaxing. She sighed disappointed as I stood up. I got a bottle of lubricant from the nightstand, pressed some on my fingers, and smeared it all over her asshole. She shivered a bit as the cool liquid touched her inner parts but didn't say anything. She knew my intentions.

I pressed more and more amounts of lubricant on my fingers and slowly entered her ass again and again, smearing more and more of the sloppy liquid inside. She was so turned on her pussy was dripping in my other palm. The inside of her ass was so hot and tight I had to apply more lube than usual.

"Ohhh..." she sighed out. "This is so good..."

When Bonnie's asshole was slippery with lube, I applied some on the anal hook as well. I smeared all over it on its head and its base, carefully, not to leave out any portion of it. Then I pressed the head of it to her rosebud which quickly contracted. I pulled back, fondled her round ass cheeks a bit, and let her relax again, then put the anal hook back into her asshole. This time it swallowed the shiny metal plug easily so I slowly pushed the hook deep inside Bonnie's asshole. She gritted her teeth and hissed out but didn't object. I knew she wouldn't. Her cute round ass was trembling slightly as the cold metal ball slipped deep into her anus.

"Ouch," she giggled. "I think I'm still a bit tight there..."

I pulled the hook slightly to make sure it was placed tight in there, then stood up, putting the collar end to Bonnie's neck. She raised her head to make it easier for me to fix it on her.

When I finished, I knelt before my beautiful lover, took her face in my palms, and kissed her. She looked so sexy with this hook in her ass, the collar on her neck and the strap hanging loosely on her back. She was wet and horny, well prepared for the action I planned for her.

"Are you ready for your birthday present, honey?" I asked.

"Give it to me!" she said, giggling.

I stood up and took the strap of her anal hook. She raised her head as she felt it. The end of the scarf covering her eyes was hanging down her shoulders aligned with her brown hair.

"Let's take a walk, my little bitch," I ordered and pulled her strap.

I led her outside the house to the patio and around the pool. The strap was tensing between my hand and her neck and ass as she followed me on all fours. She looked damn sexy in this hot fetish outfit. I felt like a mad landlord with his sex slave would have liked to fuck her right then and there but I already had other plans for her.

I led her to the place I prepared for her. I stopped her by pulling the strap, just like a wild mare. She understood it and stayed on her all fours, and trembled slightly, being the center of attention.

I looked around and checked everything once more. I thought everything was ready.

"Are you ready, honey?" I asked again, more to excite her a bit since I already knew the answer.

"Yes! Yes!" she giggled. I decided the party could be started.

Then I started singing 'Happy Birthday' along with the surprise guests and pulled down the scarf from Bonnie's eyes. She looked around and her eyes opened wide when she realized who were standing around her.

Right in front of her was standing Ule, the huge black lawyer from the firm. He had his usual elegant grey suit on, with a matching grey tie. He looked strictly business casual as he was singing the birthday song in his deep bass voice.

The other guy present was the black cop who stopped us on the highway a few months ago and was Bonnie's part-time lover before. We hadn't seen him since then, so I had to spend a lot of time investigating to find him. Once I did, however, he happily agreed to participate in the party when I outlined my plan for him.

Besides them, our cleaning girl, Yvonne was standing there in a very sexy maid costume: blonde goldilocks, black latex dress, and matching high heels and gloves, with a frilled white blouse. She didn't wear such a costume when she was cleaning our apartment, so we had to rent it from a costume rental company downtown. We had some glimpses on us when I took her there to try it on and find the appropriate size. I was happy we spent so much time selecting it; she looked like a porn star in it, with the birthday cake on a tray in her hands and singing the birthday song along with us.

Bonnie was sitting back on her ankles, her face flushed red, covering her cheeks with her fingers and giggling intensely. When we got to the part *'Happy birthday dear Bonnie...'* Yvonne leaned down to her and held the cake with the candles before her so she could blow them out. Bonnie was so embarrassed she couldn't even blow the candles the first time. But she managed to when after we ended the song and cheered and clapped a bit.

"Happy birthday, honey," I said and planted a kiss on her forehead. "And enjoy your present," I added, showing around to the men before her and the cake.

"Wow," she said, still hiding behind her hands. "That's a surprise, for sure..."

We all looked at each other for a moment. Then it was Sergeant Hancock breaking the ice: "Well, let's get the party started!" And he zipped his fly open and took out his cock. It was even bigger than I remembered; I could only catch a glimpse of it that night when he stopped us on the highway. Now I could see how long it was, already hardening at the sight of the naked Bonnie on her knees.

"Wow," it was Yvonne who said it this time, with her eyes wide. Her eyes got even wider when Ule joined, opening his fly and taking out his huge black dong.

"That's what I'm talking about, man!" the cop stated. "Now let's give this bitch what she deserves for her birthday!" He turned to Yvonne, saying, "Give it to me!" Taking the cake from her. It wasn't a huge cake, it was around ten slices. He pulled it in front of his groin and lowered it under his cock which was so long it almost reached the other end of the cake. We all watched as he carefully pushed his black cock in the whipped cream on the top of the cake. He slowly dipped it deep in the white cream, then pulled it back, and gave the cake back to Yvonne. He stepped to Bonnie, saying, "Here's your birthday dessert, baby," and held his cock into her face.

Bonnie reached for it immediately. She held the huge black cock by its base and started licking the white cream off. She closed her eyes for a moment, tasting the cream, and said, "Yummy!" and went on licking the cream all the way off the long rod. The sergeant watched, grinning as my girlfriend licked every inch of his huge member. She wandered to the base of his cock and licked off the few drops of cream from his sack.

"Yeah...," he moaned, grinning. "You didn't forget how to handle a big black cock, honey..."

"Give it to me," Ule said to Yvonne and took the cake from her. He covered his cock with the white cream just as the cop did but he pressed it deeper, smearing the whipped cream and some of the white glaze of the cake on his huge veiny cock. He covered his member everywhere with the mix of the cream and the gaze, then gave the ruined cake back to Yvonne and stepped to Bonnie. "I brought some more," he said hoarsely and pulled Bonnie closer by the strap attached to the collar on her neck. Bonnie switched to the new cock obediently and started licking up pieces of the dessert off it.

"Do you think we'll still need this?" Yvonne asked, nodding to the cake.

"Maybe later," I said. She put it down on the coffee table and stepped to me.

"I think she likes the surprise," she said, watching Bonnie as she alternated sucking the huge black cocks presented by the two horny black men.

"Now she can gratify her fetish for black cocks," I said, watching Bonnie as she bobbed on a black cock.

"Definitely," Yvonne added. "I think you organized this party pretty well. She will remember it gladly."

"I hope so."

"I think you deserve some dessert as well," she said, turning to me. I could see lust in her eyes. "Let me take care of it...," she said, and knelt down before me. She touched my bulge through my pants, grabbing and stroking it a bit. "Wow...," she murmured. "This definitely needs to be taken care of..."

I agreed. Watching Bonnie sucking those huge black rods made me just as horny as I planned it. I was happy Yvonne opened my fly and got my rock-hard cock out. She started slowly swallowing my member into her hot mouth. She started sucking me just the way I like it: with slow, elaborate moves, using a lot of saliva. She even closed her eyes as she concentrated on it. I ran my finger through her goldilocks and guided her head as she was bobbing up and down on my throbbing member. I enjoyed closing my eyes as well. She went deeper and deeper, letting my cock slide into her throat a few times.

By the time I opened my eyes, checking on Bonnie, I found things had escalated quickly. She was already on her fours again, fucked by Ule from behind. The black man was sweating in his suit; the sun was getting higher, promising a hot day. He was pounding her doggystyle, grabbing and guiding my girlfriend by the strap. His huge cock entered her pussy deep again and again, glistening with her pussy juices in the summer morning sun. The black cop was standing at her face, moving her head with abandon on his rock-hard cock. Her saliva was dripping on his sack and a few drops were glistening on the floor.

The sight of Bonnie being spit roasted made me even hornier. I grabbed Yvonne's head and started fucking her face in the same rhythm as Ule fucked my girlfriend. Yvonne released my cock and completely let me move her head on my throbbing penis.

"Let me fuck her, too," the cop said. Ule pulled his cock out of Bonnie; his huge black member was all the way glistening with her pussy juices. Sergeant Hancock sat in one of the deckchairs lying around the pool and pulled Bonnie in his lap. He quickly put his cock to her slit and pulled her down. Her pussy swallowed his huge cock right away as she gave out a loud moan, closing her eyes as she took him all the way inside. She stayed in that position for a few moments, before slowly riding the black cop under her.

"That's it, baby, ride that cock!"Sergeant Hancock mumbled. "Fuck yeaaah!"

Bonnie was riding him with abandon, with her eyes closed, and was groping her own breasts. It had to be tight for the sergeant with Bonnie's asshole filled with the hook. Now the strap was hanging loosely on her back. Ule was standing there wanking his cock in front of her face.

"Let's help this gentleman," I pointed to him. Yvonne nodded, with her lips still on my cock, but she released it. The morning breeze felt cool on my throbbing member after the maid's hot mouth. She stepped to the lawyer, knelt down before him, and got his huge black cock between her luscious lips.

"Yeaaah...," he moaned. He straightened up and started taking off his clothes. He threw down his jacket and his tie near the pool. Yvonne kept on sucking him, and while doing so, she helped him unbutton his shirt. She even fondled the huge muscles on his chest while she was bobbing on his hard cock; her goldilocks flying in the air.

"Make it wet," he ordered to Yvonne, and motioned to Bonnie, "she will need it."

Yvonne giggled, and leaned above his cock, letting a large amount of saliva pour from her lips onto the black rod. She smeared it all over with her lips and tongue, pushing his cock back to her throat as deep as she could.

Bonnie was clearly enjoying the ride. She was moaning and screaming with pleasure. The cop under her opened his jacket so she was scratching his muscular chest with her nails now. The cop raised, fondled, and kissed her breasts and nipples, then fell back.

Ule leaned to my girlfriend and slapped her ass, saying, "That's it, bitch! Ride that cock!" Bonnie shivered a bit; I could tell she was close to her orgasm.

I stripped down as well and stepped to them. I pulled the strap up so Bonnie had to raise her head to me. I kissed her hard, and asked, "Do you enjoy your present?"

"Fuck yeahhh...," she screamed. I stepped behind her and slapped her ass a few times. This made her let out tiny screams; I could tell she was really at the edge. I leaned down and grabbed the base of the hook in her ass.

"I don't think we need this anymore," I said and pulled it out. It came out with an audible 'pop'; and this was the last piece to her orgasm. She was screaming loud and clear, eyes tight shut, with her whole body trembling. The cop held his groin still so she could enjoy her moment. When she fell on his chest, Ule pulled his cock back from Yvonne"s mouth, saying,

"Thanks, honey, you lubed it well enough." And he stepped behind the panting Bonnie on the deckchair. He spread his legs and positioned himself right behind my girlfriend. He pressed his cock head to her asshole. I could see Bonnie's eyes popping open but she didn't say a word; she reached back and pulled her cheeks aside so Ule could enter her ass easily. As the large black man pushed himself into her, she closed her eyes again, concentrating on relaxing her ass so the huge black cock could slip into her. The cop was waiting surprisingly patiently underneath, with his cock throbbing in Bonnie's pussy.

"You're so tight...," Ule moaned, which made Bonnie sigh out loud. He pulled back, then pressed forward again.

"Aaahhh..." Bonnie sighed again. I leaned to her, ran my fingers in her hair, and whispered, "Relax, baby, you will enjoy it."

"I... know..." she moaned. "But I'm so... full..."

I released her head and took the strap in my hands. It was hanging from the collar; as the hook was out of her tight asshole, that wasn't needed anymore. While Ule was pushing his cock into Bonnie's ass again and again, I took down the collar off her neck and tossed it aside.

Ule started fucking Bonnie's ass hard now.

"That's it, brotha," the cop shouted from underneath. "Let's give this bitch her real present!" He joined the rhythm, pounding his cock into her pussy hard and deep.

"This is so hot..." Yvonne added. She stepped to me and started jerking my cock right away. Neither of us couldn't take our eyes away from the sight of my girlfriend getting a sandwich fucked by these two horny men.

The two huge black cocks were fucking her like a piece of meat. It was totally hot to see her ass moving in rhythm with the cocks pounding her. Her nails were digging deep into the chest of the cop below her. I could even see some drops of blood, she was scratching him so hard. He didn't care; he grabbed her head by her hair and pulled her face to himself and planted a hard kiss on her mouth. Bonnie was practically screaming as the two black cocks fucked her as hard as they could but her screams were muffled by the black guy's lips on her.

I stopped Yvonne jerking me and stepped to the deckchair where Bonnie was sandwiched between those two hung black men. I positioned myself to the end of the chair, grabbed Bonnie's head, and pulled on my cock. She swallowed me instinctively, letting my cock slide right to her throat. She couldn't really suck or lick me because the two guys were pounding her so hard; so I moved her head on my cock instead.

"Do you like it, bitch?" the cop teased her. "Do you like being fucked by three cocks at the same time?"

"Mmmmhhh...," she moaned with closed eyes, her mouth being full with my cock. The three of us banged her in full abandon, like a cheap whore at a bachelor party. All her hot holes were filled up by our throbbing cocks.

That was the moment when she came again. And as her body was trembling and spasming, she kept on screaming on my cock. I realized she was having a small series of orgasms. She always liked to cum with a cock in her mouth; apparently, the two huge black rods pounding her pussy and ass multiplied the sensation.

"Give me a break...," she moaned with her eyes still closed, and her body collapsed on the cop underneath her. She was lying and panting there for a few moments as we all stopped pounding her.

Ule stepped back, his cock getting out of Bonnie's tight ass with an audible 'pop'. Even this huge black man was panting as he stood there in the morning sun, with his huge cock throbbing and glistening with Bonnie's pussy juices.

The sergeant lifted Bonnie; he got up and put her back in the deckchair in which she was lying in her after-orgasm enjoyment.

Both Ule and the sergeant were stepping toward Bonnie with their huge black cocks pointing at her; as they started wanking them above her face, Yvonne hurried there with the already ruined cake. She held it in front of them, saying:

"Please, gentlemen, prepare her a sweet dessert!"

All of us were laughing. Bonnie was recovering, sat up, and was watching, as the two hung men were jerking off above her birthday cake. I stepped there myself as well, and it didn't take too much for my orgasm to arrive. It felt like an enormous release of a gallon of sperm; actually, I had been saving it for days for this occasion. The first spurt flew far above the cake and landed on Bonnie's thigh, but the other jets arrived into the white cream of the dessert.

My whole sack contracted again and again as I released the last drops of my hot seed on the cake. I stepped back, totally spent, and nodded with my head for Yvonne to hold the cake to the others. She turned to them, just in time. Ule aimed right into the center of the cake and released his huge load with a loud groan. He didn't continue jerking his cock, the cum was spurting out in thick streams into the cream. His whole body was trembling, and he groaned out again and again.

The cop was the last one. His cum was flying so high it shot Yvonne right on her cheek. Both of them giggled about it, and the sergeant aimed lower. The rest of his cum landed on the top of the cake, pouring in the slots the guys created with their cocks earlier.

Bonnie knelt among us, still not so stable after the hardcore fucking she got from us. She was giggling as Yvonne served the birthday cake covered with sperm to her. She didn't bother with any spoon, just pushed two fingers into it, and raised as much cream as she could to her lips. It was mixed with our white cum and she swallowed hungrily.

"That was the best birthday cake ever," she said and wiped some whipped cream off of her lips and then licked it off of her fingers. "Thank you, guys!"

"You're welcome," Sergeant Hancock said. "It was our pleasure... I mean, literally."

We were all laughing about that.

Office Sluts 4

Dirty Diaries

From Bonnie's Diary

After Dinner

"Is that cum in your hair, Clair?" She stared stonily at my reflection in the mirror and then burst out laughing. We, and when I say we I mean John, Adam, Clair and myself were enjoying a business dinner at a high-class hotel, and we ladies had taken the opportunity to powder our noses while waiting for the main course to be served.

I noticed the white stains in her hair earlier in the evening and while I adjusted my tight black dress, my curiosity finally got the better of me. Adam's girlfriend was reapplying her lipstick which matched the short, tight red dress she was wearing. The garment showed off her shapely thighs to perfection as did her sexy high heels, and a small wave of jealousy washed over me.

"Actually, it is, Bonnie," she admitted, running her perfectly manicured fingers through her blonde mane. Then she giggled and turned towards me. "I didn't want to say anything but before we came here, Adam and I had a quickie." I raised my eyebrows inquisitively and demanded details. At first, she seemed reluctant but soon started spilling the beans.

"Well, it wasn't actually that good, if you know what I mean. It was more like me on my knees, sucking cock."

"Wow!" I giggled, admiring her honesty. "Nothing like a good quickie to build an appetite, right?"

"You're so right," she said thoughtfully, checking my expression for sarcasm. Reassured I was sincere, she spoke again, only this time she seemed a little hesitant.

"And you know, what's strange?" and looked at me questioningly.

"No," I replied, wondering what she was going to say, wary of her tone.

"As we were getting ready, Adam couldn't keep his hands off me and it ended up with me leaning over the bed while he fucked me from behind." I smiled at her encouragingly, enjoying her tale. "It all happened so fast, I really didn't have time to cum but Adam did." She stared at me strangely before continuing. "I don't know what got into him but when he was ready to shoot his load, he pulled me onto my knees and began wanking his cock. But just as he started cumming, he shouted 'Take it, Bonnie!' and covered me with spunk. What do you make of that?"

"What?" I replied, shocked to my core. I'd never thought of Adam in that way, but I had to admit, he was hot. Young and muscular, I could easily picture him being masterful, but I'd never expected him to fantasize about me, let alone wish it was me he was facializing.

"Jeez, I'm sorry," I said apologetically to Claire.

"Never mind, Bonnie," she said. "Actually, although I felt a bit betrayed, it was strange and exciting at the same time."

"Really?"

"Absolutely!" She smiled conspiringly. Her eyes sparkled with excitement. "Sometimes I get so fucking bored of the vanilla shit we do in bed, so when he made me suck his cock... well when he face fucked me, knowing it was you he wanted in front of him, really turned me on."

"So... No hard feelings?"

"Absolutely not!" she claimed, leaning towards the mirror, making a final check of her makeup. "Actually, I wouldn't mind seeing it for real." She was looking at my reflection intently and I wondered if I'd understood her correctly.

"Do you mean...?" She nodded enthusiastically.

"A little swapping, yes! Wouldn't that be fantastic?"

I wasn't so enthusiastic about that, but Claire went on, turning to me:

"I would totally love to watch Adam and you fucking each other's brains out. It's a total turn-on!"

"Really?" I asked, not quite able to believe what I was hearing. She moved behind me and began caressing my body.

"But of course! Wouldn't you get turned on watching your man fucking another woman? Jeez, how could you resist touching yourself when another woman swallows his cock and he's looking you right in the eye."

Her words and hands were getting to me and I nodded. Although John and I had discussed it abstractly, I'd never really given it any real thought before. However, listening to this goddess trying to persuade me while gently caressing my body, I couldn't deny finding the idea sexy. Her hands cupped my breasts and my doubts wavered.

"We have talked about it," I admitted hesitantly, "but..."

"Super!" Claire exclaimed before I could continue and moved her hand over my stomach. "Wanna do it tonight, Bonnie?"

"W... wh..what?" I stammered. This was going too fast. I'd assumed we'd go back and talk about this with the guys, exchanging ideas, planning a date and have the time to get used to the idea, but the hands caressing my body and warm breath in the back of my neck was confusing me somewhat.

"Why not?" she insisted, one hand teasing my erect nipples while the other sought out my throbbing clit. "We could rent a room right here in the hotel and after dinner go upstairs and have some fun. What do you say Bonnie?" she asked, planting small delightful little kisses on my neck. "Don't overthink it. Adam wants you, I want you and I'm sure John won't mind fucking me, so what's the problem?"

Try as I might, I couldn't think of one good reason why not, and believe me I was trying. I looked into her eyes and felt the heat of her body through my dress. I saw the way her eyes sparkled and felt the way her hands touched me and knew there was nothing I wanted more. The lust she'd awakened in me grew and my hands reached back to touch her. We stood there caressing each other for a moment and all I could think about was spending the night with Claire and her even sexier boyfriend.

"Okay, I guess..."

"Cool." She kissed my neck and then moved away. She headed towards the door while I stood there shaking in frustration. "Game night, then!" she exclaimed enthusiastically. Before following her, I stared at myself in the mirror, knowing that now I couldn't have a relaxed dinner after this. I just wouldn't be able to shake off the thought of watching John fucked Claire while getting laid by Adam.

At the table, I watched in amazement how easily and calmly Claire conducted herself through the main course as if nothing had happened in the restroom. She chatted gaily, changing the subject subtly whenever a lull in the conversation appeared, laughing meaningfully at the men's jokes and listening avidly to their tall stories. Watching her, I couldn't help admiring her and thinking she was a perfect actress.

Then without warning, I saw her place a foot in my man's lap during dessert and watched his eyes grow as big as saucers. Shocked, he looked for my reaction and was even more surprised when I winked at him.

"What's the matter, Johnny boy?" Claire asked her shoe-covered foot pressing harder into his crotch. "Cat got your tongue." His face searched mine for a clue and found none.

"I didn't know this dinner was... a prelude," he said slowly, dangerously.

"Oh you're talking about this?" she asked, applying more pressure, causing my man to hiss out loud. "Don't worry about Bonnie here, Darling. We've already decided what's happening tonight. What do you say to a little fun and games, a little bit of wife swapping?"

"Really?" Adam asked like he just won the lottery. Grinning wildly, he checked me up and down.

"Absolutely," I confirmed. "Claire and I decided we could take a room here," my finger pointed towards the ceiling, "and see how things go," I said huskily.

"We can try some things we've never done yet!" Claire explained, the sex oozing from her pores. "We can switch partners, or just watch each other fucking…"

"I'm not sure…" John said cautiously.

"I'll even let you guys DP me," Claire promised coyly, sealing the deal.

The silence was intense and I swear I heard the guys swallowing hard. Then things happened really fast. They called the maître' d and within minutes a room was sorted out. Only when we were in the elevator did things slow down

Claire pressed the STOP button and laughed demonically as the steel box ground to a halt. "I can see you guys need some release right now," referring to the huge tent-like shapes in their trousers. She dropped to her knees in front of Adam and started undoing his flies. "Besides, I haven't had my dessert yet, boys." She fished out Adam's rampant erection and greedily opened her mouth.

"Come on baby, I really need some cum," Claire insisted and began bobbing her head. Adam wasted no time stuffing his hard cock into her lusty mouth, shoving it so deeply, it disappeared out of sight before I'd had a real chance to check it out. However, the way her throat expanded told me I wasn't going to be disappointed this evening.

Not to be outdone, John released his own monster while looking at me expectantly.

"I always knew you like to go with the flow," I said, smiling, and knelt down in front of him.

"Guilty as charged," he replied before sighing deeply as my lips engulfed his erection.

We both sucked the guys while glancing at each other, exchanging sly smiles. Both Adam and John were grunting loudly as our heads bobbed on their throbbing cocks. As if by agreement, they grabbed our heads and really began fucking our faces. It was obvious they were going for an immediate release. I watched in slutty satisfaction how they watched us performing, and from the look in their eyes, they were enjoying the view.

John was the first to explode and his hot seed filled my mouth. He pulled my head forwards, pressing his dick deeper down my throat. Beside me, I heard Adam groaning and Claire choking. I reached for her hand and she squeezed it, while the men continued emptying their balls. Time seemed to stand still but eventually, they were done and we both opened our mouths and let our men see their cream.

They raised their eyebrows approvingly and then ordered us to kiss. I quickly turned to Claire and our lips met. Our tongues entwined and we shared cum. Adams tasted surprisingly sweet and fresh as we continued our sloppy wet kiss

"Wow...," John said, and I heard the unmistakable click of a camera. We looked up at him, posing sluttily for his iPhone while he carried on taking pictures. Adam was the first to regain some common sense and quickly pressed the button for our floor. Claire and I barely had time to stand up when the elevator stopped and opened its doors to an empty corridor. Leading our men by their cocks, we made our way to the room.

"Here we are then!" Adam chuckled smugly. "Our room for the night. Let the debauchery begin." The room was tastefully decorated and neatly arranged, as if unprepared for the rampant sex that was about to take place, despite the presence of a king-sized bed. The small yellow wall lamps gave it a snug feel, as did the thick rug, and to our surprise, the floor-to-ceiling balcony window treated us to a spectacular view of a city getting ready to party.

"So...," said Claire excitedly, turning to face us. "Who wants to start?"

"Well," John replied, his voice thicker than normal. "You did mention something about swinging if I'm not mistaken..."

"I sure did," Claire stepped in front of John. "Why, are you up for it?"

"Careful for what you wish for," he warned. "Just to be clear, what did you have in mind?"

"Everything and everything!" Claire replied, biting her index finger seductively. "You can fuck me, or Adam can screw Bonnie. Maybe you want to watch me and Adam or does seeing Bonnie and me together turn you on?" I knew John well enough and didn't need to guess what he wanted.

"Any limits?" he asked.

"None, in principle but I'm not really into that sadomasochistic shit, you know, bruises and cuts which need to be covered up at work the next day. Spanking is okay so long as you're not too rough."

"Oooh I'll take good care of you...," he said simply and then turned to me. "Are you sure about this?" Our eyes locked together. I nodded.

"Do you think you'll be able to handle him?" he said, casually nodding at Adam who was enjoying the view outside the room.

"Don't you worry about me, Darling," I assured him with a big smile. "You go and enjoy yourself," and even patted his butt encouragingly. He smiled wolfishly and turned towards Claire. Seconds later his belt was wrapped around her neck like a collar and leash.

"On all fours, bitch," he ordered, his voice dangerously calm. "It's time to train you properly."

Obediently she fell to the floor for the second - well, probably third - time today and I couldn't help wondering whether her knees weren't hurting yet. John pulled at the belt while admiring her taut body, barely covered beneath the tight dress. He paraded her around the room like she was a prize poodle. When he passed the bed, he picked up the bottle of massage oil Claire had thrown down after entering the room. Then he led her towards the terrace windows and pulled her to her feet.

"Look at the view, bitch," he ordered. "Is it to your liking?" She nodded but I knew I heard her swallow hard.

"It's beautiful…," she said with a touch of uncertainty.

"It sure is..," he added. "And I'm going to fuck your magnificent ass right here, where the whole city can see it."

I was amazed at how dominant John was being. Where was my "go with the flow," guy, the man who seemed to hesitate in almost everything he did, I wondered before hearing a deep voice beside me.

"How about you getting on your hands and knees." I turned and looked at Adam.

"Are you going to parade me around the room too, with a belt around my neck?" He shook his head.

"I'd rather have you here," he patted the sofa. "I want to explore your body, Bonnie."

He settled onto the sofa, and I positioned myself on my hands and knees above his lap just like he wanted.

"Wow…," he said breathlessly. "I've fancied you for so long," and ran a finger over my spine. "Do you mind?" he asked, raising my dress over my bum, exposing it for his pleasure.

"Not at all," I answered huskily, looking over my shoulder at him before wiggling my ass invitingly. His hand caressed my buttocks softly, lulling me into a state of relaxation. Then he spanked me hard.

"Nice tone," he said as my skin reddened. I giggled at the remark and was rewarded with another spank.

He deftly removed my panties and threw the drenched garment on the sofa before moving his hands over my exposed body while he tenderly kissed my butt cheeks. Then he spread my ass, taking a moment to admire what he saw, before leaning forward and circling my exposed asshole with his tongue. Saliva dribbled down my anal crack while his fingers pressed against my cunt and clit while he tongued my ass and the cocktail of pussy juice and spittle dripped onto his lap, forming a wet spot on his light gray trousers.

I closed my eyes and bit my lip in ecstasy, this attention was getting to me. Not that I wasn't horny, quite the opposite. Claire's intimate touching in the restroom, the sexy dinner, and the hot face fucking in the elevator had all combined to get me wet and when his tongue probed my back entrance I knew my orgasm wasn't far away. I started breathing heavily. I really needed this indulgence and hoped, with all my heart, that Adam wouldn't stop before I climaxed. Then his fingers started to explore my dripping wet pussy and I came immediately. My body stiffened and I began moaning and whimpering while simultaneously trying to impale myself on Adam's strong fingers.

"Thank you," I said when my orgasm subsided. Our eyes met. "I really needed this."

"It was my pleasure," he said, grinning. "Are you ready for round two?" I nodded.

"Sure! How do you want me?"

"From behind!" he said, loosening his tie. I swiftly moved to the end of the sofa and bent over the arm. From this position, I had a good view of what John was doing on the balcony with Claire. They were naked and facing the magnificent view but I could see everything that was happening. He was entering her ass slowly, that much I could see, more from the way she held her body taut than from actually seeing him enter her, although the way John's buttocks were clenched together, I knew he was concentrating.

"Ahhhh...," Claire cried out.

"Take it, bitch" John ordered.

At precisely that moment, Adam pressed his cock against my juicy cunt and thrust his hips forward. His cock surged forward, filling my silken tunnel completely and a wave of pleasure washed over me. I let my head hang and waited for Adam's onslaught. Immediately he started fucking me, his prick sliding easily in and out of my soaking wet pussy his balls banging against the back of my thighs again and again. I reached down and fingered my clit, enjoying the way he was banging me. Suddenly our attention was drawn to the far side of the room.

"Fuck me you bastard," Claire screamed at John as he stood motionless behind her. "Fuck my ass and make me cum." My boyfriend needed no further encouragement and began pounding her back passage hard. His balls slapped into her in the same rhythm as Adam's slammed into me, and I surrendered myself to the unadulterated lust that coursed through my veins.

Our moans and the sound of skin hitting the skin filled the room and turned me on even more. Adam was really giving me a good go over and my body began its familiar tingling, but it was the sight of John sodomizing Claire that was really making me cream. John was giving it to her mercilessly now, fucking her as hard as I haven't felt him take me in months.

He was spanking her ass repeatedly while he fucked her and the stream of obscenities coming from the far end of the room made the scene even hornier. Adam agreed because he reached forward and grabbed my breasts with one hand and my hair with the other, and pulled me even harder onto his wonderful cock. Time and again he massaged my G-spot with his engorged helmet and quickly brought me to my second orgasm, and the evening was still young. The release was more powerful than the previous and I cried out loudly, my body shuddering uncontrollably as Adam's prick continued pounding my cunt.

When I finally regained my senses, I saw John standing over Claire. She was on her knees again and John had her head pressed against the wall of glass. His other hand was jerking his cock violently, aiming it at her face. I recognized his expression and knew he was on the edge. Suddenly cum exploded from the swollen glans and splattered powerfully against the tinted glass. He continued wanking, making sure he emptied his balls and even shook the last oozing drop onto the smooth surface.

"Your turn, bitch," he said, masterfully pulling Claire's angelic face closer to the window. Adam stopped fucking me and watched in awe as his blonde girlfriend leaned closer to the shiny surface and began licking at the creamy splotches of warm spunk with her tiny pink tongue. John bent over and whispered fiercely into her ear. Then he stood up straight and watched how she cleaned the glass, swallowing each large deposit until the window was clean. John pointed to some residual spots on the glass and Claire, still obeying him unwaveringly, quickly licked them clean, waiting for his approval.

"That was really something...," Adam stated, withdrawing his prick from my steaming cunt. He slumped back on the sofa and started undressing properly. As the last garment landed on the floor John guided Claire back into the middle of the room. He was leading her by her hair; his belt hanging loosely from her neck. Her hair was ruffled, and her dress was wrinkled beyond recognition. She held her heels in her hand and had the look of a completely satisfied, freshly fucked bitch.

"I think your girlfriend is ready for a proper DP now, man," John said calmly to Adam, who was staring at Claire anxiously.

"Are you, honey?" he asked, standing up and moving in front of her. His stiff cock pointed at her like a cocked gun.

"Yes...," she smiled, her eyes focusing on his swaying appendage. John reached down and yanked her head by her hair.

"What did you say, slut?" He demanded. "I didn't quite understand you." Her eyes widened in surprise.

"I want you to fuck my ass and pussy!" she said out loud, her eyes sparkling with excitement now. "I want to feel both of you between my legs." John released his grip slightly.

"That's much better," John said and let go of her hair. He grabbed her hand and pulled her towards the sofa but Adam was already there. Claire instinctively climbed onto his lap, reaching behind her and guiding his cock into her receptive pussy. Then John pushed her against Adam's chest and ordered her to spread her ass. I watched fascinated as John thrust his cock back into her asshole. Claire cried out as she was impaled but the guys didn't give her a chance to get adjusted to the thick pricks filling her orifices. As soon as they could, they started pounding her like men possessed.

I could never imagine I would just stand there and watch John fuck another woman, but here I was and more importantly, I found it a huge turn-on. Wanting to have something to look at later I decided to take some photos. I quickly grabbed my smartphone and began clicking away. The three of them were so involved in what they were doing, they never heard me but seeing this classic DP was hot as hell. Adam was watching his girlfriend as both men pummeled her body. John's back gleamed in a sweaty sheen and drops of perspiration dripped from his nose onto Claire's naked back.

She hadn't noticed: mostly because she was too busy whimpering and moaning as two thick cocks hammered into her body. Hearing her cries enflamed the boys, and they upped their efforts, pounding their pricks even harder into her orifices and it didn't go unnoticed by Claire. Her body stiffened and she let out a feline scream. I watched entranced as both men ground their balls against her receptive body, causing her to shudder violently. I pointed my cell phone in her direction and got some wonderful shots of her contorted in a mixture of pleasure and pain. I smiled as I thought about what Facebook would do if she used these as her profile pics.

The guys thrust halfheartedly while Claire collapsed on top of her boyfriend but it was obvious she was spent for the moment. Adam lifted her limp body off his erection after John withdrew from her ass and set her down on the sofa. Both men turned towards me, their rampant cocks sticking out in front of them.

"Claire's fantasy has been fulfilled today," he said matter-of-factly, standing up next to John. "She's had more cock today than she reckoned on, and she needs some rest," he continued. He reached for his cock and began jerking it wildly while grinning broadly at me. "I still haven't come yet, Bonnie so seeing as Claire's not in much state to do anything about it, I was thinking maybe you'd like to finish this."

I nodded in agreement, despite still being half-clothed. The look in his eyes made it obvious what he wanted and remembering what Claire had told me in the restroom, I knelt down in front of him and obediently opened my mouth. Adam was wanking so hard that the tip of his cock was an angry, red color and I wondered briefly if he was in pain. Then John moved into view, his hand wrapped tightly around his girth. I looked at them expectantly and stuck my tongue out greedily.

"Wait a minute," Adam cried almost in pain. He reached for my discarded panties and ordered me to open wider. Doing as I was told, he fed me my drenched thong, arranging it in exactly the way he wanted it, the smell of my arousal tantalizing my nostrils.

"Perfect, Bonnie!" Adam said and pushed his throbbing cock back into my face. It was obviously too much for him because within seconds he was cumming copiously. Huge strings of thick white cum exploded from the tip, hitting my nose first, then my lips, and then covering the strategically placed thong.

"Fuck, fuck, fuck…" Adam gasped as he emptied his balls onto the silken black material. "That's it…," he said breathlessly. "I'm done." And stepped back, completely drained.

John was next. As usual, he was silent except for the soft grunting as his hand moved in a blur. I looked at his face and saw the expression of deep concentration. His eyes were screwed shut and his lips were clamped together making it difficult for him to breathe easily. Suddenly his spunk splattered against my face, covering my mouth, thong, and chin with thick white cream. I poked my tongue into the saturated garment and tasted Adam's seed, already soaked into the porous material.

John was tapping his engorged helmet against my hidden tongue while he jerked the last amount of cum from his cock, and that's when I heard Claire making her pictures on her smartphone. I guessed the sight of me eating cum soaked panties was just as horny as the pictures I'd made of her being DP'ed and somehow I knew we'd be swapping pictures later.

"Don't worry," she said, taking another shot. She grinned teasingly. "I won't post this on Facebook. Not yet, anyway…"

Daydreaming

I spent a lot of time lying in bed this morning thinking over this one.

My Mistress's new well-endowed boyfriend is coming over, and she has plans to have me serve and please them while they enjoy each other.

Dressed in a pretty pink, sissy dress with white lace and frills, matching lingerie, and my little sissy clit encased in its cage, I kneel by the front door and wait patiently for them to arrive from their date.

When they step through the door, she has me pull his cock out and suck him off while they make out in the doorway. They become increasingly aroused, standing there caressing each other while his crotch is pressed hard into my face. Their dirty talking, plus his cock buried deep in my throat, drives me wild and after a short while, he shoots his first load of the night, into my mouth and over my face.

She calls me a filthy cum face, spunk-mouthed sissy, slaps my face and spits on me.

They leave me there for some time, kneeling while they eat and wait for him to recover. I hear him talking on the phone, and from what I can understand, they seem to be planning something special.

A short while later, the doorbell rings, and a handsome friend of my Mistress's boyfriend arrives. Ultimately, I'm on my knees, leaning over the bed with my hands bound behind my back. The new man, this total stranger, taking advantage of my prone position fucks me hard, making me moan and cry as he punishes my poor little sissy hole.

Meanwhile, Mistress's boyfriend fucks her from behind, her face positioned right in front of mine. She whispers dirty things to me while we're both being fucked, telling me how much she loves seeing me taking a big cock up the arse. When her boyfriend comes inside her, she orgasms, kissing me passionately, the intense pleasure causing her to bite my lip and make me bleed.

Once the Stranger has come, condoms are peeled from the real men's cocks and put into my mouth. I have to suck out all the cum from them, which I do hungrily. Their creamy deposits have an artificial fruity taste because of the condom, which I don't mind, but I prefer the familiar salty taste of cum, and am suitably rewarded.

Then I get sent to the bathroom to get cleaned up while listening to my Mistress being properly serviced by her two well-endowed studs.

Just a Perverted Quickie

Well... This always sticks in my mind:

1. Hubby handcuffed in chair.....

2. Me spreadeagled standing in heels on a frame - X position, a red gag ball in my mouth

3. Large black man with great abs and a huge cock fucking me in front.

4. White guy easing cock in and out of my well-lubed arse...

How could it feel, being fucked right in front of my hubby? Both of us knowing I'll soon be flooded with these strangers' hot sticky cum and there is nothing he can do about it...

Total taboo fantasy!!!!

From John's Diary

Playing Pool

It was the fourth round that night and I was on a losing streak. My friend and colleague Kyle, was busily fattening his wallet with my hard-earned dollars. With every new round, his smile continued to grow.

"Give it up, bro," he told me. "It's just not your day."

Because of my misfortune, I decided to not try again. Even though I rationalized that after losing four times, my luck had to change, I wasn't prepared to tart fate again. Putting down the cue, I decided to call it a day and that's when I spotted Lawrence coming through the door of the employee's room in the back.

"Hi," I said casually as he passed. I never understood what his sexy bitch of a wife, Madison, from the office, saw in him. Compared to her, he was a totally lame dick. Blond, hot, and a filthy mouth, she never missed an opportunity to use it. Everybody hated her, but the way she dressed made up for a lot. Her outfits weren't designed for sympathy, but more for grabbing attention. I always wondered how a limp dick like Lawrence managed to hold on to her.

"Probably money," I muttered beneath my breath. I needn't have worried, he had barely noticed us.

"Hello," he said, with empty eyes.

I held out my hand. "I'm John, a co-worker of your wife?" I said, "And this is Kyle?" I continued, pointing to my friend behind me.

"Sure..." Lawrence said, uncertainly shaking my hand. "Hi, how are you doing." He sat down in an empty chair and looked straight in front of him. My eyes met Kyle's and we nodded knowingly.

"Hey, man," I stepped towards Lawrence, "is everything okay? You look so..." I struggled to find the right word.

"Wanna have a drink?" Kyle interjected and handed over his scotch. Lawrence looked at the clear brown liquid in puzzlement and then gulped it down in one shot.

"I don't know what I'm gonna do," he almost sobbed. Finally looking at us with watery eyes he continued. "I don't know how..."

"I know it's not my business..." I asked, feeling a little uncomfortable.

"Actually, it could be your business." He suddenly stood up, grabbed my collar, and pulled me towards him. Then he looked deep into my eyes. "I've noticed how all of you look at Madison. The way she dresses."

"Sorry, man, it's just a guy thing..."

He relaxed and produced a nasty-looking smile. "That's okay, guys," he said, releasing and smoothing down my collar. "Especially now..."

We were stunned into silence and our inaction seemed to return him to his earlier lethargic state. Then he spoke again, his voice barely a whisper. "I found out Madison was cheating on me, today" he explained, staring into the void.

"Sorry, man..." Kyle mumbled behind me.

"Maybe he was looking for answers," I said, wondering whether anybody noticed the reference to the movie 'O Brother, Where Art Thou?' Nobody had, and much to my disappointment, Lawrence went on explaining his pain.

"And it's not like she fucked someone on a crazy ladies' night. No, she's been cheating on me for months, with our neighbor of all people."

"The bitch!" Kyle commiserated, although I could tell he was enjoying Lawrence's painful confession. Although the idea of Madison cheating on her lame-dick husband was funny, I just looked at him in disbelief.

"I found their sex video on her phone," Lawrence continued explaining, shaking his head angrily. "You know that bitch did everything with him. And I mean everything... Including all the things she refused me."

"Like what?" I asked, genuinely curious.

"Anal, facials, creampies. Everything nasty you can think of, she did it... with him."

"Hmmmm," I murmured a little too enthusiastically. I could think of a lot of slutty stuff.

"Wow..." Kyle said, echoing my thoughts. I looked at him sternly. "I mean, sorry man..." he quickly added sympathetically. Lawrence barely noticed.

"Anyway, as soon as I found out, I came here to confront her but as soon as I saw her, standing there in her sexy outfit, the thought of her doing all those things to me got me horny and I ended up having some really hot revenge sex back there." He waved his hand in the direction of the back room.

"Why are you so down then, man?" Karl asked in surprise. Lawrence's smile grew tighter.

"I found out the real reason for her cheating on me: Apparently, I couldn't satisfy her, like ever. Even now, she's still begging for more, but I couldn't get it up."

I patted his shoulder. "Don't worry buddy, it happens to everybody...," I turned to Kyle and winked.

"So...," Kyle started saying, "that means you two were fucking back there?" The disbelief was obvious.

Lawrence nodded and then buried his head in his hands. "Yeah, but it only lasted about a minute or so."

"And where's Madison now?" I demanded, my excitement rising.

"She's back there, craving for more cock..."

Kyle looked at me and nodded. Lawrence looked up at us and realized what we were thinking. "Hey, maybe you two could try satisfying her!"

"What? Are you kidding?" Kyle and I asked in chorus. Lawrence nodded.

"Yep!" He stood up and explained. "Just go in and fuck her senseless. I'm serious. My marriage is probably over and I don't want anything to do with that bitch again."

"And are you sure you're okay with this?" Kyle asked, unable to believe Lawrence wasn't pulling our chains.

"Sure, whatever..." and then walked out of the room.

"Do you think he was serious?" I asked.

"There's only one way to find it out..." Kyle replied pointing at the closed door.

We entered the room. The light was dimmed, but Madison, lying on her side, on the pool table was clearly visible. Her hands were tied together with a necktie, resting above her head while her blouse was ripped open. Her small, perky breasts were in view and her nipples were still erect. Her mini skirt was bunched up around her waist and her legs, clad in sexy stockings and high heels were spread obscenely.

She heard us approaching and turned her head. As we reached the table she smiled wantonly. "Hi guys..., could you please fuck me?"

"Look at this bitch...," Kyle said unbelievably. "Spread on the table... Hungry for cock..." He trailed his index finger slowly over her skin, from her face down her neck, breasts, and thighs. "What's this?" he said harshly and pointed between Madison's thighs. I leaned over. It was a trail of fresh white cum dripping from her pussy.

"Looks like hubby came around here," I giggled. Madison nodded and let out a long sigh.

"I was just getting started when he shot his fucking load. Then the useless bastard left me here like this..." She looked at us appealingly. "I'm so fucking horny, would you two like to take his place?" Madison begged. "Pleeeaaassssee, I really need some hard cocks right now!"

"Okay, bitch!" Kyle said and slapped her face hard. "You will get the fucking of your life tonight!" He had his cock out in a second and pressed it to her face. I looked around and double-checked the room was empty and the door was closed. Then I freed my throbbing cock and joined Kyle and Madison on the table. Madison motioned to me to join her, so kneeling on the table beside her, I set up shop.

She was busy sucking Kyle's cock so I slapped her cheeks with my throbbing hard-on. She couldn't move her head much, but Kyle was helping her, holding her head by her hair and pushing his cock deep into her mouth again and again. I reached down and grabbed a handful of tit while I continued slapping my meat against her face. Eventually, Madison released Kyle from her mouth, turned around, and looking me hungrily in the eye, said, "This is so hot!"

Instead of answering, I used the opportunity to shove my cock deep into the office bitch's mouth. I just held it here for a few seconds, admiring the view of Madison's filthy mouth wrapped around my cock. Then I started to fuck her face. It felt so good pushing my cock all the way, feeling my balls against her succulent lips while my helmet stretched her throat. I even managed to pinch her tits while I went to town in her mouth.

Meanwhile, Kyle was kneeling between Madison's splayed legs and was aiming his huge cock at the juicy slit. Without a word, he thrust forward, his rigid dick disappearing easily between her pussy lips. The office bitch let out a surprised yelp but quickly resumed sucking my cock as Kyle began fucking her with long, deep strokes, his rhythm building up nicely. The expression on Madison's face was one of pure ecstasy. She raised her tied hands and gripped my cock.

"Goddammit you guys, don't stop. Treat me like the little whore I am." To emphasize her words, she started jacking me off. Kyle continued to fuck her hard and after a few seconds, I removed myself from the table so they could enjoy each other. He looked up at me and winked and then really began pounding her cunt. I watched in fascination as her perky little tits bobbed up and down more violently as Kyles' body pummeled hers. Madison started moaning loudly and it was obvious she was on the verge of cumming. Seconds later we watched in amazement as Madison, the naughty office bitch, powerfully orgasmed. After she'd stopped shaking, Kyle pulled out and motioned me to take his place.

I gripped my cock and gave it a couple of pulls as I moved between her legs. I looked at her red, swollen pussy and the trail of cum, glistening on her thighs, and made my decision.

"I don't like sloppy seconds, bitch, so I'm gonna have to fuck your ass."

"Do it...," she moaned. Taking that as a green light, I placed my engorged helmet against her twitching asshole. There was a tiny bit of resistance as her sphincter opened up, but then I was inside. She moaned loudly as I pushed deeper into her back passage. It felt soooo good! Her tight ass squeezed my cock as I slid further inside her bowls and I knew she liked it there. Kyle took my place at the head of the table and fed her his thick prick. Moments later we were fucking her in unison.

I was surprised at how quickly Madison experienced another orgasm. It seemed like I'd only pumped her a few times before she started shrieking loudly and her body started shuddering violently. Through it all, I took no pity on her and kept up my onslaught on her ass. For good measure, I slapped her ass repeatedly, her buttocks turning a nice shade of angry pink.

Kyle laughed at this and pulled his cock from between Madison's succulent, thick lips. His shaft was glistening and the bitch's saliva was dripping down onto her upturned face. Seeing the begging expression she had, Kyle slapped his meat against her flushed cheeks.

"Jesus... Jesus Christ, don't stop guys, please don't stop," she pleaded, catching her breath. It wasn't clear what she was enjoying the most; the hardcore ass fucking or the dirty face slapping, but to be honest, I didn't care. Judging by what I saw happening in front of me, neither did Karl, because we just continued working her over.

"Get on your hands and knees, bitch," I ordered brusquely. "I'm really gonna punish your ass now."

Obediently, she did as she was told. From where I was standing, she looked amazing. Seeing her kneeling on the pool table expectantly, her clothes rumpled and ruined, her face and cunt dripping wet, my lust rose. I knelt behind and fed her greedy ass my cock. The wanton bitch didn't even open her eyes when I entered her but I knew she liked what was happening by the way she kept thrusting her ass backward, matching my movements.

Kyle knelt up in front of her and shoved his cock into her mouth so that she looked like she was being spit roasted. Determined to break her, Kyle fucked her face really hard, making her gag continuously but she never once begged him to stop. On the contrary, she kept her face buried in his crotch.

"How do you like being our little slut, Madison? How do you like being spit roasted?" I growled.

"I love it... Don't stop... Please... Keep fucking me," Madison gasped between Kyles's violent thrusts.

"How about we both fuck you?" I suggested it hopefully. Unable to speak with her mouthful, Madison simply nodded.

Eager to take advantage of the situation, Kyle withdrew from her mouth and laid on the table beside her. Holding his erection upright, he motioned to Madison that she should get on top of him. Taking up the invitation, Madison straddled his prick and began riding him in cowgirl fashion. Watching the two of them fucking made me eager to join in and I climbed up behind her.

"Bend over bitch, your ass is mine," I growled in her ear. As soon as she leaned forward, I rammed my cock into her vacant asshole. She screamed quite loudly, making me jump, and without thinking, I pulled out. Immediately Madison reached back and grabbed my cock and pulled it toward her proffered bottom.

"Just ignore me. It hurts like hell, but I love it," she moaned wantonly.

Accepting her explanation, I pressed my dome against her sphincter and pushed forward. Taking it a lot slower now, I kept going until my balls banged against her bum. After a moment's pause, I started fucking her. Slowly at first but it didn't take long for me to quicken the pace. Beneath us, Kyle was matching my movements precisely, and between us, all Madison could do was whimper and enjoy.

Seconds later, her body stiffened and she emitted a feral growl. It was then that I realized she'd orgasmed again. Neither of us relented and we pounded her body right the way through her climax, enjoying the way her body trembled when our stiff cocks plunged deep inside her.

"Jesus, you're a badass slut, Madison," Kyle said as the bitch from the office recovered from one of her many orgasms.

"Ohhh God... yesss...," she moaned, her head hanging suppliantly. "I really needed this... so bad..."

"Holy shit, I wish I knew you were such a slut," I said, my cock still throbbing inside her tight, hot asshole.

Madison raised her head and looked down at Kyle.

"Fuck me again," she said, "nice and hard, just how I like it."

"My God, we've discovered an honest-to-god nympho," replied Kyle in disbelief, as he continued pummeling her pussy. It was strangely erotic feeling his prick rubbing against mine through the thin flimsy veil of skin separating her orifices.

Being part of Madison's sandwich was beginning to take its toll and I felt my knees aching. I heard greedy sucking sounds coming from beneath the blond-haired slut and assumed Kyle was sucking Madison's perky round tits. Madison kept moaning as both pricks bored into her, each one thrusting harder and harder.

Despite being overcome with ecstasy, she matched our maniac thrusts easily and I was surprised to see she was still full of energy. She must really get off on this rough handling, God knows she was acting like some dye in the wool porn star. I felt Kyle stop moving and that allowed me to pump her hard, my thrusts impaling Madison onto Kyle's rigid manhood.

"You're such a dirty slut, Madison," Kyle said through gritted teeth.

"I... am..." Madison agreed, her voice a little more hoarse than it usually sounded.

"Do you like the way our cocks are fucking your holes?" I asked.

"Yes..." Madison began saying but was cut off by Kyle shoving his finger into her mouth. She didn't even flinch. She sucked it deep in, letting a lot of saliva drip on my friend's hand.

"Good God you're fucking crazy," Kyle said in wonderment.

"Just fuck me, guys!" Madison wailed. "Make me cum!"

"Look at this fucking slut," Kyle said. "You think she can take two cocks in her pretty mouth?"

"She has got a pretty wild mouth," I said thoughtfully, "so why don't we try? What do you think, Madison?" I asked, fucking her asshole very hard. Seeing her nod, I gave her one final fuck and then withdrew from her gaping asshole. I stood there, watching them climb off the table, leisurely wanking while I waited for Madison to get on her knees. Without instruction, our afternoon's fuck toy knelt on the dirty floor and I was amazed to see how skanky she looked. With her hair messed up, her face flushed, and her ruined blouse barely covering her chest, she looked like a true professional. Then she grabbed our cocks and put them in her mouth. Although our cocks pressed against each other, the situation was so crazy, it didn't seem to matter.

Much to our surprise, Madison managed to fit them inside her filthy little mouth, wiggling her tongue between our cocks while looking up at us. Her eyes sparkled mischievously as she struggled to accommodate two raging hard-ons between her cherry-red lips.

Despite both of us trying, it soon became apparent that this was more for fun than fulfillment, and seconds later Kyle withdrew his cock and gave me an encouraging smile.

"She's all yours, John," he said generously, stepping back to enjoy the view. Madison didn't flinch a bit and went on sucking my cock. She let it slip from her lips and said huskily, "Fuck my face you big pricked bastard."

I started humping her face, not too hard at first, but determinedly pushing my cock deep into her throat, time and time again. I suddenly realized her arm was moving and was amazed to see her playing with her swollen clit. She really was insatiable. This was a huge turn on and I began fucking her face in earnest now. Between my wild thrusts, I heard her muffled moan.

"I'mfff cumminghhh!"

I grabbed her head and fucked her throat even harder, pounding her mouth while her orgasm ripped through her body, and was astounded when she grabbed my balls with her free hand and gave them a good squeeze. Her orgasm seemed to last ages but eventually, she calmed down, and much to my relief, she loosened the grip on my balls.

I pulled out of her mouth and saw her breathing hard. A knowing smile appeared across her face.

"My God... This was so dirty...," she said, panting.

"You think we're done here?" Kyle asked in disbelief, standing beside me. He slapped his cock against her face. "You think we're here for your pleasure? God, you're a spoiled bitch." He continued spanking her face with his meat. "If that's what you think, then you're sadly mistaken. You've had your fun, now it's our turn."

The wanton expression on her face told us enough.

"Well, why don't you two studs give it to me," she said huskily, "all over my face."

Kyle looked at me and winked. The two of us moved into position and began jacking our cocks. I thought we'd explode immediately, but somehow we'd both managed to keep it together during the whole session. I guessed some of that was due to the fact neither of us wanted to pass up the opportunity to fuck Madison and both of us were determined to see it through to the end.

"Open your mouth, slut" Kyle ordered.

"Why don't you finish us off, bitch," I added just as brusquely. Madison obeyed our wishes and grabbed our throbbing cocks. With a sly smile, she began jerking us off.

"Anything you say, stud. What kind of spoiled slut would I be if I let you all do the work?" she said coyly, her arms moving rapidly.

Kyle was the first one to cum. He moaned out loud and came with huge white drops spraying on her tongue. "That's it...," he moaned. "Drink my spunk you fucking whore."

Copious cum and saliva dribbled out of Madison's mouth and trickled down her chin before dripping onto her exposed chest and the floor. Finally spent, Kyle stepped back to admire his handy work. Seeing the blond office bitch, kneeling on the floor with cum dripping down her face was simply mind-blowing.

"Do you like swallowing spunk?" I asked, as she wildly jerked my cock.

"Hmmm," she moaned, her tongue flicking quickly across her cum smothered lips.

"Good," I replied coolly, "because I'm cummin."

Madison poked out her tongue again, but that was not what I wanted. I pushed her hand away and grabbed my pulsating prick, aiming it at her face.

"I wanna cum all over your pretty face, slut," I said masterfully. "Let me paint your face."

"Hmmm, cum for me baby," she replied hungrily. "I've always known you wanted me to be your little slut." That was the last straw.

I shot my load all over Madison's face and hair. The first thick rope hit her cheek, which had turned a rosy red from the intensity of the moment, while the second thick salvo landed in her hair. The third and fourth expulsions covered her face from her forehead down to her chin and covered everything in between.

"Wow, look at you... you little cumslut," Kyle said in admiration.

"Hmmmm...," she moaned, licking cum off her fingers. Her face was covered in goo, which was insanely hot because it showed just how much of a nasty slut she was.

I looked at Madison, kneeling there, one last time, marveling at the body we had used as a communal fuck toy. Her pussy was red and swollen and I guessed her asshole would hurt for a few days, such was the ferocity with which I'd fucked her.

Her pale skin was blotchy red where we'd grabbed or slapped her and her hair was so wild and messy, it went beyond the "just-been-fucked" hairstyle. This was definitely in the, "I've just been sandwiched" territory, a place usually reserved for porn stars and backdoor hookers — not a successful businesswoman. Kyle grabbed his phone, taking pictures of the apparition in front of us. Madison looked at him wantonly and blew him a kiss.

"Just making sure I don't forget how you looked after the fucking we've given you," he said casually, snapping more photos.

Late Night Office Slut

Cindy was the kind of girl who looks hot because she did everything possible to look hot; hair dyed blonde, heavy slutty make-up, and a keep-fit regime that guaranteed her a killer body. Although these things disguised her strong personality some things can't be hidden. Things like her straight thin lips, her strong nose, and her cold blue eyes, gave the careful observer clues to her real nature. "Clothes," someone once said "make the man" and Cindy took this seriously.

Her fashionable clothes did her body justice, making her look hot and sexy. Every guy in the office liked the way she looked and smelt. Some had even confided in me that they would have fucked her in a New York minute. I'll have to admit she had an effect on me but really... Her ice queen bitch style ruined everything.

Anyway, It was a regular Wednesday night shift and I was sitting in my boss's, The Worm, comfortable swivel chair. He ordered me to take charge for a while because he had some personal stuff to sort out and needed about an hour or so free. I agreed and then he disappeared without another word. This was a perfect chance for me to snoop around his office and after sampling the whiskey I found in the desk, cheap, I decided to check out the private shower behind the office. Nothing special.

I was lounging in the expensive chair with my feet on the desk, admiring the smoked glass cabinets along the far wall. Watching my reflection cleaning out my nails with the antique letter opener I found in one of the Worm's desk drawers, was very entertaining. Waiting for the telephone to ring, the boss hadn't said it would ring for certain but if it did I should answer it, and to be honest, I was bored out of my mind. That's when I heard the tiny knock. Surprised, I quickly checked to see if everything was where it should be and then crossed the room to open the door. My surprise grew when I saw who was knocking.

"Oh, sorry," Cindy said and I could tell she wasn't expecting to see me here. "Uumm is Carl here," she asked hesitantly. I shook my head.

"No, he's had to leave. Something important came up and he asked me to take over for a while," I elaborated, taking a step backward and allowing her to enter. "Can I help you with anything?"

"Maybe...," Cindy nodded absently and walked into the room. Watching her move towards the desk gave me the perfect chance to check her out. She was wearing tight jeans and I was busy taking in her shapely pins when out of the corner of my eye, I caught her watching me. Now it was my turn to pass the inspection.

"You know, I have a little problem here..." she said a little awkwardly while looking at me intently. Then as if making a decision, she shrugged noncommittally and continued speaking. "You know, I have a fiancé..." Lucky bastard.

"Yes," I nodded for emphasis. "I've heard he works here as well." Now it was her head that moved up and down.

"Exactly. And even though we're still organizing our wedding, we've decided not to wait until then and we are trying to conceive."

I was surprised by this intimate admission but said nothing. Undeterred, Cindy went on. "Yeah... We've stopped using protection and try to catch every opportunity to get me pregnant." Again, I nodded politely wondering where the hell this was headed. "But we haven't succeeded so far," she continued.

"Sorry to hear that," I said, trying to suppress the mental image of me fucking her silly and cumming all over her slutty little mouth.

"Thanks," she said, a little distracted. She cast another glance around the office, as if making sure it was empty. "So anyway, the past few months have been kinda stressful for me and..." She paused before carrying on. "And I thought maybe you could help me relax, you know... if you're interested?" I raised my eyebrows inquisitively.

"Really? How?"

"You could fuck me," she said huskily, looking into my eyes. "You could fuck me hard."

I felt my mouth go dry. Seeing my expression, she emitted a tiny giggle.

"I'm bored," she said contemptuously. "I'm bored with our sex life, only fucking when we can fertilize my eggs. I don't want to have to keep measuring my body temperature while constantly checking the calendar. I need sex and lots of it. In fact..." She didn't finish the sentence, instead giving me the come hither look. "Of course, I could wait for Carl unless you're up for it." I just stared at her.

"Oh come on John, don't make me beg for it. Do you want to fuck me or not?" I cleared my throat and continued staring. "I need it, you know... a good hard fuck, right here and right now. Are you up for it?"

"Of course, I'm in!" I replied, barely able to believe my ears.

"But remember," she said, pointing a warning finger at me. "You cannot finish inside me." Her pretty face would do nicely.

My surprise was total. Surely this kind of thing only happened in cheesy porn movies. Making my decision, I moved in front of her and grabbed her hair. I stared into her eyes, glancing briefly at her face, admiring her cherry-red lips and breathing in her exotic perfume. She kept her eyes on me, never wavering.

"So you wanna fuck?" I asked softly, watching her for a reaction. Her eyes sparkled mischievously but she didn't say a word. I got the impression she didn't think I was serious about her proposal.

"Yes, John," she whispered tightly. "I want to get fucked tonight. I want you to take me any which way you can and don't be a gentleman."

"I'm gonna fuck you now, bitch," I growled. She said nothing, just continued to stare challengingly at me. She knew what effect she had on men and me in particular, and she knew I'd never back down from a chance like this. Jesus, I bet that was what she was gambling on. Not surprising really, when you consider what a manipulating bitch she is. Our battle of wills continued for another couple of seconds. Finally, I couldn't take it anymore, and grabbing her arms, I turned her around and pushed her towards the desk. Surprised by my actions, she stumbled and almost fell but the desk gave her something to grab and recover her balance. Seeing her standing there, leaning on the desk had its benefits. Her arse was sticking out towards me and she'd spread her feet shoulder breadth in a perfect "fuck me" position. I needed no further encouragement, I reached around and found the buttons and zipper keeping her jeans in place. Seconds later I pulled the tight garment over her peachy bum, bunching it around her knees. Her pale ass cheeks greeted me and I was enamored to see how her pretty pink panties disappeared between her shapely buttocks before reappearing to cover the small bulge of her fragrant sex. I noticed the decorative tattoo high on her left cheek and was impressed. Gazing at her perfect arse, I almost bent forward and licked and bit her but I decided to play it cool and spanked her. A sharp stinging little slap bringing color to her skin.

"Ouch," she cried and was rewarded with a few more stinging slaps. Now her bum was nice and red.

"Be quiet, bitch," I ordered her. "After all, this is a workplace."

This made her giggle so I spanked her a few more times as punishment but I could tell she was enjoying it too much, so I ceased.

"I've been waiting so long for this," I admitted, sliding a hand over her burning skin before pushing a finger beneath her panties. My first impression wasn't wrong. The dainty undergarment was saturated from the slick juices seeping from her willing pussy.

As my fingers brushed against her pussy lips, I immediately understood exactly how much she wanted this, She was dripping wet. Pushing her down on the desktop I removed my hand, hearing her sigh of disappointment, and reached for the discarded letter opener. It was sharp as a knife so I carefully inserted the point under the elastic and lifted her sopping garment. Then moving the opener back and forth, I watched how the sharp implement sliced open her delicate panties. She hissed loudly, which got me more excited, and taking hold of the biggest piece of cloth, I folded it over, exposing her arse some more. Just to keep her on edge, I ran the sharp blade over her bare skin and was rewarded with a subtle shiver.

"Relax," I said gruffly. "This is not what you should be afraid of tonight."

"I hope so," she answered with a smile.

Saying nothing, I pushed a couple of fingers deep into her pussy. It was as good as I had imagined it would be. Her longing was so hot, it had superheated her pussy juice and it felt like I was dipping my fingers into hot oil; hot, fragrant, pussy oil. The image of this hot, tight little cunt being fucked by me, while her fiancé thought he was the only one who rightfully had access to it, really got me hard and my cock throbbed painfully in my trousers.

Smugly enjoying the thought, I fingered her pussy for about a minute, and from her reactions, eyes closed, tiny erotic noises, and some labored breathing, I could tell it had been a while since this bitch had felt any real satisfaction. Well, that would change tonight.

I withdrew my fingers and purposely smeared the copious pussy juices over her tight little asshole. I twitched and she hissed angrily but that didn't deter me and I carried on pushing deeper and deeper, the tightness of her rectum surprising me. I would have bet my life that she took it up the bum but considering how long I had to finger her, I wondered if she was an anal virgin. Maybe her fiancé wasn't into that. Finally, I felt her loosen up and my fingers were soon moving in a blur. Looking at her gorgeous bum, I was once again tempted, no I really wanted to kiss it, lick it. Pull her buttocks apart and force my tongue deep inside her back passage, but this was not the time or occasion for it. Tonight she would lose her anal virginity.

Collecting all the saliva my dry mouth could muster, I spat at the delightful brown orifice and spat. I watched in satisfaction as the large glob of spittle landed just above and dribbled slowly towards her asshole.

"I don't have any lubricant, Bitch," I hissed into her ear. "So this will have to do. It's better than dry fucking your slutty ass, anyway."

Her eyes were screwed shut but the wanton smile told me all I needed to know. Hastily standing up, I unzipped my trousers and let them fall to my ankles. Next, my boxers, and then the beast was free. There was a tear of joy in its one eye and I could barely restrain myself. Stepping forward, I aimed my cock and leaned over her. It felt pretty nasty pushing my cock into her asshole and at first, her sphincter seemed reluctant to grant me entrance.

"This is what you want, Bitch, don't pretend otherwise, or you wouldn't be here." I pressed harder and felt her resistance waning. My helmet finally slipped past her tight opening.

"Yesssss...," I heard her hissing. I moved my hips some more.

"What was that?" I asked angrily, not stopping and feeling the snugness of her back passage gripping me. Cindy kept her mouth shut while I continued pressing home. Finally, she emitted a small whimper as I bottomed out and ground my pelvis against her fleshy buttocks. Satisfied with her reaction, I pulled back until only my engorged dome helmet was inside her and then thrust forward.

A small cry escaped her lips but I ignored it. Again my pelvis bumped against her bum.

"Yesssss!" she cried out. "Come on you bastard, fuck my ass!"

And that was what I did. I grabbed her waist and started fucking. Not soft or gentle, I pounded her hard and fast, and to my amazement, she fucked me back. Every time, my cock disappeared easily, burying itself to the hilt, and with each thrust, I felt her anal muscles gripping me tighter and tighter.

"Fuck yeaaah...," she cried out as I took her ass powerfully. She even liked it when I spanked her ass, the timely slaps increasing the heat in her rear.

I lost track of time because all I was interested in was fucking her as if there was no tomorrow, but even I knew I'd reached her sweet spot because at once she and breathing heavily. Then she cried out loud and her body began shuddering uncontrollably. Not really caring about her state of mind, I continued fucking her ass, driving my cock so deep my balls banged against her soaking wet cunt, soaking them in the process, prolonging her orgasm. In fact, it was all too much.

I grabbed her hips, thrust as deeply as I could, and came deep inside her ass. My body jolted violently with each ejaculation, forcing my cock deeper into her back passage while I held onto her heaving rear end. Eventually, my balls were empty and my carnal lust subsided. I looked down at her, sprawled across the desk, still impaled on my cock, her eyes closed in ecstasy, and a smile of real satisfaction on her pretty face.

"I fucking ruined your asshole," I hissed into her ears, admiring the cum dripping out of her gaping well-fucked orifice.

"You don't have to tell me," she sighed wistfully, barely moving beneath me.

"We're not done yet, bitch!" I said gruffly and pulled her to her feet. The surprised and fearful look she gave me was very gratifying and feeling very masterful. I placed my hands on her shoulders and began applying pressure. The look of disdain in her eyes told me she understood what I was demanding even if she disliked the idea. Reluctantly she dropped to her knees and came face to face with my dripping cock.

"Suck it," I ordered loudly. She looked up at me again, probably hoping to see me relent but there was no chance of that. I'd waited too long for this moment.

"But it's been...." She began objecting.

"I know exactly where it's been, bitch," I replied masterfully. "It was up your ass. Your gorgeous, tight little ass," I said triumphantly. "Oh and by the way, it was a pleasure fucking it, but now I want more. I've fucked your ass and now I'm gonna fuck your face. Problem with that?" Slowly she shook her head. "That's right, bitch. Now open that fucking slutty mouth of yours and get on with it." My tone left her in no doubt who was in charge.

Obediently her lips parted and the head of my cock disappeared between them. I felt her tongue slide up and over the engorged dome before pushing into my tiny piss slit.

"That's right, slut," I sneered encouragingly. "Suck that fucking dick," and pushed it deeper into her wet mouth.

Her eyes flared defiantly for a second and I'm sure she would have said something insulting if the opportunity had been available but it wasn't and she couldn't, not with a mouthful of dick. I pushed my cock into her cheek from the inside, watching with satisfaction how it disfigured her face. To increase her humiliation, I patted her cheek lightly, asking her condescendingly, "D'ya like that, bitch?"

She moaned, but it wasn't one of disdain. It sounded like someone thoroughly enjoying something they thought they'd dislike intensely.

"That's it, bitch. Suck my cock, make it nice and hard again."

Having gotten over her preconceptions, Cindy's head immediately started bobbing up and down, producing lots of saliva, just like a pro. I absently wondered how many cocks she had blown in the past to be this practiced and couldn't help smiling at the thought of her schmuck fiancé and what he would say if he could see her now. My cock throbbed and grew harder in her soft warm mouth, reminding me of my intention.

I saw her body tense when I grabbed her blond hair. Like a pro, she was preparing herself for my onslaught and I didn't disappoint her. I thrust my hips forward and was rewarded with the sight of my prick disappearing completely from sight. I held her face against my pelvis until I felt her struggling to breathe before releasing the pressure.

Then in a move that surprised me, Cindy tried bobbing her head forward. Although it pleased me to see her taking some initiative, it wasn't what I'd planned. So pulling her head back to look up at me, I wiggled a finger at her.

"Oh no, you don't, slut. I'm in control here."

Relaxing my grip a little, I let her head drop and thrust my cock as hard as I could down her throat. Like a real trooper, she accepted the reprimand and knelt there compliant as I started fucking her mouth. I went for it hard, driving my cock down her throat fast and deep, watching with satisfaction how she closed her eyes while letting me have my way. It was noisy, messy, and fucking wonderful. Excess saliva dribbled down her chin and dropped onto her silken blouse, the soft material becoming immediately darker. Hidden from sight except for the erect nipples poking against the smooth fabric, her perky tits moved freely and I wondered if she was wearing a bra. I watched Cindy move a hand between her thighs. Then it started moving vigorously and I smiled admirably at her sheer wantonness.

I continued fucking her mouth, sometimes pulling her head hard against my body, forcing my cock deeper. Apart from the occasional gurgle, Cindy made no sound but by the way she was violently fingering herself, I knew she was enjoying this as much, if not more than I was.

Suddenly I pulled out and grabbed my greasy manhood, watching her take some deep breaths. While she was looking up at me, panting heavily, I slapped my throbbing cock onto her upturned face, seeing how her saliva smeared her exquisite makeup. I don't know what turned me on the most; the fact that I was getting ready to shoot a load of spunk over her face or the fact she was dying for it.

I grabbed her hair again and buried my cock deep into her hot mouth. Instinctively knowing what I wanted, Cindy closed her eyes again and waited.

"Let me see your fucking ass, bitch. That's it, slut, pull them apart," I ordered. She immediately reached back, pulled her cheeks apart, and in the smoked glass cabinets, I saw the reflection of her exposed asshole. Then it occurred to me why Carl, The Worm, had chosen these cabinets. I briefly wondered how many willing sluts had been fucked here by him and couldn't help whistling. Looking at Cindy's reflection, I saw how shiny her asshole and thighs were and couldn't help grinning. As if reading my mind Cindy's starfish puckered and another glob of cum dribbled down towards the carpet.

This was such a turn on and I began fucking her face harder. How many cum stains were on the dark carpet, how many sluts had emptied their creamy deposit here and left it there, letting it dry into the woven material, making it almost impossible to remove. Guessing Cindy wasn't the first and wouldn't be the last I quickened my pace.

Expertly judging my condition, Cindy reached up, grabbed my balls, and squeezed, sending me spiraling over the edge. With her lips clamped around the base of my cock, I released another torrent of hot spunk into her body.

She gagged while swallowing and then moaned hungrily. I kept my cock where it was the whole time and watched in satisfaction how she didn't spill a drop from her lips, my spunk disappearing down her gullet. Her eyes were closed but I didn't care. She'd asked for and got what she wanted. She was a true cum slut.

I pulled out and watched her panting in front of me. Then I grabbed a fistful of her hair and pointed her head to look behind her.

"Look what a mess you've just made." She looked at the dark damp spot on the carpet and giggled wantonly. She turned and looked at me, a mischievous glint in her eyes. I grabbed her blond tresses and wrapped them around my cock and wiped it clean. I couldn't help smiling smugly as I saw her hair matting together from the combination of saliva and spunk, knowing she'd have to work the rest of the shift looking like that.

"This is good for my hair, right?" she asked, giggling again.

"That's right," I answered. "More natural than any other hair product." Her giggling started to annoy me so I silenced her by slapping my erection against her face. Taking her cue, Cindy began sucking me again. I watched as she cleaned my cock completely before letting her stand up. I watched her hitch up her jeans, once again admiring her body. My cock throbbed again and I knew I had to have her again. Once she was decent, she walked to the office door and opened it. Following her, I was surprised to see her hesitate before leaving.

"Next week?" she asked. Saying nothing I pressed my hand against her ass and pushed her out the door. She stared at me expectantly but I simply closed the door in her face.

John Smith's Rules on How to Be A Good Office Slave

● Make sure you keep the butt plug in place for the whole day, especially if your Master orders you to

● You are only allowed to release the pressure after notifying your Master. He will tell you exactly where and when to show up for the release

● Once at the determined spot, wait patiently, making sure you're on your knees, your hands holding your high heels, your mouth wide open and your tongue sticking out expectantly

● Your Master will push his cock inside your mouth and will fuck your face hard; remember, this is not an occasion for long and sensual lovemaking, especially when you're in a public place, being his slave, working for his pleasure

● Make sure you use a lot of saliva during the face fuck as it also acts as a lubricant later on; for good measure, try to coat his balls with it, especially if he makes you deepthroat him, pressing his cock balls deep into your mouth

● When your Master's cock is hard and wet enough, he will make you stand up and turn around; lean onto the window or mirror on the wall, based upon what he selected for a location

● Your Master will reveal your ass by lifting your skirt and pulling your panties down to your knees; only then will he pull the plug out of your ass and place it where you can see it - if you can lick it from this position, you will serve your Master better

• Your Master will enter your ass now. He will fuck you with quick, elaborate thrusts which you shall enjoy by leaning forward, arching your back, and closing your eyes

• Your Master will not ruin your clothes throughout this hardcore ass fucking; however, he may or may not slap your ass, based on how open the selected area is

• A few minutes will be enough for your Master to spray his hot seed into your asshole; make sure you milk his cock so you get every drop of sperm he has to offer

• He will pull out and quickly press the butt plug back into place to make sure not a drop of his fresh semen dribbles out; be careful not to move at all during this sensitive operation

• Readjust your thong and skirt and thank your Master for the precious gift to you

• Wear your butt plug proudly through the rest of the day!

How to Start Your Day in the Office

As usual, the door of my office opened but it wasn't Bonnie who entered, as she should have done this early in the morning. It was Alissa, the brunette bitch, from the service center.

"Hi...," I said, confused as to why she was here. "How can I help?"

"Hi right back at you," she replied huskily, carrying a silver tray with coffee, sugar, and milk. "Bonnie asked me to step in for her today because she had something to deal with, something personal."

"To step in..." I repeated unnecessarily. She nodded knowingly. I hadn't a clue what was going on and I wondered how much she knew about the morning ritual Bonnie and I took part in every morning. My mind pursued this train of thought while my eyes slowly inspected Alissa. I had to admit, she looked stunning, but then she always did. Her brown hair hung neatly around her cute cheeks and her eyes sparkled, but it was the playful smile that convinced me that she and Bonnie had few secrets. This happy thought was confirmed when she knelt down in front of me, after depositing the tray neatly on my desk.

"I know how you like your morning coffee, *Sir*," she said, smiling broadly, her agile fingers quickly opening my fly. I felt a lump in my throat, but that wasn't the only one I could feel. "And you've no idea how long I've wanted to do this," she continued as if nothing out of the ordinary was happening.

Really? Everyone's favorite beauty queen wanted to suck my cock? It seemed like a cheap porn scene but hey, who am I to argue. I decided to go with the flow.

Looking down, the opening in her blouse revealed not only her deep cleavage but also her beautiful apple-shaped tits. "Uh-huh," I've always admired those puppies. Luckily, she made no move to correct this oversight in her clothing, as she freed my cock and studied it carefully.

"Hmmm," she hummed, "Bonnie was right, it really is a nice one, isn't it?"

"Thank you, honey..."

"And I hope you taste as good as she promised," she said eagerly, interrupting me.

I swallowed hard while my heart raced. 'Did these girls really talk about the taste of cocks between themselves?' I wondered absently. 'Maybe I should hang out with them more often.

Alissa grinned like a hungry hyena, hungry for meat, while she held my rapidly swelling cock. She heard my surprised gasp, and her smile widened. "Can you imagine my surprise when Bonnie told me she was going Christmas shopping this morning? She couldn't have given me a better present if she'd tried."

"What about your fiancée?" I asked, recalling some vague office talk about her getting engaged recently.

"Hmm, let's just say I'm not prepared to go onto a strict diet right now." She replied, tightening her grip. "Why stick to one thing, when the menu looks so interesting? Her eyes shone like diamonds. "And I'm not averse to trying something different if you know what I mean..." Then she began rubbing my hard cock.

"Hmmm..." Her moan was truly erotic as she leaned forward, pressing her voluptuous breasts against my chair, and undid my belt. Pulling my pants and undershorts down my thighs, my cock sprang proudly in front of her face.

"Oh, my," she said playfully, gently rubbing the spongy head with her soft, dexterous fingers. "Someone's definitely pleased to see me."

I would have replied, but I was too busy moaning in ecstasy as this magnificent woman smeared my leaking pre-cum all over my throbbing member. When her thumb slipped around the sensitive ridge of my dome, I groaned again. Alissa really knew what she was doing. Pleased with my reaction, she held my dick like a greedy child would hold a lollipop and looked me in the eye. Then her beautifully made-up lips parted.

"Aaaahhhh!" I groaned loudly as her mouth enveloped my throbbing flesh. Her tongue flicked over my helmet before she started sucking. The inside of her glorious mouth felt incredible, like hot, wet, pulsating walls pressing down on my cock from all sides. It felt so good, I was surprised I didn't cum immediately. Without stopping for breath, Alissa took the whole length in her mouth, the muscles in the back of her throat squeezing my prick deliciously. Who could have guessed the innocent-looking beauty from the service center could deepthroat like a pro?

She raised her head, stopping when the tip was still buried between her full, gorgeous lips. Her tongue swirled around the ridge of my head, paying special attention to the most sensitive bit, just beneath the underside of the ridge. She swallowed me again, coating my member with saliva, and then used her tongue to mix our fluids. My prick throbbed powerfully, under her touch, and I couldn't contain myself any longer.

Deciding it was time Alissa learned how I really used Bonnie, I stood up abruptly, my movement sending the ergonomic chair crashing into the wall behind me. However, I was the surprised one. Without missing a beat, Alissa immediately grabbed my butt, her long nails digging sharply into my skin and pulled me forwards. Her boobs slapped against my legs as she moved back and forth, her mouth violently milking my cock. I ran my hands through her silky brown hair, combing it out with my fingers, gently playing with it while subtly holding her head in position. She groaned her approval.

Her tongue began swirling, licking, lathing layers of saliva onto me with renewed vigor and I pushed my hips forward. Another groan. I took this as a green light for some serious mouth fucking and grabbing her head, I thrust my cock as far down her throat as I could. She took it like a champion. In fact, she held me there, deep inside, her hands resting determinedly on my buttocks. Seconds later, I withdrew completely, an obscene plopping sound coming from her mouth. Panting heavily, she couldn't disguise her disappointment. She pouted.

"Hmmm, so far so good, Mr. Smith. Now please give it to me!"

"I'll give it to you, you dirty fucking bitch," I said, spanking my greasy cock over her upturned face. She giggled and closed her eyes as drops of saliva dripped from my cock onto her exquisitely made-up face. Greedily her mouth opened and I accepted her invitation. This time I didn't stop. My prick slid effortlessly between her lips, her tight throat swallowing time and time again my thick shaft. Despite a mouthful of cock, Alissa moaned lewdly, a sound that only increased my fervor. I felt my orgasm rapidly approaching as a tsunami of hot satisfaction spread throughout my loins from my dick.

"I'm going to cum!" I gasped, my spunk rising. Bonnie's substitute didn't blink at the news, as I felt my lust pass the point of no return. Her sharp, manicured fingernails pressed deeper into my ass, and she looked up at me with her big brown irises. Her intent was obvious. She applied vacuum-like suction to my cock, melting it, milking it, trying to ingest every inch. It was too much for me. Taking hold of her head, I stared at her and arched my back involuntarily. Then my hips bucked and I had the most intense orgasm of my life.

I groaned uncontrollably as huge wads of white-hot lust exploded from my cock, splattering the sides of her throat. Unable to contain myself, I kept spurting, string after string of thick creamy cum into Alissa's mouth, unloading everything I had. While my body shuddered, I looked down, enjoying the erotic sight in front of me. I'd never felt more alive than now, everything was intense. Her soft brown eyes seemed to memorize me, while the soft locks of hair entwined in my fingers felt like silk, she'd set for me. Her sharp fingernails gouged into my buttocks, causing me to gasp from the pain while her tongue sent shivers down my spine.

She sucked on my cock, her expert mouth extracting every tiny drop of cum she could, as I continued to unload. Finally, I was spent and my body gradually calmed down. Her eyes sparkled as she pulled away, a single string of cum hanging from her lips, still connecting us. Sluttishly, she opened her mouth, showing me the white, gooey deposit still there. Then she dipped her finger into it and slowly raised it in front of her face, her expression marveling at the sight. Then, determined to show how bad she really was, slowly closed her pink lips and swallowed.

"Wow," she giggled hungrily, "it really is as good as Bonnie claims." She swallowed again, the sight very arousing. I watched entranced, my cock rapidly hardening again, as she ran her fingers into her hair, the sperm adding an extra shine.

Then she stood up.

After adjusting her blouse, her hand flew to her mouth.

"Oh no, Mr. Smith," she said apologetically. "I forgot to finish the way Bonnie told me to." She winked saucily. "I know I was supposed to milk you into my coffee and use your cum like some creamer, but I was too greedy and swallowed it all. I hope you don't mind?"

No, I didn't mind it at all.

Long Time No See

Just after submitting my final report, my cell phone buzzed. Checking it, I found the caller was Megan. Strange – I haven't talked to her for years. So I thought, she's calling me to apologize, calling to ask me to forgive her. Forgive her for screwing me over and kicking me to the curb like a dog.

I checked my watch. Six-thirty PM. Time to go home. The last time I'd checked, it had been nine. I just decided to call Megan back to see what the hell she wanted after all those years when my cell buzzed again. It was on vibrate, sitting on my desk so I grabbed it and answered the call.

"Hello, Megan?"

"Hello," said a guy's voice. It made me pay more attention. The voice was low and husky, reminding me of beer. Lots of beer.

"Is this a certain John Smith?"

"Yeah, it is Ryan. Who's this?"

"The name is Ryan," the guy replied. "You don't know me, but I hope to change that soon."

What the hell was that throaty voice talking about? And why was he calling from Megan's cell?

"Are you there, John?"

"Yeah," I said. "I'm here. What are you talking about? Who are you?"

"I'm a friend of Megan's," he said, and he laughed out loud. "A very good friend, indeed," he added.

"Okay...," I said.

"And the fortunate events of tonight turned out so Megan needs you."

"Pardon?"

"That's right, John." He said in his creepy voice. "Let's just say she's... been a bad girl, that's why she's in trouble," he said, laughing.

"What the fuck?" I asked.

"Let me tell you a little more about myself, John. I'm a whiz master."

I blinked, not sure I'd heard him right.

"Uh, what did you say?"

That laugh again. "I'm a professional master of sex, John. Women come to me for manhandling, sometimes even humiliation. Do you have any problems with that?"

"No," I said, lying through my teeth.

"It's okay, I don't bite," he said, adding, "Unless the client asks me to."

I shook my head, saying, "So Megan has been behaving badly lately, and you're punishing her? And what are you calling me for, Ryan, or whatever your name is?"

"I'm calling because her punishment is not completed yet. And after I checked out her Facebook profile, I was wondering if you could help me as one of her oldest friends?"

I almost dropped the phone.

"Is this some kind of joke?" I asked angrily. "I haven't even talked to her for two years!"

Ryan spoke again, unruffled. His voice was as smooth as when I'd first answered the phone.

"No, John, it's not a joke. In fact, just the opposite."

I waited for him to go on, still not certain about what was really going on. But there was silence.

"Well?" I snapped. "Are you going to explain what that means?"

"It means that our little friend Megan was a bad girl and I need your help to punish the slutty little whore."

"What the fuck are you talking about?!"

"Calm down, man." The iron tone of command in his voice startled me.

"For what I know, you can be one of her friends," I said. "Trying to mess with my head."

"That's true, John, and there's no way for me to prove I'm not. Not at this point. But I think you're interested in what I have to say. Interested enough to keep talking, anyway. Am I right?"

I couldn't deny that I was curious now.

"And why did you choose me among her Facebook contacts?"

"I called you because I've seen some pics on her profile in which the two of you were smiling pretty happily. And I still got the feeling you wanted to fuck the hell out of her. So I thought you'll be the perfect choice to help me punish this slutty whore tonight. Am I right or am I right?"

He paused, and I heard noises in the background. They sounded like muffled thumps as if someone were moving furniture around.

When he spoke again it wasn't to me but to someone there with him. His voice sounded more distant as if he was facing away from the phone.

"Stop moving, slut! If you do that again, I'll put the nipple clamps back on!"

"What the hell?" I thought.

"My apologies, John. Megan hasn't stopped... misbehaving." Another chuckle. "Anyway, another thing you probably don't know about your ex is that she is a submissive. That means-"

"I know what it means," I said. "She's there? Prove it. Put her on the phone."

"Of course. She's restrained right now, so I'll bring the phone to her."

I heard some steps on a hard floor. Then Ryan spoke again.

"I'm going to remove your gag for a moment, bitch. Your ex-boyfriend is on the phone, and he'd like some kind of proof that you're actually here."

I heard muffled grunts, the sound of a catch being unfastened, and heavy breathing.

Then Megan's voice spoke, and there was no mistake: the sultry voice that aroused me so well back then.

"Master, may I speak?" she said.

"Yes, bitch, you may speak," answered Ryan. "Talk to the phone. Tell us what a filthy little submissive slut you are."

Megan's voice again, much closer to the phone, right in my ear. "I'm a filthy little submissive slut."

Holy shit, I thought. That's Megan on the other end of the line, saying shit about herself.

"Again, louder," said Ryan sharply, in the background.

"I'm a filthy little submissive slut!" said Megan, loud enough to make me hold the phone away from my ear. But damned if I wasn't enjoying this! The bitch I always wanted to fuck was degrading herself right here over the phone. I suddenly noticed that my cock was more than shifting in my pants now; it was fucking rock hard. My balls felt swollen, and there was a faint ache starting deep in my groin.

After a moment, Ryan came back on.

"Megan visits me from time to time and tells me all her sins I should punish her for. When I poked around in her Facebook profile and saw your pics, I thought you would lend an ideal helping hand to punish her this time."

"Well, that's very generous of you," I said, wanting to sound snarky, but my voice sounded a little shaky in my own ears.

"Yes, I think so," said Ryan seriously. "Wait a minute."

I heard the sound of those heavy steps again, and he came back a minute later.

"I went to another room. I don't want Megan to hear this. She is restrained and completely helpless." He paused, letting that sink in. "And, she is blindfolded so she won't know it's you unless you choose to reveal your identity."

My dick was throbbing now. The thought of fucking Megan, or making her blow me, or doing any number of other things to her while she was tied up almost made me cream my jeans.

Ryan continued. "Megan will think you're a total stranger, brought in to use her for his pleasure as part of her sub training. That last part is true, by the way. If you take me up on my offer, it will kill two birds with one stone. You can fuck her as you wish, and I'll be able to put her through an important stage of her training program."

Training program, I thought. He takes this shit seriously.

I was silent for almost a minute.

"John? Are you interested?" Ryan said.

"Fuck, yes, I'm interested."

"Good! Can you come now?"

"Yeah." I would have rescheduled anything for this crazy adventure if I had anything planned.

He gave me the address and told me to be there in an hour.

****

The address was in the industrial part of town, in a block of warehouses that seemed to stretch for miles. After some searching, I finally found the right building. It was completely nondescript - no business name on the door, no signs on the front, no indication that it was occupied at all.

The parking lot was nearly deserted except for a green Jeep Cherokee. I parked next to it, killed the engine, got out, and locked the car, making sure the anti-theft system was on. Then I walked to the rusty door with the address Ryan had given me printed on it. There was a doorbell and I pushed the button. I didn't hear anything from inside the building. The door didn't open. I waited a bit, then hit the doorbell again. Still nothing. There was silence except for the faint buzz of the parking lot lights. I banged on the glass door hard enough to make it rattle in its frame.

"I'm here!" I heard the guy's voice from the other side of the door. After some clicking the door opened and there was Ryan. He was a tall muscular man, at least five-ten, square-shouldered. He was wearing plain jeans and a dirty singlet, just like Bruce Willis in the Die Hard movies. He had black rubber boots on his feet.

He looked behind me, checked out the parking lot, then nodded and let me in. He immediately closed and locked the door behind me.

"John?" he asked. His voice was much more powerful in person.

"Uh...yeah, I'm John Smith," I said, looking around. "Where is Megan?"

"I'm Ryan, your Master for tonight," he said jokingly and offered his hand. I took his hand and shook it. His grip was strong and straight.

"Well," he said in a businesslike tone. "Shall we?" He gestured to an open inner door.

I nodded and stepped through. Ryan came through behind me and closed the door.

We were in the kitchen. It was just as messy as the lobby, with unwashed tableware and empty pizza boxes everywhere. A typical bachelor flat.

"A beer?" he offered, pointing to a chair at the kitchen table.

"Yeah, why not," I nodded. He opened the fridge and took out two bottles. "I only have Rolling Rock. Do you mind?"

"Not at all," I said, taking the bottle he offered. He opened both of them with a Rolling Rock branded bottle opener, then he said, "Cheers!" and drank a huge one. "Fuck, I needed that," he said. "Your friend Megan has drained me for good," he said and laughed.

"Is she okay?" I asked, still not sure what to think about this crazy guy.

"Sure she is, don't worry!" He nodded and sat on the other chair. "You arrived just in time, I needed some rest after the first round of her punishment. Are you ready to jump in?"

"Actually, I have to tell you probably have the wrong impression," I said. "The thing is, we have never been together with Megan."

He looked at me, thinking, then asked,

"What about your pictures where you are together?"

"I have always had a crush on her but she hasn't accepted my feelings," I admitted. "I was in her friend zone for a while but got bored of it so I stopped getting in touch with her."

"Then this time you can make your dreams come true, right?" he said, grinning.

I nodded. "Yeah. I guess..."

"So are you in?"

"I'm definitely in!"

"Good!" he said and finished his beer. I did the same while he stood up and opened a grey locker room in the corner. He took out a matching pair of black boots.

"Take that goddamn suit off," he said. "And put these on."

It was strange to get naked in front of this strange guy but I decided I would play by ear. So I put my suit and shirt on a hanger, got naked quickly, and put on those pair of rubber boots. They were perfect on my feet which made me wonder what other sizes we share. Well, I will find out soon.

"Oh, I almost forgot," he added. "Put these on." And he handed a gas mask over. He shrugged when he saw me hesitating. "I know, it's crazy but the bitch likes it. Plus, it will hide exactly who you are."

Both of us put on a mask and I took some deep breaths. The filters were working perfectly – the air felt even cleaner through them.

Ryan stepped to a metal door in the wall and swung it open. Behind the door, in a large room, blindfolded and bound tightly to a small ordinary workbench, was Megan. She was nude and tied down in a doggy position, her wrists and ankles tightly bound in place by big leather cuffs with heavy buckles. There was even a black collar on her neck. Her legs, spread wide, left her pussy and bare ass completely vulnerable, open to any kind of use or abuse. To complete the scene, there was a table beside her laid out with an assortment of whips, crops, canes, dildos, and other toys.

Megan was moaning softly when the door opened, but when she heard it, she looked at us and started speaking.

"Master? Is that you? God, who is this guy with you? We haven't agreed on anything like this! Will you untie me? Please?"

She was whining. Ryan, who was standing just behind me, said loudly "Shut your filthy little cocksucking mouth, slut. Just for speaking without permission, you'll get ten extra slaps which will be performed by our guest star here."

Megan groaned and I could see a glimpse of happiness in her eyes.

"Yes, I have the guest I promised you." Ryan went on, grinning. "His identity is not for you to know unless he chooses to tell you. He may be someone you know. He could just as easily be a stranger."

Ryan walked slowly into the room until he was directly in front of Megan, his belly touching Megan's hair. He leaned down to her and kissed Megan deeply for several seconds, running his strong fingers up and down Megan's cheek and neck. I could hear Megan whining softly during the kiss, like a small animal trying to get to a delicious piece of food that was just out of reach.

Finally, Ryan broke the kiss, leaving Megan panting. I stepped closer and noticed her pussy leaking some white fluid.

"Our guest has just noticed what a filthy whore you are, having fresh cum leaking out of your pussy." Ryan said to her. "Tell him, whose cum is that?"

"It's yours, Master," she answered. "You have just fucked me hard and you came so big I can't keep it in my pussy."

"That's right, bitch," he said, pulling her ass cheeks apart so I had a better view of her pussy and the cum dripping out of it. "You had aroused me so much I came in gallons. Do you like the view, stranger?"

"Hell yeah," I answered. My voice sounded pretty strange under the mask.

"Now I give my permission to this stranger to use your body for the evening in any way he chooses. You will not be able to stop him. You will not be able to protect yourself. You will not even be able to see him. He will have total mastery over you until the session is complete. Do you understand, slut?"

"Yes, master," Megan said softly.

Ryan leaned closer to Megan's face.

"Louder."

"Yes, master, I understand!"

"Good. I will turn you over to our guest now."

Ryan turned away from Megan and walked back to me. I was still standing in the doorway. Ryan patted Megan hard on her bare naked ass cheek and whispered, "Enjoy it, baby!"

By this time, my cock was rock-hard and pulsing heavily, and my balls felt swollen with cum. My heart raced and my breath had become ragged. As I stared at Megan's helpless form strapped to the workbench and her pussy spread wide open, I was tempted to fuck the shit out of her right then and there. It would have been so easy; just bend a little at the knees, position my cockhead against her pussy lips, and thrust upward.

I managed to resist this impulse. I wanted to have fun with her, toy with her, and make her feel some humiliation and helplessness.

"Hello," said Megan timidly. "Are you there? Who are you?" She sounded scared. Good, I thought.

I didn't speak but made sure she was aware of my presence by walking slowly and deliberately closer to her. The floor was bare concrete, and my footsteps in the rubber boots sounded loud in the small room. Megan turned her head to figure out how close I was; I could see her eyeing me up and down to guess who I could be, but she couldn't. I stopped about five feet behind her, and just stood there for a moment. I could feel Megan's excitement.

"Hello?" Her voice was quavering now. "Hello? Sir? Please say something! Please! Who are you?"

I said nothing, but instead inspected her ass and pussy.

"You like what you see?" Ryan asked, then spanked Megan's ass again. She hissed but stayed silent.

"Do you have any lubricants?" I asked Ryan.

"Why?" he asked. "You don't find her pussy wet enough?" he said, pointing to the cum dripping out of her pussy. "Wait... You mean you don't like sloppy seconds?"

"Not really," I admitted. "Besides, I always liked her ass..."

"Good point," Ryan said and I could swear he was grinning behind his mask. He took out a small bottle of lubricant from his pocket. He was surely prepared. Megan let out an incoherent cry of panic followed by a flood of words.

"Oh, God, please, Sir, please, I'm begging you, please not my ass, please don't, oh, fuck I'll do anything, oh, please, oh fuck..."

"Be quiet, bitch." Ryan said. "Our special guest has my permission to ass-fuck you tonight, and you will take it like the good whore you are. And you will thank him afterward. And, you'll remain quiet while he does it." said, stepping to her face. "Fuck she's so hot I'm hard again."

He opened his jeans and quickly pushed them down. My guess was right: his cock was about the same size as mine, but his body was more muscular in general and this was true for his abdomen, as well. He quickly grabbed Megan's face and pushed his rock-hard cock into her wet mouth. It forced her lips to stretch open wider than I would have thought possible. Megan's eyes bulged and drool almost immediately began to leak from around the cock. I could hear her trying to make noise, but the hard tool muffled it almost completely.

"There," said Ryan, admiring his work. "That should keep the little slut from bothering you. Now, take her asshole, man."

He didn't need to tell me twice. I stood directly behind her, legs on either side of hers, my cock just inches from her asshole. Her little rosebud was pink and clean, puckered like a tiny mouth that had just eaten something sour.

I got the pad of my thumb wet by slipping it onto her anus gently and began to massage it softly, trying to loosen it up a little. It was locked up tighter than a bank vault. After a few circles, I began to feel her sphincter muscle relax a tiny bit.

"That's right, you little whore, open up that sweet ass for me," I said. I pushed a little harder with my thumb and heard Megan gasp through cock in her mouth.

"He's going to ass-fuck you now," he said matter-of-factly. "For as long as he likes. He is going to blow his load into your ass. When this is done, you will thank him for it. If not, you'll pay the price. Understood?"

Megan nodded weakly.

By this point my dick was oozing precum and pointing to the ceiling, bobbing and twitching. I poured some lubricant between her ass cheeks and inserted my index finger into her rectum. I slowly but firmly pressed my finger inside her. Her hands flexed involuntarily. I finished by doing a small circle inside her asshole, making her gasp.

Okay, I thought, time to get down to it.

I waited a few seconds, letting her get used to the feeling of my finger in her ass. Then, I pressed deeper. She screamed, trying to struggle against the unyielding restraints. I pushed in really deep, and I worked my hand around in a small circle to map her tight hot rectum. She whimpered in response.

"Fuck!" she yelled, her fingers convulsing again.

After a few seconds, I pressed deeper, this time to the hilt. She shrieked; I watched her body stretch and bend deliciously.

"Oh, God, please tell me who you are!" she begged.

"She's tight, isn't she?" Ryan asked, totally ignoring her pleas.

"She sure is," I said and started really enjoying the game. "Thanks for not stretching her out."

"Sure man," Ryan laughed, patting me on my shoulder.

Slowly, deliberately, I started fingering her. Her asshole felt really tight and hot on my finger. Ryan watched it, then, without warning, spanked her ass cheeks hard.

"Ahhhh, God!" Megan screamed. "Please! Who are you? Tell me who you are!"

It was my turn to laugh out loud. I really enjoyed this horny bitch lying in front of me, on this dirty workbench after so many years dreaming of fucking her. When I woke up this morning, I wouldn't have imagined I would finger her ass tonight. And yet here I was, Megan whining with her asshole on my finger and this crazy stranger slapping her ass hard.

I poured some lubricant into my middle finger and pressed it into Megan's hot asshole along with my index finger. Her breath was coming in short, panicky gasps now. Sweat trickled down her face and chest. I watched with fascination as a drop of sweat rolled down her right tit and perched on the end of one swollen nipple.

"Man, I like your work!" Ryan laughed and offered me a high five. I couldn't help taking it and found myself laughing. This guy could be crazy but I had the fun of my life for sure.

"I think you'd loosened her up already," Ryan said. "Go ahead and fuck that ass!"

He took out a condom from his pocket and tossed it to me over Megan's body. I quickly pulled out my fingers from the girl's hot asshole, opened the condom up, and pulled it on my throbbing member. I could hear Megan gag and moan with her mouth on Ryan's cock while I was adjusting the rubber on my cock.

It was time for me to switch gears so I poured some lubricant on my condom-covered throbbing cock, and pulled her round ass cheeks apart. I touched her asshole with the head of my cock. She wanted to say something but Ryan's cock in her mouth muffled her voice.

"That's it, man!" Ryan ordered, pushing his cock deep into her mouth. "Fuck her ass!"

I placed my swollen cockhead against her asshole and began to push. It only took a few moments before her ass relaxed a bit and my head popped in. When it did, I heard what was probably a scream but came out as a faint whine thanks to Ryan's cock. The feel of her sphincter clenched tight around the base of my cockhead was absolutely incredible. Goddamn, but she was tight!

Slowly, gently, I continued to push. The lube reduced the friction a lot, but I could still feel that tight ring of muscle gripping my shaft as it went in deeper. Megan's screams turned to moans, and her hips squirmed.

I slapped her ass hard. "Stop moving."

She obeyed immediately. I kept pushing until my shaft was buried in her rectum to the balls. Then I slipped it back out until the head was the only part still inside her. After waiting a few seconds, letting the time drag out, letting Megan's apprehension build, I shoved back in with a sharp thrust. Megan's head jerked back in response, making her hair fly. I slapped her ass again, and again. I alternated cheeks, each time aiming at one of the slutty little tattoos.

A savage rhythm established itself. Thrust in, smack, pull out, smack, repeat. The pleasure coursing through my cock was beyond belief. Meanwhile, Ryan was enjoying the hot wetness of her mouth.

I began to thrust harder and faster, and I realized Megan was moving her hips in sync with me. Every time I pushed in, she arched her hip upward as much as her restraints would allow. I realized she was trying to let me in even deeper. She wanted more of me in her ass. She was loving it!

I spanked her ass again, and she screamed louder this time. Then I waited several long seconds, enjoying the way Megan's panting became gasping, and listening to the low keening sound that had started in her throat. She probably wasn't even aware she was making the noise, I thought.

I began to fuck her ass with long, hard thrusts. My cock slipped in balls deep again and again. Her keening became louder and turned into a continuous whine, interspersed with barely intelligible pleas for mercy. Her entire body jittered in the tight restraints, spit-roasted between the two hard cocks. Her face began to turn bright red. Ryan fucked her face just as I did her ass. I watched his balls hitting her jaw again and again.

The whole situation was so hot I decided to go one level further. I pulled out and enjoyed a bit how her asshole gaped in front of my eyes. Then I pulled down my rubber and tossed it on Megan's sweaty back. In my fantasies, I always fucked her bareback – why not right now?

It was such a great feeling entering her hot, slippery, tight asshole with my naked cock. Although she was loosened up nicely from the hard fucking I gave to her, her asshole still gripped my cock tightly. I had to sigh out, it felt so good.

"That's right, little slut, you're spit-roasted," Ryan said as a matter of fact. "A stranger on one end and your Master on the other. And you're going to take it like a good whore."

Megan nodded frantically, her hair flying up and down. I reached out and grabbed a handful of it and yanked back, hard. Megan cried out in pain. Her head was now tilted back at an uncomfortable angle, but it gave Ryan full access to Megan's mouth.

"Thank you, man! What a nice gesture! Keep her head just like that!"

"No problem," I said. I twisted a loop of hair through my fist and held onto it as I began to fuck Megan in earnest, ramming my shaft in and out of her tight ass, feeling my balls slap her wet pussy every time I pushed in. Megan arched her hips into each thrust, greedily trying to get even more of me inside her slutty little ass. I buried my cock as deep inside her as it would go, forcing little screams from her mouth with every thrust.

"She's enjoying your cock in her ass!" said Ryan. "Very nice job, buddy!"

I didn't answer; I was too busy wallowing in the intense pleasure of having my cock squeezed and massaged by those tightly toned ass muscles. It was taking all of my willpower not to cum yet.

Ryan was face-fucking Megan in earnest now. The bitch probably gagged every time the big cock went in. Ryan had Megan's head between her hands, holding it perfectly still, making her a passive receptacle, completely helpless to resist having her mouth violated. But I could tell by the tightness around my cock that this little bitch loved being treated like this.

Ryan and I got a nice rhythm going so that Megan had a cock deeply inserted into her at all times. She rocked her body back and forth on the workbench, as much as the restraints would allow, trying to maximize the pleasure of each thrust into her ass and mouth. Her moans turned into screams of ecstasy, combined with whimpered pleadings to fuck her harder and faster. I was deliberately fucking at only a moderate pace, to keep her from cumming. I also wasn't touching her clit, except for the slapping it was receiving from my swollen balls. It must have been driving her fucking crazy. I knew how badly she needed to cum.

In the middle of this ass fucking I saw Ryan strip off his dirty singlet. Without breaking the face-fucking rhythm, he pulled it over his head, swiped the sweat off his forehead with it, and then let it fall to the floor.

I grabbed Megan's swollen breasts and started fucking her hard. I really enjoyed the sensation of her hot rectum on my naked cock and her wet pussy touching my balls at each thrust. I straightened up, fucked her hard and deep, grabbed the condom from her back, and spanked her with it. She laughed out hard but her voice was muffled by Ryan's cock again, and even turned to serious moaning as I entered her ass again and again. She gasped for breath. Sweat poured freely down her body. Drops of it sprinkled the concrete floor beneath her.

Ryan let his cock out of her mouth and slapped her cheeks with it.

"Oh, fuck, please, please tell me who you are!" Megan begged. "I can't fucking stand it, you can do anything you want to me, just please say something!"

I observed her while I was pounding her tight ass. Tight, toned, athletic body; long brown hair, now dark with sweat; cute sorority-girl face with perfectly even, white teeth; firm B-cup tits; long, sexy legs. She'd been quite a catch, I thought, the hottest chick at the university where we'd both studied. I remembered how hard it felt to be in her friend zone. Now I knew that she got off on kinky stuff like domination or threesomes.

I threw the wet, sloppy condom on Megan's back and fucked her with abandon. Ryan smeared his pre-cum and her saliva all over her cheeks making her look like a bitch in heat while I was pounding her ass hard. I could feel the heat coming from her sweating body. Hair hung down across her eyes.

I slapped across her ass cheeks as I was fucking her. She drew in a sharp gasp, and her neck and cheeks began to flush under Ryan's cock. My hand left a bright red mark.

"Oooohhhh...," moaned. "Ohhhmmmmm..."

Ryan even pushed his balls between Megan's panting lips and let her suck them. He was watching me pounding the brunette's ass and although I couldn't see under his mask, I could swear he was grinning.

"Wanna DP her, man?" he asked.

"Sure!" I said quickly and pulled out. Megan's asshole was gaping again, as though missing my cock. Ryan leaned down and opened the cuffs on her hands and ankles. Megan stood up slowly, her whole body was trembling. The condom fell on the floor.

"Are you ready for your well-earned sandwich, bitch?" Ryan asked, looking deep into her eyes from under the mask.

"Yessss....." she hissed.

"Good little bitch," Ryan said and pulled a finger over her face. Then pulled out a dirty mattress and leaned on his back. "Come and sit on my lap!" he ordered Megan. She quickly obeyed which made me guess this wasn't the first time she was punished by this crazy "Master".

"Mmmmppphh!" she cried when his cock entered her dripping-wet pussy.

"Shit I like sloppy seconds," Ryan moaned. "Come on, man, let's give this bitch a serious double fucking!"

I knelt behind Megan and admired her luscious body again. I knew right then I would remember this evening for the end of my life. But Ryan didn't let me daydream about her: he pulled her ass cheeks apart for me to enter her asshole which looked so inviting. So I pushed my cock head to her rectum and slowly entered her again. This time, her hole felt even tighter with Ryan's cock present in her pussy.

"Mmmpphhhh!" she moaned out loud, closing her eyes shut. "Ohhhhhh!"

"Yeah?" I said, laughing. "Yeah? You like two cocks in your body?"

"It's.... fucking great..." she moaned, still with eyes shut.

"You seem to really enjoy it, slut," Ryan said, slapping her ass cheeks. "Do you enjoy two men double fucking you?" Slap. "You don't even care who..." slap "the other guy is?" slap.

"Just.... fuck me...," she moaned and it was my turn to slap her ass which I happily did. I entered her hot ass balls deep, grabbing her breasts and pounding her again and again. She began to moan and whine, letting her body be completely used by us. Ryan started fucking her pussy hard and I tried to adjust my movement to his thrusts. He went on talking dirty to her and slapping her round ass cheeks.

"That's right, baby," slap "Take our cocks." slap. "You need this." slap. "Just enjoy it." Slap.

"Ohhhhh...," she moaned again and again. "Ohhhh..."

Her hands were grabbing the dirty mattress and trying to hold herself steady. Her feet wriggled like trapped little animals.

I counted out fifteen thrusts, then stayed steady in her ass, feeling Ryan pounding her pussy from below. I kept my cock balls deep in her hot ass for a while, then started moving again. She started moaning again immediately. The suction of her asshole around my cock felt fucking amazing. My cock was throbbing and quivering.

I counted fifteen thrusts again then stopped moving. Megan let out whooping gasps, filled to her limits. Her face was red and sweaty.

"Do you like being double fucked, Megan?" I asked and spanked her ass again. "Does it feel good?"

"Fuck meeeeeaaaahhh...," she moaned as an answer.

I pulled my cock out but left my head in, and started fucking her with small, powerful thrusts, counting 'till twenty this time, enjoying the feel of her hot ass. More whooping gasps. Her chest heaved, making her titties jiggle nicely.

"You're really a bitch," I admitted. "I never guessed you are such a dirty whore."

"Who..." thrust "are..." thrust... "you?" she asked, still panting.

"Someone who has really wanted to fuck your ass for a long time now...," I said, fucking her in unison with Ryan. "Someone who really enjoys fucking you now...," slap.

Still panting, Megan turned around and tried to check out my face under the mask.

"God...," thrust, "if I knew...," thrust "I would...," thrust "have done...," thrust "anything..."

"It's too late, bitch," I said and slapped her ass again, making her moan out loud. "Now take my cock in your ass like a pro!"

She leaned back on Ryan, closed her eyes, and enjoyed the serious fucking we gave her. I shoved two fingers into her mouth and forced it open, letting her saliva pour on Ryan's mask. She couldn't move too much; we were fucking here like wild animals. I slid my length all the way into her ass again and again and felt Ryan doing the same in her pussy.

"Take it, bitch," I hissed into her ears, "Take it all."

That's when she turned her head back, looking into my eyes again. I let my cock stay buried in her ass for a minute, savoring the tightness. Then I withdrew until just the head.

"Yeah, that's right. You like my cock, don't you?"

"Yess...," she moaned and pushed herself back onto my cock.

"You really are a cock loving bitch, baby," I said and began to thrust in and out again, fucking her ass with my last power. She was helpless to resist it.

"Oh, fuck!" she yelled. "Oh fuck, fuck, fuck, please fuck me deep with that fucking thing!"

I obeyed her with all my heart and fucked her ass deep. Every time my cock went balls deep into her asshole, there was a little splashing sound. I fucked her faster, enjoying the sound and the hot feeling of her ass. All the time this was happening, Megan was whimpering from deep in her chest, whimpering in enjoying fucked to the limit.

I could feel Ryan fastening up. He pulled the mask off of his face.

"Fuck I could hardly breathe in this thing," he moaned, enjoying Megan's hot pussy. He threw the mask away, saying, "I don't need it anyway," and grabbed Megan's waist, moaning out loud, adding a new dose of load into her pussy with strong, powerful jerks.

The noises she was making changed, and her thighs began to quiver. I knew she was close so I fucked her as hard as I could.

"Please, please, don't stop guys, please make me cum, oh fuck, please make me cum," Megan begged softly. "Yeeaaahh...," she cried out loud and had her own orgasm. Her whole abdomen was pulsing and getting tighter. Her red nails dived into the grey mattress and she trembled heavily.

I decided this was my moment. I pulled off my mask and threw it on the floor, near the lonely condom lying there. Megan noticed it and glanced back above her shoulder.

"John!" she recognized me instantly. "How did you...?"

She didn't have the time to ask her question; this sudden revelation pulled my trigger. I thrust my cock deep into her hot ass and came a huge one. I pushed her head down on Ryan's chest and thrust a few last ones as I shot wave after wave into her body.

Slowly, gradually, the ecstasy faded into a warm glow. I felt my cock begin to soften and pulled it out of Megan's asshole.

All three of us laid down next to each other on the dirty mattress, trying to catch our breaths. Ryan got back first, stood up, and hurried out of the room. Megan and I remained there, face-to-face with each other. Her face was deeply flushed from pleasure, looking beautiful. She had a glimpse of lust in her eyes as she was moaning softly.

"I didn't think it was you," she panted and looked deep into my eyes.

"Well, I didn't think I would have a chance until my phone rang tonight," I admitted. "But I enjoyed it like hell."

"Me, too," she nodded. " Thank you for ass-fucking me! You had a wonderful stamina, John. It felt incredible! If I knew it back then…" she said softly.

Yeah, it would have been nice, I thought. But I didn't want to go down that road. Instead, I pointed at my cock, saying, "Here's something you still have to clear, honey."

She smiled and knelt up immediately. I could see her pussy and ass, both dripping fresh white cum. She was oozing slick warmth there.

"Your holes are fucking sopping!" I said while she was leaning on my cock and took it deep between her lips. Her mouth got stuffed with my dripping cock, so she was unable to answer.

That's when Ryan returned. He was holding an open bottle of beer in his hand.

"That's it, bitch, clean that cock!" He said, grinning, as he leaned to the door frame. Megan quickly ran her tongue all over my cock, making sure she licked up and swallowed every drip of my cum.

I really enjoyed the feeling of her pinky tongue on my throbbing tool but it went kind of sensitive after all the hard ass fucking I gave her. So I withdrew my dick. Megan panted heavily, her mouth hanging open, and drool fell to the mattress in long strings.

"You still want cock, bitch?" Ryan asked. "Hell I already came twice in you today but I'm gonna fuck your face anyway."

He quickly stepped next to the mattress and shoved his already hard cock into Megan's mouth which she happily accepted, even moaned taking it between her lips. As she leaned on Ryan's cock, I could see our cum dripping out of her pussy and ass to the mattress. It ran through my mind how much cum this mattress had to drink up in the past.

I stepped back and watched Megan being face fucked by this stranger Ryan. He just pulled his cock out, leaving a trace of saliva and cum hanging between his cock head and her lips.

"Open wide," he ordered. She stretched her mouth as wide as it would go. He examined it like a doctor then nodded, and shoved back in, and resumed the face-fucking. She looked amazing on her knees, sucking like a horny bitch.

They didn't seem to care about me now that I didn't participate in the act. Megan moaned and sighed during the hard face fucking she got from Ryan. I had to admit he had good stamina and as they were moving like a well-oiled machine together, I realized he was really a match for her. He could really satisfy her needs and maybe this crazy guy was exactly the one Megan needed.

I walked back to the kitchen and dressed up. As I finished, I looked back into the other room. Megan whimpered on her knees, with Ryan's cock balls deep in her throat and Ryan was pouring beer on her hair. The white bubbles soaked her brown hair and she giggled with the cock muffling her voice. Ryan drank another gulp from the beer, then threw the empty bottle on the mattress, and asked, "What did you say?"

He pulled out of Megan's mouth. She took a deep breath, and answered,

"Piss on me!"

At first, I thought I misunderstood it but Ryan just laughed out loud and pointed his cock to her breasts. He was clearly struggling to be able to piss through his erection. She laughed, too, and slapped his cock. Ryan grabbed her hair and made her stay right in front of his cock. He was aiming again and this time he managed to let out a thick stray of piss on her breasts. I watched the light yellow liquid pouring down on Megan's hard nipples, red breasts, flat belly, and on her dripping pussy. He pissed so much it was actually washing down sweat and cum off her body, right into the dirty mattress.

Megan reached down, smeared some of the remaining cum on her clit, and started rubbing it in small circular motions.

"You liked it, baby?" Ryan asked, panting and spanking her cheeks with his hard cock.

"Yes," she said immediately. "Now fuck my face..."

"What did you say, bitch?" Ryan said loudly, slapping her cheek with his cock again.

"I said... fuck my face properly, Master! Please..."

"That's better," Ryan said. "You have to know who the boss is around here."

I felt it was time for me to leave. I closed the door behind me and went straight to my car. I sat behind the wheel and took a last glance at the old warehouse. Then opened the gallery on my phone and ran through the few pics I had shot about Megan and the crazy Ryan. It felt so unbelievable to sit there after I just fucked this bitch I longed for so long. I wouldn't have imagined this today afternoon, sitting in the office.

Hell, I will never forget this evening.

At the Hairdresser

This other man and I were sitting at the hairdresser's, waiting to begin something none of us had ever tried before. I wasn't too well acquainted with the man across from me, but he was Bonnie's ex, Steve, the one before me. She told me about a few occasions the two of them had sex, which I found really exciting and made me horny every time she brought them up. As we were always joking about having a threesome, I thought her ex could be a perfect choice for it: he had already proved to be a match for Bonnie sexually, and he had a private place (the beauty shop) where we could do it, and he could easily be convinced to join us.

So there I was, on a rainy autumn day, anxiously waiting for Bonnie as she was preparing in the staff room.

The wheels had been in motion for the most memorable night of my life for a week. I just had to find out this guy's number and talk to him briefly. He was in from the start, I didn't even have to explain the details.

"Whatever you want, man," he said. So I only had to finalize it with Bonnie to have a plan for a hot evening of dirty sex. I was excited at the prospect of finally being able to double fuck my lovely girlfriend.

We arrived by a cab after a long and silent drive. Bonnie had an elegant black coat on, revealing her perfect thighs and the black sexy high heels. I couldn't help fantasizing about how we will fuck her tonight.

"So you're John." The guy shook my hand after we entered the beauty shop and closed the door behind us. We entered the shop and watched as Steve turned the "CLOSED" sign over and put up the shutter. Then he turned to us and greeted Bonnie with a kiss on her cheek.

"Long time no see," he said to her, causing me instant jealousy. "So you really want to do this?" he asked both of us. Bonnie turned to me, with a shy smile.

"Sure," I said, nodding and swallowing hard.

"That's great!" he said and stepped to the mirror. There was champagne in ice there which he opened quickly.

"I've prepared for this," he said, pouring some champagne for us and said, "Cheers!" We were all smiling and drinking.

"John here told me about the threesome the two of you planned," Steve said. "But we didn't really have the time for details. So... what are the rules?"

"Well... what kind of rules?" Bonnie asked.

"You know, you've probably talked this over. What's in it for you, and for you," he pointed to Bonnie and me one by one. "What is your thing in it? What makes you excited?"

"I think the whole idea is exciting for us," Bonnie told him. "And as for the rules, there aren't any."

"So everything is free?"

"Absolutely."

"I can do whatever I want?"

Bonnie looked at me, again, for approval.

"Yes, Steve," I answered. "You can do whatever you want."

He checked her out again.

"Can I fuck her any way I like?"

"That's right."

"What if I wish to cum at a certain place on her body?"

"Then you do."

Steve nodded, smiling, and put down his glass.

"So," he said after a moment of silence, "how shall we proceed?"

We both looked over to Bonnie, the sole attraction, who took off her coat so her sexy body with her hot lingerie came into full view.

Bonnie clearly prepared for this dirty occasion, as her body was covered in a knee-length pair of black stockings with matching bra and panties. Her red polished, pedicured toenails peeked out from the six-inch black high heels she balanced on, matching her manicured fingernails. Her heels clacked on the hardwood floor as she made her way toward us. Her grin was seductive and eager but it also betrayed her nerves as she strutted to her fate.

The halves of the bra, trimmed in fluffy black, met diagonally in the middle of her chest where they were tied together with a red silk bow, revealing her huge cleavage.

"Let me show this gorgeous body off," I said. Bonnie stood there, proud of being the subject of our desire.

Never more aroused in my life, did I start presenting my girlfriend to her ex just like a piece of art on an auction. A beautiful, yet dirty sculpture.

"Look at her pretty face," I started, pulling Bonnie's brown hair away from her face. "I have always liked her smile."

"And I liked her cheeks," Steve added.

"You liked to spray your cum on it?" I asked provocatively.

Steve smiled and asked, "So she told you?"

"Of course. Every single detail."

He was laughing, and I went on showing Bonnie's breasts.

"Look at her breasts," I said, pressing them together with my palms. "Look how luscious and perfect they are."

"Yeah...," Steve said, and I could see his jaw stretching so I thought he was starting to get really excited. So I pushed Bonnie's tits together and squeezed them a bit.

"Turn around," I told Bonnie and as she did, I presented her backside to my fellow for this night.

"Look at this ass," I showed her butt. "Round, firm cheeks. They are so hard you could break a nut on them." I said and slapped her ass cheeks loud and hard. Bonnie hissed a bit but didn't say a word.

"Still the same," Steve said and reached out and slapped Bonnie's other ass cheek, causing her to giggle this time. She was looking back at us, smiling and biting on her finger. This made her look even more like a porn star.

"Spread your ass for us, my sweet little bitch!" I ordered her. She did and my eyes were glued on the black panty hiding her moist pussy and dark asshole just in front of us.

Soon, her ex and I were naked, our cocks free at full mast, and we escorted Bonnie to the large chair in which the hairdresser usually cuts hair. I planned another usage for it tonight.

We made her sit down in that massive chair, she was still looking very sexy while still wearing the heels, thong, and bra. I could barely take in how hot she was at that moment, preparing for the hardcore fucking she was here for.

We wasted no time, getting right to it as Bonnie's ex obediently stood to her left side, I stepped to the right. Our hard cocks were pointing right at her face and she sucked them, first one then the other. For the next couple of minutes, she was switching between our cocks sucking them deep with her eyes closed, savoring our taste in her hot mouth. It felt a little uneasy at first to watch my girlfriend suck off some other dude, even if it was her ex. However, I paid my attention to Bonnie, to her pretty mouth sucking the length of that dick and the joy on her face as she did so.

As both of our cocks were nice and lubricated with her spit, I decided to fondle her a little, to let her enjoy the presence of the two guys. So I just stepped between her legs and sat down on the floor which felt a little bit cold but at least relaxed me a little after that hot sucking. Steve went on enjoying Bonnie's hot mouth by grabbing her hair and pushing deeper and deeper into her with every thrust. I enjoyed the show of the hot mouth fucking for a while then just leaned between her thighs and pulled aside her black thong. I could see her labia ajar and glistening with her fluids from her excitement.

Her ex's hard cock probably was a large cause for this because I recalled how much she licked a cock in her mouth, it even made her come while we were doing 69 sometimes.

I started to lick her pussy just along the thong. She accepted it with a happy moan and her sucking speed slowed down a bit. Encouraged, I licked deeper into her pussy, around and around again.

Steve stepped back, letting her enjoy the cunnilingus for a moment. He jerked off a bit while he was watching us, and Bonnie just leaned back, closed her eyes, and moaned out loud again and again.

Things started to heat up: Steve climbed and knelt up on the arms of the chair and just positioned himself above Bonnie's head. He only needed to touch Bonnie's cheek with the end of his cock, and Bonnie looked up immediately; she opened her mouth and let the hard cock slide in deep. At that moment, I felt a bit of jealousy rising, but that feeling faded quickly. As her ex's cock slid into her throat, Bonnie let her head back to the headrest of the chair. Steve groaned as Bonnie sucked him deep, grinding him briefly. It was such a sight! Then he lifted himself, only to drop back down before doing the same thing again and then again, only more quickly. I went on licking her out while I was watching from below how this stranger was fucking my girlfriend's mouth. It was really hot to see my good girlfriend in her lingerie as a stiff, hard cock was moving in and out of her mouth, letting her saliva drip down on her breasts. Her ex held onto the chair, going balls deep as he fucked her lovely mouth right in front of me.

I decided to fill Bonnie's pussy with a little more than just my tongue at this point. I pushed one, then two fingers inside her hot wet pussy and went on licking her clitoris. Bonnie moaned with her mouth muffled with Steve's cock. She grabbed the arm of the chair harder. I almost forgot to breathe as I was licking her hard, fingering her deep. Her juices were dripping down on her ass, making the leather surface of the armchair wet and slippery.

I knew this was a good opportunity for her to come. I switched up a little bit by moving my fingers in and out faster. I was committed to making her come and I knew the cock pounding her mouth would help me. Her contact with my fingers finally marked my success; she started trembling and moaning harder; her pussy convulsing. Her nails were digging into the leather surface of the arms of the chair and she had a violent orgasm.

I knew her pussy would be too sensitive after such a strong experience so I backed up, pulling out my fingers from her dripping wet pussy. Steve wasn't so gentle; he went on fucking her mouth no matter what. His cock slipped balls deep into her mouth again and again; she couldn't even turn her head away – not like she would have wanted to. He even let his cock in there for a few seconds; when he pulled it out, she was breathing heavily for a few moments.

"That was just... wow!" she panted. But Steve didn't really give her time, pushed back his cock into her mouth immediately and went on pounding it again.

I stood up and enjoyed the sight. I will surely look at hairdresser chairs differently from now on. I even jerked off a bit while watching the hot and dirty mouth fucking session in front of me.

Finally, Steve pulled out. Bonnie was panting again,

"You're crazy, guys..."

"And we haven't even really started," Steven stated.

"Let her stand up," I said, "she's probably not feeling her legs."

"It's not so bad," Bonnie said smiling, while standing up, "actually, it felt pretty good."

I took her hand and guided her to the other artifact at the hairdresser's: the big mirror with a sink in front of it. I stepped behind her and admired her body in the mirror.

"Look at all that fluid all over your body," I said. "And the evening hasn't even really started yet."

She looked over herself and leaned slightly on the sink. She watched her own face close in the mirror. I used the opportunity and reached down to her magnificent round ass cheeks.

"Look at this," I showed them to Steve. "Look how firm and tight she is!"

"Yeahh..." he said, leaning close.

"You wanna fuck her ass?" I asked, recalling what Bonnie had told me about Steve not really being an ass man. But I was and surely wanted to bring out of the situation as much as I could.

"Well...," he hesitated, but I could see the sight affected him. I released Bonnie's ass cheeks and just spanked her hard.

"Doesn't she have a perfect ass? Just made for a good pounding!"

Steve stepped closer:

"May I?" he asked and reached for her black panties.

"Be my guest, pal!" I said. After he fucked Bonnie's mouth, I wouldn't really mind him stripping my girlfriend. He pulled down Bonnie's panties slowly, all the while watching her ass.

"You like it, don't you?" I asked and spread her ass cheeks apart again. Seeing her asshole for the first time tonight was so hot! I immediately leaned down on her and let some saliva pour from my mouth on her asshole. I smeared it all over her ass with my index finger, even pushed some into her tight asshole. "See how tight it is?" I presented it to Steven like a treasure.

"Yeah," he said, still holding the black thong in his hand, jerking himself with the other.

"Come here, and fuck this hot piece of ass," I told to him. I spread Bonnie's ass cheeks even more apart.

"Yes please....," Bonnie begged like a kitten. "Please fuck my tight little ass hard..."

Steve got the message, stepped right behind Bonnie, and pressed his cock to the entrance of her back tunnel. I could hear Bonnie hissing as he penetrated her ass slowly. He let her adjust for a few moments, then spread his legs a bit, grabbed Bonnie by her tits, and started fucking her with deliberate movements. Bonnie closed her eyes and enjoyed the hot ass fucking she was receiving from her ex.

I released her ass cheeks now and let Steve fuck her ass real hard. He pressed her to the mirror and entered her sloppy asshole to the hilt again and again, grunting and moaning. His huge balls and sack hit her pussy lips every other time. Bonnie enjoyed this with closed eyes, practically screaming.

I wouldn't think this party would go so well. Steven really got the taste of it, he pounded Bonnie's ass in a stable rhythm. Bonnie opened her eyes and looked in the mirror, and I could see her admiring her naked, wet body pounded from behind by her ex. It really was a sight, I was jerking off beside them like a madman.

After only a few minutes of this raw ass fucking, she started shuttering and trembling, her knees almost letting themselves go but she grabbed the sink and let her body give in to the orgasm. Steven didn't care, he fucked her ass deep, without mercy. He even grabbed her hair and pressed her head to the mirror, and both of us guys were watching Bonnie's face doubled by the mirror, convulsed by the mix of pleasure and pain. Her body trembled a bit but she regained her consciousness soon, opening her eyes and licking a wet spot on the mirror. The sight of her licking her own tongue in the mirror got me wild. I grabbed her hair and pulled her head down to my lap. She managed to lean down to my cock without stepping aside from Steven so his cock remained deep in her ravished asshole.

The second Bonnie's wet tongue touched my cock, I moaned loudly and put my hands on Bonnie's head. I pushed straight forward to fit as much of my dick into her hot mouth as possible. As my cock slipped into her mouth to the hilt, Bonnie reached down to undo the bow on the front of her bra, allowing it to fall off her body as she took a cock at either end of her. Now revealed, her huge boobs shook with her body and hair, swinging around wildly amid the intercourse as her ex thrust repeatedly into her ass while I enjoyed a blowjob at the other end. I could hear Bonnie's body slap against her ex's as she took the base of my cock back in her hand and started to slurp on my cock. She looked good with a pair of cocks in her, and the main course was going to look even better.

Bonnie's lips and tongue played with my cock for several minutes, preparing me for the real fun as I started to clench my hands, pulling on her hair. After sucking the entire length for a little while, she focused on the head and tip, flicking her tongue against it and licking it gently. Then she went back to stroking and sucking me off, as all the while her ex was slamming into her ass from behind.

Finally, Bonnie pulled her head back from my cock with a gasp but continued to stroke it as she received the hard anal pounding. Those piercing eyes met mine again as her beautiful mouth uttered the last words I'd heard before the real pleasure began: "Fuck me both of you!"

What had sold me on this opportunity was Bonnie's specific mention of the fact that double penetration was something she had wanted to try since her college days. To be completely honest, sandwiching Bonnie was something I had always wanted to do. That kind of thought was something I'd often fantasized about. In my mind, nothing was hotter than the thought of Bonnie's sexy little body sandwiched between two dudes who were filling her holes and stretching out her taint.

With Bonnie's words, nothing stood in my way. I knew better than to overthink the situation. I needed to just do it.

Bonnie and her ex came to a stop from their fucking and their bodies separated. Steven stepped to the chair where the hairdressers usually wash the hair of the clients. He sat down, and let his head slip into the headband. Bonnie climbed on him, reached down, and slowly sat on his cock. She hissed again, twirled her abdomen to get used to the cock from this angle, then looked back at me:

"Let's get it on!"

I stepped behind Bonnie. Her pussy was completely filled with her ex's cock, but she helped me find the alternate entrance by lying down on the chair and spreading her ass cheeks nice and wide. I squatted down behind her, my gaze transfixed on the vacant dark hole.

My mouth went dry as my breathing fluctuated. Meanwhile, my heart pounded anxiously in my chest. I was still completely turned on, though, and with my rock-hard cock in my hand, I leaned forward some more, aiming for that tight asshole that would forever etch this night into my memory.

Bonnie was breathing faster too while she was holding her ass open and her ex pressed her in place against himself. I was just moments away from fulfilling my dirtiest fantasy and, even though the time elapsed was probably about 10 seconds, it felt like another five minutes before the head of my cock poked Bonnie's ass, guided by my hand. Bonnie whined quietly when my tip made contact with her flesh. I swear I could feel my cock get even harder as I continued to look steadfastly at my lover, whose twat was filled to the hilt with another cock already while I attempted to fill the neighboring hole simultaneously. I pushed forward just enough to wedge the head of my cock into her before releasing my cock and taking another deep breath.

Her eyes wincing shut, Bonnie cooed as I thrust forward slowly, entering her asshole inch by inch. I had to grab the base of my dick a couple of times to help push it in, but there wasn't too much resistance despite her tightness. Her breathing became more ragged, and her red nails dug into her ex's shoulders as more and more of me filled her. I could feel the hard cock on the other side of the membrane that separated Bonnie's ass and pussy. The feeling was weird and incredible at the same time. The pressure added by the other cock was only enhancing the experience of plugging Bonnie's asshole.

Again, the actual time and my perception of it didn't match up. That first thrust into Bonnie probably took only a few seconds, but it felt like much longer as I took it all in. I slowly exhaled a few times, balancing myself on her ass with one hand as I sank deeper and deeper into her until, at last, my balls rested on Bonnie's taint and my body made contact with her ass. Bonnie cried out either in pleasure or pain; I couldn't tell. I put my hands on Bonnie's hips and held onto her as my cock adjusted to the pressure inside her. It was a tight fit, but the sensations were amazing even before reality sank in.

I had been entranced with Bonnie's asshole, but now that I was to the hilt inside her, I looked up to see that Bonnie was looking back at me. I could see just the corner of her mouth over her shoulder as she grinned, clearly madly amused, but those beautiful brown eyes caught my attention as I gazed back at my beloved, naked friend. It was at that moment that my situation finally took hold of me.

The past few minutes seemed to be in slow motion, but upon making eye contact with Bonnie, it was as if the play button had been pressed to return us to live action. I looked away from Bonnie's face and looked down to see again that I was balls-deep in her asshole. I leaned over to check out her stretched-out taint and stuffed pussy, a sight that drove me wild with unquenchable lust. Not only was I inside Bonnie but she was stuffed in both holes! Her tight pussy and asshole filled to capacity raised the bar for the hottest thing I'd ever seen, and the sights and sounds were going to get only hotter as the activity progressed. Meanwhile, Bonnie looked beyond pleased to finally be filled by two guys at once.

The only sound now was our heavy breathing and a couple of giggles from Bonnie as we all adjusted to the pressure and prepared for one hell of a fucking, which this girl needed. Leading up to this moment, I had worried about how I would perform with another guy involved, but I had underestimated Bonnie's sexiness. Having her body as the meat in this sandwich made me wholly willing at that moment to give myself over to this sinful act of depravity.

With renewed gusto, I inched my cock back until only the head was still inside Bonnie's ass. Bonnie moaned softly as the veins of my cock slid against her insides. Then I pushed forward, steadily sinking my whole length back into her, which caused a gasp and a louder moan from the girl as she lowered her head and again sank her nails into her ex. I held onto her more tightly and began to fuck her ass just as her ex began to stir underneath her.

Bonnie cursed and then planted her hands on the arms of the chair on either side of her ex, holding her body up halfway between the two of us as we double-penetrated her. I held myself up by her hips as I hovered over her ass, leaning over her and sinking my cock into her asshole a few more times before getting the hang of it. Meanwhile, her ex had started to steadily thrust in and out of Bonnie's pussy as Bonnie tensed up, threw her head back and moaned. Her hair brushed my shoulder as she jerked back. Her jerking movements caused the chair to rock and tremble below us.

Before we guys could really get going, Bonnie grew more comfortable with her predicament and started to fuck us instead. She started slowly rocking her body back and forth on our cocks but quickly grew more eager and slammed back into us hard and fast. I continued supporting myself on her hips while her ex was holding onto her shoulders as she was sliding up and down the full length of our cocks. My balls were continuously slapping against her taint as I stayed still and let her polish my knob with her shitter. She cried out with sounds of both joy and agony as she took us deep into both her holes.

I held my breath as I watched Bonnie fuck us. Her body thrust back and forth, being penetrated in both her ass and pussy simultaneously. The bitch rocked her body with remarkable stamina for a couple of minutes, moaning and panting as she did.

Bonnie couldn't keep up the fucking, though, and after a while, I think the discomfort became too much for her. She slowed down, gasping for breath and whining a little as she sank down onto her ex after doing an otherwise terrific job of pleasuring two men at once. I took this opportunity to begin fucking her ass again, thrusting in and out of her steadily while her ex ground up into her other hole. The experience was hot and wild on the sole fact that Bonnie was getting nailed like a whore. She was so close to me that I could feel the heat emanating from her body.

Having Bonnie's ass would be the culmination of years of sexual frustration. The fact that she was being double-penetrated was the icing on the cake. I was shoving the head of my cock inside her, neighboring her ex's cock that was already deep in her pussy.

I could feel the hard dick on the other side of the membrane. I was balls-deep in Bonnie's ass as my body slid up against hers. Her body was already slick with sweat and her own fluids dripping everywhere.

I couldn't contain my moan of pleasure as I took in the fact that I was inside Bonnie's ass. Seeing her being sandwiched made the experience all the more intense, and I could see her head was up against Steven's, her mouth at his ear, her boobs pressed against his neck while I ground up on her. The sound of her heavy breathing filled the ear, joining the sound of my own. The heat from her body was already making me sweat while my heart was pounding so hard that it almost hurt. Bonnie sank her nails into Steven's chest as she enjoyed with closed eyes being double-stuffed.

We went on fucking hard and continued taking in the reality that Bonnie was being sandwiched. All that was left to do was for her ex and I to work together and shift our bodies and Bonnie's body before we had her angled just right. What ensued was the most enjoyable experience of my life.

"Fuck her harder," her ex exclaimed, and we got right to it. Bonnie's moans almost sounded like sobs as we thrust into her holes slowly and roughly but steadily. I was so lost in lust that I barely considered Bonnie's comfort for the moment as I gave myself wholly to the experience. The sexy bitch's slick flesh gyrated between us two as we simultaneously made love to her cunt and asshole.

I backed up off Bonnie's body to look down and admire the brunette beauty, who was starring as the meat in our sex sandwich. I gazed on in disbelief as our hard cocks plunged in and out of her steadily, filling her ass and pussy while pulling at her taint. My eyes traveled up to her messy hair and sweaty back, as she moaned and took our steady fucking. All the while, Bonnie's legs remained at the two sides of her ex's, giving us full access to her sex holes as we both went to the hilt inside her.

After a couple of minutes of working our way through the experience, her ex and I began to pay more attention to what each other was doing to really heighten the enjoyment for all three of us. We established a rhythm where he would sink into her pussy when I pulled back inside her ass, and vice versa so that we were essentially taking turns going balls deep inside of her. It helped relieve the pressure that Bonnie was feeling while also ensuring that one of her holes was filled at all times.

I continued to admire Bonnie's glistening and writhing body for a few more minutes before I lay back on top of her, over her right shoulder. Her flesh was hot and damp as her breasts pressed against Steven's body. Meanwhile, her ex was situated over her other shoulder, so neither one of us was a distraction to the other as we focused on our respective holes and kept Bonnie pinned helplessly between us.

At this point, the threesome became really hot and a ton of fun. As I gave myself completely over to this shameful act of debauchery, Steven and I were firmly fucking Bonnie as she had never experienced before as we held her in place. The pleasure intensified to the first match and eventually exceeded my wild expectations as I began to thrust harder and harder into Bonnie's ass. I increased my speed, forcing her ex to keep up the pace in her pussy.

We both pumped back and forth into the bitch, sawing in and out of her. I could hear her ex grunting beneath her and realized I was groaning myself as Bonnie writhed and squealed between us, occasionally laughing as her head and legs swung between our thrusting bodies. I could feel the pointed heel of her right shoe poking my knee as she reacted to being pressed between and stuffed by the two of us men. At last, it seemed like Bonnie was sincerely enjoying her situation while I sank into her over and over and over again.

I remember distinctly how hot the room became. I briefly pulled back to admire Bonnie again and saw beads of sweat on her neck and her back. It felt like time slowed down again as I viewed her body, the entirety of which gleamed in the dim light from the perspiration. Her sweat-soaked hair was matted against her neck and shoulders and hanging down into her ex's face, her arms bracing herself as she took the double penetration and as she reveled in being the meat in our sandwich. Her breasts heaved as low, pleasured moans escaped from her throat, joining a myriad of other sounds, including the creaking of the chair beneath us as it supported us during this raunchy activity. Her ex and I kept up our pace as we pushed in and pulled out of Bonnie faster and faster. At this point, joining the sounds of our moaning was the squelching of her wet pussy and ravished asshole. I could feel the heels of her shoes press into my knees as her leg bounced in rhythm with our fucking. The smell of sweat mixed with Bonnie's perfume became almost overwhelming as it joined with the sights and sounds of our group sex.

Forcing my cock as deep into Bonnie's ass as I could with each thrust, I focused hard to continue my rhythm with her ex, who pushed even deeper into her pussy, separated from my cock in her ass by only the thin membrane. The two of us held her still and tightly between our bodies so that the sweaty, gasping bitch lay there, getting double-penetrated and crying out with blissful agony with each thrust into her as her legs thrashed in the air, pinned within a mass of human flesh.

I had never felt more alive in my whole life. The incredible sensation of feeling my cock slide beside another inside this hot woman would soon be more than I could take. By now, we were fucking Bonnie like a well-oiled machine, our cocks moving with the force and consistency of pistons. We boys grunted harder and harder while Bonnie was practically screaming at this point. Turned on only more, we sawed in and out of the writhing, sweating, moaning brunette between us harder and faster, rocking her entire body as she was helplessly caught in this hot, wet, delicious sandwich.

We continued to fuck her in unison on that chair, which now was probably stained with sweat. Of course, at that moment, I don't think anyone would have cared less. We were having the time of our lives. I was even slipping against Bonnie's damp body occasionally, but I would quickly straighten myself out and go right back to hammering her ass and doing my part in this threesome. Bonnie's body, of course, was slick with sweat from all three of us, but it suited her all the better. She continued crying out while her legs bounced wildly on either side of Steven, for some reason, turning me on only more. If she hadn't been enjoying the double penetration so far, she most certainly was now. I know as sure as hell was and I didn't want it to end ever.

The threesome continued for several more minutes as the sounds of slapping damp flesh and squelching holes joined our cries and moans of intense pleasure to fill the room. Finally, our continuous thrusts into her sex holes made Bonnie cum. Her slick body slipped effortlessly between our sweaty flesh as her ass squeezed me, her nails dug into Steven, as she experienced her orgasm. Her body rocked and shuddered between us as she came, screaming as she did and pushing me close to the edge myself. Filled with new-found confidence, I announced, "Let's cum on her face!" just as Bonnie was coming down from the most intense portion of her orgasm.

I wasn't going to let this experience be absent of the cherry on top, which meant a sticky facial for this bitch. Just the thought of cum streaming down Bonnie's face was almost enough to get me off right there. Plus, I could recall how Bonnie told me about an occasion when after making her hair, they had sex and Steven's cum drained her hair in this same place so he had to do the hair washing and drying again. Lucky adventures of a hairdresser...

As Bonnie continued to shudder from her climax, I pulled off of her, slipping out of her ass with a loud popping sound before the used bitch fell on Steven's chest limply. She took a couple of seconds to catch her breath, but her ex forced her off him.

As we two guys stood up, Bonnie was finally able to stretch out her legs before quickly squatting down in front of me. Her ex hurried to stand on the left side of Bonnie while I stood on her right, and we both jacked off, pointing our cocks at her. Within a few seconds, I came.

Bonnie closed her eyes as she was waiting for her reward which she had worked for hard. I moaned loudly as my cock finally erupted, blasting Bonnie in the cheek first and then unloading all over her pretty face. As if the experience wasn't close enough to perfect, Bonnie's ex began to cum just a second or two after I did.

"Make sure you shoot some on her hair!" I reminded him. He was grinning and aimed at her forehead and hair. Steven and I were painting Bonnie's face and hair in unison, in the same manner that we had fucked her body.

Time seemed to slow down again. I looked down with pervert satisfaction as cum shot from both our cocks simultaneously and splattered all over my lover. My cumshot covered her cheek and chin first, then her dark hair while her ex splashed onto her chin, nose, eyelid, and hair, of course. Still cumming, I moved my aim to blast her other eyelid and then her forehead, while my counterpart continued plastering the side of her face and then moved down to her neck. By the time we finished cumming on her, we had covered her whole face while leaving residue in her hair, and still, more jizz was dripping down her neck down to her boobs.

As soon as I was satisfied, I exhaled heavily and collapsed in the easy chair behind me, while Bonnie's ex headed off to the toilet, I think, probably to clean up. As I took a minute to catch my breath and cool off, I sat in utter disbelief at what had just transpired and admired yet another hot sight I had helped create tonight as Bonnie slowly stood up and wiped the cum from her eyelids, grinning from ear to ear as she did. She ran her fingers through her hair, enjoying the feeling of cum in her curls.

"This was sooo greaaat...," she sighed happily.

"Yeah...," I moaned since I couldn't really speak in longer sentences at that moment.

As she strutted over to me drenched in jizz and sweat, dressed in only her high heels and a smile, she assured me that tonight was everything she had hoped it would be and that we would be doing this very same thing again.

Extra Short: Cuckold Shoot for Onlyfans

The steam was swirling up from our mugs, the scent of cocoa, and the dim, warm glow of the living room as we nestled into the couch. It was one of those rare evenings when the city's chill seemed a world away, kept at bay by the soft throw blanket and Bonnie's weight against my side. We were halfway through some Scandinavian crime series, subtitles flickering beneath the icy blue glare of the screen when she paused it.

"John, I need to ask you something a bit... unconventional," Bonnie said, her voice softer than the cashmere socks she'd slipped on her feet earlier.

"Shoot," I replied, curious about the hesitation in her tone.

"Clarissa... she's doing something new for work. OnlyFans stuff." Bonnie turned to me, her gaze steady.

"Sure, that's... popular these days," I responded, not quite catching her drift yet. I wasn't surprised, though. Clarissa has always been a top 10 fine young lady, all the men turned after her when she passed the office. Her hot long legs and dirty blonde hair amazed everyone.

"The thing is, she wants to shoot a really hot scene. And well, she needs someone with a... creative mind. Someone like you."

"Me?" I choked on my hot chocolate, coughed, and finally caught my breath. "Bonnie, why would she want me to—"

"Because," Bonnie interrupted, her hand found mine, "you have this perverted streak that you think nobody notices. But I do, and so does Clarissa. Plus, there's your past with her."

True, I had had my share of adventures with Clarissa before, but I always considered those occasions as she was playing with me, actually. And now she's specifically asking me to indulge in her dirty shooting?

"Doesn't that bother you?" I asked, my mind racing as I tried to reconcile my girlfriend's calm demeanor with the bombshell she had just dropped. Was this a test? A trap?

"John, I trust you. Completely. And I want you to enjoy yourself," she explained, giving me a reassuring squeeze. "You don't know all the details, but yes, there will be some... intense sex. Just show up freshly showered, and Clarissa will fill you in."

"Intense how?" The lawyer in me wanted contracts, clauses, and boundaries. Yet, the man in me felt an illicit thrill at the idea of being invited into such a private, carnal world.

"Let's just say, Clarissa is very open-minded." Bonnie's voice held a hint of mischief. "And she values your... discretion and creativity."

"Open-minded" echoed in my head as I sipped the now lukewarm chocolate, eyes fixed on Bonnie's earnest expression. Trust – that's what this was about. She trusted me enough to send me into the arms of another woman, knowing I'd return to hers. It was a gift, a responsibility, a dare.

"Okay," I whispered, setting my mug down. "I'll do it."

"Good." Bonnie leaned in, kissing my cheek. "I'll message her right away." she opened her phone. "And remember, John, have fun. But also, respect the scene, okay?"

"Got it." My heart thrummed in my chest, equal parts nervous and excited. What had I agreed to? What did Clarissa, that blonde ice queen with her serious eyes and deceptively sweet curves, want with an average guy like me?

"Thank you, babe." Bonnie snuggled closer, hitting play on the remote. As the characters on screen chased shadows, I found myself chasing thoughts of Clarissa, wondering what lay ahead in this strange new role I'd been cast into.

***

The drive to Clarissa's felt like a crawl through quicksand, my pulse an erratic drumbeat against the steering wheel. I parked outside the nondescript suburban home, stopped the engine, and used a minute to think it over the last time. This ice queen invited me to participate in a dirty shoot with her. What could go wrong?

Stepping out, I could feel the crisp air fight against the heat flushing my cheeks. I was freshly showered, as instructed, the scent of citrus soap still clinging to my skin.

A young guy opened the door before my knuckles could rap against it, his thin frame shadowed by the dimly lit hallway. "John, right on time," he said, adjusting his glasses with a practiced motion. There was a professional tinge to his voice, the kind used to maintain distance in intimate settings. He ushered me into the living room with a sweeping gesture, one that hinted at a rehearsed civility.

"Make yourself comfortable," he offered. I nodded, letting my gaze wander, and there she was, standing naked, in high heels only, in the middle of the living room — Clarissa, the embodiment of erotic confidence. She lounged with regal indifference, her naked form adorned only by a stark black collar, a contrast to her pale skin. Her serious eyes locked onto mine, an unspoken challenge in their depths.

"So you've already met my boyfriend!" she chirped and planted a light kiss on my cheek.

"Boyfriend?!" I asked. Bonnie didn't tell me Clarissa had someone. This complicated things, at least. But I had to take a moment to adore her nipples pointing at me erected, at the toned flat belly above her tight pussy, which had only a landing strip above it, neatly trimmed.

To my surprise, it wasn't just my hosts waiting for me in the living room. Two of my colleagues were already there, looking at me as if waiting for the party to start.

Carl, the fellow lawyer at the company, slicked-back hair reflecting the low light, tilted his chin up in greeting from the sofa, while Ule's, the sole black attorney's massive silhouette unfolded from his seat, a nod punctuating his acknowledgment. The energy in the room crackled with anticipation, and I took my place among them, the fabric of the couch unfamiliar beneath me.

"Thank you all for coming," Clarissa began, her voice threaded with a silvery command. As hot as she looked, she still seemed strange standing with her legs apart, naked, with all of us guys sitting around, fully clothed. But she just went on, like a director. "As you might've guessed, tonight's performance will be... special." Her lips curled around the words, a sly smile playing at the edges. She touched her bare pussy with her well-manicured long fingers involuntarily. "Our audience has been clamoring for a cuckold gangbang scene, and who am I to deny them?"

My heart hammered as she laid bare the nature of our gathering.

"Alex here," she gestured to her boyfriend, whose presence seemed to shrink ever so slightly, "will be our gracious cuck. He'll be on the receiving end of verbal barbs and menial tasks." The rawness of her declaration stripped any pretense; we were not just participants, but instruments of humiliation. "And you guys, are invited to be the bulls for the evening. You will have to fuck me as hard as you can, make my followers satisfied! Don't hold back," she urged, her gaze touching each of us in turn. "I want it as hard as possible. No limits."

A shiver raced down my spine, part fear, part exhilaration. The air seemed thicker as the gravity of her request settled on my shoulders. Could I embody the role she asked of me? My mind churned with the possibilities, the boundaries I'd cross tonight.

"Anything goes," Clarissa reaffirmed, locking eyes with me. It wasn't just a statement; it was an invitation to explore the darkest corners of desire.

"Understood," Carl drawled, his arrogance now laced with a hint of eagerness. Ule merely grunted, his deep voice resonating like a distant storm, ready to break.

"Good," Clarissa purred, satisfaction gleaming in her eyes. "Let's give them a show they won't forget."

"Let's begin," Alex said, almost inaudibly, his role accepted if not embraced.

This was the point of no return, and I was already too far gone to look back.

In the charged silence that followed Clarissa's decree, I watched as Alex, like some solemn priest preparing his temple, began to set the stage for our carnal rite. His slender fingers adjusted the two high-resolution cameras, their lenses glistening under the halo of the ring lights that hung above.

"Perfect," he murmured to himself, a hint of pride in his voice as he circled around, inspecting every angle with a meticulous gaze through his glasses. "Here," he said, handing the end of a black leash to Clarissa, the leather strap contrasting starkly against the alabaster smoothness of her skin. As it clicked into place around her collar, a shiver ran down my spine—the symbolism was unmistakable.

"Stand over there, guys," the naked blonde directed, pointing to a spot just outside the camera's view. Carl and Ule moved without a word, their silhouettes casting long shadows that stretched across the living room floor like dark omens. I took my place beside them, feeling the heat of anticipation coursing through my veins.

"Are you ready?" Alex asked, his voice low and steady. It wasn't just a question; it was an invitation to cross a threshold I'd never even approached before.

"Born ready," Carl replied, his smirk audible.

"Let's do this," Ule added, his tone betraying no emotion, yet his eyes gleamed with a predatory hunger.

I also nodded, unable to find any words.

"Rolling," Alex announced, his finger hovering over the record button before pressing it with an almost reverent touch. The red light blinked on, signaling the start of something irreversible.

"Remember, make them feel every second," Clarissa whispered, her eyes locked onto the lens as if she could see through it, into the souls of those who would later witness this spectacle.

"Trust me, they will," I thought to myself, my pulse quickening at the prospect of unleashing our dirtiest desires. Bonnie had given her blessing, but it was Clarissa who had thrown down the gauntlet—I was here to prove that I could pick it up.

"Action," came Alex's soft command, and with that single word, the world narrowed to Clarissa. She sat on the sofa, crossing her long, slender legs, her high heels swung in a comfortable motion. She opened up a magazine from the glass table and started flipping through it clearly bored. It was a BDSM magazine, I realized. The images were visibly showing scenes of men and women dressed in black latex, being whipped, bound, and fucked in various positions. Clarissa held it so the dirty scenes were clear for the cameras. Stopping at a particularly filthy double penetration, she put it in front of her on the grey carpet of the sofa and opened her legs with a sigh. Even though she had played the role of the lovely hostess naked tonight, this was the first time we could see her open, wet pink pussy.

Locking her gaze on the model in the image, she started fondling her clit. I looked at my fellow invitees for this filthy night: Carl and Ule were watching her frenzy of masturbation grinning, with lust glistening in their eyes. Clarissa closed her eyes, let her head lie back on the arm of the sofa, and her well-manicured fingers spun quickly on her clit.

All of us in the room could hear her sexy voice as she was moaning and enjoying herself. Clarissa looked absolutely stunning while being lost in pleasure, with her long blonde hair cascading down her back and those perfect fingers working diligently between her thighs. Her soft moans filled the air as she continued to ride out waves of intense sensations.

Meanwhile, Carl and Ule standing nearby, their erections straining against their pants, eagerly watching her every move. They could barely contain themselves, knowing full well that they would soon have complete control over Clarissa's body and mind.

"Alex!" the blonde shouted with a frustrated tone in her thin voice. "Could you help me out here?"

The guy adjusted his glasses and stepped forward.

"Yes, honey?" he asked, swallowing a hard one, eyeing his girlfriend up and down.

"Come here," she pointed to her crotch with a nasty grin on her face. Alex knelt obediently and leaned between the blonde's sexy thighs. He looked up at his lover once more, who only nodded, pointing at her pussy. Alex ran his hand all along her legs, leaning closed, and began pleasuring her with his tongue. With a mixture of submission and authority in her voice, she pulled his head right into her wet opening.

"That's it, baby," she moaned, closing her eyes. "Lick my pussy deep!"

As her fiancé was licking and sucking on Clarissa's sensitive folds, the girl leaned back against the armrest of the sofa, letting out occasional gasps of pleasure."

As the cameras captured their every move, I felt my cock hardening in my pants. Glancing at Ule and Carl, I could tell they were getting just as horny as I was.

"Fuck me hard, Alex!" Clarrisa ordered him. "Make me feel like your bitch!"

Alex straightened his back hesitantly, with his fiancée's wetness on his face. He approached Clarissa's wet pussy, pushed down his pants, and set his cock straight to her pussy. We all watched his dick pointing to her dripping entrance. He pushed in, and moaned out loud, maybe too loud. Probably for the cameras.

He started to move slowly at first, but under Clarissa's insistent demand, he eventually picked up speed, slamming into her with force.

"That's it!" Clarissa moaned loudly, opening her eyes now, and looking into her lover's eyes. "Harder!" She even slapped Alex with her open palm, the harsh sound surprised us all.

"That's not enough, Alex! Fuck me harder! Make me feel like I'm your slut!"

Alex stopped dead in his tracks, looking at Clarissa with a mix of confusion in his eyes. But Clarissa didn't mercy him, pulled his body inside her with her legs deeper. So, with a sense of reluctance bordering on desperation, Alex resumed thrusting into Clarissa's gaping pussy.

"Is this all you got?" she asked. "It's not enough!"

She pushed him away. The guy looked at the cameras with eyes wide. Now Clarissa invited us with her index finger. We looked at each other, and all three of us stepped into the picture.

"Let us take care of her," Ule improvised to the scene. Carl and I also pulled out our erections and held proudly in front of Clarissa. She looked around at the array of throbbing members in front of her, feeling both excited and nervous about what was about to happen. With Alex leaving now to the back corner of the room, the three of us surrounded the lovely blonde on the sofa, preparing to take turns using her as our personal plaything.

"I want to taste your big black cock," she said to Ule. "Please give it to me."

Without hesitation, Clarissa took the thick black meat into her mouth and started sucking on it enthusiastically, swirling her tongue around its length and teasing the tip with her lips.

Ule moaned appreciatively, obviously enjoying the attention Clarissa was giving him. The rest of us watched intently as the lovely blonde's angelic lips completely engulfed the black cock, making our own members twitch with anticipation.

"Yes, baby," Ule moaned in his deep voice. "Take my hard cock, bitch! I'm gonna make you... my personal cum dumpster!"

He positioned himself at the edge of Clarissa's face and grabbed her blonde locks with both of his hands. He began to drive into her mouth aggressively, with her saliva dripping on his balls, on her chin and tits.

Clarissa eagerly swallowed the huge cock deep, relishing in the taste and power dynamic of the situation.

"Mmm...," he moaned. "I love how deep you take it!" He continued to pound Clarissa's face, pushing her limits and making her work harder to take everything he had to offer.

Her cheeks bulged with his cockhead buried deep in her throat, and she could barely breathe through the tightness as she struggled to take in as much of his essence as possible.

Ule decided to give her a bit of mercy and pulled back.

"You're a really talented cock sucker, baby!" he stated. "It's been a really long time somebody took my cock deep in her throat like that."

Clarissa nodded appreciatively, still trying to catch her breath as she looked at me. I didn't waste any time, stepped in front of her, to be the next with this living sex toy. Ule stepped back, with Clarissa's saliva still glistening on his cock.

I positioned myself at the entrance to Clarissa's waiting throat and began to plunge my member aggressively into her waiting orifice. Clarissa eagerly accepted my cock, eager to show off her skills as a skilled cuck-sucking professional.

Carl didn't wait anymore, also stepped beside me and leaned down to hold Clarissa's hand. He put it on his throbbing member, which she started jerking vividly. She seemed to show devotion to pleasuring multiple men at once.

Clarissa looks up at him gratefully, with my cock still deep in her mouth. I glanced at Alex in the corner, he was watching eagerly to see if she can handle two cocks at once without breaking her focus on servicing their needs. She pulled back, releasing my throbbing cock from her hot mouth, saying,

"I'm happy to please both of you at the same time, gentlemen."

She moves fluidly between our members, taking turns sucking Carl and me deeply while maintaining eye contact with each of us. The sight of her working so diligently to satisfy multiple men at once sent a shiver down my spine. We exchanged approving glances with Carl as we were watching our plaything in action.

"Cut!" Clarissa's voice sliced through the thick air, abrupt as a clap of thunder. I reeled back, my heart lurching with a cocktail of concern and adrenaline. She sat upright, an imperious queen holding court even while on her knees. "Water," she demanded, her voice a blade that could cut through steel. Alex hurried to her with a bottle which she accepted gladly.

I watched, captivated, as her full lips parted to take in gulps of the clear fluid, the droplets cascading down her chin like pearls of dew on golden morning leaves. Her throat worked in delicate swallows, yet her eyes never left ours.

"More," Clarissa commanded, setting the glass aside with a clink that echoed off the marble floor. "I want it rougher, harder. Don't hold back, guys"

I exchanged a glance with Carl and Ule—both men now silent sentinels to the blonde siren's decree. The room seemed to contract around us, the heat turning viscous, wrapping around my skin like a lover's caress.

"Sure thing, babe," Ule growled, his voice low and predatory. And just like that, we were back in motion, the camera's red eye winking at us once more.

"Alex, get over here," Carl barked, and Alex moved with the obedience of a well-trained pet, his glasses catching the glare of the ring lights as he approached.

"Strip us," Carl ordered, a smirk playing upon his lean lips. Alex's hands trembled slightly as they reached for our clothing, undoing buttons with meticulous care, folding each item with the precision of a man whose role had been reduced to servitude.

I felt the fabric fall from my shoulders, leaving me bare and exposed, skin prickling under the scrutiny of both the camera and Clarissa's ice-blue gaze. There was no modesty here, no place to hide—we were all laid open, raw, and visceral under the scrutinizing lens.

My thoughts raced as I watched Alex, the cuckold, fold our clothes with such deference, his own arousal evident despite his humiliation. This was the game, the dance of dominance and submission, played out in the most intimate of theaters.

"Good boy, Alex," Clarissa cooed as she turned her attention back to us, taking Carl and myself back into her wet, hot mouth again. Her mouth resumed its work, warm and wet, and I found myself lost in the rhythmic push and pull, the slick sounds punctuating the silence. My mind wandered briefly to Bonnie, to the trust she placed in me, and I wondered if she knew just how deep into the abyss I'd willingly plunged.

"Look at her go," Carl muttered, pride and lust coloring his tone. "Bet you've never seen her like this before, have you, Alex?"

The bespectacled man shook his head mutely, eyes glazed as he beheld the scene unfolding before him—a tableau vivant of debauchery and desire.

"Keep it going, let the camera see everything," I murmured, the lawyer in me momentarily surfacing, ever-conscious of the performance, of the need to provide a show that would be immortalized in the annals of digital fantasy.

"Everything," Clarissa echoed, her voice a sultry promise as she drew us further into the depths of the evening's sinful symphony.

The chill of the air-conditioned room brushed against my skin, a stark contrast to the heat emanating from our entwined bodies. Carl's grip on Clarissa's hair was unyielding, his fingers wrapped tightly as he directed her head back and forth between himself and me. The sight before me was an intricate dance of flesh and desire, punctuated by the slick sound of Clarissa's lips sliding over our throbbing cocks.

I could see Ule getting around, sitting on the sofa, jerking his huge black cock. I could already tell he was planning the next move, fucking our lovely blonde hostess.

"Hey Alex," Carl's voice cut through the heavy atmosphere, casual as if discussing stocks over lunch, "grab me a beer, would you?" His eyes never left Clarissa's face, watching every movement with the intensity of a hawk.

Alex, ever the obedient voyeur, scurried to the kitchen, his movements quick and eager to please, while we were fucking his girlfriend's mouth with abandon. Our cuck host soon returned with a chilled bottle, condensation beading along the glass like sweat upon our skin. Carl took it without glancing away, the click of the cap skittering across the marble floor lost in the cacophony of moans and grunts.

"That's a good one!" Carl stated, after gulping a large one. Ule took advantage of this, and ordered the girl: "Get here, bitch!"

The blonde walked to him on her hands and knees, like a good slut. She began to take his huge member into her mouth instinctively, but Ule pushed her lovely face away.

"Get lower, baby!" he ordered her, laying back on the plush sofa with the ease of a man accustomed to command. His legs raised in a deliberate invitation. "Show them how you worship!"

Her response was immediate, that wicked grin curling her full lips as she lowered herself between his spread thighs. There was a glint in her eye, a spark of feral pleasure at the debasement yet to come.

"Oh yeah, that's right, lick my ass, baby!" he stated. "You really know how to make a guy feel special."

Clarissa lowered herself down onto her knees and began to worship Ule's rear entrance, licking and probing with her tongue. She took extra care to cleanse his hole thoroughly, showing just how dedicated she was to serving his needs completely.

The other men watched with interest, wondering what new depths of submission and devotion she would reach during this part of her performance. While rimming the huge black man, she also began jerking his cock which might have been hard to focus on. But she did so vividly, pulling back a bit, saying "This is exactly what I've been craving for, baby!"

Ule grabbed her head right away:

"Let me give you a little reminder of who's in charge here, sweetheart." And then gave her a light slap on her pretty face before pushing her face firmly against his buttocks. Clarissa giggled and gasped in surprise but quickly adjusted to the new position, determined to continue pleasing everyone present.

I could see Ule getting around, sitting on the sofa, jerking his huge black cock. I could already tell he was planning the next move, fucking our lovely blonde hostess.

"Hey Alex," Carl's voice cut through the heavy atmosphere, casual as if discussing stocks over lunch, "grab me a beer, would you?" His eyes never left Clarissa's face, watching every movement with the intensity of a hawk.

Alex, ever the obedient voyeur, scurried to the kitchen, his movements quick and eager to please, while we were fucking his girlfriend's mouth with abandon. Our cuck host soon returned with a chilled bottle, condensation beading along the glass like sweat upon our skin. Carl took it without glancing away, the click of the cap skittering across the marble floor lost in the cacophony of moans and grunts.

"That's a good one!" Carl stated, after gulping a large one. Ule took advantage of this, and ordered the girl: "Get here, bitch!"

The blonde walked to him on her hands and knees, like a good slut. She began to take his huge member into her mouth instinctively, but Ule pushed her lovely face away.

"Get lower, baby!" he ordered her, laying back on the plush sofa with the ease of a man accustomed to command. His legs raised in a deliberate invitation. "Show them how you worship!"

Her response was immediate, that wicked grin curling her full lips as she lowered herself between his spread thighs. There was a glint in her eye, a spark of feral pleasure at the debasement yet to come.

"Oh yeah, that's right, lick my ass, baby!" he stated. "You really know how to make a guy feel special."

Clarissa lowered herself down onto her knees and began to worship Ule's rear entrance, licking and probing with her tongue. She took extra care to cleanse his hole thoroughly, showing just how dedicated she was to serving his needs completely.

The other men watched with interest, wondering what new depths of submission and devotion she would reach during this part of her performance. While rimming the huge black man, she also began jerking his cock which might have been hard to focus on. But she did so vividly, pulling back a bit, saying "This is exactly what I've been craving for, baby!"

Ule grabbed her head right away:

"Let me give you a little reminder of who's in charge here, sweetheart." And then gave her a light slap on her pretty face before pushing her face firmly against his buttocks. Clarissa giggled and gasped in surprise but quickly adjusted to the new position, determined to continue pleasing everyone present.

Carl only nodded but I leaned down and slapped Clarissa's tight ass cheek hard. "Tight and fit," I added. "She's really well-trained and devoted!"

"A real cum slut, if you ask me!" Carl added, fondling his cock again.

Meanwhile, Clarissa was sitting still on Ule's lap, trying to regain her composure after such intense stimulation.

Taking advantage of the brief pause of the hardcore action, I stepped behind her and set my throbbing cock to Clarissa's tight anal cavity. I was determined to add another layer of humiliation and pleasure to her special onlyfans scene. The room falls into a temporary lull, allowing me to carefully insert his erection into Clarissa's waiting rear entrance.

She let out a sharp cry of surprise and pleasure as she experienced the sudden intrusion, causing the others to look over in curiosity.

Ule and Carl exchanged amused glances, impressed by Clarissa's ability to handle such intense stimulation being penetrated in both of her orifices.

As Clarissa began to ride Ule's cock steadily again, I managed to enter her asshole to the balls, causing her to let out a loud moan of pleasure mixed with pain.

The sight of our penises invading her body at once left everyone in the room speechless, caught up in the raw power and intimacy of the moment. Clarissa's body trembles with pleasure and discomfort, her pussy and ass twitching from the intense double penetration she received from us.

Alex was jerking himself off so hard he was out of breath now. He even had a drop of saliva falling out of his mouth without caring at all.

Clarissa's screams filled the air, signaling her total submission and pleasure from being sandwiched.

"Ahhhh! Ahhhh!" Her voice rose in volume as she succumbed to the sensations coursing through her body, unable to contain her ecstatic cries any longer.

Ule looked at me with a satisfied grin, proud of his ability to bring her to this level of pleasure and submission.

The other men in the room were equally impressed by her willingness to endure such an intense experience for our enjoyment. Or the Onlyfans' viewers.

"Please... I can't take it anymore...," Her voice broke with emotion as she struggled to continue speaking between gasps for air.

"The cum, bitch!" I whispered, leaning to her ear from behind. "Come on our cocks!"

And that's exactly what she did. She came being sandwiched between our bodies with vivid trembling, screaming out loud.

"Shut this bitch up!" Ule said laughing, not caring about her enjoyment at all. Carl stepped to Clarissa's head, grabbed it, and pushed her agape mouth on his cock deep. This really muffled her joyful screams which even intensified by the triple penetration.

Ule and Carl exchange concerned glances, recognizing that they have pushed her to the brink of physical and emotional exhaustion. But rather than showing any concern for her well-being, they simply smiled knowingly, pleased by the sight of her breaking point.

Alex was watching us closely, eager to see just how far we could push Clarissa before she finally broke apart. The waves of her orgasm were ruling her body again and again. With three large penises invading her body – one in each orifice – Clarissa let out a muffled groan of anticipation and resignation.

Clarissa started to choke on the triple penetration, signaling her complete submission and vulnerability As she tried to accommodate all three penises simultaneously, she began to struggle slightly, her eyes watering and her face turning red from the effort. "Mmmph... mmph..."

Ule and Carl shared a smug grin, amused by her predicament and the way she was working so hard to please them. I didn't hold anything back now, going at her tight asshole mercilessly. I could feel Ule's cock also penetrating her pussy through the thin walls separating her orifices. She would have been screaming if Carls wouldn't silence her with the cock in her mouth. He even slapped her face a few times with his cock deep in her mouth.

"Oh God... I'm going to cum...," my voice trembles with excitement and pleasure. I could really feel the sperm growing in my balls, eagerly waiting for my release in the blonde's asshole. But I suspected the shoot we were working on needed some more visual ending.

"This bitch is too tight...," Ule also groaned beneath us. "I can't take it any longer anymore..."

"Let's shoot it on her face," Carl added, shoving his cock into Clarissa's throat again and again. "Let's make a great... money shot!"

All of us withdrew our cocks from Clarissa's throbbing orifices, leaving her feeling empty and exposed after experiencing such intense pleasure.

"Kneel before us, my pet," Ule panted. with a teasing tone, jerking his huge wet cock as all us others followed suit, holding our members in our hands.

Clarissa dutifully knelt down in front of the men, waiting to receive their hot seed all over her face as a symbol of her complete submission and servitude. She stood there quietly, her eyes cast down submissively as she prepared herself for the upcoming act of degradation. We grinned wickedly at Clarissa, excited about the opportunity to mark her face with our fresh, sticky proof of ownership. As we prepared to release our ejaculate onto Clarissa's upturned face, she remained still and obedient, accepting this final humiliation without resistance or protest.

Clarissa became ultimately aroused by the anticipation of being covered in cum and started furiously rubbing her clit, driving herself closer to the edge. Her hips began to buck involuntarily as we surrounded her like eagles the innocent prey, jerking our throbbing members inches away from her face.

"Mmmph...," she moaned softly, unable to contain her growing excitement any longer. Just as Clarissa reached peak pleasure, Carl was the first to finally release his load onto her cheeks, causing her to flinch slightly. Clarissa received the full force of Carl's load, taking every drop onto her face and even swallowing as much as possible. As the stream of hot cum rained down onto her cheeks, Clarissa opened her lips wide, eagerly accepting every last drop. Her tongue darted out to catch as much of it as possible, and she swallowed eagerly, showing her complete submission and dedication to her guest.

"That's it, baby," Carl moaned in his deep, satisfied voice. "Take it all..."

I couldn't take it anymore, stepped closer, and added my load to my colleague's on the blonde's lovely face. I shot four times, each one spraying a fresh white dose of hot cum onto her nose and cheeks. She took his giggling, playing with her clit feverishly.

As I stepped back, she pushed out her tongue again and turned to her fiancé. Alex was jerking his cock just as crazily, as his fiancée.

"My face! Come on!" Clarissa pointed at her cum covered features with both of her index fingers.

"Oh, sorry," Alex understood and stopped jerking off, picked one of the cameras off, and zoomed on the blonde's face. Kneeling on the carpet, she smiled and threw a kiss to the viewers.

"That's enough," Ule stepped in and grabbed her head once more. He pushes his throbbing member deep into her mouth, using her open orifice as a conduit for his final act of degradation. Clarissa gasped in surprise but remained obedient, accepting this last act of domination without resisting or fighting back.

Clarissa struggled to breathe and choke while Ule continued to fuck her face relentlessly, using her body as a receptacle for his seed and a symbol of his power over her. As Ule went on pounding Clarissa's throat and mouth, she gasped for air and coughed weakly, her eyes watering as she tried to take in enough oxygen to sustain herself. "Mmm... Mmff..." She manages to say between gulps of air, indicating her struggle to breathe while taking his cock deep into her throat.

Even now, with our cocks completely spent, it was amazingly arousing to watch how our black lawyer colleague fucked this blonde girl's face relentlessly. The mix of our cum stuck onto his black member but he didn't care, just fucked her throat deep to the balls.

Clarissa was clearly overwhelmed by Ule's size and power, unable to speak or breathe easily due to the intense sensations coursing through her body. As Ule's large cock pushed deeper into her throat and filled her esophagus completely, Clarissa began to choke and gag, finding it increasingly difficult to breathe or speak coherently.

"G... Gg...," She managed to wheeze out between gasps for air, indicating her extreme submission to Ule's dominance, all the while playing with her clit furiously.

And when Ule even slapped her face while having his huge member inside her mouth, she just came. We could all see her body trembling, her tension going away, all her control lost. She became a doll in our black friend's hands, a twitching mess of sexiness.

Satisfied with his display of control over Clarissa, Ule withdrew his cock from her throat and let loose a massive burst of hot seed onto her upturned face, leaving her covered in sticky strands of cum that ran down her chin and neck.

"Ahh... Ahh..." he moaned loudly, reveling in the sight of her submission and his ability to claim ownership over her body.

Ule sat back on the sofa, and Clarissa was left completely covered in cum, highlighting her vulnerability and submissive nature, and emphasizing the extent of the humiliation she has endured. After being filled with cum multiple times throughout the scene, Clarissa was now completely covered in sticky white strands of seed, which adorned her pale skin, blonde hair, and naked breasts. She looked like a living canvas of submission and debasement, completely at the mercy of these powerful men who had taken control of her body and mind.

We all stepped back and admired our filthy handiwork. Carl nodded approvingly at the sight of Clarissa covered in cum. He then turned to Ule and said,

"Well done, buddy. You really made her look delicious."

"Your followers are gonna love this sight," Ule agreed.

"There's only one thing missing," Carl said and his evil grin appeared on his face again, looking curiously at Clarissa's stained body. "Alex, would you join us, please?"

Alex, the engaged man, knelt down beside Clarissa and gazed upon her face which was now covered with our cum. He leaned in close to Clarissa's face, studying every detail of her now-disheveled appearance. His engagement ring sparkled on his finger, serving as a reminder of the commitment he had made to marrying her and subjecting her to this humiliating treatment.

"Wow," he whispered softly, "these guys really had their ways with you, right, baby?"

"It was so great..." Clarissa added with a satisfied smile.

"Clean her up," Ule said, grabbing a camera and zooming on the kneeling blonde's face. Alex looked up surprised, this cuckold cleanup perversion was clearly not planned for their shoot today.

"Come on, man," Carl added. "The followers will love that shit!"

Alex looked back at his fiancée and seeing her glad smile, he didn't hesitate anymore. He leaned closer to Clarissa and began licking up the fresh cum off her face. He dipped his tongue into the pool of cum on Clarissa's cheek and started lapping it up slowly, savoring each drop as if it were a delicacy. His eyes never left hers, maintaining constant eye contact during this intimate moment.

"Mmm... This is so tasty," he murmured between licks, and I wasn't sure if he was telling it for the camera or if he was really enjoying the taste of our seed. Ule leaned close to him anyway, zooming on this dirty feast with the camera.

While being licked clean by Alex, Clarissa struggled to keep herself from making any sudden movements or reactions but ultimately remained relatively still and submissive. Her breathing became slightly heavier and more irregular as she tried to process this last filthy cleanup happening to her.

"This is so hot...," she managed to utter weakly, but quickly fell back into silence once again.

Alex showed off his skill in removing every last bit of cum from Clarissa's face, emphasizing the level of devotion and attention he was willing to give to their shared fantasy of degrading her As he meticulously cleaned Clarissa's face with his tongue, he paid careful attention to every detail, ensuring that not a single drop of seed remained on her delicate features. His lips were sliding smoothly across her skin, leaving it feeling cool and refreshed after being coated in warm bodily fluids moments ago.

"And... cut!" Clarissa stated with a tired smile on her face. She stood up, trying to gain balance on her high heels. "Thank you, guys... I appreciate your help." Her words were clear now, and she even planted a kiss on our faces. It was strange to feel this kind of slight gratitude after being balls deep in her orifices – but still made the cherry on the cake.

***

Several days passed. Work and life made it almost impossible to rest even a tiny bit. But when Saturday arrived, and I managed to start watching my favorite show, the X-Files again, Bonnie surprised me with some news:

"Clarissa called," she said lustily, which made me turn the volume down. "The video was a success! She received so many tips like never before! And guess what!"

"Yes?" I asked carefully. "She's already planning part two! So get ready, big boy!"

I leaned back, watching special agents Mulder and Scully investigating another case on the big screen. And recalling the night I spent at Clarissa's, my cock twitched. Yeah, I will definitely be ready.

THE END

Characters Cheat Sheet

Tired of keeping in mind all the characters in Office Sluts? I've got you, here's you cheat sheet reference:

Bonnie: a 30 years old brunette, the main female character of the story. Expert in real estate cases. She works for Walden, Inc. and gets romantically involved with John.

John: a 30 years old lawyer. Begins to work for Walden, Inc. as Office Sluts 1 starts.

Carl: a cocky lawyer, John's pal.

Helen: works at HR, a shallow but chubby black haired girl, adores blowbangs as the purest form of entertainment.

Clarissa: the dream girl of the office, a slender blonde with long legs.

Mr. Tagamoshi: senior executive of a client company in Japan.

Sergeant Hancock a.k.a. Patrick Donovan: a black cop serving on the highway.

Janet: blonde secretary.

Ule: black lawyer from South Africa.

The Worm: the manager of the department Bonnie and John are working in.

Andy: John's former crush from high school, a one night stand later.

Asa: the brown haired thin Japanese teacher hired by the company. She had been working as a porn star previously.

Lori: an intern, innocent and cute but catches up with the debauchery quickly.

Hannah and Dorothy: new interns at the company, John helps them get on track.

Mrs. Yakamoto: a very nice elderly lady, the widow of a late executive of a client in Japan.

Doctor Surlove: rich, muscular, confident client in Japan, also a dom.

Brigitte: sexually overheated co-worker from accounting. Addicted to cum swallowing.

Yvonne: the personal maid of Bonnie.

Adam: John's old friend.

Claire: Adam's girlfriend, a bimbo with a high sexual drive.

Kyle: John's friend and colleague.

Lawrence: Madison's cuck husband.

Madison: John's colleague, Lawrance's wife, hot and horny as hell. Nymphomaniac by the book.

Cindy: a slutty blonde working for Walden, Inc. A cold ice queen. Occasional secret lover of Carl.

Alissa: brunette bitch from the service center.

Megan: a lovely, curvy brunette John had a crush on but she only friend zoned him.

Ryan: Megan's current lover, he likes to tie her up and punish her for her real or not-so-real sins.

Steve: a hairdresser, Bonnie's former occasional lover, John involves him to participate in a filthy threesome with him and Bonnie.

Alex: Clarissa's cuck fiancé, a typical nerd.

Suggested Playlists for Making Sweet Sweet Love To

- Sexy Night[1] - hand picked songs for a filthy getaway from yours truly

- Timeless Love Songs[2] - The ultimate romantic playlist by Spotify

- Reputation by Taylor Swift[3] - and a detailed description on how to use it on Literotica[4], written by yours truly

- Future Nostalgia (The Moonlight Edition)[5] by Dua Lipa

---

1. https://open.spotify.com/playlist/6ddbBOoDQW4Z7uZoyg54Q6

2. https://open.spotify.com/playlist/37i9dQZF1DX7rOY2tZUw1k

3. https://open.spotify.com/album/6DEjYFkNZh67HP7R9PSZvv

4. https://www.literotica.com/s/how-to-use-reputation-for-sex

5. https://open.spotify.com/album/0E3wRkztEF32ZdYICXBuBf

Also by the Author

Cuckold Birthday

John Smith starts his work as a freshman at the biggest law firm of the U.S. Join him in his quest of being involved in hot office sex, wild orgies and finding true love.

Check it out at https://www.smashwords.com/books/view/307658

Just A Little Favor

John and Bonnie have an open relationship. Join them as secrets are revealed from their past and temptation shows up at hot orgies and wild adventures in elevators, office spaces, parties and many more!

Check it out at https://www.smashwords.com/books/view/383606

Inside The Cube

What if you wake up in a cubic room with strangers beside you? The porn parody of the popular indie scifi-horror movie.

Free download: https://www.smashwords.com/books/view/456545

About The Author

I started writing erotic stories just after finishing my uni years. I write off my hidden desires mixed with some of my wildest experiences, so as you read the book, you're looking over my shoulder as I create the steamy sex scenes I wouldn't dare to admit publicly.

Besides writing, I love to cook pasta, soups, and desserts with my fiancé and to give him blow jobs for breakfast. Besides sex, writing, and cooking, I also like yoga, reading, and an occasional drink of liquor.

Follow my author profile at Smashwords:

https://www.smashwords.com/profile/view/sandymonroe

My blog:sandylikestowrite.blogspot.com[6]

Get in touch at sandy.likes.to.write@gmail.com

Follow me on Twitter: https://twitter.com/SandyMonroeXXX

---

6.   *http://sandylikestowrite.blogspot.com*